CONSUME ME

Club Genesis - Chicago, Book 2

USA TODAY BESTSELLER

JENNA JACOB

CONSUME

Me

USA Today Bestselling Author

JENNA JACOB

Consume Me

Club Genesis – Chicago, Book 2

Published by Jenna Jacob

Copyright 2023 Dream Words, LLC

Edited by Raw Book Editing: www.http://www.rawbookediting.com

ePub ISBN: 978-1-952111-40-2

Print ISBN: 978-1-952111-41-9

Previously published as *Masters of My Desire.*

They made my wildest fantasies come true until…

I'm **Savannah Carson**—sane, sensible archeological activist. I never envisioned starting my much-needed vacation by wrapping my SUV around local wildlife and totaling my vehicle. I also never imagined being rescued from the wreckage, an impeding blizzard, and certain hypothermia by two gorgeous knights in a shiny pickup. As they swept me away to safety, I realized my attraction to them was far more dangerous.

At the mercy of **Nick Masters** and **Dylan Thomas**—drool-worthy construction owners—their commanding compassion unravels my inhibitions and ignites a primal passion that consumes my very soul. Trapped in isolation for seven glorious days, they wreck me as they capture my heart. But all too soon, the snow stops and the reality that the world won't understand my complicated love life intrudes. So, I flee, resuming my lackluster existence and tiding myself over with memories.

But Nick and Dylan have other plans. They track me down with an ultimatum: take the safe path and walk away…or embrace their unconventional love and let them…*Consume Me*?

Previously published as *Masters of My Desire.*

Chapter One

"Oh my God, I just killed Bambi."

My body trembled, and tears stung my eyes. While the thunderous beat of my heart and the cacophony of shrieking metal still echoed in my ears, the punch of adrenaline slowly bled from my system. I couldn't erase the image of the regal buck or the sickening thud of flesh exploding against my SUV from my mind.

Peering through the web of the shattered windshield, I pressed a hand to my stomach. Blood and chunks of fur-mixed flesh, covering the hood of my vehicle, looked like something out of a bad horror movie. Saliva pooled in my mouth. Dragging in several deep breaths, I swallowed rapidly to keep from throwing up all over myself.

I shouldn't have looked.

Guild and sadness wended through me. The pain of my shoulder, where I'd bounced against the doorframe, paled in comparison to the anguish I felt for taking the innocent animal's life. I was a murderer.

"I'm so sorry, Bambi. You probably have a mate and babies that will wonder where you are."

Unsure how long I'd been sitting in the middle of the deserted, gravel road, I finally realized I needed to call a tow truck or the police...someone who could help me. As I went to reach for my purse,

I discovered it had been tossed to the floorboard. But after unbuckling my seatbelt, and gingerly reaching across the console, my head began pounding like a million busy jackhammers were trying to bust out of my scalp. My stomach pitched once more, like a kayak in a hurricane, as I snagged the strap, and slowly sat upright before pulling out my cell phone.

But before I could tap in 911, the growl of an engine and crunching gravel snagged my attention. Lifting my gaze to the rearview, I caught a glimpse of a huge red truck as it slowed, pulled up beside me, and stopped.

When the window of the truck lowered and the passenger stuck his head out, my heart skipped a beat. Even though worry lined his face, the man staring at me was devastatingly handsome. The concern in his dark, charcoal-colored eyes sent butterflies dipping and swooping in my stomach. Clearly, he was Native American with his long, blue-black hair, sun-kissed skin, and high exotic cheekbones. I could have gazed at him for hours.

When he sent me a curious look, I peeled my gaze off him. Then, with a *thank you* poised on my tongue; I pressed the button to lower my window, but it didn't budge. I raised my finger, motioning for him to give me a second, then slung the strap of my purse over my shoulder.

As I opened the door, the driver leaned forward and poked his head around the stunning Native man's shoulder. The sight of his hypnotic blue eyes and rugged jaw dusted in a light scruff matching his ash blond hair, combined with the icy wind swirling around me, stole my breath.

The driver was as dangerously delicious as his passenger. They were two of the most decadent and sinfully handsome men I'd ever laid eyes on. The kind that, without even trying, intimidated me to the point of being nervous and tongue-tied.

But, Lord…were they ever gorgeous.

"Wait," the passenger barked.

So focused on his deep voice flowing over me like warm honey, I ignored his command and eased from the driver's seat. As I stepped onto the road, a nauseating squish echoed in my ears while my foot plunged, ankle deep, into the warm, thick center of the deer's bloody carcass.

Revulsion crawled up my spine and tore from my throat in a guttural groan before landing like a brick in my stomach. While the slippery sensation and grotesque sound pounded my brain, I jumped over the remnants of the deer. Kicking the bloody goo from my foot, I ran to the back of my SUV and tossed my purse aside before doubling over and promptly puking up every ounce of my four dollar and eighty-seven cent cup of coffee into the ditch.

"Hold her hair," the passenger ordered.

While strong fingers gathered my mane, the Native man gripped my hip and leaned over my body.

"Let it out, little one," he murmured.

His hot breath fluttering over my ear sent a different kind of shiver quaking through me. But it wasn't enough to stop the next wave purging from my belly. After coughing it out, I released an un-ladylike spit and groaned.

"I'm sorry," I whispered, embarrassed beyond comprehension.

"You don't have a thing to be sorry for," assured the blue-eyed man, still cinching my hair. "I think we need to get you to a hospital."

"No, please. I don't like hospitals," I begged before swallowing the bitter taste staining my tongue. "I'm fine, just…grossed out."

"You're not *fine*. You're shaking like a leaf," the Native man corrected, strong hand singeing my hip.

"I'm just cold."

It wasn't a lie. But that wasn't the real reason I was trembling. It was because of *him*. His dark, mysterious eyes. His wide shoulders. His tall, powerful body. And his soul-stealing beauty.

"Are you done?"

I nodded and slowly stood upright.

"Good girl."

His innocent words sent a blast of heat straight to my core. My nipples hardened with a sharp ache, and a rush of slick warmth spilled onto my panties. Completely caught off-guard by my instant arousal, I swallowed back a gasp and peered over my shoulder. Though worry still stormed in his eyes, a kind smile tugged his lips while his luscious heat surrounded me.

"If you want to take her to the truck so she can warm up, I'll call for a tow," he stated to the other man while the wind violently whipped through his long hair.

"No hospitals," I reminded as he gathered the wild strands in his fist before tucking them in the back of the black tee hugging his sculpted chest.

While I ogled him as if he were a fat, juicy steak, he cupped his wide, warm hands around my cheeks and held me with a stern stare. "You need to get checked out, pet."

Pet? Oh, hell! He's a Dominant?

My mouth went dry as a massive tremor quaked through me.

I'd read about Doms and subs…read every book I could get my hands on. I'd even spent hours combing the web, drinking in all I could about BDSM. Pet, a common nick-name that Dominants called their submissives. So were terms like girl, precious, kitten, and little one.

Oh hell.

He'd already called me little one earlier.

Suddenly, I couldn't breathe. Black spots began clouding my vision. And my heart thundered like a drum line. Fearing I was about to pass out, I closed my eyes and dragged in a ragged breath.

"Easy." His rich velvet voice echoed in my ears as his hands tightened upon my face. "Relax, little one. Take a deep breath."

Little one. There it was again.

"What's your name, kitten?" the blue-eyed man asked.

Little one? Kitten? Holy shit!

The chances of both men being Dominants pinged through my brain while every cell in my body danced and cheered. Images of them binding me, spanking me, and submitting to their every whim sent tingles racing down my spine. While my favorite kinky fantasy was sailing the seas on a luxury yacht with two commanding Sheiks, being Dominated by these two gorgeous hunks now rescuing me on this deserted gravel road, turned me on even more.

Was fate or divine intervention at play? Had I actually just won the grand prize in the kinky sexual lottery?

You're not that lucky, chided the little voice in my brain.

"S…Savannah. Savannah Carson," I stammered, inwardly cursing my usual tongue-tied response.

"I'm Nick Masters." The Native man smiled, releasing my cheeks.

Master Masters? I nearly snickered, but instead, cried out in surprise as the blue-eyed man suddenly hoisted me off the ground and into his burly arms.

"And I'm Dylan Thomas," he said, flashing a dazzling smile. "Come on, let's get you inside our truck so you can warm up."

Gaping at the man intimately nestling me against his steely chest, I clutched his wide shoulders as more lurid images—that included him *warming me up* in other ways—flashed in my head. As he carried me toward their truck, his name finally soaked through the lust saturating my brain, and I blinked up at him. "You mean like the poet?"

"Yeah." He sheepishly chuckled. "Like the poet."

Easing me onto the bench seat, he turned up the heat, then closed the door before jogging around the vehicle. I leaned forward and placed my fingers on the vents as Dylan climbed in behind the wheel beside me.

"Where were you headed before the accident?"

"Kit's Korner. It's a bed and breakfast down the—"

"I know exactly where it is. Nick and I are staying there, too. We stay there every year."

"So do we."

His brows knitted together as his blue eyes delved deeply into mine. "Do you need us to call someone for you? A husband…or boyfriend to let them—"

"Oh, no. I'm not…I don't have either," I muttered, gazing into his dangerous eyes. "I'm meeting my sister, Mellie, at Kit's. It's our annual Sisters Getaway. We usually meet up at Kit's in the summer when it's nice and warm. But we couldn't do it until now because we've both been too busy working and…well, you know…life happens. People get busy, and…"

I pinched my lips together to keep from yammering on and on, then turned my attention out the passenger window. Like a rope, the sight of poor Bambi lodged beneath what was left of my Escalade pulled me back to reality and the pain pulsating through my body. My head throbbed like mad, and an unrelenting ache drummed from my shoulder all the way down my arm.

"Is your sister already at Kit's?"

"No. She's flying in from Arizona."

And doesn't know you've been in a wreck, the little voice reminded.

A rush of panic sped through me. "Ohmigod, she's going to freak out. I need to call her."

"We're out of cell range right now. Not sure if you know it or not, but the area we're in is a dead zone for cell service."

"I knew that. I just…forgot. I'm still a little shaken because of the deer and all."

"You have every right to be. Don't worry. Nick has a satellite phone. I'll go get it from him so you can call your sister. Okay?"

As Dylan flashed another drool-worthy smile, I simply nodded like a damn bobble-head doll while drinking in his masculine beauty. But when he innocently patted my leg in reassurance, I jolted as a surge of electricity bolted straight to my core.

"Easy, Savannah. We're not going to hurt you. I promise. Sit back and relax. We'll take good care of you, kitten."

As Dylan climbed from the truck and shut the door, the word *kitten* circled my brain.

"Is this really happening?" I murmured, gently pinching myself. "Or did I hit my head in the accident, too?"

While a delightful throb churned between my legs, my head, shoulder, and arm ached in pain. I was beyond ready to get to Kit's and soak for hours in the big, luxurious spa tub inside my room.

When Nick and Dylan returned to the truck, a gust of icy air whipped through the cab, sucking out all the toasty warmth. But as they eased in beside me, their decadent body heat enveloped me like a fever and made my hands tremble when Nick passed me his satellite phone. Focusing on my sister, I dialed up Mellie, but she didn't answer. I left a condensed message in her voice mail, explaining my escapade with Bambi and reassuring her that I was okay. Next, I placed a call to my insurance company and secured a rental car to be delivered to Kit's.

While we waited for the tow truck, Nick and Dylan transferred my luggage from the back of my SUV and loaded everything into the back of their truck as sirens wailed in the distance. I could tell there was more than one headed our way.

Turning in my seat, I sent Nick a scowl. "You called for an ambulance, didn't you?"

"I did." He nodded firmly. "You *will* be checked out by a medical professional, even if I have to tie you to the gurney myself. Is that understood?"

My pulse spiked.

My body hummed.

And another rush of slickness spilled into my panties.

"Yes, Sir."

As the submissive reply tumbled off my lips—totally shocking me—a slow smile tugged his lips.

"Good girl," Nick purred. "I knew the minute I gazed into your eyes."

"Knew what?" I asked, feigning innocence.

"Once we know you're all right, we'll sit down and have a talk. I have a feeling we have lots to discuss."

The inflection in his whiskey-smooth voice told me he hadn't bought my act for a second. To keep from digging myself in deeper, I pressed my lips together and peered in the rearview as a patrol car and ambulance barreled our way. As they drew closer, the screaming sirens made my head want to explode.

The EMTs poked and prodded before announcing I didn't have any broken bones. When they offered to transport me to the hospital as a safety precaution, I adamantly refused, despite the angry scowls on Nick and Dylan's faces. Instead of pressuring me to go, they intently listened to the EMT as he listed off a litany of symptoms that would need immediate medical attention.

"We'll keep a close eye on her," Nick promised.

"If she needs to go to the hospital, we'll hog-tie her and drive her there ourselves," Dylan assured.

I rolled my eyes at their overbearing comments, but deep down, I dreamed about them binding me in rope. At least until I saw my SUV being hoisted on to the back of a tow truck—wobble over the remains of the poor deer—before my vehicle limped down the road.

When I was finished answering the sheriff's questions, he handed me a copy of the accident report and left. Before we climbed into the big, red truck, I dug through my suitcase and found the bottle of pain pills I'd tossed in that morning.

"Do you have any water?" I asked Nick, who watched me as if waiting for me to explain the little brown bottle in my hand.

"Sure thing." Dylan smiled as he flipped open the cooler in the truck's bed and plucked out a fresh plastic bottle.

"What are those?" Nick asked, nodding toward my fist.

"Pain pills."

"Why do you carry pain pills?"

"I had dental surgery a couple of weeks ago. While I was packing this morning, I grabbed them in case my tooth flared up again."

"Were you a Girl Scout?" Dylan grinned, handing me the water.

"No." I chuckled before downing two of the tablets. "I just like to be prepared."

"So do we." Nick smirked, holding the passenger door open for me.

It felt like hours before we were finally on our way to Kit's. Meshed between the sinful men, their body heat and masculine scents surrounded me and wreaked havoc with my hormones.

"How did you manage to pulverize that big bastard?" Nick asked, capturing me with his decadent black eyes.

"I didn't mean to kill the poor, innocent thing." The weight of my guilt was oppressive.

"Innocent, huh? Kind of like you?" he asked with a wolfish smile.

"I'm not innocent," I protested, but my tone was far from convincing.

"Right," he derisively drawled.

"It wasn't the deer's fault. I should have been paying more attention to the road."

"What were you doing?" Dylan asked, briefly glancing my way.

"Turning up the heat. I'd only taken my eyes off the road for a second. And when I looked up, he was right in front of me. There was nothing I could do."

"Do you need us to turn up the heat?" The velvety tone of Nick's question left no doubt he wasn't talking about the temperature in the truck.

Desire slashed through me like a hot knife and scalded my cheeks. I lowered my head to hide my embarrassment. "No. Thanks, I'm fine."

"You might be warm enough, but you're not fine, kitten. You've just been in a wreck. Don't bullshit us. We don't tolerate that very well," Dylan warned.

"How long have you been in the lifestyle?" Nick's forthright question caught me off-guard.

The air in the truck instantly turned as thick as mud.

"I don't know what you're talking about," I lied.

"Yes, you do," Nick scoffed before leaning in and lowering his lips close to my ear. "You don't need to be ashamed or hide who you are, little one. If this is all new to you, we'll help you through it."

I scowled and defiantly stuck out my chin. "I'm not hiding anything, and I'm sorry, but I don't know what *this* even means."

"Ordinarily, we spank little subbies for lying, but on the off-chance you really don't know what you are, we'll give you a pass."

Though Dylan's smile was warm, his tone teemed with such command I couldn't stop myself from dropping my gaze to his broad hands gripping the steering wheel. Yes, I wanted to know what his big, beefy paws would feel like spanking my ass, but I wasn't about to confess my kinky fantasies to either of them. Clearly, they had real life experience in the lifestyle. The only knowledge I had was pressed between the pages of the deliciously dirty books I read.

"I know exactly who and what I am... A successful businesswoman who has no intention of handing over her power or subjugating herself to a man," I replied curtly.

Nick arched his brows as a brilliant smile exploded over his face. "How do you know it's a power exchange, pet?"

Great! Open mouth...insert foot.

"This discussion is over," I announced in the haughty tone I reserved for the assholish lawyers who questioned my findings at work.

"Oh, it's far from over, little one. But we'll table it until you feel better."

Nick's dazzling smile was so intoxicating, I felt like a drunken sorority pledge.

Deciding my best defense was to simply keep my mouth shut, I did. Thankfully, the pain meds finally kicked in. Closing my eyes, I laid my head back against the seat, but my brain refused to shut down.

Being surrounded by two Dominant men who exuded more confidence and power than I could ever possess was wreaking havoc on my hormones and crowding my mind. While a part of me felt like a kid in a candy store, another part felt like a frightened rabbit cornered by two blindingly beautiful, famished wolves.

Worried they could smell my fear, I realized neither Nick nor Dylan knew a whit about me or my boring life. If I was brave enough, I could shed my timid skin and reinvent myself. Hell, I could be as wild as Mellie for once. My talented, interior designer sister was forever trotting the globe, working with some of the most famous and influential people on the planet. Mellie was forever having flings in exotic continents with filthy rich millionaires.

Sadly, I was nothing like my sister. Mellie had grace, poise, and confidence.

I didn't.

Dylan and Nick would probably laugh themselves silly if they knew my last dating disaster had been nine long months ago with a boring paralegal from Topeka. While I'd be the first to admit I lacked sexual prowess, nothing had prepared me for Wayne. He pegged the needle on the Nerd-O-Meter. Compared to him, I was a promiscuous sex kitten. But when Wayne's sinuses began to drain halfway through our date and he slapped a mentholated strip across his nose at the table of the restaurant, I faked a headache and called an Uber.

My love life sucked.

You can change that if you want, taunted the voice in my head.

If I found enough courage, I could live out my BDSM ménage fantasy with Dylan and Nick. It wasn't like I'd ever see them again. I wouldn't have to worry about hearing any awkward platitudes like, *Thanks, we'll have to do this again sometime,* or *I'll call you in the morning.* The only thing stopping me from enjoying—because, seriously, how could I not?—the most epic experience of a lifetime was fear. If I could erase that, I'd take home way better memories from this trip than killing Bambi.

My thoughts grew fuzzy. And as the hum of the truck's engine filled my ears, the dark haze crowding my brain dragged me under.

After what felt like mere seconds, a deep masculine voice dragged me from the depths.

Lost and floating in a thick fog, it took a hot minute for me to realize I wasn't in the truck, but flat on my back in a warm, soft bed. But it wasn't my bed. The scent of cinnamon and spice filling my senses added to my confusion. Briefly lifting my heavy lids, I instantly recognized my surroundings. Since they each looked alike, I knew I was in one of the bedrooms at Kit's Korner. Relief wended through the drug-induced blanket enveloping my brain. I closed my eyes, anxious to slide back into the inky abyss.

But Nick's angry, clipped voice quickly yanked me back to the surface.

"No, I will *not* allow her to reschedule the damn deposition again, George. This is bullshit. I'm sick of her playing the victim card. I sure as hell didn't force her to sign the prenup. She did that all on her own, then lied, cheated, and stole from me. She can leave with everything she walked in with…her former Pimp-daddy's Bentley and all her designer clothes. That's it. Period."

Prenup? As in divorce?

"I'm done," he snarled.

Forcing my lids open, I spied Nick, wearing a grim expression and sitting in a chair at the foot of my bed. Sat-phone pressed to his ear, he lifted his other hand, and pinched the bridge of his nose. He was clearly distraught, but try as I might, I couldn't keep my eyes open. I wasn't purposely eavesdropping, but with him there in my room, it was impossible not to. Though his voice was strained with irritation, it didn't stop tingles of need from skipping through me.

Forcing myself to focus on something else, I filled my lungs with the rustic scent of the barn. It wasn't really a barn. Kit simply called the modernized outbuilding situated alongside her Victorian mansion *the barn*. Her B&B offered rooms, both in the main house and the barn. Mellie and I always opted to stay in the outbuilding each year because we enjoyed the privacy. We could stay up late drinking wine, giggling, and spilling the tea without keeping other guests awake.

"Thanks, George. I appreciate you handling this for me." Nick's tone softened. "How are things going at Genesis? Is Leagh still keeping you on your toes?"

I could hear George's baritone voice through the sat phone, but not enough to make out what he said.

After a short pause, Nick let out a deep laugh. I forced my eyes open, just to see his smile.

"She loaded your toy bag with clothespins and bunny floggers? I can't wait to hear how you plan to punish her for that when we get back...*if* we get back. We're in the crosshairs of a fucking blizzard that's heading our way." Nick paused again. "All right, man. Thanks for everything. Later."

"Who are George and Leagh?" As my words tumbled over my rubbery tongue, they came out slurred.

"They're friends of ours." He smiled. "Good morning...err rather, good afternoon."

"What time is it?"

"It's about four-thirty," Nick replied, easing onto the edge of the bed. His long hair spilled over his shoulders like an inky veil. I wanted to reach out and touch it...rub the blue-black strands between my fingers to see if they were as soft as they looked.

"How's your headache?"

"It's gone, but I'm loopy, and my throat's so dry it feels like sand."

"Hang tight. I'll get you some water."

As he stood and walked to the bathroom, I gingerly sat up. When the sheet slid down my body and pooled at my waist, I realized I was totally naked. With a gasp, my cheeks caught fire. I quickly yanked the bedding to my throat as Nick swaggered back into the room.

"Who the fuck undressed me?" I barked, embarrassment blazing through my veins.

He narrowed his eyes and scowled. "Seems I should have grabbed the soap so I could wash out your filthy mouth, little one."

"Dream on. You'll need a court order to do that," I bit out.

"Will I now?" he challenged. "Dylan and I undressed you. We also washed the blood off your foot, ran your clothes up to Kit, who's trying to get the stains out as we speak. Oh, and your shoe is in the dumpster out back. It was beyond saving."

With a disapproving frown, he thrust the glass toward me. Waves of guilt rolled through me as I took it and pressed the rim to my lips. Ignoring his stern expression, I guzzled the cool water while my throat basked in relief. I owed Nick an apology, but I was hard-pressed to actually say the words. It didn't matter that I'd been whacked out on pain meds. The fact that two men, two *strangers*, had stripped me naked was unsettling. Knowing they'd seen every imperfection on my body was humiliating. The realization they could have touched and fondled me—not that I would have minded *if* I'd been awake—only added fuel to my embarrassment.

As if he'd read my mind, a flash of disappointment zipped across Nick's eyes.

Another wave of guilt—for thinking them so deviant—crested through me. They were Dominants, not rapists. Taking indecent liberties with me while I was unconscious went against the BDSM code of *safe, sane, and consensual.*

Still, I couldn't get past the mortification of knowing they'd seen me naked.

No one but my doctor—who supplied me with a flimsy cotton gown—had seen me nude since puberty. Back in college, I couldn't muster the courage to take my clothes off or leave the lights on the two times I'd had clumsy, disappointing sex.

Holding me with a penetrating stare, Nick crossed his arms over his chest. The stance made him appear even more Dominant, forceful, and intimidatingly delicious.

"We're adults, Savannah. You're not the first woman Dylan and I have seen naked."

"I know. I'm sorry. I don't mean to sound ungrateful for everything you two have done for me. It's just…I didn't expect to wake up *naked*."

"Do you honestly believe we undressed you with sexual intent?"

"No."

"Good, because we didn't. Trust me, little one. When it comes time for us to explore your wicked body, you'll be wide wake for every touch, kiss, and caress."

My heart rate tripled.

My throat went dry again.

"Which brings me back to the question I asked you earlier. How long have you been in the lifestyle?"

Instead of confessing I had zero experience, I mulishly pressed my lips together.

Nick frowned. "Why do you do that?"

"What?"

"Pull up walls and hang out a 'no trespassing' sign the minute you realize you're not in control?" He leaned down and stroked a warm finger along my jaw. "Letting go, especially for someone like you, is an amazing experience."

"I have no idea what you're talking about," I lied, as I jerked back and set the empty glass on the nightstand with a heavy thud.

"Yes, you do."

"I hate to burst your bubble, pal, but I'm not a submissive. I'm a strong-willed woman who's always in control."

"You've already used your free pass, little one. That lie is going to cost you." A wicked grin spread across his gorgeous lips. "Not tonight, but soon."

A ripple of need skipped up my spine, but I lifted my chin defiantly. "Look, Nick. I'm not here to play games. I'm here for a week of relaxation with my sister."

Though all the right words to disguise my true feelings rolled off my tongue, I couldn't quash the dirty fantasies of playing Dom/sub games with him and Dylan dancing in my brain.

I mentally shook the erotic visions away.

Nick's insistent questions about my experience, or rather lack of, only fed my doubts and insecurities. He and Dylan could have any woman they wanted. They probably had gorgeous, experienced submissives willingly falling to their feet on a daily basis. Why on earth was he wasting his time planting unrealistic seeds in the mind of a plain, boring girl like me?

After peeling his dissecting stare off me, Nick walked to the window and drew back the curtain.

"Speaking of your sister," he began, gazing out at the barren cornfield. "She called the sat phone while you were asleep. They closed the airport in Omaha and had to divert her flight to Oklahoma City. She's not sure she can make it, but thanked us for helping you." He turned my way with a wicked smirk. "I assured her Dylan and I would take *good* care of you."

A toxic cocktail of arousal and heart-sinking despair singed my system.

It wasn't fair. I'd been looking forward to our getaway all year. It was the only highlight of my life. Mellie knew how to pump me up. How to support and encourage me to survive another year of work, sleep, rinse and repeat. After our parents died, she took me under her wing and gave me strength. The fact she might not be coming made tears sting my eyes. As they spilled down my cheeks, I hung my head.

"Don't cry," Nick cooed, easing onto the mattress again. Cupping my chin, he tipped my head back. "I'm sure she'll do everything in her power to get here. I can tell spending time with her means a lot to you."

"It does," I sniffed, clutching the sheet tighter. "I miss her."

Nick sympathetically nodded as he softly wiped away my tears with the broad pads of his thumbs. It boggled my mind how the man could be so commanding and powerful, yet tender and caring. But the longer he gazed into my eyes, the more I wanted to lean in closer and press my lips to his.

Easing back from his touch to keep from doing it, I glanced at the open door. "Where's Dylan?"

"When we brought in your purse, it slid off the table and some of your things fell out. We found the list of groceries you were going to buy for the week with your sister. He ran to the store for you."

"Are you telling me you went through my purse?"

"No, we simply put everything back inside. Well, except for the list. I give you my word, we didn't desecrate the secrets or sanctity of a woman's purse. We know better. Also, no children or animals were harmed in the processes, and no wars were started," he said with a smirk.

"You're a smart ass, you know that?" I chuckled.

"So, that's what it takes?"

"That's what *what* takes?"

"To drag a smile out of you. I like it. You've got a beautiful smile."

My cheeks caught fire, and I dropped my chin. I wasn't used to hearing compliments.

"He didn't have to do that. I could have borrowed Kit's car," I protested.

Though I was grateful Dylan had taken the initiative to get the groceries for me, the fact they'd taken over the task was unsettling. I was used to doing everything on my own.

"He wanted to. Besides, you're in no condition to drive."

"I *could* have. I feel fine now." Nick sent me a skeptical stare. "Can you step out for a minute so I can find my robe?"

"No. I'm not leaving you alone. You already said you felt loopy. I'm staying to make sure you don't stumble and fall. If you hit your head again, you will be going to the hospital."

"I'll be careful. I promise. I just need to go to the bathroom."

"Then go," he said, sweeping his arm toward the doorway.

"I'm not getting out of this bed naked while you're here."

"And I've already said I'm not leaving you alone. Don't make me repeat myself again, little one. It goes against my nature."

"Ah, yes. Because you're a big-bad-Dominant. How could I forget?" I taunted with a sarcastic smile. "Just because you've seen me naked once doesn't mean I want you seeing it again. Now leave."

Nick pursed his lips and silently studied me with an intensity that seared my bones. Then he took a step back and widened his stance before squaring his shoulders and tucking his hands behind his back. The uncompromising command rolling off his chiseled posture flattened me like a paper doll.

Goosebumps peppered my flesh, and a tingle crawled up my spine.

"You have two choices, little one. Get out of bed and go to the bathroom, or lay there and soil the sheets. I don't care which option you choose, but I'm not leaving you alone. Understood?"

His censuring tone was reminiscent of my father, *God rest his soul,* when he caught me shaving the family cat when I was six. Yes, I was being overly modest, but no way would I lie there and piss the bed.

"Fine," I bit out, tossing the covers off my body before climbing out of bed.

At that exact moment, Dylan entered the room. His eyes widened and an approving smile stretched his lips. With a yelp, I slapped an arm across my breasts while covering my pussy with my other hand.

"No need to be shy, kitten. We've seen every gorgeous inch," Dylan said as his smile widened.

The enticing dimple on his cheek suddenly blurred as my vision darkened. Blinking at the inky veil closing in fast, I took a step, but my legs turned to Jell-O.

"Shit!" Nick cursed.

As I reached for the nightstand to steady myself, both men rushed toward me, wedging me between their hot, rock-hard bodies. My hormones zinged and pinged like fireworks.

It was the single most divine moment of my life.

"Back to bed," Nick barked.

"I'm fine," I argued, tamping down the rush of lust. "I just stood up too fast."

"You're a stubborn one, aren't you?" Dylan growled.

"No, I just need to go pee."

The combination of their heated bodies and twin erections pressed against my mound and butt cheeks sent an arc of lightning to my core.

"Then let's get you to the toilet," Nick growled against my ear before they led me to the bathroom.

After convincing them I could take care of business without their help, they grudgingly left me alone and closed the door. When I heard their muffled voices on the other side of the portal, I shook my head and grinned. They were hovering over me like a couple of mother hens. I didn't hate it.

Standing at the sink, washing my hands, I saw my toiletries neatly aligned on the vanity. They'd unpacked for me.

"Thank god, I didn't bring my vibrator," I softly muttered, grabbing my toothbrush.

"You okay in there?" Dylan asked as I rinsed the paste from my mouth.

"Yes, Dad," I drawled, rolling my eyes.

"In case you didn't notice, we're both wearing belts, kitten."

"There's also some cotton rope and a whole drawer full of wooden spoons and spatulas in the kitchen, little one," Nick added.

Like a brush fire, heat rolled up my body.

I opened the door to find both men wearing cocky grins, and my robe dangling off the tip of Dylan's finger.

"Is that your idea of a threat?" I challenged, lifting the silky fabric in my fist.

"No, kitten." Dylan winked.

"It's a promise," Nick assured.

I flashed them tight smile, then shut the door in their faces.

Chapter Two

After tying the robe firmly around my waist, I emerged from the bathroom. Nick was gone, but Dylan was still standing sentinel. No longer being naked filled me with a sense of control. At least until Dylan gently slid an arm around my waist before leading me back to bed. The heat of his hand cinching my hip bled through the silky fabric, sending a quiver skipping through me.

As we rounded the mattress, Nick reappeared at the doorway with a mug of hot tea and ordered me back into bed. Without arguing, I climbed under the covers and sipped the steaming liquid beneath their watchful gaze. The way they pampered me was endearing, but a bit overwhelming.

"We're going to head out to the other room so you can rest," Dylan announced as they both stood and turned for the door.

I felt a little guilty for the wave of relief that washed over me.

"Hey guys?" I called out. "I just want to say thank you both for… everything."

Their matching broad smiles warmed my heart.

"We'll let you shower us with appreciation later." Dylan winked with a devilish grin before closing the door behind them.

My heart drummed in my chest. Surely, he wasn't talking about showering them sexually, was he?

Oh, you wish.

"Right," I whispered. They were far too suave and urbane for a plain Jane like me. They had swagger, and lots of it. I had GPS coordinates and typographical maps.

But they don't know that about you, unless you tell them.

"If they did, they'd turn tail and run," I mumbled.

And why was I thinking such ludicrous thoughts in the first place? They weren't interested in having sex with me. This was just some kind of game they obviously liked to play. They weren't going to follow through with their sexual asides, were they? Doubts volleyed through my mind like tennis balls at Wimbledon. And trying to analyze them was impossible, not to mention, pointless.

I tried to sleep but couldn't. Restless and bored, I slowly stood and walked to the window, then pulled back the curtain. Snow fell from the sky in a swirling, violent rage, and covered the ground in a thick white blanket.

"Mellie can't drive through this shit," I whispered despondently.

While I was relieved she was safe and sound in Oklahoma, I had no clue what I was going to do the entire week without her. Saturated in sadness, I sat on the edge of the bed and watched the snow continue piling up outside.

A wide hand clasped my shoulder. Jolting with alarm, I snapped my head around and looked up at Dylan.

"Sorry, kitten. I didn't mean to scare you," he said, trailing his hand up and down my arm.

Though there was nothing remotely sexual about his touch, my hormones pinged as if it were a precursor to foreplay.

"It's okay. I didn't hear you come in," I replied as the scent of savory herbs filled my nose.

Dylan tucked a strand of hair behind my ear while holding me prisoner with a potent stare. Lost in his shimmering, ocean-blue eyes, I wanted to stay drowning in them forever.

"I guess I should have knocked," he somberly murmured,

skimming a knuckle down my cheek. "Damn, Savannah, do you have any idea how fucking beautiful you are?"

No.

Though the words spilling off his tongue made me feel beautiful, I subtly shook my head.

"Trust me. You are." He smiled and extended his hand. "Come on. Dinner's ready."

"Nick knows how to cook?" I asked, placing my fingers in his palm.

"We both do." Cupping my elbow, he helped me off the bed, then led me toward the door. "You're in for a treat. Two of the most amazing chefs on the planet have fixed you dinner."

"Is that so?" I chuckled. "I guess that means we're having frozen pizza tonight, right?"

Dylan gasped and sent me a feigned scowl as he dramatically clutched his heart. "Your lack of faith in us wounds me deeply."

"My apologies, I suppose you two pulled out all the stops and whipped up some Michelin Star TV dinners, huh?" I asked with a sassy grin.

"Not even close." He winked as he escorted me to the large dining table.

At the freestanding island in the middle of the kitchen, Nick looked up and flashed me a heart-melting smile before focusing his attention back to the steaming pot on the stove. The delicious aromas filling the air made my stomach growl and my mouth water.

"Wait till you taste what we've created for you, kitten," Dylan preened, pulling out a chair for me. "Sit and relax. Your dinner will be served in a minute."

Serving was a submissive's job. Doms weren't supposed to wait on a submissive, at least not in any of the books I'd read. There was something fundamentally wrong with the whole picture.

"But I thought…"

"You thought what?"

"Never mind." I bit my lips together.

I didn't want to open Pandora's Box and bring up the topic of BDSM with them again.

"If you have something to say, speak up. We're good at a lot of things, but mind reading isn't one of them." Dylan smirked.

"I have no doubt what you two are good at." As the words spilled off my tongue, I wasn't sure who was more shocked; me or Dylan. The look on his face was pure intrigue. I wanted to die. "I mean... I don't doubt that you guys are good cooks. It smells delicious."

Dylan leaned in close to my ear. His warm breath wafted over my neck and drew a shiver up my spine. "For some reason, you don't believe we punish little girls who lie. Trust me. We do."

My heart galloped.

My palms turned sweaty.

And my mouth went dry.

In order to keep from stammering a response, I grabbed the bottle of wine on the table and started to fill the empty glass at my plate. Without a word, Dylan wrapped his wide hand over mine. Then, before a drop even crested the rim, he guided the bottle back to the table.

"That's your water glass. You don't get wine tonight in case you need another pain pill."

After spending most of my life making my own decisions, his edict chafed.

"I wasn't going to take any more pain pills. I feel fine," I protested as Nick placed a steaming plate of herb-crusted fish, sautéed snap peas, and sweet potato fries in front of me. My eyes grew wide as I peered up at him, then arched a brow at Dylan. "Ohmigod, this looks amazing. You two really *can* cook."

"Brat," Dylan chuckled.

The meal was amazing, but watching them enjoy the wine rankled me. Pushing back, I pressed for a glass until, grumbling in disapproval, they finally relented. Yes, it was a small, meaningless victory, and even though I secretly wanted them to devour me—like they were their food —I needed to firm up the ground beneath me...at least for as long as I could.

We talked, ate, and laughed, and as I learned more about them, a sense of calmness settled through me.

Dylan was like a game show host, constantly dropping snarky and funny one-liners. Nick had a great sense of humor, too, but was definitely more serious and pragmatic. I suspected it had a lot to do with the divorce conversation he'd earlier had with George. While it was refreshing the way Dylan made me laugh, my demeanor was a lot more like Nick's.

Instead of letting me help clean after dinner, they led me to the couch in front of a roaring fire and draped a soft cotton blanket around me. Staring into the flickering flames, I exhaled a satisfied smile. My belly was full, and for the first time all day, I felt at peace.

Long minutes later, they joined me. As they eased onto the couch, nestling me between their hard, warm bodies, Dylan handed me a mug of hot chocolate.

As I sipped the rich, creamy sweetness, Nick absently massaged my neck, and Dylan traced his fingertips up and down my arm while we talked about our lives. Though their blissful touch aroused me, it also calmed me in ways I couldn't explain.

The pair had been best friends since first grade and claimed one another as a brothers. Nick owned a construction company in Chicago. Dylan was a veteran Marine who'd served three tours in Afghanistan. When he returned home, he became Nick's foreman.

I told them about my career as an archeological activist, which, after learning about Nick's company, filled me with anxiety. I'd lost count of the number of construction company owners I'd pissed off over the years, having to slap injunctions on their projects when a historic relic was unearthed at a dig site. Nick bristled, but became sympathetic when I explained most of the artifacts unearthed were Native American in origin.

It had been difficult to tell them about losing my parents at sixteen. I'd never told anyone other than Myron, my boss, how they'd died on an icy road in the Ozarks. They'd been driving home after closing up our lakefront cabin for the winter when they'd encountered the unexpected storm. Witnesses said after my dad crested a hill, he lost control on a patch of black ice and flipped down a steep embankment. Mellie had been away at college, but moved back home to raise me until I graduated high school.

I hadn't realized I was crying until both men leaned over, pressed their lips to my cheeks, and sipped my tears. A sizzling arc of electricity zipped through me before landing between my legs with a steady throb.

"Is there any more wine?" I blurted. My body stiffened, even as their masculine fingers continued caressing and soothing.

"Not for you," Nick murmured. "We want you clearheaded and sober for the next topic."

I wiped my cheeks, swallowed tightly, then glanced up at him. He was wearing his bad-assed Dom face. A powerful tremor shook my entire body.

"Are you cold?" Dylan asked.

"No, just scared," I confessed without thinking. "It's late, isn't it? I think I should go to bed. We can always talk tomorrow."

"It's barely ten o'clock, little one. Surely, you can stay awake a bit longer, can't you?" he asked, arching his brows.

"Okay," I whispered.

"Good girl." Dylan smiled.

I shivered again. Each time they praised me, a surge of heat rolled through me.

"No more evading," Nick warned. "What have you experienced in the lifestyle?"

"Nothing." I dropped my gaze and clasped my hands to stop them from shaking.

"Who told you about it?" Nick's calm tone didn't falter, neither did the sublime rhythm of his capable fingers kneading the back of my neck.

"I've read books and researched the internet."

"Are you intrigued by it?" Dylan asked, sidling closer, still stroking my forearm.

While their interrogating questions sent my anxiety level through the roof, I felt weirdly safe and protected. Though I was stepping into unchartered territory, I somehow knew they wouldn't let me fall. Maybe it *was* time to be brave and honest about the desires I'd been hiding for so long.

"Yes."

"Tell us what intrigues you," Dylan pressed.

"Everything," I whispered on a shaky breath. "I'm always in

control of my life and my job. I have to be. What I do comes with a huge amount of pressure. So much so, I can't help but dream of letting go."

Nick's fingers stilled before he palmed my nape. With firm, but gentle pressure, he turned my head toward his. Placing his palm along my jaw, he spread his fingers along the side of my neck in a bold and blatant display of possession.

My head was already swimming when he leaned in and pressed his lips to mine. The warmth and texture of his kiss sent a moan splintering the silence…*my moan*. Dragging my hand up his thick arm, I sank my fingers into his silky hair. As I savored the sharp contrast between his rock-hard body and soft mane, Nick deepened the kiss. Unable to hold back, I met the growing intensity of his kiss—giving back as good as I got—while his low growl of approval hummed against my lips.

"That's hot as hell," Dylan softly growled.

Suddenly self-conscious, I tried to pull away, but Nick held me in place and glided his tongue over the seam of my lips. When I parted to welcome him in, his fingers tightened on my neck as he swept in deep, exploring every crease and crevice with slow, languid strokes.

Dylan skated his fingers down my arm before kneading and squeezing my thighs with a calming touch. Engulfed in a thick haze of surrender, I relinquished control. Enveloped in serenity, the heady sensation felt like a powerful drug, one I could easily become addicted to, if I wasn't already. One demanding kiss had me sailing higher than the clouds.

Nick eased back. My eyes fluttered open only to be captured by his decadent gaze.

"Thank you for being honest, little one. It means a great deal to us."

"Uh-huh," I moaned on a quivering sigh as lava pumped through my veins.

"I need a taste, too," Dylan announced in a raspy voice.

Nick's hands slid away, and Dylan took over, as if they'd practiced the move a hundred times. He didn't say a word. He didn't have to; his hungry expression spoke volumes. Dylan pressed his soft but firm lips against mine. But there was no gentle coax this time. No, he claimed my mouth with his tongue, letting me taste his urgency. I clutched his shoulder and wrapped my fist in his shirt, anchoring myself to him for this wild ride.

"That's it, little one. Let him explore your wicked mouth," Nick growled against my ear before trailing fiery kisses down the column of my neck. Stopping at the thundering pulse point, he flattened his tongue to my flesh and growled.

My body hummed as they set blaze to yearnings I'd kept locked away. The need to unleash all the hunger and demand screamed and clawed to be set free.

Dylan skimmed his broad palm over my throbbing nipples. Swallowing my muffled whimpers, he cupped my breast beneath my robe. Tongues tangling, I ached to feel his strong hands on my bare flesh. No longer concerned about them seeing me naked again, I ached to strip off the barrier of clothing between us and drink in the warmth of his skin.

With a slow, torturous glide, Nick slid his lips up the side of my throat, then nipped the fleshy lobe of my ear. My swollen clit throbbed in time with my pounding heart. The little bud, desperate for relief, longed for their skillful fingers to delve between my cream-soaked folds and rub its misery away. As the need to come climbed through me, I rocked my hips, pitifully whimpering. But when Dylan released my lips, I cried out in frustration.

"Shhhh. Easy. We're not going to push you. Let's just sit here and talk." Dylan crooned.

Talk? Was he on crack? Had they seriously set me on fire like this...to *talk*? I didn't want to talk, I wanted them to put out the flames and fuck me. Fuck me hard for hours. Fuck me until I lost count of orgasms...lost consciousness.

"Talk?" I whimpered, panting like a porn star, and darted glances of disbelief between them.

"How long has it been since you've...been with someone?" Dylan asked.

Oh hell.

Swallowing tightly, I tried to steady my breathing. There was no way I was going to confess I hadn't had sex in over four years. They'd fall out laughing or think I was frigid and awful in bed, which I probably was. I had no idea if I was a good lover or not. I suspected I was pretty lousy, since neither guy back in college came back for a repeat performance. But how did one know if they truly sucked in the sack? It's not like I'd handed out scorecards at the end of the deed. I didn't want to think about my lack of sex, much less discuss it.

Nick cleared his throat. When I turned to look at him, he pinned me with an impatient stare. "You're stalling, little one. Stop trying to candy coat your answer. We know it's been…a while. We simply want to know how long."

"How do you know it's been a while?" I snapped with indignation. "I could have had sex last week. It's not stamped on my forehead like the expiration date on a milk carton."

"I have no doubt you *could* have. You're a beautiful, alluring, and extremely erotic woman. But you *didn't*." Nick smiled, seeming pleased with his ability to read me like a damn book. "You're making me repeat myself, little one. Just to let you know, I'm keeping track. Now answer the question. How long has it been?"

There it was again, that commanding Dom voice that made me turn into a gelatinous pile of marshmallow fluff. *Damn him!* I glanced at Dylan, hoping he might save me from spilling my guts.

But he didn't.

He simply chuckled. "The game you're trying to play will never work. We're not going to let you play us against one another. Now, answer the question."

His voice was as stern and commanding as Nick's.

I was screwed.

Lowering my head so I didn't have to see the pity or shock on their faces, I quietly murmured, "Four years."

"How many times have you had sex?" Dylan asked in a gentle coax.

I closed my eyes as all my grandiose dreams of pretending to be a free and wild spirit, and any hope of living out a Dom/sub ménage, swirled down the drain.

Dylan and Nick would soon discover I was nothing but an

inexperienced geek. I knew from experience; gorgeous men like them didn't sex up nerd-girls. No matter how much smoke I blew up my own ass, or how alive they made me feel, fantasy time was over.

"Look, guys, it's late and I've had a horrific day. Whatever we're doing here…it isn't going to work. Let's just save ourselves and end this awkward conversation. I'll hang out in my room until Mellie gets here. If you want, I'll come out from time to time to play cards or board games. Hell, I'll let you give me cooking lessons, but let's stop wasting each other's time playing pointless games, okay?"

Without waiting for a response, I started to stand. But before I could lift my ass off the couch, Nick leapt to his feet. Anger blazed in his eyes as he stuck out his hand. Fear and indecision gripped me by the throat.

"What are you doing?"

"You said you were ready for bed. That's fine, but we'll escort you to your room."

His voice was low and bathed in warmth, but his eyes still held an edge of fury.

Dylan stood and extended his hand as well. Though his expression was unreadable, his blue eyes had turned dull…lifeless. Their displeasure was palpable, but instead of caving, I squared my shoulders and stood without their help.

"I'm quite capable of tucking myself in," I replied coldly.

As Nick wrapped his hands around my waist, my robe shifted, exposing more of my breasts. Though they'd both seen me naked, his gaze seared a path to my cleavage.

"We've no doubt you're quite capable of…a lot. But our questions weren't meant to make you run and hide."

"Quite the opposite." Dylan slid his fingers through my hair before tucking the long strands behind my ear. "We were actually getting ready to ask if you'd like us to teach you submission…until you slammed up your walls and locked us out."

They want to… train me?

My heart sputtered.

I clenched my jaw to keep from gaping.

"What are you hiding from us?" Nick asked.

I opened my mouth to answer him, but nothing came out.

"We can't take you on the journey until we know what makes you tick," Dylan explained. "And the only way we can figure that out is by communicating. Surely, that was covered in the books and articles you've read, correct?"

I nodded.

It had been driven home, like a spike…in everything I read. Trust, honesty, and communication were the cornerstones of a good, healthy BDSM relationship. Yet, I hadn't been honest for fear they'd reject me. I hadn't trusted them enough to share my secrets.

"I'm honored you wanted to train me. I'm sorry—"

"*Want*, not wanted…if you'll let us," Nick corrected.

"Will you?" Dylan arched a brow.

"Yes, I-I'd like that a lot."

"Good. The first thing we need you to do is knock down your walls and let us in. Can you do that?" Dylan asked, holding me with a hopeful stare.

"I'll try. I'm scared."

"Of us?" Nick asked.

"No. Of screwing up. There's still a lot I don't know or completely understand."

"We don't expect perfection, little one, just the willingness to learn and to grow—"

"And to be completely honest with us," Dylan interrupted. "About everything…your joys, sorrow, and fears. Understood?"

"Yes, but I need to tell you, I have a lot of fears."

"We know. But if you let us, we'll help you work through them," Dylan assured.

"Which means we first have to earn your trust," Nick added. "We'll never hurt you, or take advantage of the power you give us, Savannah. You have our word."

"A minute ago, you were so angry with me. Why?"

"It wasn't anger, little one, it was frustration. We keep trying to find ways to see inside your soul, but you keep opening and closing yourself like a clam," Nick explained. "We'll never force your submission. We can only take what you're willing to give us. You understand that dynamic, right?"

Suddenly, I realized the mixed signals I'd been sending them. "Yes. I do."

"Good." Dylan smiled and cupped my hand before helping me off the couch. "Come on, let's get you tucked into bed. Tomorrow morning, we'll start your training."

Butterflies dipped and swirled in my stomach as Nick slid an arm around my waist before they guided me to my room. Pausing at the side of the bed, Nick released the sash of my robe as Dylan skimmed the silky fabric off my shoulders. I sucked in a gasp and gripped the ebbing fabric before it exposed my breasts.

"Let go, little one. You're perfectly safe," Nick whispered as he gently clasped my wrist and lifted my hand away. "We're simply tucking you in. Nothing else."

The robe fell away on a gentle sigh, and I fought the urge to cover myself with my hands. Nick leaned over and pulled the sheets down, then patted the mattress. With a timid nod, I settled in the middle of the big bed. As Nick drew the covers up, Dylan crawled over me and lay atop the blanket next to the wall. I turned and stared at him with wide, curious eyes. He simply smiled as Nick settled on top of the covers behind me.

"Sleep, kitten. We'll keep you safe," Dylan whispered.

Safe. Oh, I felt more than safe, a hell of a lot more. My body hummed with need I couldn't sate with them in the room.

Nick turned on his side, spooning me, and began massaging my scalp. Dylan lifted onto his elbow and propped his chin in his palm before tracing a finger down my cheek.

With a moan of delight, I closed my eyes as the abstract patterns their fingers painted lulled me into darkness.

Chapter Three

A shrill screech filled the room, jerking me awake. I tried to sit up but was tangled in a web of heavy arms and legs. Nick groaned and pawed at a leather case on his hip while the incessant alarm continued blaring. At the same time, Dylan scrubbed a hand over his face, then turned my way.

"Good morning, gorgeous," he said, as a lazy smile spread over his lips.

"Hello," Nick growled into his sat phone. "Yeah, just a sec. It's for you," he announced, handing me the phone.

"Hello?"

"Sanna? Please tell me you're not hurt," Mellie frantically demanded.

"I'm not hurt."

"Oh, thank god. How bad is your car?"

"Completely totaled."

"Well, shit. I'm sorry."

"Me, too. What are you doing?"

"Well, I was sleeping, but…" I chuckled.

"Are you telling me you're in bed with the guy who answered the phone?"

"Yeah, I mean…no," I stammered. "Not like you're thinking. I'll explain later. Where are you?"

"I'm home," she said with a dejected sigh.

"No," I whined as I tucked the covers around me and sat up. "You really can't get here?"

"Have you looked outside? Of course, you haven't. You're in bed with Mr. Dreamy Voice," she laughed. "I was stuck all night in the Oklahoma City airport, watching the weather channel. You're in the middle of a one in a thousand year blizzard. They cancelled every flight from Omaha to Chicago…indefinitely. I finally said fuck it and caught a red-eye back to Phoenix. I'm sorry, baby. I'm not gonna make it."

"Well, shit," I sighed.

Nick cleared his throat. When I glanced his way, he scowled and mouthed, "Soap."

"I'm sorry I woke you two up so early. I hope I didn't interrupt anything," Mellie teased with a wicked giggle.

"Three of us," I mumbled without thinking, then cringed.

"Oh, little sis, we're going to have a nice long talk when you get home," she furtively whispered. "I'm gonna need a play-by-play of all your sweaty deeds."

"There's nothing to tell," I muttered, then quickly changed the subject. "You're really not coming?"

"Baby, they've not only shut the airports down, but they've also closed all the highways as well. The only way you could get back to Kansas City for a while is with a sled-dog team."

"Aww, dammit," I groaned.

"I know. I know. But hey, it's not all bad. You're snowed in with Mr. Seduction Voice, and whoever else. And since I can't get to you, I'm going to crash for a few hours, then repack and head to Cancun. Alejandro is waiting for me on his yacht. We're going to sail up to Baja for a few days."

"You lucky little bitch," I giggled.

"Oh, kitten," Dylan warned in a low growl.

When I rolled my eyes at him and huffed, Nick pinched my nipple beneath the sheet. Jolting in surprise, I bit back a yelp and sent him a scowl.

"I don't blame you for chasing the sunshine and warm temps. And just for the record, we are *not* planning this trip in November *ever* again. It's cold as fu—" I amended my words when I caught the look of censure etched on Nick's face. "It's cold here."

"I hear you, baby. Hey, when is Myron shutting down the office for the holidays?"

"He already did. We wrapped up our last case for the year last week. He and Helen should be in the Caymans by now."

"Oh, good. So, you don't have to go back to work until February, right?"

"Yeah,"

"Great! Come spend Christmas with me. Alejandro can take us on a cruise to St. Kits so we can soak up the sun."

I hated to quash her excitement, but spending the holidays with Mellie and her current *flavor of the month* held zero appeal. I'd only be a third wheel, and in the way.

"We'll see," I answered vaguely. "Let's talk about it when I get home, okay?"

"Hey, I'll see if he has a friend for you...maybe two, since you're obviously into kinky shit like that," she giggled.

"No!" I gasped. "Please, Mellie, don't. I said we'll discuss it *later*."

"Fine. You can bring Mr. Bedroom Voice and whoever else is in the sack with you." She laughed. "I gotta tell you, sis. When you break out of your cocoon, you go all the way. I never would have suspected you were a closet sex kitten."

"I'm not. Dammit, Mel...hush."

"Okay. Okay. I'll stop teasing you, but what you're doing is so... juicy. Promise me one thing."

"What?"

"Don't do anything I wouldn't enjoy."

It was impossible to stay mad at Mellie while her sweet laughter filled my ear.

"I won't."

"Sanna..." she said in a somber, haunted tone.

"Yeah?"

"Promise me you won't try to drive anywhere until the roads are clear."

"Cross my heart. I won't even think about it until it's safe. You've got my word."

"Thank you, Sanna. Okay, I'm gonna go crash and burn. I'm exhausted. I'll try to give you a call when I get back from Baja. Is it okay to call on this number again? I wouldn't mind hearing your dude's voice again. It's…luscious."

"I'll call *you* when I get home."

"Aww, come on. I don't want to steal him. I just want him to talk dirty to me." She chuckled.

"*Goodbye*, Mellie," I sighed.

"Bye, baby."

After ending the call, I handed the phone back to Nick, who sat on the side of the bed wearing a cheeky grin.

"What?"

"First, how are you feeling this morning? Is your headache back?"

"No. I feel fine. My muscles are a little sore, but other than that, I feel…perfect." I was going to say normal, but being in bed with two studly men was anything but normal.

"That was an interesting conversation, little one."

My face turned hot. "You heard all that?"

"Every word. The bad thing about sat phones is…they're loud. You can overhear what the caller is saying." The knowing smirk on Nick's lips had me mentally replaying my conversation with Mellie. While I couldn't remember every word, I suspected he'd heard more than I'd wanted him to.

"So, are you ready to keep breaking out of your cocoon, kitten?" Dylan asked with a broad smile. "We're more than ready to show you how to spread your wings and fly."

Spreading my wings to fly wasn't the lurid image that flashed in my brain, but spreading my legs and flying to the heavens sure was…in living color.

"Who wants coffee?" I squeaked. "Either of you hungry? I'll make breakfast." I was just about to scramble from beneath the covers when

I remembered I was naked. "Nick, could you please hand me my robe?"

He sobered and scowled, then cupped my cheek. "You will address us both as Sir from now on and your safeword is red."

My gut seized, and I swallowed with an audible gulp. Ready or not, Submission 101 had begun.

"You do know about safewords, correct?"

I nodded.

"All right. We'll start out with some basic rules then. We will only give orders, once. Failure to comply without a valid reason will earn a punishment. If you are in emotional or physical pain, you will use your safeword."

"If you call red to avoid punishment," Dylan began. "You'll earn a harsher punishment."

"You won't be needing your robe today," Nick informed. "In fact, you won't be wearing clothes for quite a while."

Surely, they didn't expect me to frolic around all day in the nude… did they?

"But…" I swallowed tightly. "It's cold."

"Then your nipples will be deliciously hard for us," Dylan added with a carnal smile. "Don't worry. We'll make sure you stay nice and warm."

"We'll cover more rules in a bit," Nick announced as he stood and extended his hand. "Right now, coffee sounds wonderful. Please go to the kitchen and make us a pot, little one."

Good grief. What had I gotten myself into? Last night, the thought of submissive training sounded like heaven. But this morning, after Nick delivered his first command, I realized I was in way over my head.

"You're not already testing the rules, are you, kitten?"

As Dylan's question raked my skin, I shook my head. "No…Sir."

"Good. I'd hate for us to start off on the wrong foot." He smiled.

Gathering my courage, I tossed the covers off my body. My nipples beaded instantly, sending a delicious throb to drum between my legs. But before I could rise from the bed, Dylan cupped my shoulder.

"Just one thing before you go…" He bent and latched his mouth over my nipple. Drawing deeply, he swirled his tongue over my crinkled flesh before lashing it against my hardened tip.

"Ahhh," I exhaled in a breathy sigh.

As the breathy sigh escaped my lips, he pulled back and gazed at the glistening tip with a hungry smile. "That's to help keep your focus on us while you make the coffee."

"Yes, Sir." I quivered.

As I eased out of bed, I prayed my trembling legs didn't buckle. While praying they weren't staring at the cellulite on my ass, I somehow made it out of the room without tripping over my own feet.

As I worked on making coffee, my hands shook, my body ached, and my nipples throbbed to feel more of Dylan's hot mouth. I could hear their deep, muffled voices coming from my room but couldn't make out what they were saying.

"Probably plotting ways to make me squirm," I mumbled under my breath.

As I filled the carafe, some of the water splashed over my swollen nipple. A low moan escaped my throat.

To keep your focus on us…

"You have no idea how focused I am right now," I whispered. "And it's not on coffee."

While the coffee maker gurgled and the caffeine's rich aroma filled the kitchen, I arranged some cream and sugar on a serving tray before filling and loading three mugs. Taking slow and careful steps, I made my way back to the bedroom without spilling a drop.

Dylan and Nick sat in the matching wingback chairs near the window. Between them, a pillow lay on the carpet. Even though I'd never attempted a true submissive serve, I'd read about them. Determined not to fail my first lesson, I cast my gaze to the floor, then carefully eased my knees onto the pillow before placing the tray on the floor in front of me.

Suddenly, anxiety flooded my veins. Not because I was naked or kneeling at their feet. But because I had no clue who I was supposed to serve first.

"Very nice, little one," Nick praised as he leaned forward, trailing his fingers over my cheek.

"Beautifully done, kitten," Dylan complimented with a matching caress.

I sat frozen, my mind whirling with indecision.

"May I ask a question?"

"May I ask a question, *Sirs*," Nick corrected.

"Right, sorry. May I ask a question, Sirs?"

"Yes, of course. Raise your head and speak, kitten."

I peered up at Dylan then cast a wary glance at Nick. "I don't know who to serve first, Sirs." My voice had turned almost meek, mirroring the smallness now consuming my soul.

"Ah, of course." Dylan nodded. "You're trying to figure out if there's a hierarchy between us, aren't you?"

"Yes, Sir."

"Good girl." He smiled. "You will always serve Nick first, not because I'm a lesser Dominant, but because he's wired a bit more hardcore than I am."

I'd already surmised *that* based on their demeanor. Nick's Dominance was definitely more intimidating.

Nick chuckled and shook his head. "That was a very… tactful way to put it.."

Dylan shrugged and grinned. "I try."

Tinges of envy snaked through me. Their friendship was solid, like marble. Aside from Mellie, I'd never had a best friend.

Focusing back on my task, I peered up at Nick. "How do you like your coffee, Sir?"

"Lots of cream and lots of sugar. I enjoy sweet things…like you." He smiled.

A shiver raced up my spine as I prepared his mug. I could feel his gaze following my every move. With trembling hands, I turned the cup until the handle faced toward him, then raised it above my head. Keeping my eyes cast toward the floor, I prayed the coffee wouldn't slop and burn his thigh. When his broad hands encased mine, I exhaled a sigh of relief.

"You're doing fantastic, kitten." Dylan's praise bolstered my confidence. "I prefer mine black, please."

"Yes, Sir. Thank you."

Nick's touch calmed my trembling hands, but did nothing to slow my thundering heart. The need to please them, to prove I was worthy of their time and energy, pressed in all around me. But at the same time, their reassuring praise drew deeper yearnings to the surface. I couldn't wrap my head around the satisfaction flooding my veins; I knew it was because of their Dominance.

Nick released my hand, then fisted the mug. "You may serve Dylan now, little one."

Repeating the motions a second time was definitely less scary. Especially, when Dylan kissed my fingers before lifting the mug from my hand.

"Excellent job, kitten. You may enjoy a cup, too."

"Thank you, Sir."

Pride sluiced through me. I couldn't help but wonder what their next task might be as I added cream and sugar to the last mug.

I sat back on my heels and sipped my coffee while we chatted about the weather. I tried not to squirm as their hungry stares roamed my naked body. Though they were only caressing me with their eyes, I could feel their touch sliding over my flesh.

When our mugs were empty, Nick stood. "We're going to fix some breakfast, little one. Why don't you go relax and soak your sore muscles in your spa tub. We'll come get you when it's ready."

"Yes, Sir. Would you like me to take the tray back to the kitchen for you?"

"No, kitten. We'll take care of it," Dylan assured. "We'd rather you take some time for yourself and mentally prepare for your first day of training."

"I will, Sir."

This submission stuff was great. Well, all except for trekking around nude.

While the tub filled with water, I poured my favorite jasmine bath oil into the steaming water, then brushed my teeth. After shoving my hair into a clip, I stepped into the luxurious water and engaged the jets. My eyes nearly rolled to the back of my head as pulses of hot, liquid bliss thrummed at my sore muscles.

Long before I was ready to give up the tub, Nick strolled through the door and announced that breakfast was ready. His held open a big, towel for me as I flipped the drain and stood. Heat rushed through me as his hungry stare caressed my slick body. As I stepped out, he wrapped the soft cotton around me before he began drying my body. His reverent touch felt far more intimate than the kiss we'd shared last night.

As he dragged the towel over my legs, I clung to his bunching and flexing shoulders. And when he began drying my throbbing pussy with gentle pats, I held my breath and focused on the steam-clouded mirror at the sink to keep from rocking against his hand.

When he finished, I slowly exhaled and removed the clip from my hair. After setting it on the vanity, I looked around for my robe before I remembered it wasn't allowed. Suddenly, I didn't want to leave the deliciously warm, humid bathroom. The barn was heated, but I was going to freeze my ass off once I stepped into my room.

"I laid some clothes on the bed for you. Put them on, then join us at the table, please."

"Oh, gawd, thank you," I rejoiced.

Nick arched a brow. "Thank you, who?"

"Ah, I mean, thank you, Sir."

"Much better. Hurry before your breakfast gets cold."

"I will, Sir. Thank you." I nodded as he left my room.

Rushing to the bed, I sighed in delight at the sight of my cotton pajama bottoms, a long-sleeved thermal shirt, and socks sitting on the mattress. Though there were no panties or a bra, I didn't care. I was just thankful I had warm clothes to wear.

Breakfast was incredible. Fluffy blueberry pancakes, country ham, hash brown potatoes, orange juice, and coffee. But the fact that Dylan and Nick were unusually quiet, didn't go unnoticed. I had no clue if they were in Dom mode or if they were simply waiting to spring my next task. The not knowing what they had in store for me was as exciting as it was scary.

When the meal was done, I stood and started to gather the dishes.

"Sit down, kitten. We didn't give you permission to clear the table," Dylan stated with a tight smile. Anxiety spiked as I eased back into the wooden chair. "Do you know why we wanted you dressed this morning?"

Honestly, I'd been so ecstatic about staying warm, I hadn't thought there was a reason...until now. "No, Sir."

"Why do *you* think we wanted your body covered?" Nick asked.

My heart clutched as dread thundered through my veins.

"Because you don't want to look at me naked anymore?" I murmured.

"Why on earth would you think that?" Nick scolded.

"I-I don't know...because I don't have the body of a model."

"We need to work on your self-esteem," Dylan bit out with a frown. "Try again."

"Because I failed you both somehow," I whispered, dropping my chin. When they both softly scoffed, I peered at them under my dark lashes.

"No. If you fail us, we'll let you know...on the spot," Nick assured. "We let your cover your sexy body because we knew it would make you more secure. We're not going any farther until we've learned more about you. Dylan and I are going to ask you some specific questions."

"We want nothing but absolute honesty, understood?" Dylan added.

Great. I'd rather have stayed naked as a jaybird than endure their inquisition.

"Yes, Sir," I said on a bitter sigh.

"I detect some resistance, kitten. Why is that?" Dylan asked expectantly.

"I'm afraid that once you find out I'm nothing special, you won't want to waste your time training me and call it off."

"Your honesty is appreciated, little one," Nick replied as he cupped my fingers. "We're not going to do that. You may not think you're special, but we do. When we came upon you on the road yesterday, before you even opened the car door, we knew you weren't like any other woman we'd met."

Oh, he's done this before.

Nick was blowing such smooth, lush smoke, I almost believed him.

"So, our first question is one we asked last night. How many times have you had sex?"

His words hit me like a freight train. Once they found out I was as inexperienced with sex as I was the lifestyle, this was going to end in one of two ways.

They'd either tie me up and fuck my brains out, or laugh their asses off.

If I was a betting woman, my money would be on the latter.

I'd thought serving them coffee was hard. I wasn't wearing enough layers of clothes for this *honesty* task. They'd gone from holding my hand and taking baby steps to pushing me off a damn overpass.

Gathering up my courage, I lifted my head and stared at the oil painting across the room. Until now, I'd never noticed how ugly it was, or how the symmetry of the big, gaudy flowers in unnatural tones matched my feelings of inadequacy.

Steeling myself for the worst, I mumbled, "Two."

"Okay. Tell us about the two men," Nick instructed. "What were they like?"

Okay? That was it?

They weren't falling out of their chairs laughing. Hell, they didn't even snicker. Why not? I doubted either of them had gone more than a week without sex, let alone years. And now Nick wanted to know... *Oh, hell. What did he just ask me?*

"I'm sorry, Sir. What was the question?"

Nick raised his brows, and his lips drew into a tight, thin line. "You know the rules. If you want me to repeat myself, stand and bend over the table, little one."

"No. I-I mean, I *heard* your question, but I was thinking about something else and I don't remember it. Honestly, Nick."

A devilish smile curled his lips. "It's *Sir*, little one. Now stand and bend over the table. Consider this a reminder to keep your mind clear and focused on my words from now on."

My body shivered—not with fear—but arousal.

Finally, I was going to feel a real spanking at the hands of a Dominant...not from my own hairbrush. Body humming with anticipation and fear, I swallowed tightly and stood.

Dylan pushed the dirty dishes to the other end of the table, then placed a wide palm between my shoulders. With firm but insistent pressure, he pushed me flat against the polished wood before gathering my wrists in his wide hand.

"Don't move, kitten," he breathed against my ear as he stretched my arms out across the table.

Self-conscious about my vulnerable position, I worried they'd think my ass too big. But when Nick landed a hard slap against my ass, I jerked and moaned as a brilliant fire spread over my orbs, down my legs, and crawled up my back. Yes, it stung, but quickly numbed by the needy throb gathering in my clit and the rush of wetness spilling onto my pajama bottoms.

"Oh, yes," I hissed, arching my ass higher in the air. "More. Please."

Nick swore under his breath as Dylan expelled a gravelly chuckle.

"This is supposed to be punishment, little one." I couldn't miss the laughter in Nick's voice as he leaned over my body and brushed the hair from my nape.

"It feels good, Sir," I confessed on a dreamy sigh.

Savoring the lingering sting, I didn't object when one of them tugged off my cotton pants. The contrast of the cool air meeting my heated flesh sent a shiver through me as the sound of chairs scraping over the tile floor filled the air. I wanted to sneak a peek to see what they were doing, but kept my forehead pressed against the table and waited while kinky thoughts crowded my brain.

"Spread your legs, kitten," Dylan instructed as he gripped my thighs and helped me widen my stance. "You're wet. I can see and smell your sweet cunt, and it's making my mouth water."

Dylan's crude words were like an aphrodisiac.

Moaning, I rocked my hips against the table's edge.

Without warning, another sturdy slap landed across my bare flesh. I sucked in a hiss, welcoming an even brighter surge of fire, before exhaling in several hard puffs.

Basking in the swelling burn, I whimpered as a succession of wicked slaps lit up my ass.

As the mounting pain layered one over the other, I tossed my head back and screamed.

"Your safeword is red," Nick reminded with a feral growl. "Use it if you need it."

"No, Sir," I gasped as tears spilled down my cheeks. "More. Please."

"Take a look at that," Dylan murmured with a hint of awe.

"Son of a bitch," Nick moaned. "I think you need to help her out, man."

Enveloped in a haze of fire and demand, their voices sounded distant.

Suddenly, I felt thick fingers press against my folds before spreading me open. I cried out in surprise and gratitude, then held my breath. As Nick's wide palm smoothed my inflamed flesh with slow, unhurried circles, I writhed and moaned against the table.

"Touch my clit, oh, please. Please. I need it," I begged with a brazen plea.

"Oh, I'm going to touch it, and a whole lot more," Dylan vowed near my waist.

As he pressed his slick tongue against my core and dragged it up my center with a slow, languid swipe, my knees buckled and my pussy crashed over his face. No man had ever put his mouth on me there before. The sensation was so savage and intoxicating, I growled like an animal.

"Easy, little one," Nick murmured, gripping my hips. "I've got some questions for you."

Questions?

No. They'd have to wait. My whole world was focused on Dylan's wicked mouth, guzzling my nectar while his sinful tongue scraped my clit and laved, lapped, and stabbed my quivering pussy.

"What were the men you had sex with like?" Nick growled in my ear.

"What?" I panted, lost in the euphoric splendor of Dylan's masterful mouth.

Nick landed a harsh slap upon my ass.

"Oh, fuck," I screamed.

Another brutal smack brought me up from the table as a cry of searing delight tore from my throat.

"Watch your language and answer my question," Nick growled, pressing me back onto the table.

"They weren't men, they were boys. The sex was…boring," I panted.

As if being rewarded for my answer, Dylan plunged two fingers inside me.

"Oh, my god," I wailed when he found my G-spot.

My tunnel clasped down hard around his wiggling fingers.

Lights flashed behind my eyes.

My entire body seized.

And just as a tsunami of bliss crested, Dylan pulled his fingers from inside me and tore his lips off my clit.

A wail of panic and frustration pealed from my throat.

"You don't get to come yet, Savannah," Nick taunted. "We're going to keep you poised right here…on that razor's edge until you answer all my questions."

"Then ask them, dammit. I need to come," I barked.

An evil chuckle rolled off Nick's lips as he landed a blistering spank.

"You don't make the rules. And you're never allowed to use that tone of voice again, little one," he growled.

Riding the wave of pain searing through me, I whimpered an apology.

"Let's continue. Are you dating anyone?"

"No," I whimpered as Dylan's fingers began toying with my pussy, chasing the pain away.

"Why not?"

"I'm too boring," I sniffed.

A brutal spank rocked me to the core. Crying out in pain, I began to sob.

"We need *honest* answers," Nick thundered.

"I am being honest," I wailed as my tears spilled onto the table.

"Explain your answer," Nick demanded, gently caressing my throbbing orbs.

I tried to focus and engage my brain. I knew the sooner I told him everything he wanted to know, the sooner I could come and quell the frenzy of demand clawing through me. But when Dylan started dragging his tongue against my pussy again, my mind went blank.

"Guys don't see me inside the dusty courthouse, researching land rights," I began as if reciting shorthand. "Only men I see are wrinkled security guards, and asshole lawyers. Last date, years ago, nerdy paralegal. I suck at sex. That's all I know."

I prayed Nick wasn't going to insist I explain my jumbled words. If he did, I'd fail. I was too focused on Dylan's driving tongue, sucking lips, and masterful fingers.

"What do you do for fun?" Nick pressed. I groaned and rocked my hips in need.

"Nothing but read."

"You don't go to clubs or out to dinner with friends?"

"No," I panted, bearing down on Dylan's tongue. "Please...Oh, god, please."

"I love to hear you suffer, kitten," Dylan growled. "But since you didn't ask correctly, I might just have to leave you like this."

"No! Please don't, Dylan Sir. Please..."

"Please don't what?" Nick challenged.

"Stop touching and licking me, Sir."

"Touching and licking what?" Nick taunted.

"Oh, god," I moaned. "Don't make me say it."

"If you don't say it, kitten, you don't get it," Dylan warned with a hit of humor.

"Please, Dylan, Sir. Touch my pussy with your fingers and your tongue."

"With pleasure," he roared before his entire mouth enveloped my needy mound.

Driving his tongue deep inside me, he drank my juices with pure possession. Lost in the splendor of the sizzling sensations, I moaned, bucked, and writhed.

Nick gripped my hair and pulled me upright, his brawny chest—like a slab of marble—pressed against my back as he nipped the lobe of my ear. "Arms above your head, little one."

As I raised my hands toward the ceiling, he snaked his fingers up my shirt before tugging, squeezing, and rolling my hard nipples.

Soaring to heights I'd never known; I closed my eyes and basked in their mind-bending sensations.

"I can't wait to taste your sweet pussy."

Nick's warm breath fluttered over my ear as his fingers floated from one aching hard nipple to the next as he rolled, pinched, and plucked a carnal symphony of whimpers and moans from me, Dylan's tongue zeroed in on my clit, while his fingers sought that magical bundle of nerves deep inside me.

My limbs grew numb and my body hummed as the gathering storm within grew bigger.

As my orgasm mounted, pleasure and pressure pressed in all around me until my needy whimpers and moans morphed into keening cries of demand.

"That's it, little one. Fly for us," Nick coaxed.

While Dylan sucked my clit between his lips and scraped it with his tongue, Nick tugged and pinched my nipples—one after the other—before sinking his other hand in my hair. Tugging my head back, he sank his teeth into my neck with a growl, then released me and roared, "Come for us, Savannah. Come...Now!"

Lightning exploded down my spine before splintering through me.

Blinded by the brutal waves of ecstasy crashing through me, I screamed in bliss. My tunnel violently spasmed, and clamped around Dylan's fingers as Nick's teeth bit into my flesh once more. Ecstasy thundered through me like a cyclone, sending every sizzling cell in my body swirling. As Nick whispered all the depraved and immoral things he ached to do to me, Dylan slurped and lapped my flowing juices until they'd wrung every drop of pleasure from inside me.

As they finally eased me back to earth with soft strokes and glowing praises, Nick scooped my sated, boneless body into his arms. Dylan stood and pressed himself against us before plunging his tongue deep in my mouth. I tasted my essence for the first time. It was warm and a bit salty with a hint of some undefined spice. Tasting myself was strange but not repugnant, and I greedily swirled my tongue around his, capturing more of the unique flavor.

"It's time to take this party to the bedroom," Nick growled with a naughty grin.

Chapter Four

I was still basking in the afterglow as Nick tugged off my shirt before easing me onto the bed. Though my butt cheeks were tender, I barely noticed it at all. I was too busy floating on clouds of pleasure.

"It's not nap time yet, kitten," Dylan chuckled as I snuggled against the mattress. "We're just getting started."

Lifting my heavy lashes, I watched him yank off his T-shirt.

I was definitely wide awake now. Turning onto my side, I dragged a greedy gaze over his tanned, chiseled body. My mouth watered, and my fingers itched. Watching me with a cocky grin, he tossed his shirt to the floor.

"What? No butt wiggling? No hip thrusts? What kind of striptease is this?" I laughed.

A muffled chuckle came from behind Nick's shirt as he peeled the dark fabric off over his head. Like a magnet, my gaze drank in his sculpted, toffee-colored torso.

They both looked as if they'd just stepped off the pages of a fitness magazine.

"Where's your money?" Dylan teased as I rolled to my belly, cradled my chin in my palms, and raptly watched them strip. I licked my lips, still stained with my own salty nectar, as a coy smile blossomed over my mouth.

"I can pay with kisses, Sir," I giggled.

Hunger replaced the smile on Dylan's face as he quickly kicked off his shoes and started working the button at his waist. Nick was in perfect sync with his friend's movements. As they shed their jeans, in tandem, their big, glorious cocks sprang forth. Both were erect, engorged, and ready. My breath caught in my throat as I stared at the captivating sight of the twin crystal beads clinging to their wide purple crests.

"Is this what you want to kiss, kitten?" Dylan smirked, stepping forward and fisting his thick shaft.

The clear liquid bead grew larger.

A sizzle of lust pulsated through my body. I was barely able to peel my eyes from the enthralling sight when Nick stepped in close. His eyes blazed with desire. When I dropped my gaze and stared at the thick veins pulsating along his fat cock, his shaft jerked in need.

My palms itched to feel their straining flesh.

Anxious to slide my tongue over each inviting glistening drop, my mouth watered.

Acting on instinct, I eased off the bed and to the floor. Tucking my feet beneath me, I thrust my shoulders back and cast my eyes to the floor.

A sense of submissive surrender surged as I waited for their commands.

"Raise your eyes and tell us what you want, little one." Nick's tone was deep and thick.

A shiver of fear mixed with excitement slithered up my spine as I raised my head and stared into his hypnotic dark eyes.

"Please, Sirs. I need to taste you…both."

A beastly growl rumbled in Nick's chest as he gripped his shaft and ruthlessly pumped his generous length. The clear bead slid over his crown and drizzled down his fingers.

Stepping in front of my face, still stroking his steely shaft, he cupped my jaw. "Open that wicked mouth of yours and taste me," he instructed in a low whisper.

"I…I…" Fear and embarrassment spiked.

"You've never done this before, have you?" he asked in a compassionate voice.

"No, Sir."

"Then we'll be honored to teach you. Stick out your tongue and slide it over my cock."

Nick cupped my trembling hand and guided it to his erection before wrapping my fingers around his warm girth.

A powerful intimacy washed over me. I could feel his savage need and hunger as if this one touch had linked me to his very soul. I opened my mouth and extended my tongue. With a timid swipe, his slippery liquid exploded over my taste buds. I savored his salty essence as well as the masculine musk filling my nose.

"Mmm," I moaned, dragging my tongue over his crest again.

"That's it, take your time…satisfy your curiosity," Nick coaxed as he threaded his fingers in my hair and massaged my scalp. "When you're ready to take me inside your mouth, relax your throat, and breath through your nose."

Delighting in the unique flavor coating my tongue, I nodded.

Growing bolder, I swirled my lips over his broad crest, then traced the edge of it with the tip of my tongue. Nick's hiss of approval sent empowerment rushing through my system.

Dylan guided my free hand to his shaft. I began to stroke him, rubbing my thumb over his silky, wet cap. Cupping my fingers over the slick tip, I coated them before stroking my fist up and down his thick cock.

"Fuck," Dylan snarled, wrapping his hand over mine. "Stoke it like this."

Gripping my hand tighter, he set the tempo and pressure he wanted while guiding my fist up and down his steely shaft.

My confidence bloomed. I opened my mouth and wrapped my lips around Nick's wide, dripping crest. He gripped my hair as I suckled the tip, drawing out more of his tangy essence.

"You're killing me, pet," Nick growled as he tilted my head back by my tangled hair.

Filled fuller with the new position, I rolled my tongue over each distended vein while stroking both their cocks. Nick wrapped his hand over mine, stilling my movement, before he guided me to the base of his cock, squeezing my thumb and finger tightly around him.

"Hold me like that, pet. No more stroking. Your hot mouth is all the motivation I need right now. You keep stroking me and I'll be done before we get started."

I grunted my affirmation, feeding inch after glorious inch of him inside my mouth. The texture of his velvety hard flesh, his masculine scent, and the pulsating veins drumming against my tongue awakened something primordial and feminine deep inside me.

"That's it…suck him down deep," Dylan urged. "Show Nick how much you want to please him."

"Fuck," Nick hissed, then gripped my hair and shuttled a frenzied tempo before he pulled from my mouth with a feral roar.

"On the bed, kitten. It's time to brand and claim you," Dylan directed.

Brand me? Fear thundered through my veins. Glancing around the room, I searched for whatever nefarious tool they intended to use. Surely, they weren't planning to carve my flesh with a branding iron or knife…were they? I swallowed then skimmed a scared glance between them.

"You're going to do what?"

"Brand you, little one, with our come. Mark your breasts and belly with our seed," Nick explained, his eyes glazed in desire as he jerked his cock with vicious strokes. "We're going to claim your power as we brand your mind, heart, body, and soul."

My…heart? *No.* They could have my mind and body all they wanted, but my heart was off-limits. They didn't need my heart. This was only a training exercise, not a love connection.

They can only take what you're willing to give, reminded the voice in my head.

Relief whipped through me. As long as I locked my heart away, everything would be fine.

With a timid nod, I forced a smile, then rose from the floor and onto the bed. As they joined me—Nick on my left, and Dylan on my right, I realized I was proffering myself to them, like a sacrificial lamb.

Nick gazed down at me. Hunger etched his face while command and power oozed from every pore in his body.

"Who do you belong to?" Dylan asked as they continued stroking their thick cocks.

"You, Sirs," I whispered, unable to look away from their forearms bunching and flexing with each of their punishing strokes.

"What is your purpose, pet?" Nick pressed in a voice thick.

"To please, Sirs."

"Very nice," he moaned, sweat glistening upon his impeccable body.

"Spread your legs. Use your fingers and open your pussy for us, sweet slut," Dylan instructed.

Slut. I'd always viewed the word as demeaning and filthy, but Dylan said it with such endearment and affection, it annihilated all preconceived vulgar implications. It made me feel aroused, calm, and stunningly submissive.

No longer coaxing my surrender, they commanded me with deliberate, Dominant precision. Stretching my thighs wide, I spread my saturated folds open and watched their eyes widen at once. As their labored breathing filled the room, Nick and Dylan inspected my wet slit while the clear fluid dripping from their crests glazed my breasts and stomach. The desire to feel their hot come splattering and branding my flesh…to be claimed and owned, if only for a brief moment, climbed to maddening heights. Spreading my folds wider, I stroked my hard, aching clit.

"Beg for us to claim you, sweet slut," Dylan choked.

Sweat dotted his forehead, and a grimace of lust tugged his lips.

Nick's expression was much like Dylan's…rife with need and hunger.

They wore their power, command, and control like a well-tailored suit.

My tunnel contracted and my heart soared at the sublime splendor of it all.

"Please, Masters. Please mark me. Make me yours," I moaned on a ragged whimper.

"Ours," Nick roared as thick, hot streams erupted from his shaft.

Dylan followed him over almost instantly. Together, they branded me with fiery possession as ropes of creamy come showered my stomach, breasts, nipples, and chin.

As I softly whispered, "Yes. Yes. Yes," tears filled my eyes.

The magnitude of the moment blindsided and overwhelmed me so deeply, sobs tore from my throat. Nothing could have prepared me for the onslaught of emotions pelting me. I felt small and treasured, pleasing and pampered, wanted and arousing. *Was this what submission felt like?*

The last of their release dropped to my skin. They each coated their fingers with their hot seed before lifting them to my lips. Gliding my tongue over their silky treasure, I sucked their fingers, imprinting their flavor to memory.

Long minutes later, they climbed from the bed and returned with a warm washcloth and a bath towel. Reverently and tenderly, they cleaned me up, but didn't erase the indelible mark they'd branded inside me. Still, I couldn't help but notice how they seamlessly worked together. I knew deep down inside they'd practiced theses same moves on dozens, if not hundreds of other women. But before childish jealousy could stab me too deeply, Nick crawled in beside me and hugged me to his chest. Dylan followed from behind, pressing his warm body against my back.

Cocooned within their steely bodies, emotions swirled.

I felt small and safe, yet at the same time, sliced wide open.

Overwhelmed, I tried to dissect and compartmentalize my feelings, but couldn't. I was as fragile as bone China, and crumbling quickly.

Tears began spilling down my cheeks.

"Savannah?" Nick whispered, combing my hair away from my face.

"I'm sorry. I don't know why I'm crying," I moaned.

It wasn't a lie.

I couldn't reconcile the barrage of emotions whipping through me. Something amazing and far beyond my comprehension had been unlocked inside me. Something raw and vulnerable was unraveling within, while at the same time, a strange sense of peace flowed through me.

"It's okay, kitten."

"No, it's not," I sobbed. "I don't know what's happening. Why can't I stop crying? Thank you both for what you just did. I know it sounds stupid, but I never would've gotten to experience such an incredible experience if it weren't for you both. I'm sorry. I know how pathetic I sound right now, but…"

Choking on a sob, my tears continued to flow.

"What's happening is perfectly normal. Tasting submission for the first time is often overwhelming," Dylan whispered, gliding his wide hand over my hip.

"It is. I don't have words to describe what I'm feeling…it's all so powerful and foreign."

"We know," Nick assured. "It's okay. Cry it out if you need to."

"We're not going anywhere," Dylan promised.

Their understanding of what I couldn't comprehend was like a safety net. I was completely free-falling, but they were right there to catch me.

It took a while, but I finally regained my composure and stopped crying. Of course, my mind still wandered down a labyrinth of confusion, and a kernel of fear took root in the pit of my stomach.

How was I supposed to go back to my uneventful life after experiencing…this? Struggling to harness the panic clawing to break free, I focused on the rhythmic sounds of their breathing and the soothing cadence of their fingers and hands gently stroking my body. It didn't take long before I was able to shove a lid on my fears of the future and bury them deep within my mind.

I was here now and determined to bask in every sensation they were willing to give me.

Nuzzling Nick's chest, I closed my eyes and inhaled his masculine scent before branding it to memory. Then I threaded my fingers through Dylan's hand, still resting on my hip, and imprinted his gentle and reassuring touch to my soul. I may not be able to live this fairy tale forever, but I could carry these precious memories with me until the end of time.

I couldn't hide from the fact that they'd changed me. Freed me. Opened me to something magical. Forced me to see the parts I'd tucked away were beautiful and natural. With a clarity I'd never known before, a veil had been lifted. I was a submissive, and it was pointless for me to deny it ever again.

I had six days…six short days, to learn all I could about submission from these two amazing Doms. And I had no intention of wasting a single moment. I sniffed and inhaled a ragged breath, welcoming the sudden calm, centered feeling washing over me.

As we laid in a tangled web of arms and legs, we talked and talked. My insecurities disappeared…at least for now, and it was much easier to confess all the curiosities I yearned to experience. My list wasn't long, and their eager remarks made it clear they were going to take immense pleasure in introducing me to the joys of paddles and bondage. Their gentle words, wicked chuckles, and reassurance filled me with excitement. I was anxious for them to test my limits.

It was hours before we eventually climbed out of bed. As Nick and Dylan tugged on their jeans, I peeked out the window. Snow had drifted halfway up the glass.

"Unbelievable," I muttered, in awe of Mother Nature's frenzy. "You guys have to see this."

As they eased in beside me, Nick shook his head and chuckled. "Looks like we'll have to find a way to occupy our time. We're definitely not hunting."

"I'm sure we'll come up with something fun to do." Dylan winked with a crooked grin. "You know…like the dishes."

"Oh yeah, that was the first thing on my list," Nick quipped sarcastically.

As we cleaned up the kitchen—me naked once more, and them wearing nothing but low-slung jeans—their proximity became a test of self-control. Every cell in my body wanted to drag my tongue over their sculpted bodies. But I couldn't. I didn't have permission. Of course, that didn't stop me from torturing them as much as they were me.

Purposely spreading my legs and bending at the waist to put the frying pan away, I caught a furtive glimpse of Dylan watching me. As he cursed under his breath, I grinned. It was all the encouragement I needed. Taunting them with suggestive poses, I continued putting the dishes away. But their playful swats, gentle caresses, and possessive gropes had me aching for more. My plan had totally backfired, but my hormones weren't complaining.

While I wiped down the stove, Dylan strode down the hall to his room, only to reappear a few minutes later carrying a big, black duffle bag.

"You were reading my mind." Nick grinned.

"What's in the bag, Sir?" I asked.

"A good Dom is like a boy scout. They always come prepared," Dylan replied as he set it on the dining table. "Trust me, kitten, we're damn prepared."

"For everything," Nick stressed. "Especially curious subs stranded on the side of the road."

"Why do I get the feeling something scary is inside that bag?"

"Is that how you speak to us, little one?" Nick's brow arched.

"I mean, Sirs," I amended with a grimace.

"Only scary for subs who don't remember proper protocol," Dylan chided.

"Yikes," I gulped. "I promise to do better, Sirs."

"Then nothing in there should be scary to you…only fun," Nick stressed.

As Dylan slowly opened the bag, I inched close to the table. Though the snick of the heavy-duty zipper heightened my curiosity, I was too hesitant to look inside. So, I simply watched Dylan pull out several thick bundles of white, cotton rope.

Excitement bloomed.

"Dylan is a Shibari master," Nick announced. "Have you read about Shibari, little one?"

"No, Sir."

"It's Japanese rope bondage. It's quite lovely to look at and even more impressive for the sub that's bound in so many intricate knots."

A tiny quiver slid through me as I watched Dylan unwrap various lengths of rope and drape them over the table.

When he was done, he smiled at me and crooked his finger. "Spread your legs and raise your arms out to the side."

Without hesitation, I complied as Nick eased in beside him.

Together, they worked the rope around my waist, under my arms, and beneath my breasts. Pausing along the way, they tied the rope into knots. The combination of their warm, capable hands and the braided cotton gliding over my flesh filled me with a type of peace I'd never felt before.

Dropping my chin, I watched as they continued binding and aligning dozens of intricate knots between my breasts, around my waist, and up my back. Lost in the sublime sensation of being restrained, I closed my eyes and sighed before floating away to a silent corner in my mind.

I purred as a length of rope slid between my folds—laving a wicked kiss over my clit—before bisecting my ass cheeks. Dylan mumbled something about my wet pussy, but I was too far gone to process his words. Suspended in ethereal clouds of serenity, I continued sailing, never wanting to touch back down.

At once, their hot mouths engulfed my breasts. I was still moaning as Nick and Dylan drew demandingly on each of pebbled peak before pressing the sensitive nubs to the roofs of their mouths. Skimming their strong hands over my tingling flesh, they nipped, laved, and sucked my heavy breasts until I was panting and writhing. Each rock of my hips sent an enticing burn blossoming over my clit as the strategically placed knot burnished my pearl like a lover's thumb. Pulses of electricity streaked through my body as I uninhibitedly ground myself against the cluster of knots.

When a hard slap landed on my ass, my eyes flew open and a squeal tore off my lips as both men lifted their sinful mouths from my breasts.

"Welcome back, kitten. I take it you're enjoying the ropes?"

"Mmm," I purred. "Yes, Sir. They're amazing."

"I think you like this knot the best, little one," Nick teased as he tugged on the rope between my legs.

"Yesss," I hissed. "Especially that one."

My admission made them chuckle.

"Tell us how you're feeling," Dylan asked, staring at me intently.

"Wonderful...amazing even, Sir. I feel like I'm floating in clouds. The ropes are tight but they don't hurt, in fact, they feel incredible. I've dreamed about being bound, though never like this, but I never imagined it would make me feel so safe...and whole." I paused and frowned. "It's more than that, but I can't find words to describe the bliss I'm feeling right now."

"What way did you dream about being bound?" Nick asked.

"The regular way, Sir. You know...tied to the bed. But this...this is mind-blowing."

"We're glad to hear that." He grinned.

"Do you feel safe enough for us to bind your arms?" Dylan asked.

"Oh, yes, Sir. Please."

"No more trying to get yourself off, little one," Nick scolded. "That's our job. Do it again and we'll cut that rope between your legs. We like watching you suffer. Orgasm denial is a good thing."

"I don't like the sound of that, Sir."

He laughed. "I'm sure you don't."

"Personally, I think edging might be a nice...experience for her," Dylan interjected, guiding my arms to the front of my body before pressing my wrists together. "Hold your arms like this, and don't move."

"I won't, Sir. But what's edging?" I asked as he began wrapping and looping the rope through and around my wrists.

"Edging is a bit more sadistic than orgasm denial." His blue eyes sparkled mischievously. "It involves taking you to the brink of orgasm then bringing you back down, over and over, until the combination of frustration, delirium, and need completely consumes you. It's an effective tool for punishment."

"That doesn't sound fun at all. Don't you two implement fun punishments...Sirs?"

"No. That defeats the purpose of a *punishment*." Nick grinned. "However, some punishments backfire on Doms. Like your spanking earlier."

"How did that backfire?" I asked as Dylan continued securing a beautiful row of knots from my wrists to my elbows.

"You enjoyed it," Nick growled.

"All done," Dylan announced, smiling at his stunning artwork. "This isn't the type of Shibari I'd put you in for a suspension scene at

Genesis. I simply wanted you to get a sense of what the ropes feel like."

"What is Genesis?"

"It's our BDSM club back home," Nick responded, dragging an approving stare up and down my bound body. "You look absolutely gorgeous."

"We should have brought a frame with us," Dylan groused.

"If we'd known we were going to be playing, instead of hunting, we probably would have," Nick smirked.

"It would have been fun to suspend our sexy girl and watch her float away to subspace."

Subspace?

"Is that the dreamy feeling I kept experiencing?

Dylan smiled and combed his fingers through my hair. "Yes, kitten. You were definitely floating in subspace."

"Are you sure?"

"Yes. We could tell by the way your eyes grew glassy and unfocused."

"It's definitely a peaceful place. But it's strange, too. My mind and everything around me falls quiet, but I can still hear and feel what you both are doing to me. I like it."

"That's how it's supposed to be," Nick proudly assured.

"So...now that you two have me trussed up like a turkey, what's next?" I smirked.

"Greedy much?" Nick teased.

"I can't help it. We've only got..." Instead of reminding them our days were numbered, I let my words die off. Like a sponge, I wanted to absorb every sensation and emotion they were willing to share, but feared we'd run out of time. "I mean, I'm anxious to learn, Sir."

Nick spanked my ass with a growl. "This all stops if you can't be honest."

I gasped as the sting climbed up my spine. "We only have a few short days, Sir. I want to learn it all."

"Much better." There was a disquieting edge to Nick's voice as he and Dylan exchanged a somber glance. "We'll teach you all we can in the time we're given."

My throat tightened and my eyes stung. I'd inadvertently pointed out the elephant in the room. And with it, the disquieting realization that, I'd not only allowed them to bind my body, but my heart was already tangled in the ropes of their Dominance as well.

It wasn't supposed to happen. I wasn't supposed to let my heart get involved.

A rolling wave of panic washed through me.

"I'm sorry to ask this after you've gone to all this trouble of tying me up, Dylan, Sir, but I need to use the restroom. Could you take off the ropes now, Sir?"

Chapter Five

It was a cowardly way out, but I needed a few minutes to gather my thoughts...to cordon off my heart and set some internal boundaries. As they released the ropes, I closed my eyes. My freedom was bittersweet. As each strand fell from my body, a layer of submission went with it.

The slap of reality was too harsh. I wasn't equipped to handle it. The power they wielded was far more potent and persuasive than I'd dreamed possible. They'd stolen my heart so fast—even after vowing not to let them—I had to reclaim it now.

When the last piece of rope slid from my flesh, I forced myself to walk—not run—to my room. Desperate to compartmentalize my swirling emotions, I raced to the bathroom. After shutting and locking the door, I sat on the edge of the spa tub and scrubbed a hand over my face.

I hadn't even started sorting a damn thing out before the doorknob twisted and rattled.

"Open the door, Savannah," Nick's deep voice thundered from the other side.

"I'm almost done," I screeched, lurching to my feet and flushing the toilet in ruse.

"You've just earned a round of edging. Open *now* or we'll find even more evil ways to punish you, little one."

Shit. Shit. Shit.

Gripping the knob, I pulled the door open. Their faces were etched in matching disapproval. My stomach knotted, and not in the fun Shibari kind.

"Why are you punishing me? I didn't do anything."

Dylan scowled and grunted before walking toward the bed and pointing to the floor. "On your knees and over the bed."

"But, I—"

"You don't have permission to speak," Nick growled.

Trembling like a leaf, I somehow made it to the bed. As I knelt alongside the mattress I saw the black duffle bag on the floor. I had no doubt it contained plenty of wicked devices for unruly subs.

But I *wasn't* unruly.

I was simply confused and needed time alone to sort out my feelings.

Okay, so I hadn't been honest when I asked Dylan to untie me. But did I have to pay a price for wanting to get my head on straight?

"Lean over the bed and stretch your arms out. We don't want to see a pinky move. Understood?" Nick barked.

Complying, I closed my eyes. Angst galloped through me like a herd of wild horses.

A foot slid between my legs, nudging my knees apart once, twice, three times, until I was wide open to accept my punishment. Cool air wafted over my exposed pussy. I had no doubt they could see how wet I was.

A broad hand splayed over the small of my back as the bed dipped. Nick's scent surrounded me as his warm breath danced over the shell of my ear.

"You asked why we're punishing you?"

"Yes, Sir."

"Because you shut down on us like a light switch. We'll give you ten seconds to explain what trigger flipped in that beautiful head of yours."

Though his harsh command made my pussy ooze and throb there

was no way I could confess I had feelings for them…that I'd given my heart along with my submission. I might as well tattoo *pathetic loser* on my damn forehead.

I'd take their punishment then find a way to secure my heart. Instead of explaining myself, I mulishly pressed my lips together.

"Nothing to say?" Dylan taunted.

I shook my head and tensed in anticipation of the pain they were going to inflict.

But when two fingers plunged deep inside my core, I jerked in surprise. And when a masterful thumb began strumming my clit, I moaned, "Oh, god."

"We're not gods, girl. We're just two tenacious Masters determined to tear down your walls. You'll communicate with us and tell us what's bothering you, even if we have to keep you here all night."

There was no malice in Dylan's tone, just the buttery promise that they intended to slice me wide open with pleasure.

Their determined and decadent fingers toyed and teased my pussy, setting me on a collision course with the stars. Struggling to force down the orgasm rising inside me, I jolted when one of them began massaging something wet and cold over the puckered rim of my ass.

My nerve endings ignited like fireworks, sizzling and exploding in mind-bending sensations I'd never felt before.

All notion of holding back the pleasure roaring inside me went up in smoke.

"Too much. Too much," I wailed.

Unable to harness my orgasm, I tried to sit up to keep from failing them.

"Easy," Nick commanded, splaying his hand at the small of my back. Holding me in place like an anvil on a fly, he leaned in close to my ear. "It's only lube. You've never experienced ass play before, have you?"

"No, Sir." I tensed again, waiting for his fat cock to invade my virgin opening.

"You'll need to get used to it, little one." He chuckled. "We'll need to do a lot of anal training before you can take us both together."

The sinister fingers strumming my pussy suddenly pulled away.

With a pitiful groan, I writhed in frustration until a familiar buzzing sound filled the room.

"It's time to take you to the edge," Dylan taunted, pressing the tip of the vibe to my clit. "Remember, kitten, you don't have permission to come."

"No, you don't," Nick seconded. "But you will simmer for us. Maybe then you'll be willing to answer our questions."

Within minutes, I was on the cusp of orgasm. Squirming, I tried to escape the vibrating demon. Desperate for release or reprieve, my limbs grew numb and my tunnel expanded. The orgasm barreled down on me like a freight train. Keening in panic, I gripped the sheets.

And as release crested like a tidal wave, Dylan removed the vibe, stalling my orgasm.

I slumped against the mattress as a groan of frustration bubbled from the back of my throat.

"Why did you shut down on us earlier?" Nick asked in a deep, whiskey-smooth voice.

So, they wanted to play twenty questions with my arousal again. Dammit, I hated this game. Determined to stick to my story, I didn't understand why they couldn't let me get away with one little white lie. We could move on to bigger and better things...like the massive orgasm clawing inside me.

"I had to go to the bathroom."

A humorless chuckle rolled off Nick's lips as the vibrator whirred to life again.

"You don't have permission yet," he reminded with an evil smile.

"Surprise. Surprise," I bit out defiantly, then whimpered as Dylan pressed the vibe against my clit.

In a matter of seconds, the threat of release thundered through me. Screams of need and panic tore from my throat.

"Don't do it." Nick's commanding roar melded with my carnal shrieks.

"I...c-can't...h-hold...back," I wailed.

And just as I started to shatter, Dylan jerked the vibe away.

My screams of protest and pitiful sobs echoed off the walls.

"N-no more. P-please," I begged.

"You hold the power to stop it," Dylan replied, caressing his wide hand up and down my spine. "Answer the question, and we'll let you shatter into a million pieces, kitten."

"I don't want to answer the fucking question, I just want to come," I wailed.

"*Why* don't you want to answer it, our filthy-mouthed slut?" Nick growled.

"Because it's personal," I whined, sagging against the mattress.

"That's all the more reason to tell us, little one."

"No. Some things I want to keep private, all right? We're not in a relationship. You simply giving me lessons."

Nick wedged his burly arm beneath me before flipping me onto my back. Then he climbed onto the bed and hovered over me with a lethal scowl.

His words sliced me open like a scalpel.

"We're not going to let you fall, little one," he whispered. "Not today, not tomorrow, not even next week."

"You can't promise that." My voice cracked as tears stung my eyes. "When this is over, you and Dylan will be back in Chicago, and I'll…"

"You'll what?" Dylan asked, climbing onto the bed beside me.

His eyes, brimming with warmth and compassion, unraveled me.

"I'll go back to…to dreaming about all this."

"You can do more than dream about it." Dylan smiled, then bent and sipped the tear that escaped my eye.

"How?" I sniffed.

As he sat up, he and Nick exchanged a knowing glance before Nick subtly nodded.

"Mika. He's the owner of Genesis and a good friend. We can reach out to him and ask him to find you a lifestyle group and a club you can join when you go back to Kansas City."

"You can?"

"And we will," Dylan confirmed. "There's no way we're going to open you up and draw out your submission without also giving you a safety net. Unfortunately, we can't be that safety net, no matter how much we want to."

The offer was a responsible one.

But the reality that I let myself envision where they would give me more than they could offer, along with losing my heart to them, burned like acid.

But what else could Nick and Dylan offer besides passing me off to some club or group in KC and hope I found a Dominant willing to claim me?

The sad truth was…nothing.

Until I found a way to erase my foolish fantasies and insulate my heart, I couldn't take one more step down this precarious path with Nick and Dylan.

With a gulp of steadfast determination, I quelled my tears. Somehow, I'd find a way to tuck away my foolish dreams, draw a hard line in the sand, then carry on with my training. I'd take the knowledge they were willing to give me, then seek out a Dominant of my own, when and if I decided to. There was no need for them to fix me up with a stranger. I didn't want a stranger, I wanted Dylan and Nick. And if I could only have them for a short time, then so be it.

"I appreciate your concern, but I'd rather you not contact Mika. I'll find a Dominant on my own."

"Nobody said anything about fixing you up with another Dom," Nick snarled.

"Easy, bro," Dylan warned with a cautious stare.

"No," he challenged. "If we expect her to be open and honest with us, then we have to do the same."

"Nick," Dylan chided, his cerulean eyes flashing in silent warning.

"Savannah." Nick gazed at me, ignoring Dylan. His charcoal eyes softened as he smoothed a hand through my hair. "We're not looking to hook you up with a Dominant. The thought of you kneeling before someone else and looking up at him with your beautiful, trusting brown eyes makes me want to slam my fist through a lead wall."

"I don't understand." I was afraid to breathe…afraid to hope.

"You've touched me, little one. In here." He patted his heart. "And when this week is done, I'll be carrying a piece of you with me."

His words made my mind whirl like a carnival ride. Nick wasn't making a declaration of love by any stretch of the imagination, yet despite the tension it was causing between him and Dylan, he was being honest.

"And you with me, Sir," I replied softly before glancing at Dylan. Would he be taking a piece of me with him, too?

"I'm sorry, kitten." Dylan's expression was filled with sorrow and guilt.

I had my answer.

"You've nothing to be sorry for, Sir."

"I'm good with a joke, but when it comes to relationships and shit…" He shrugged and shook his head.

When I caught sight of his emotional fortress, I realized I wasn't the only one hiding parts of myself behind walls. As memories of Psych class back in college roared through my brain, the lesson about the various ways people hid their pain and trauma behind masks— especially masks of humor—had the puzzle pieces snapping into place. My heart ached for Dylan, not with pity, but sorrow for the ordeals— most likely in Iraq—he'd been through.

Desperate to help ease his fears, I cupped his cheek. "I promise I won't ask you to marry me then."

As he blinked at me in shock, I couldn't help but grin. And when he tossed his head back and laughed, relief sailed through me.

"I like this sassy side of you, kitten. Claws and all."

"I'll remind you of that the next time you decide to punish me with edging, Sir. That suc…stunk, really stunk." I glanced at Nick then flashed an innocent smile.

"Better, but you have a long way to go." Nick smirked. "Where did you learn to cuss like a sailor?"

I shrugged. "I grew up in a house with colorful language. Sometimes, it just slips out."

"Like when you talk to your sister?" Dylan grinned.

I nodded. "You can't tell me that you two choir boys don't swear. I've heard you."

"True, but we don't like to hear *you* curse."

"You're in construction, for crying out loud. It's not like you've not heard those words and worse. I was at a site once and a guy asked if I wanted to see his purple headed yogurt slinger. I was like…seriously?"

Dylan started to laugh. Nick cupped his hand over his forehead and gaped at me as if I'd grown a third eye.

"Did you tell him yes?" Dylan asked.

"No. I did *not*!"

When Nick started laughing, I inwardly exhaled in relief. The weight of our awkward discussion had been purged, and the sounds of their happiness smoothed my ragged nerves.

"Fair enough, little one. Just watch your mouth with us. And Dylan, make sure no one on our crew ever mentions purple headed yogurt monsters."

"You got it." Dylan grinned and cupped my breast. "Speaking of business, don't you think it's time we got back to it?"

"Yes Sir. I think that's a marvelous idea." I thrust my shoulders back, greedily lifting his palm.

Nick eased from the bed, stripped off his jeans, then positioned himself between my legs before spreading my thighs.

"You're dripping wet, little one. I think you liked the edging. Were you lying to us?"

I gasped as Dylan sucked a nipple in deep, flicking the sensitive tip with his tongue. The sizzling current surged straight to my clit.

"I wasn't lying, Sir. My body has a mind of its own when I'm with you two, Sir."

Nick chuckled, sending his wet breath floating over my needy pussy. "Ah, but you don't know what we have planned. And I don't remember saying anything about you enjoying it."

"Please, Sir, I've had enough torture for one day."

"You haven't begun to suffer for us, yet." His words were like rich, smooth chocolate…decadent and delicious.

I had no doubt Nick could make me suffer unimaginable agony. The thought alone made me even wetter.

He spread my folds with his broad thumbs, then swiped his slick tongue all the way up my center. The whimper that slid from my throat melded with his growl of approval.

I opened myself to his desires, and he devoured me like a starving animal.

While his tongue laid siege to my clit, his fingers invaded my quivering core. A wet finger rimmed my anus as Nick circled the gathered flesh in a delicate massage. Pulses of electricity arced in a dazzling fire, spreading outward from my virgin hole in an obscene ripple. Dylan nipped and laved my turgid nipples with urgency.

Lost in every sensation they commanded; I was at their mercy. While their fingers, tongues, teeth, and lips claimed my surrender, they tossed me toward the heavens like a sapling in a hurricane. I welcomed the building pressure, basked in the gathering electricity numbing my limbs, and savored the carnal fire pumping through my veins.

"Please. Please. Please," I impatiently mewled.

"You beg so fucking sweetly," Dylan praised as he tugged my throbbing nipple between his teeth. "Shatter for us, kitten. Come now. Come hard!"

His words sliced the fragile threads of my control.

Dylan sank his teeth into my nipple, pinching the other with a brutal squeeze.

As Nick's broad finger breached my puckered rim, driving deep inside my dark passage, I screamed and arched my hips and completely shattered.

A feral roar splintered the air as Nick ripped his fingers from inside me.

My tunnel fluttered in abandonment as a mournful wail tore from my throat.

"Hang on, baby," Nick hissed impatiently. "I have to feel you, pet."

The sound of a condom wrapper slowly registered in my brain as I writhed and bucked at the savage emptiness inside me. And just when I thought I was going to burn alive, I felt his hard crest nudge my slit.

"Yes, please. Fuck me, Nick. Fuck me hard."

"Fuck her, Nick. Do it," Dylan demanded on a feral whisper.

Nick slapped the broad head of his cock against my clit and I screamed as the orgasm continued to toss me in its tempest.

"It's Sir, my luscious little slut," he roared as he pushed his fat crest through my narrow opening, then drove deep inside my clutching tunnel. His cock was huge, but the pain of my yielding tissues as the most exquisite torture I'd even felt.

"Sir...Sir, fuck yes. Oh yes, Fuck me...hard," I begged, meeting his measured strokes with frenzy.

While Nick continued thrusting in and out of my pussy...dragging his thick head over my ignited G-spot, Dylan shoved a pillow beneath my head before tapping his cock on my lips.

"Open, kitten. Swallow me down that glorious throat. Suck my cock, baby."

Parting my lips, I extended my tongue. The muscles in my throat tightened as I gazed at Dylan's shorn sac, tightly drawn in narrow ripples; separating his orbs was a thick rigid line. As I inhaled his potent, masculine scent, I slid my mouth over his swollen crest.

Working him inside my mouth, inch after glorious inch, a symphony of whimpers, hisses, grunts, and growls filled the thick and pungent, sexually saturated air.

As Dylan's cock nudged the back of my throat, I burrowed my nose against his thick pubic hair and breathed in his savage musk.

Nick drove deeper and faster into my blazing core, surging the crescendo higher and harder. Unable to focus on their individual sensations, I surrendered, allowing them to claim me any way they wanted.

Nick brushed his finger over my sensitized clit, and once again, I took flight. Lost in splendor humming through me, I sailed higher and higher.

As my muffled cries of ecstasy vibrated over Dylan's cock, he gripped my hair and bellowed, "Now. Come now!"

An animalistic cry of triumph tore from his lungs as his hot, thick come jettisoned down my throat.

A split-second later, Nick released a thunderous cry.

As he spilled his seed into the condom, I swallowed, screamed, and gurgled on Dylan's come and fragmented. My entire body convulsed as my pussy gripped and milked Nick's cock.

Panting and sweating, I forced my heavy lids open.

Bliss etching his face, Dylan eased from my mouth, then gently caressed my cheek. Wearing a satisfied smile, Nick slowly pulled from my pussy and winked.

"You're amazing, little one," he panted.

He then rolled off the bed and padded to the bathroom.

While glorious aftershocks quaked through me, Dylan flopped down beside me. We were both still panting as if we'd run a marathon when Nick returned and gently wiped my sensitive folds with a warm cloth.

As he dropped onto the bed on the other side of me, I placed a palm on their wide chests. When they twined their fingers with mine, I closed my eyes and savored our connection. Though limp and sated, I'd never felt more alive and invigorated.

The shrill sound of Nick's sat phone caused all three of us to jump in surprise.

"I'm going to throw this fucking thing out the window," he groused as he sat up, snatched his jeans from the floor, and freed the phone.

"Hello," he barked with a scowl.

"Are you three doing okay? How is Savannah feeling today?"

I could hear Kit's voice through the earpiece and watched Nick's expression soften. A slow smile tugged the sides of his mouth.

"She's doing fine. I know she's sore, but she's not complaining." He grinned mischievously. "She cries out now and then and sometimes whimpers and moans."

His body shook with silent laughter as my eyes widened in horror. I had to bite my lips to keep from screaming at him.

"Do you have enough groceries? If not, I can try to dig a path and bring you some food."

"We've got plenty. We don't need a thing. I promise. Stay inside and keep warm. We're just hanging out down here and getting to know Savannah better by the minute." Nick flashed me a wicked smile. "Is everything okay up at the house?"

"Me and these two cuties from Des Moines are doing fine," Kit laughed.

"You're not corrupting them, are you?" Nick teased.

"I wouldn't remember how," she chuckled before her voice dropped. "I haven't heard a word from Mellie. I'm sure Savannah is worried sick."

When Nick relayed the news that her sister was safe and sound back home, Kit was happy and relieved, then reminded him there was dry wood in the mudroom. After thanking her and reassuring her, once again, that we were fine, he ended the call.

"I can't believe you said all those things to her," I gasped.

"What?" Nick blinked in a poor attempt at feigned innocence.

"You told Kit I was sore and moaning and that you were…" I raised two fingers on each hand and wiggled them in a quotes symbol. "Getting to know me better. She's going to think we're down here having sex."

"We were."

"Argh," I groaned. "I don't want her knowing."

"Why not?"

"Because it's private."

"And?"

"And…" *Dammit*! Why was he always digging at me? "I just don't want her to know."

"That's not a reason."

"Do we embarrass you?" Dylan frowned.

"No. God, no!"

Nick picked up the vibe and turned it on. "Need another reminder about honesty?"

"No. Put that away."

Nick tsked as Dylan sat up and held my legs open while Nick rubbed the vibe along the insides of my thighs. "Who gives the orders, little one?"

"You both do, Sir."

"That's right. Now answer Dylan's question…do we embarrass you?"

"No. It's just… I don't want her thinking I'm a slut who engages in one night stands, or one week stands, or any other kind of stand."

Without a word, Nick turned off the vibe, then stood and walked to the bathroom.

Dylan released my thighs with a heavy sigh.

"What did I do now, dammit? You're the ones who wanted me to be honest."

"Nick, bring back the vibe," Dylan barked.

"No. Please," I groaned as I sat up. "No more edging."

Nick stood in the frame of the doorway. My gaze skittered over his naked body, greedily absorbing the bounty of tight muscles stretched beneath his toffee skin. When I glanced at his face, he pinned me with a look that screamed Dominance *and* disappointment.

"Okay, look. I'm really trying here, you two. But you can't expect me to open up and vomit out all my feelings, then turn around and get pissy when you don't like what I say."

"Nobody's gotten pissy except you, kitten." Dylan smirked.

"You two are wearing pissy expressions. I can see them."

"But we're not the one throwing the tantrum now, are we?" Dylan's blue eyes twinkled as a sarcastic smile spread over his lips.

"Did you forget who you were addressing, little one?" Nick's dark brows slashed as he scowled and walked toward the bed...vibe in hand.

"No, Sir. I'm just trying to communicate. That's what I'm *supposed* to do, right?"

My tone was too sassy, but they were backing me into a corner. Call it a personality flaw, or pride, or whatever, but I always pushed back.

Dylan wrapped a hand in my hair, then stood...lifting me off the bed with him.

A wicked smile curled Nick's lips as he turned off the vibe and strode toward me.

"Shall we start this conversation over, little one?"

I swallowed the lump of fear in my throat and nodded before casting my eyes toward the floor. Well, as best I could with Dylan gripping my hair so tightly my scalp burned.

Nick placed the vibe on the nightstand and nodded. "Trust me. Submission will get you a lot further than arguing."

When he caressed my cheek, a part of me wanted to bite his fingers. Instead, I closed my eyes and tried to center myself and pound out the dents in my wounded pride.

"You're very beautiful when you let go," Nick said, pressing his lips against my ear.

"Thank you, Sir."

Dylan released my mane, then settled his wide hand on the small of my back.

"We're not happy hearing you equate what we're doing to something as insignificant as a one night stand." Dylan placed the fingers of his other hand beneath my chin, forcing my gaze. "If all we wanted was sex, we wouldn't waste our time searching for ways to unlock your submission, or praise and reassure you."

"What we're doing involves emotions far deeper than sex, Nick added. "Do you honestly not feel connected to us?"

Yes. Too much.

Flickers of concern and rejection reflected in his eyes. And as an oily wave of guilt spilled through me, I realized the roots of my submission weren't planted in how many orgasms they gave me, but finding my fulfillment in submitting to them.

"Yes, Sir. You both have touched me, too. But I didn't mean it the way it sounded."

"Then what did you mean?" Dylan asked, gently squeezing my neck.

"I meant that Kit knows me. She knows I'm…inexperienced. We're girls. We talk about things like that, especially after a shi… a few glasses of Merlot." I closed my eyes and exhaled, finding it hard to correct my words while trying to make a point. "I didn't want her to know what we're doing here because I didn't want her to think I was a kinky freak."

"Does it matter what people think?" Dylan asked.

"Yes. I know it shouldn't, but Kit's a friend. And why I share a lot of things with her, I can't share this. I'm not even sure I can tell Mellie about what we're doing. I don't know that she'd understand how you two make me feel…how submission fills the empty spaces inside me. I don't even have words to describe what's happening to me." My gaze flittered back and forth between them, searching for a glimmer of understanding.

"We don't want to be your dirty little secret, nor will we ever allow you to be ours." Dylan frowned. "We hope what we're teaching you will help you grow past your fears and erase the preconceived notions of how you think you're supposed to behave or conform. All we want is for you to see yourself and your desires in a new light. Does that make sense?"

"Yes, Sir," I whispered.

"Good." Nick smiled. "I vote we take a break and all go soak in the spa tub. We can't tackle everything in one day."

His suggestion sent hope soaring. Maybe taking a bit of the pressure off, I could finally get all this submissive stuff down, or at least sort it out.

Dylan cupped my chin, then claimed my lips with a potent, drugging kiss. "Don't forget, we're going to be here, right beside you, every step of the way."

They would, for a week at least. After that...

Chapter Six

Though the tub was designed for two people, it was large enough for three. The hot, bubbling water soothed my sensitive folds, but the way Dylan and Nick pampered me was far more relaxing. As they passed me between them, their reassuring hands never left my skin while they gently washed my body, then shampooed and conditioned my hair.

Tranquil and boneless, I snuggled against Dylan's brawny chest while Nick draped his strong body over my back. If I'd had the ability to stop time, cocooned in their silent affection, I would have chosen that moment to do it. Though I was in uncharted and unfamiliar territory, nothing in my life had ever felt so right, or granted me such inner peace.

"How sore is your pussy?" Nick asked in an enticing whisper.

"Mmmm," I purred. "Just a little bit."

Nick nipped the lobe of my ear. "Just a little bit, what?"

"Sir. Just a little bit, Sir," I replied on a dreamy moan.

"Then we'll leave it alone for a bit and begin your anal training."

My eyes flew open, and I jerked my head off Dylan's chest, nearly colliding with Nick's chin. "My what?"

A devilish grin spread over Nick's lips. "Your anal training."

"Oh, no, Sir. I misspoke. My clit is fine. Honest."

Lifting from my back, he eased in beside Dylan before cupping my face. "Have you already forgotten what you get for lying? Or do you secretly enjoy edging?"

"I do and I don't." I exhaled. "My pussy is a little sore, but not so sore you two need to ignore it, Sir."

"That's not your decision. Why are you so scared to start anal training?"

"I'm afraid it's going to hurt."

"Have we hurt you yet?" Dylan asked.

"Of course not, Sir."

"Then you have no actual reason to fear it." Dylan winked.

He was right. They'd done everything to earn my trust. The misunderstandings we'd had so far were born of *my* fears and insecurities. I knew in my heart they'd never intentionally hurt me, but it didn't erase my apprehension of them shoving things up my butt.

"How does it work, Sirs?"

"That a girl." Nick smiled. "But don't worry, we'll start out small."

An hour later I found out that *small* was a matter of perception. Small for Nick was *huge* and uncomfortable in my opinion.

After climbing from the tub and drying off, they eased me to my knees and bent me over the bed. While plying me with soothing words and encouragement, Nick slathered my puckered rim with lube before Dylan slid a slim, silver butt plug—adorned with sparkling purple jewels on the base—straight up my butt.

I never knew how much concentration it took to clench the sensitive opening in order to keep the plug in place. Each movement ignited a war between my body and mind. My body screamed to remove the unwanted intruder, while my mind screamed to do whatever it took to please my teachers.

Shuffling to the couch, I slowly eased onto the cushion. Though I was grateful I didn't have to parade around the room, I struggled to cope with the dull throb engulfing my little rim. Though I didn't enjoy this part of my training, Nick and Dylan took great pleasure and pride in my discomfort.

Nick built a fire so I could warm myself and relax before he joined

Dylan in the kitchen to prepare dinner. It was still snowing outside. A part of me wanted the blizzard to rage on forever. Except for the plug up my ass, the fantasy they'd created was practically perfect.

I listened to their banter and grinned as I watched the flames dance and flicker.

By the time dinner was done and darkness fell, the combination kitchen/living room was warm and toasty. The plug was less distracting and painful, but I didn't strike any provocative poses putting the dishes away this time. I was too scared the damn thing would pop out.

After we finished cleaning the kitchen, Nick grabbed a bottle of wine before the three of us eased onto the couch.

My first day of training was done, and both men were anxious for me to give them feedback. Trying to put my feelings and emotions into words was hard, but I managed to convey the peace I found being bound. I didn't candy-coat how I felt about edging, but after tons of ribbing from Dylan, I had to confess when they finally allowed me to come the power of my orgasm ranked somewhere between heaven and life-altering.

"And what about the plug?" Nick chuckled. "How does it rate?"

"At first, a minus ten. Now, it's okay. I know it's part of the preparation."

Preparation to fulfill my ultimate fantasy. Well, one of them anyway. I dreamt of visiting a fetish club almost as much as I yearned to experience double penetration. The latter filled me with trepidation, even with anal training. I wasn't sure I could accommodate both their massive cocks. But before I let my fears get the best of me, I mentally blocked it from my brain.

"What is Genesis like, Sirs?"

"It's amazing," Dylan began. "The members are genuine and kindhearted. It's hard not to think of them as extended family."

I could feel the love surrounding his words. "What do they do there?"

"Every kind of power exchange you can imagine," Nick chimed in. "From soft erotic scenes to blood dripping edge play."

A shiver skittered up my spine. "The blood thing sounds scary."

"It's all consensual and negotiated," Dylan assured. "While we have a private room, like most of the regular members, there's something to be said about sitting in the dungeon and watching all the various scenes play out before your eyes."

"A private room? I guess you two play with a lot of subs, huh?" I tried to mask my sudden spike of jealousy, but clearly failed when Nick turned and studied me for several long seconds.

"Yes, we have. But that doesn't lessen what we're sharing here with you. Understand?"

"Of course, Sir. I didn't honestly think you two were choir boys." I smiled, making light of my foolish insecurities. "So, what's your private room like?"

"It has a bed, bathroom, and a large play space with a suspension rack, bondage table, and a cross."

"Our equipment isn't as big as the ones in the main dungeon, but they serve the same purpose," Dylan added.

Images of all the ways they could use me inside their room swirled through my head. Fearing I'd leave a puddle on the couch, I quickly changed the subject. "George, the man you were talking to yesterday, is he a club member, too?"

"Genesis has strict rules about anonymity, but since you heard me talking to him about Leagh and punishment, yes. He is a member, as well as my lawyer. George is much older than his mischievous sub, who goes by the name Dahlia at the club. She definitely keeps him on his toes."

Dylan laughed loudly. "That's an understatement, bro. She's a hellcat. But, you're right. She's exactly what he needs. Dahlia's antics breathe life into George and give him an energy you can practically feel."

"I remember you saying something about bunny floggers." I grinned at Nick. "How much younger is his sub?"

"George is pushing seventy and Dahlia is probably...mid-twenties." Dylan nodded.

Forty plus years was a huge age difference. Why would a woman close to my age want to submit to a Dom so much older?

"Age isn't an issue for most in the lifestyle," Nick replied as if reading my mind. "Like the vanilla world, we're all puzzle pieces. When you find the one that's a perfect fit, nothing else matters."

"I'd love for you to one day meet Emerald, kitten." Dylan smiled.

"Emerald?"

"That's her club name. She mentors new subs and knows a lot about the lifestyle."

"Club name. You mean that's not her real name?"

"No. Lots of Doms and subs choose a club name to protect their identities. Even though Mika has implemented a rigorous vetting process, there are some high-profile members. Anonymity is a must so people don't lose their kids or their careers. Like Nick said, who you see and what they do at the club stays inside its walls. It's a cardinal rule."

"Do you both have club names, Sirs?"

"No." Nick shook his head. "Neither of us have kids, and since I own my own company, there's no risk if we're outed."

"And you think there is a club like Genesis in Kansas City?"

"Maybe not exactly like it, but I know there are lifestyle groups and like-minded people in the city who will welcome you with open arms." Dylan smiled, but it didn't quite reach his eyes.

I nibbled my bottom lip and nodded as my mind whirled.

Being with Dylan and Nick felt as if they were the right puzzle pieces for me. Were there really other Doms out there who I could connect with the way I did them?

As I lowered my head, an ironic smile tugged my lips. I'd been naked nearly all day and not once had I been embarrassed by it. Even crazier, being naked around them felt like the most natural thing to do. Had they really changed me that much in two short days? Would I ever be this relaxed around another Dom or Doms?

As I mentally continued down that rabbit hole, the thought of kneeling for anyone other than Dylan and Nick made my heart ache.

Your heart has no business being in the middle of this mix, the little voice reminded.

No, it didn't. The best I could do was etch every minute I spent with Nick and Dylan to memory, then go home and find a Dom who could continue teaching me everything I needed to know.

"You're thinking awfully hard, little one. Share with us," Nick coaxed.

"I'm just taking it all in. The thought of being in a club like Genesis is…intriguing."

An unusual silence fell over the room.

"Once I get home, I'm going to have to look into finding a club to join."

A fierce scowl appeared on Nick's face, and his body tensed. Even Dylan's relaxed demeanor took on a visible edge. I wasn't trying to demean their training, but my attempt to convince them I was self-reliant had totally backfired. Then I remembered what Nick had said about me kneeling before another. What was I supposed to do, erase all these wonderful feelings they'd unlocked inside me and go back to *reading* books about the lifestyle? That wasn't fair.

"You don't like that idea much, do you, Sirs?" I asked, studying their stormy expressions. No, they didn't like it at all. "Is there another alternative to pursue the lifestyle that I don't know about."

"No," Dylan replied curtly.

"All right, then why does my seeking out a Dominant to finish training me piss you two off? I can't just go back to my life again. You two have opened me up. There's no way I can shove all these wants and needs down inside me again."

"We realize that, kitten. But doesn't mean we have to like it," Dylan grumbled.

"I don't like the idea of having to get comfortable with another Dom either, but I'll do it. I'm a strong, capable woman. I'll do whatever I have to until I find a Dom or Doms who are as patient and understanding as you two are." I sent them both reassuring smiles, then without asking permission, I kissed each of them on the cheek. "Thank you for opening my eyes."

As I leaned away from Nick, he gripped my hair and dragged my lips to his before searing me with a raw, urgent claim. I could taste his desperation. I and met his frenzied kisses head on before realizing it wasn't a contest. He *needed* to give me his power. I relaxed and softened my lips before parting them and opening for his tongue.

A low growl rumbled up from deep in his chest as he cinched my hair tighter and took total control of the kiss. As he urgently devoured me, claiming every inch of my mouth, I clutched his broad shoulders.

While his inky hair danced over my fingers, Dylan dragged his tongue up my spine and over my shoulder. Scraping my flesh with his teeth, he nipped and laved the hammering pulse point at the base of my throat with a hungry groan.

My pussy clenched, forcing the muscles of my ass to constrict around the plug. Splinters of lightning ignited outward, setting my clit ablaze. Without invitation, I climbed my way up Nick's body and straddled his lap while he wrecked my mouth with blistering kisses. Whimpering for relief, I ground my throbbing pussy against his hard cock trapped inside his jeans.

"Fuck, Savannah," Dylan whispered as he eased off the couch and knelt behind me.

As Nick fed on my desperate cries, Dylan tapped the jeweled base of the plug, sending a lurid drum echoing over my electrified nerve endings.

Talons of need tore through me as I ripped my lips from Nick's mouth.

"Please, Masters. Please help me," I begged.

As Dylan continued tapping at the plug, I writhed and raked my aching nipples over Nick's hard chest like a cat in heat.

"Fuck! I need a condom," Nick roared as he gripped my hips and lifted me off his lap before freeing his cock in a frenzied rush.

Gazing at the glistening wet tip, I wriggled free and slid to my knees beside Dylan.

My flesh stretched tight around the plug, sending me sliding down an avalanche of spine-bending pleasure.

Desperation multiplied to demand.

Dylan launched to his feet and raced away. I didn't watch where he was going, I was too mesmerized at the sight of Nick's weeping erection to look away. Unable to resist the need to taste his salty essence and glide my tongue over his angry, distended veins, I opened my mouth and leaned in.

"No. Not yet," he barked as he fisted my hair, and pulled me away from his crest. Staring into my eyes with a fervent stare, he shook his head. "You don't take what you want from me, sweet slut. You beg."

"Please, Master. I need to taste your cock."

"Such a sweet, insatiable slut," Nick growled. "No. You're going to do more than taste me, girl. You're going to worship my cock... worship it with that sinful mouth of yours...and worship it with all your heart."

Cinching my hair tighter, Nick guided my lips to his thick, weeping crest.

Opening wide, I engulfed his swollen crest, moaning in delight as his slick nectar glazed my tongue.

Dylan groaned behind me as the duffle bag hit the floor. "Ass in the air, kitten. It's time to play."

Rising to my knees, I cupped Nick's balls with one hand and stroked the base of his shaft with the other, then smiled around his cock as he let out a hiss. When Dylan tapped the inside of my thighs, I spread my legs as I continued bobbing, sucking, and swirling my tongue around Nick's thick cock.

"You're dripping wet, kitten," Dylan drawled. "I think you like the plug."

As Dylan gripped the base of the plug and spun it like the hands of a clock, I cried out over Nick's shaft. With a bellowed curse, he pulled my mouth off his cock and lifted my head.

"I want to hear your cries while Dylan prepares your tight ass for a bigger plug."

"Bigger? Oh, god," I moaned.

My clit throbbed incessantly while Dylan continued to swirl and tug on the wicked plug...sending shards of electricity sputtering outward before skipping up my spine and down my legs.

Torturously long seconds later, he slowly pulled the plug from my ass. My gathered rim began constricting and releasing in an attempt to return to normal. But before that could happen, Dylan smeared a glob of cold lube to my quivering backside before coating me completely with his thick finger. The sensation was so excruciatingly arousing I wanted to crawl out of my skin.

"You've dilated beautifully. You're definitely ready for a larger plug," Dylan announced still thinning and stretching my puckered rim.

"No, please. Put the other one back in, Sir. I can't handle a bigger one."

"Sure you can. And you will because it pleases us," Nick announced, guiding my head toward his lap. "Put your mouth back to work on my cock, little one. And no more screaming. The vibration makes me want to lose control."

While Nick fed each glorious inch into my mouth, Dylan continued widening and stretching me open. My nerve endings were screaming with a sublime mixture of pleasure and pain. I couldn't wait to come.

Bobbing up and down on Nick's cock, I slurped and moaned while shamelessly rocking my hips, all while clutching around Dylan's finger with my virgin hole.

"We're almost there. Just a tiny bit more." His hot, wet breath floated over the cheeks of my ass, adding to the growing fire inside me. "I can't wait to bury my cock in your tight, silky ass. It's going to be fucking heaven."

"I can't wait until we're both inside her," Nick said in a thick, gravely growl.

"Fuck, yessss," Dylan hissed, adding more lube before pressing the cold tip of another plug to my throbbing flesh.

Swirling the new plug, he slowly pressed t in deeper and deeper.

Flashes of light exploded behind my eyes.

My body trembled and quaked.

Pressure mounted beneath my clit.

It was too much.

Too intense.

I needed relief…now.

Lowering my hand to my pussy, I boldly strummed my clit and moaned before thrusting my hips back, driving the plug in deeper.

Yanking me off his cock, Nick gripped my wrist before pulling my hand from my pussy.

"We didn't give you permission to touch our clit, girl. Place your hands flat on my things, and don't move them. Understood?"

Mewling in frustration, I nodded and complied, still rocking against the plug.

"Relax, kitten," Dylan whispered as Nick filled my mouth with his cock once more. "We're almost there. You're doing beautifully. We're so fucking proud of you."

His praise sent me soaring until I floated through the heavens. Silence surrounded me as I basked in my surrender and the sinful sensations they drowned me in.

Nick's veins pulsated on my tongue. I could practically feel the sweet hum of arousal vibrating off his heated shaft. As Dylan slid the plug into place, I reveled in the burn enveloping my throbbing, taut ring.

"Get inside her quickly, bro. Her lush mouth is about to make me come undone," Nick confessed.

Dylan grunted, then pressed his latex-sheathed crest between my folds. "You ready for me to fuck you, kitten...ready to see what it feels like to be stuffed completely full?"

Shivering with excitement, I moaned a muffled gurgle, then bore down, silently begging Dylan to fill and stretch me.

Their hungry curses filled the air as their fingers plucked and pinched my nipples. When Dylan finally drove balls deep into my fluttering core—a blissful burn of pleasure, pain, and pressure consumed me. I'd never been filled so fully or stretched so tightly in my life.

Wedged between their hot, thrusting bodies, their carnal grunts and groans melded with the thick veil of sex hanging in the air.

My dark forbidden fantasy had come to life.

It was more surreal than anything I'd ever imagined alone in my bed.

With each driving thrust, they marked my soul.

These two incredible men had completely severed me from my boring existence and brought me to life

I knew, without a shadow of a doubt, I was never going to be the same woman again.

"Feel us, little one? Feel the power you're give us?" Nick hissed. "Feel your precious gift coming back to you, Savannah?"

I mewled and nodded as I sucked him deeper.

"Good. Touch your clit, little one. Take us with you when you shatter, gorgeous."

Sliding my hand from his thigh, Nick seized my hair and lifted my mouth to the tip of his cock before manically shuttling it to the back of my throat.

I strummed my swollen clit, driving myself higher and higher while Dylan gripped my hips and pounded my pussy with fast, unrelenting strokes.

Their power surged through me, sending a conflagration of possession, dominance, and command igniting every cell in my system.

Like a bomb, I exploded.

And as the brutal orgasm ripped through me, their thunderous cries reverberated through my body. Blinded by the powerful waves of ecstasy crashing through me, I gulped Nick's come jettisoning down my throat and coating my tongue while Dylan slammed his shaft deep and followed us over.

Spent and spineless, I collapsed over Nick's lap. His glistening cock lay hot and twitching against my cheek. As Dylan eased from my quivering tunnel and stood, I realized each exchange we shared was more beautifully brilliant and more powerfully potent than the last.

Each time they claimed me, they branded their Dominance deeper inside me.

I quivered and jolted when Dylan pressed a warm cloth to my enflamed folds before gently cleaning me. When he finished, he leaned down and smoothed the hair from my neck before placing a soft kiss to my skin.

"I'm all sweaty," I mumbled, still absorbed in the afterglow.

"We like making you sweat." He chuckled.

"Because we *love* hearing you scream." Nick smirked.

"I like the way you two make me sweat and scream," I slurred, drunk on endorphins and swimming in a foggy haze.

Dylan lifted me from the floor and cradled me in his arms. From beneath my lashes, I watched Nick stand and refasten his jeans. Dylan sat on the couch; his hard cock nestled against my hip.

Nick arched a brow as he gazed down at me. "How do you feel?"

"Dreamy." I smiled.

A gorgeous grin stretched his mouth. The man defied the gods with his unadulterated beauty. I could have stared at him for hours. When he sat down and pulled me onto his lap—cradling me in his arms—I snuggled against him and drank in his decadent body heat.

Dylan placed my feet on his lap and began to massage my arches. With a soft moan, I closed my eyes, savoring their blissful aftercare while the fire crackled and hissed.

Long silent moments later, Dylan asked, "Is she asleep?"

"I think so," Nick replied.

I wasn't, but I didn't correct him. Right or wrong, I was curious to find out what they were thinking.

"We're in over our heads, man," Dylan drawled. "Especially you."

"Don't pin this all on me. I saw your face when you were balls deep inside her, man."

"I know. But this whole thing is getting FUBAR'd beyond belief."

"Not if we don't let it," Nick assured.

"Really? What happens when we have to leave?"

"You mean, what happens when we have to leave *her*," Nick corrected.

"Like I want to think about that now?" Dylan sighed. "I finally figured out how she climbed so deep inside us."

I felt Nick turn his head as I remained silently breathing evenly.

"So, it's not all on me, huh?" Nick asked with a hint of sarcasm in his tone.

"No, man."

"What have you come up with Doctor Phil?"

"Don't bust my balls just because I'm in tune with my feelings, and you're not. I'm cautious for a reason."

"What's that?"

"It keeps me from getting in too deep with women like her."

"No. It's just mortar for your walls, asshole." Nick chortled.

"True. You want to borrow some? I think you need it."

"Nah, I'll be fine. We both will."

Though stunned by the revelation I had touched them as deeply as they had me, the tone of Nick's voice made me wonder if any of us would be fine when this powerful connection was severed.

"We both know this isn't going to go anywhere, right?" Dylan bit out.

"Man, why are you always so fucking negative when you can't cover something up with a joke?"

"Do you know why you married Paige?" Dylan asked, ignoring Nick's question.

"Yeah, because I was thinking with my dick instead of my brain."

"True," Dylan scoffed. "You're in love with the idea of marriage, family, and taking care of the little woman."

"Do I need to carry Savannah to bed, so I can lie down on the couch while you dissect my brain, Doctor?"

"Come on, Nick. How many times have you helped me see the forest for the trees? Too many to count. It's time I do the same for you, man." Dylan paused as Nick grunted. "I get it, I do. I know you want to settle down and have a family. Even before you married Paige and we went through our shit, I secretly hoped she'd warm up to the idea of us sharing her. But she didn't."

"I know, man. And I'm sorry for what it did to us. I learned a lot of lessons from that mistake. The biggest ones being, we're no good alone and I have lousy judgment when it comes to women."

"No, you don't. Look at that woman in your lap. She's perfect," Dylan whispered. "But I'm no poster child for happily ever after. The minute things start feeling like a ball and chain, I'm asshole and elbows running the other way. You know that. But Savannah...well, she's a whole different story. She blindsided us because she's so fucking real. She's so honest and pure. She's like an oasis in the middle of the desert. We're never going to find another like her at Genesis...or anywhere else."

"So, why aren't you running for the hills?" Nick pressed.

"Because I can't. I don't want to. Believe me, I've tried. She's like a magnet. I'm so fucking drawn to her. Do you realize how perfect she'd be for us, if—"

"If she didn't live in Kansas City and wasn't going to look for a Dom when she gets home?"

Their entire conversation had me warring with a whole host of emotions…mainly hope.

With so many revelations being unearthed between them, I curled on my side and nuzzled my face against Nick's chest. I feared my expressions might give me away.

"Savannah?" Dylan whispered.

I didn't respond. Yes, eavesdropping was deceitful and wrong, and if they ever found out I was playing opossum, they'd probably edge me to death. But I knew their conversation wasn't over, and I had to hear more.

"She's out," Nick whispered. "There's nothing we can do, man. We'll teach her as much as we can in what little time we have and pray she finds a good group back home where she can keep growing and learning. Maybe we can plan several trips to Kansas City and check in on her from time to time."

"Are you crazy?" Dylan snarled. "I don't want to show up at one of the clubs in Kansas City and watch her with some other Dom. Once she finds a group, the Doms are going to be lining up to slap a collar on her within the first five fucking minutes."

"Listen to you, 'Mister Don't Tell Her How You Feel'," Nick drawled. "Listen, I can't even go there, bro. Her with another Dom makes me want to—"

"That's the shit you have to stow away, man."

"So do you."

"Look, the last thing either of us wants to do is hurt her. But all that innocence just waiting to be tapped into is a fucking powerful thing."

"It is." Nick sighed. "We've got to be careful. I know. I know."

My head spun. They had feelings for me far outside the realm of just teaching me. That powerful connection between the three of us wasn't my imagination. Yet they weren't going to act on their feelings. They were going to ignore the giant elephant in the room, and what? Think I wouldn't notice? Men were so damn clueless. I didn't want to join a local club and find a Dom, I wanted them.

"We have a few more days. We'll go with the no strings, no promises route and enjoy her as long as we can before we say goodbye, all right?" Dylan asked in a flat tone void of emotion.

Nick issued a heavy sigh and brushed his fingers through my hair for several long, silent minutes.

"If that's how it has to be, that's how it'll be."

Their game plan was a lot like mine. Close off the heart and ignore the emotions. While it made sense for me, it didn't for them. They were Doms. They were supposed to set the bar for open, honest communication.

People in glass houses.

I inwardly cursed the fact that all three of us were playing a stupid game of subterfuge. Still, I searched for a glimmer of gratitude. It wasn't hard to find. If not for Dylan and Nick, I'd still be locked in BDSM dreamland, hopelessly wishing to experience all the desires they'd effortlessly given me. Yes, it would be easy to plop my ass down on the pity pot and wallow in despair for not being able to have a long-term relationship with them, but the harsh reality was… it simply wasn't in the cards.

Dylan eased off the couch and returned a short time later. The smell of scotch wafted over my nose. Their conversation turned to work and the upcoming projects they'd bid on. Their voices held great passion as they talked about a community center for underprivileged youth scheduled to break ground in the spring. The big, bad Doms had a soft spot for children and those less fortunate. It was somewhere during their discussion of politics, City Hall, bureaucratic red tape and corruption that sleep pulled me under. Rousted awake, I discovered Nick carrying me back to my room as the fireplace glowed with dying embers.

"I'm sorry we have to do this to you, little one, but we need to get that plug out." Nick lowered me to the cold sheets, then turned me onto my side.

I shivered when he pressed my knees to my chest. "We'll get you warmed up in a minute, little one. Just take a deep breath, then let it out and push."

I closed my eyes as Nick's broad fingers gripped the wide base. Following his instructions, I exhaled and bore down. A whimper escaped my lips as the widest part slid free. Then, while Nick strolled off to the bathroom, Dylan climbed onto the bed and held me against his chest.

"We're proud of how brave you've been with the plugs," he praised, combing his fingers through my hair.

But not proud enough that I earned a way for you to keep me.

Shoving the cynical thought from my brain, Nick returned and washed my throbbing rim with a warm cloth. I was still shivering when he joined Dylan and me in bed, but quickly warmed when Nick pulled the blankets over us. I drank in their body heat while marveling at their steely bodies surrounding me. Too tired to continue wrangling my myriad of emotions, I closed my eyes and drifted to sleep.

Chapter Seven

B linding sunlight streamed in from beneath the curtains.
The storm had passed.

A melancholy ache filled my heart. No matter how desperately I wished it, time wasn't going to stand still.

On the left of me, Dylan lay on his back, snoring softly. Slowly rolling to my side, I studied his handsome face, memorizing every contour of his rugged features. I longed to draw my nails through the blond stubble covering his jaw and chin, to feel them prickle my fingers. Light lashes rested against his cheeks, shrouding his beautiful blue eyes beneath the smooth lids. Staring at his full lips, I could still feel how soft and commanding they were when he kissed me. My gaze wandered down his wide neck and over his broad tanned shoulders before stilling on his flat, dusky brown nipples. Hard muscles bulged beneath his flesh as if a master sculptor had spent a lifetime chiseling him out granite.

Curling my arm beneath the pillow, I raised my head and drank in the rest of him. Having kicked off most of the covers, his impressive, flaccid cock lay resting on his thigh. I stared in utter fascination. I'd never seen a totally soft cock before.

"No matter how long you stare at it, kitten, it won't suck itself," Dylan teased in a sleepy voice.

I jerked my head up, surprised he was awake. A goofy smile spread over his gorgeous face, causing his sexy-assed dimple to grow even more pronounced.

"Starting lessons before coffee?" Nick mumbled in a gravely tone as he sat up and tenderly kissed my shoulder.

"Maybe," Dylan smirked. "I think Savannah might need breakfast in bed. She looks kind of hungry."

"Very funny," I said in a dry tone. "I was just looking at…"

"My cock, yes, I know. Feel free to crawl on down there and take a closer look."

"I need to brush my teeth first," I said and began to scamper out of bed.

"Bring the tube back with you, little one." Nick instructed with a mischievous twinkle in his eyes.

"The tube of…toothpaste?" I asked as my brows wrinkled in confusion.

"Yes. The tube of toothpaste, *Sir*," Nick said, pursing his lips as if trying to think up some form of unpleasant punishment.

"Yes, Sir… that's exactly what I meant." My words rushed together. I didn't want or need any more punishments.

"That's what I thought." Nick winked, then flashed a dazzling smile.

I swallowed back a wanton moan and hurried to the bathroom.

After completing my morning rituals, I padded from the bathroom, toothpaste in hand.

Their gazes scraped my naked flesh with every step I took. My nipples pebbled and my heartbeat faster as their cocks simultaneously sprang to life. The devilish smiles adorning their faces told me they were up to something. Hopefully, a happy ending.

"So, do you have some kind of kinky toothbrush lesson planned?"

Nick chuckled. "Something like that." He extended his hand, and I passed him the paste. "Come, lie down."

I eyed him suspiciously as I climbed over his stretched out legs.

Taking my time, I gazed at his thick erection before settling between him and Dylan. Nick removed the cap slowly, as if he were opening a container of plutonium. The mischievous smirk on his lips and his dramatic demeanor were probably meant to heighten my anticipation. But it was a tube of toothpaste, for crying out loud. How dangerous could it be?

"Spread your legs, kitten," Dylan instructed with a devilish grin.

"I hate to break this to you, guys...but I don't have teeth down there." I laughed as I parted my thighs.

"Guys?" Nick admonished.

"Oops, sorry. I mean, Sirs."

"We're well acquainted with your cunt, girl. We can both attest there are no teeth. But we also know how much you're going to squirm when we lick the minty toothpaste off your sweet, hard clit."

"You can't put that on my girl parts," I gasped and slapped my thighs together.

"Of course, we can," Dylan refuted. "And it's your clit, kitten."

"I know what it's called. What I don't know is why you want to put toothpaste there, Sir."

"That's what we intend to show you. Lay back and enjoy." Dylan's strong hands pried my legs apart as Nick smeared a fingertip of paste upon my sensitive nub. I yelped, startled by the coldness, then held my breath as a strange tingling sensation enveloped my nub. Gripping the sheets, I anchored myself and tried to prepare for what would happen next.

Dylan climbed between my legs and lowered his head. His wet, warm tongue swirled over my pearl, and when he blew a gentle breath over the swelling bud, I nearly launched to the ceiling fan. A shrill cry ripped from my throat. I could have sworn he'd pressed an ice cube straight over my clit. As the shock to my system ebbed, the tingling sensation started again, accompanied by an enticing burn. Repeating the process over and again, Dylan licked and sucked with dizzying precision, while Nick iced and painted my straining nipples with the paste. Currents of electricity pulsated through my cells, crashing headlong upon one another before pooling beneath my sweet spot in pulsing urgency. Every touch, lick and kiss spiked my need to come.

The demand grew higher and harder, like a rolling ocean tide, surging and racing toward the craggy shore.

"Have you ever read about orgasm denial, little one?" Nick asked as I panted and writhed.

"What?" I gasped as I opened my eyes. I tried to focus on his face hovering close to mine. Even with my mind thick like syrup, I recognized the flash of disapproval in his eyes before a smile of retribution tugged his lips.

Crap! I wasn't paying attention, again.

Why had he chosen that exact moment to start interrogating me again?

He knew I was coming undone. They'd been fervent with the toothpaste. Coupled with Dylan's magnificent tongue and his nimble fingers, it was a miracle I'd not failed them and come like a virgin. "No. No, Master. Please. No edging."

"I love it when you call me, Master, little one. But I can promise you hours of edging if you don't answer me." Nick stroked his cock in long, slow glides as he glanced at Dylan, still devouring me with a vengeance.

I had to focus and think about what he'd asked me. Something about orgasm denial. "No, Sir, I haven't."

"Haven't what, little one?"

"I haven't read about orgasm denial, Master."

"Very good," he praised before claiming my lips with a hungry kiss.

I opened, extending him a greedy invitation, yet he simply teased the rim of my lips without sweeping his tongue inside my mouth. The need to suckle him deep rode me hard, but Nick wouldn't allow it.

When I mewled in frustration, he pulled back with a laugh. "Oh, little one, you're not calling the shots here. Don't tell me you haven't figured that out yet."

"No, Master. I mean, I know who holds the power." I writhed as Dylan continued his blissful oral torture.

"*Your* power, Savannah, and it's delicious. But it's time for more anal training." An evil smirk tugged one corner of his mouth.

I groaned and tossed my head from side to side in protest as I ground my pussy against Dylan's masterful mouth.

"Oh, but it is, you rebellious little vixen," Nick replied with a chuckle.

Suddenly, Dylan pulled from my pussy and sat up. My juices glistened over his mouth. With a playful wink, he rolled off the bed and began rummaging through his bag of wicked toys.

I wanted to scream. Denying me an orgasm was not going to make me a better submissive, just a frustrated, pissed off woman. And that damn plug! What was the thrill of shoving that thing up my ass? I was certain I could accommodate their cocks now just fine… *if* they took it nice and slow. If I failed to take them both, they could *then* bring out that annoying metal bastard and shove it up my backside.

"Remember, pet, this isn't all for you. It's for us, too," Nick soothed.

With a deep sigh, I closed my eyes and nodded. I'd never get far on my submissive journey if I expected to get my way. But dammit, they had no clue how uncomfortable that damn plug was. How could they? Dominants didn't parade around wearing jewel encrusted plugs up their butts.

"On your knees," Dylan instructed with a roguish grin.

"Yes, Master," I grumbled as rolled over and braced myself on all fours.

While Nick assumed the role of 'Master butt plug shover,' Dylan's decadent fingers, slathered with lube, prepared my rim.

In seconds, a conflagration of heat seared my system while the demand for release snarled inside. I begged and wailed for permission to come as the broadest section of the plug passed my impossibly stretched rim. Instead of granting me reprieve, Nick landed a sharp, punishing slap on both of my ass cheeks.

As pain overrode pleasure and I quickly tumbled from the edge of no return, Nick slid an arm around my waist and hauled me up to my knees.

"Let's go make some breakfast, little one."

"Now?" I screeched, panting and dazed. "You can't be serious, Sir!"

"Oh, but I am." He smirked.

"But…I need…what about…"

"I asked if you'd read up on it, little one. You told me no. We decided you needed to experience it firsthand."

"Welcome to orgasm denial," Dylan winked, scrubbing a hand over his nectar-coated chin. Clenching my jaw to keep from screaming, I moaned. "Come, kitten. It won't be quite so frustrating when you focus on something else for a bit. Besides, we enjoy watching you simmer."

Shaking with need and frustration, I closed my eyes, then counted to ten. It wasn't enough numbers. So, I counted again…and again.

"Can I at least put some clothes on, Sirs? I'd rather not fry bacon nude," I huffed.

"Since you used that snarky tone of voice, you don't even get to wear an apron." Nick frowned.

"I'm sorry, Master," I mewled. "It's just that I'm—"

"Wet? Ready? Needy?"

"And climbing out of my skin." I nodded.

"Good." He smiled.

"Why is that good? Sir."

"Because it pleases us. And because we know when we finally give you permission to come, it's going to be an epic explosion."

"Biblical," Dylan seconded. "You have no clue how erotic you look and feel when you shatter."

At least, I had something to look forward to…eventually.

As Nick and Dylan donned their jeans, I took guilty satisfaction in the pained expression on their faces as they tucked their swollen erections into the denim. I wasn't the only one suffering.

Either I was too horny to care or growing accustomed to the plug, but it no longer felt like I had a giant sequoia shoved up my butt. My tender ring continued to throb and I had to remain focused on clenching the base, but I managed to keep the anal intruder in place better than the day before.

When breakfast was over—thankfully, Nick fried the bacon—and the dishes done, the two men carried in more wood from the mud room. I held the door for them, shivering as the bitter cold wind wafted over my naked body. The sun shining through the kitchen window suggested warmth, but it was only a guise.

"Dammit, Savannah," Dylan groused. "Your lips are purple and you're trembling like a leaf. Get your ass into a hot bath or back in bed. We've got this."

"Thank you, Sir," I replied as my teeth chattered.

Stretched out in the bubbling hot spa tub, I savored my time alone. I was used to my isolation…it was familiar. But after several short minutes, I realized I missed my Doms. How had I grown accustomed to their presence so quickly?

The question you should be asking is how did you fall in love with them so quickly?

The tiny voice in my head unleashed a torrent of fear.

Sucking in a deep breath, I closed my eyes. I couldn't be in love with them. My mind was simply confusing love with gratitude. It was perfectly normal to feel indebted to them. They'd not only rescued me, but brought the submissive inside me to life.

As I tried to rationalize away my feelings, it grew increasingly obvious I was merely lying to myself. Isolating my heart was impossible.

The bubbles churned and gurgled as I began to dissect the emotions they'd brought to life. By their own admission, they cared about me, but not enough for them to open their hearts or rearrange their lives to include me. And how narcissistic was it of me to expect them to?

The way they pampered me and fed my submission only made me want to please them more. Their patience was so unparalleled that, like a bridge, it built a solid foundation of trust.

It was going to gut me when our time was through. But I knew in my heart neither of them would smile and tell me to have a nice life when I walked out the door. They'd never purposely hurt me… physically or emotionally. That, in itself, was a priceless, golden safety net.

So what if I loved them? Loving someone wasn't a bad thing. I loved several people in my life. After all Dylan and Nick had done for me, it was only natural to add them to the list of those near and dear to my heart.

Besides, they weren't geared for a serious relationship any more than I was. Even if they were, I certainly wouldn't be in the running to capture *their* hearts. They probably had more subs at Genesis than I could shake a stick at. Sure, I might be special to them, but I suspected there were a lot of women far more special to them than me. Harboring stupid sophomoric fantasies was futile.

We were snowed in. I was convenient. By the end of next week, they probably wouldn't give me a second thought. I'd be nothing more than a notch on their proverbial flogger.

I sank deeper in the tub with a disgruntled sigh and let my thoughts run free.

I've known them less than seventy-two hours. That's hardly enough time to make a love connection.

They want a week of "no strings, no promises." No matter what feelings I have for them, they're not going to be reciprocated. I need to keep from setting myself up for a fall.

They live in Chicago. Long distance relationships rarely work.

Yes, the sex is phenomenal, but relationships can't survive on sex alone, no matter how mind-blowing it is.

But on top of that, they're basically still strangers. For all I know, they have a collared sub, or multiple collared subs, back in Chicago.

Without warning, a green-eyed monster of jealously monster reared its ugly head before spilling its envious poison over me like a black, oily sludge.

"Fuck! I could have done without that thought filling my head."

"If you're curious to find out what soap tastes like, you don't have to curse. I'll gladly give you a taste."

I jumped and whipped my head toward the sound of Nick's censuring voice to see an unhappy scowl on his face.

"No, Sir. I'm sorry, I wasn't thinking. It just slipped out."

"I see. What negative thoughts were running through your head? he asked, easing onto the side of the tub.

Shit. Was nothing sacred with this guy? Could I not have a single emotion without being obligated to vomit it out? I cast my eyes toward the water and sighed. If I told him it was nothing, he'd drag me out of the tub and edge me till morning. Even then, he'd likely find an even harsher punishment. Either way, I was screwed.

"I was thinking about the fact that I don't know very much about you or Dylan, Sir." It was the truth in a convoluted way.

"Go on," he prompted.

I swallowed tightly. "Do you two have a collared submissive?"

"No. Next question."

"Do you always share women? I mean, you two seem so… comfortable. Like you've…" I couldn't finish the sentence. I was tripping over my tongue as jealousy spiked again.

Nick was quiet for so long, I hazarded a quick glance to find him staring at the wall with a faraway look in his eyes. After a long moment, he turned and gazed down at me.

"I'm not sure how much of my conversation with George you overheard, little one. So, I will tell you a bit about me. I was married for a short time. It was a mistake. One that nearly ruined my friendship with Dylan. And yes, we've been sharing women since the summer we graduated high school."

"That's a long time," I whispered without thinking.

Nick laughed. "We're not *that* old, pet."

"No, Sir. I meant…"

"I know what you meant, girl. Relax, it's all good," he chuckled. "We grew up in a small town out in the country. It was a hot and humid summer night. Dylan and I were driving home from a big field party when we came across a girl walking down the gravel road crying. When we realized it was Abby, a girl we'd gone to school with all our lives, we pulled over and stopped. Long story short, she and her boyfriend had been parked in a cornfield down the road. She'd wanted to lose her virginity before she went away to college, but her boyfriend had gotten drunk and passed out on her."

"So, you and Dylan…"

"Took care of her little problem and drove her home."

I wasn't sure if I admired their chivalry or deplored their motive for snagging a convenient piece of pussy.

"What other questions are rolling around in that pretty head of yours, girl?" He smiled.

"Too many," I confessed with a nervous smile. "How did getting married almost ruin your friendship with Dylan? If I'm being too nosy, Sir, please tell me."

He leaned down and kissed my lips with a tender caress. "No, little one. Your questions deserve answers. I met my ex-wife, Paige, right after Dylan came home from Iraq. She liked to align herself in high social circles. We met at a fundraiser. Admittedly, I drank too much champagne and invited her back to my house. One thing led to another and a few weeks later we were in a relationship. She's strong-willed, and while I find that extremely attractive in a submissive, Paige didn't have a subservient bone in her body. But I thought I was in love and could abandon my Dominant desires. I may have been able to."

He shrugged and frowned with a sour expression. "Who knows? I never got a chance to test that theory. After the wedding, she changed...like overnight. There were two sides of Paige. She had a loving, carefree, playful side and a vindictive, hateful, and manipulative side. Unfortunately, I didn't discover the latter until *after* the wedding. Dylan was the only one who saw through her façade. He'd tried to warn me that she was only interested in my money and climbing the social ladder. Instead of listening to him, I got pissed and accused him of trying to sabotage my happiness because she wasn't a woman we could share. I almost lost him over her. I've spent a lot of time kicking my own ass because of it."

"But you thought you were in love." I reached out and squeezed his leg, leaving a wet handprint on his jeans.

"No, I was in love with the idea of being in love. I knew in the back of my mind I was making a mistake as I stood before the minister. But my own stubborn pride kept me from turning on my heel and walking out of the church doors. The marriage was destined to fail before it began. We've been divorced two years, yet she's still trying to drag me back to court, contesting the prenuptial agreement."

"Can she do that?"

"She can try, but she'll fail. My lawyer has a box filled with proof that she'd been fucking other men since we got back from our honeymoon. I didn't know it at the time, but her prized Bentley was a gift from one of her rich fuck buddies, an old man she kept on the side because he gave her credit cards to buy whatever she wanted."

"Why did she even bother marrying you in the first place?" I asked in disgust.

"I asked her that, once. She told me it was something she hadn't tried yet."

"Wow." I was speechless. What kind of heartless bitch did that to a guy? I couldn't wrap my head around the fact that she'd used him. My blood began to boil. I wanted to find that nasty snatch and bitch slap her into next week. "I'm so sorry you had to go through that, Sir."

"It taught me an important lesson; guard my heart and never get married again."

Paige had damaged Nick so deeply that his entire outlook on relationships had been tainted. She'd stripped him of the hope of ever finding his happy-ever-after. And somehow, I knew if Paige ever discovered how deeply she'd crushed him, she'd take great joy in that fact. Women like her gave our gender a bad reputation.

"Do you have any other questions, pet?" Nick asked with a solemn expression.

"No, Sir. Thank you for your honesty," I whispered, wishing I could take his pain away.

"It's part of the exchange, Savannah. You've lowered your walls so impressively, I'm glad I've had the chance to do the same." A broad smile spread over his lips and his eyes sparkled with pride. The joy I'd brought to him sent a rush of warmth through my body.

"You can relax a bit longer if you'd like, pet, then come on out and join us. Dylan is building a fire. We want to keep you warm. Very, very warm." An evil smile tugged the corner of his mouth as he reached down and plucked a nipple.

"Warm? You two keep me hotter than a raging inferno."

"Then we're doing our job, little one." Nick stood and walked out of the room, chuckling as he left.

The emotional torture Paige had put him through made my heart ache. And the fact that the evil bitch was still making his life a living hell had me seething with rage. I'd never wanted to hire a hit man like I did then.

Naked and cold, I padded back to the large common area where I was met with two hungry smiles and a blazing fire—not only in the fireplace, but in my veins. Amazed by their ability to ignite my desires with just a look, I darted a nervous gaze between them.

"You're scaring me, Sirs," I giggled as I eased between their warm bodies and sat on the couch.

"Your fears are unfounded, kitten," Dylan winked.

"Thank heavens," I sighed in gratitude.

"We'll remind you that you said that." Nick grinned.

"Remind me? When, Sir?"

"Don't look at me like that." Nick laughed. "We'll make certain you feel no pain."

"No pain with what, Sir?" I gulped.

"You'll find out later."

Nick's cryptic reply sent my heart racing. Obviously, they had something planned that had the potential to include pain. My mind filled with possibilities, none of which brought me an iota of comfort.

"Nick tells me you two had a nice talk in the bathroom. Is there anything you want to know about me?" Dylan offered.

Oh, they were smooth as silk. Nick dropped a bomb that ratcheted my fears off the damn charts, and Dylan swooped in to dust the shrapnel away by changing the subject. And silly me, I let them keep me on my toes like a ballerina in a performance of *Let's Mind Fuck the Submissive*. I liked it better not knowing when I was going to be blindsided versus waiting, wondering, and worrying what they planned next.

"Still reinforcing my trust, right, Sirs?" I asked with a knowing smile.

"Exactly," Nick grinned. "You're learning fast. Good girl."

Goosebumps peppered my flesh and my nipples drew up tight from his praise.

"I'm an open book, kitten, ask me anything." Dylan preened with a bright smile.

"What were your tours in Iraq like, Sir?"

He looked as if I'd asked him to cut off his arm.

Like hot oil, guilt rushed through me. "I'm sorry, Dylan...err, Sir. You don't need to tell me. It's none of my business."

"No. It's fine. There's much you don't know about us and you'll never know unless you ask. No subject should be off-limits. We know how precious and fragile trust is. I don't want you to feel that we're less than honest with you about everything. Understood?"

"Yes, Sir." I nodded. "But we can talk about something else if you—"

He pressed a finger to my lips, silencing my offer.

"At first, I was excited when my Unit Commander recommended me for sniper school. Each time we qualified on the range, I fired High Expert, so I tried out and was accepted."

"He had the highest scores in his class. Don't let him fool you, Savannah. He's good."

"That's impressive," I agreed.

"Who's telling this story, bro?" Dylan teased before the unusually serious expression fell over his face again. "My unit was deployed six weeks after I completed sniper school. After we arrived in Bagdad, we were sent to the Anbar Provence. It's a place where more U.S. soldiers were killed than anywhere else in Iraq. General Sherman said, 'War is hell.' It really is."

The tortured tone of his voice filled me with sorrow. I knew revealing this part of his life was killing him. I wanted to tell him to stop, but I knew he wouldn't.

Sucking in a deep breath, he scrubbed a hand through his short, spiked hair and continued.

"After Anbar, we spent time in Ramadi. It was a fucking mess. Buildings blown to shit, rubble everywhere, mothers carrying crying, bandaged babies down the streets. It was bad. Burned out Hummers clogged the streets with charred bodies of fellow servicemen inside."

Dylan closed his eyes and rubbed his forehead with his hand. "I lost a lot of good friends in that godforsaken place. If it hadn't been for Nick, I would have probably voluntarily eaten a bullet by now."

My blood ran cold at the thought of Dylan in such a dark place that he'd contemplated suicide. "Oh god, Dylan. Don't say that. This world would be a sad and lonely place without you."

My voice cracked as a tear slid down my cheek. I soothed my hand over his shoulders and leaned against his strong body, holding him tight, praying his painful memories wouldn't haunt him the rest of his life.

His jaw ticked before he turned and looked into my eyes.

"It changed me, Savannah. I wish you could have met the man I used to be."

I choked back a sob and shook my head. "It wouldn't have mattered. The man I see before me is the one who has touched me in ways I've never known. I'm honored to take him just the way he is."

Tears brimmed his eyes as he pulled me against his chest and held me close. "I don't deserve you, kitten."

"Yes, you do," I choked against his warm neck as tears spilled from my eyes. "You deserve someone a whole lot better than me."

"There is no one better than you, princess, and there never will be."

Chapter Eight

My heart hurt for his pain and exploded in celebration that he'd bravely bared his inner demons to me. I held him for a long time in the silence of the room, trying my best to give him comfort.

"Your journey back has been a tough road, bro. But you *are* back, man. Don't lose sight of the work you've done." Nick's words were thick with emotion, and slathered in praise and admiration. I could only imagine how scared he must have been trying to help Dylan cope in those early dark days.

"You and I both know life is always worth living, dude." Dylan softly smiled.

"We do. So, come on, let's make it exhausting, too."

Without another word, Nick plucked me from Dylan's side and lifted me into his powerful arms. The carnal smirk on his face left no doubt what he had in mind. It was the shot of medicine Dylan desperately needed. I watched his desolate mood transform before my eyes. His haunted expression dissolved, giving way to a broad, knowing smile.

I reached out, extending a hand to him. "Please, Master. I need you."

"You've already got me, Savannah," Dylan growled as he stood and laced his fingers in mine.

Side by side, they carried me into the bedroom.

Splayed out on the bed, I watched as they peeled off their jeans. Helpless to do anything but stare at their mouthwatering erections and scrumptious sculpted bodies, I greedily drank in every hard rigid and plane.

"It's time for that plug to come out, kitten," Dylan announced in a husky voice.

My heart clutched. Were they going to impale me with a bigger one? Or would they finally claim my ass and pussy together? Gazing at the size of their thick cocks, I suddenly worried I wouldn't be able to accommodate them both at the same time.

"No, little one. It won't hurt, you have our promise," Nick soothed. He'd somehow read my mind again. "Climb on top of me, and trust us, pet. We're not going to do anything except make you feel good."

Nick positioned himself in the middle of the bed and extended his hand, helping me straddle his waist. Easing his hands to my hips he glided me down until I sat on his washboard abs.

"Kiss me, girl," he growled, cinching a hand in my hair.

With an acquiescent moan, I lowered my breasts to his chest as he pressed his lips to mine. Instead of commanding the kiss, he allowed me the freedom to explore his mouth. Handing over his control felt foreign, yet strangely empowering. I pulled back with a quizzical stare. His passive expression had a devilish smile tugging the corners of my mouth. I latched onto his bottom lip, giving a playful tug before sipping the plump flesh inside, suckling it sweetly. And still, he allowed me free reign until I tugged his lip again. Savagely gripping my hair, he seized me with a blistering kiss while tingles skittered over my scalp. Undaunted, I returned the savage passion he dished out.

Dylan moved about the room. The scrape of a drawer dimly registered as I fed on Nick's mouth in wild abandon. The crinkle of a condom wrapper peppered the air before the mattress dipped behind him.

"Here, man, sheath up," Dylan urged.

Nick released my hair, then dropped his hand behind my back and gripped his cock, nuzzling against my ass. After rolling the latex in place, he fisted my hair again and drew my chest to his.

"Lift your hips," Dylan instructed, softly caressing my thighs.

Raising my ass in the air, Dylan removed the bulbous plug while Nick swallowed my muffled groans of gratitude.

But my relief was short lived.

Dylan drove his lube-covered fingers inside my throbbing ring… swirling and stretching my tender tissue, and readying me for… what, I didn't know.

Nick wrapped a hand around my waist, eased me up, then slowly guided me onto his steely shaft. The cool, latex-covered tip warmed instantly as my greedy pussy sucked at his shaft…pulling him deeper inside me. While Nick thrust in and out of my hungry core, pulses of lightning splintered my system as Dylan continued stretching me wider and applying more lube.

"I can't wait to drive my cock balls deep in your tight little ass," Dylan bit out.

Anxiety spiked and anticipation mounted. This was it. They were going to claim my pussy and ass all at once.

Nick searched my eyes with a probing stare before a compassionate smile speared his lips. "Don't be scared. Dylan will fully prepare you. I promise."

"Yes, I will. After I get you opened up, we're going to take you nice and slow. Relax, kitten. We're going to take good care of you. I promise."

Their reassurance erased my apprehension.

Basking in the fiery ripples of pleasure pulsating outward from my stretching rim, I rocked against Nick's driving hips. And while his wide crest scraped my G-spot, he plucked and pinched my nipples.

"You're so fucking gorgeous, Savannah. Your cunt feels like wet, hot silk. So smooth and tight. So fucking tight," he growled, driving deeper with each measured stroke. "Open your pretty little asshole for Dylan. Let him inside so we can blow your dirty little mind."

Pressing the tip of his cock to my dilated opening, Dylan eased his fingers out, one by one. Nick stilled while Dylan pressed his cock against my tingling rim. The pressure was savage, nearly unbearable.

When he finally squeezed his fat crest through my burning hole, I tossed my head back and cried out as a euphoric mixture of pain, pleasure, and pressure streaked through me.

Staggered by the onslaught of sensations, I melted and let them take control.

"Fuckkkk," Dylan hissed before sucking in a deep breath. "Relax your muscles, baby. You're strangling my cock."

"Is he hurting you?" Nick asked, dragging a knuckle down my cheek.

Panting frantically, I shook my head and focused on rising above the burn.

"Slow breaths, little one. Relax and let your body grow accustomed to him. We're not going to move until you're ready. You're doing amazing, beautiful. Just relax and focus on letting him in."

I nodded, then concentrated on slowing my breathing and relaxing the screaming muscles surrounding Dylan's cock. Nick lowered his hand and circled my clit with his broad thumb. Almost instantly, pleasure fused with the pressure and fire. As sizzling currents arced through me, I began rocking myself on their embedded shafts.

Dylan's cock retreated but still remained inside me as Nick's cock surged into my pussy. Back and forth, they alternated thrusts, establishing a spine-bending rhythm that tipped my whole world on its axis. I couldn't tell up from down or left from right. Time lost all meaning as I streaked across the heavens like a shooting star.

Consumed by the sputtering pulses igniting my system, I rocked against their driving shafts while dazzling bursts of light flashed behind my yes.

"That a girl," Nick murmured. "We're both inside you…fusing ourselves to your body, your mind, your heart, and soul. Can you feel what we feel for you, little one? Can you feel the glorious power you've given us? We can, and it's astounding."

Nick's words pierced my psyche like a spike.

Tears filled my eyes.

They weren't simply teaching me and plying me with fabulous sex. They were imprinting themselves inside me. *Me.* The woman who'd never had a lover more than once. The shy loner who fantasized of having this kind of connection with a man, never once believing it would be possible with *two*. I mattered to them in ways I'd never thought possible. No longer able to deny the love taking root in my heart, and though Dylan and Nick would never be mine, I branded them to my soul.

My muscles trembled.

Beads of sweat dotted my flesh.

And as they drove in and out of my body, the sublime pressure consuming me mounted.

Swirling in the whirlpool of surreal sensations, I tossed all inhibition aside and rode them like a tempest in a sea of carnal splendor. My pussy and ass rippled, clutched, and fluttered around their surging cocks while our grunts, growls, and cries of rapture bounced off the walls.

Pulses of fire singed the thin membrane separating their driving cocks, as tiny explosions detonated in my veins.

Possessed in their erotic passion, demand spiraled higher.

Quivering and clasping around their driving shafts, I drank in their feral curses and grunts thundering in my ears and rode them in wild abandon as they dismantled my walls and annihilated my soul.

Though they were emotionally splitting me wide open, I remained wrapped in a blanket of safety, protection, and unequivocal love.

Sailing past the heavens, beyond the stars, and flying toward the sun, thunder and lightning collided inside me. High-pitched cries of demand pealed from my throat as the massive orgasm clawed and screamed within.

"Look at me," Nick barked. "Open your eyes, Savannah. I want to see and feel you explode for us. Now, little one. Come for us…Now!"

His command sliced through me like a white-hot blade.

Demand spun into a giant orb of euphoria and exploded in a blinding flash of fire.

My entire body seized.

Suspended in another dimension, pleasure pulsed before brutal convulsions detonated deep in my womb. Screams of ecstasy burned my throat as the monstrous orgasm ripped me to shreds.

Cursing and growling, Nick and Dylan pounded their cocks through my convulsing body with frenzied thrusts.

My muscles greedily sucked at their driving shafts.

Their thunderous roars vibrated my bones as they shattered and erupted at once.

Every muscle in my body gave out, and I fell to Nick's broad, heaving chest. His arms banded around me in a hold so sublime, tears spilled from my eyes. Overwhelmed by the staggering onslaught of emotions, I sobbed.

Dylan eased from my ass then draped his hot, slick body over my back. His warm lips danced on my shoulders and spine before he burrowed his face against my neck and nuzzled in close.

Encased in their sweating, panting bodies, their murmured praise spilled over me like warm honey. I could palpably feel the magnitude of their protection, devotion, and care. And for the first time in my life, I truly felt accepted and unconditionally loved. Not as a daughter, or a sister...but as a woman.

Uncontrollable sobs wracked my body. I no longer felt like their student, but their submissive. Walking away from them was going to kill me. Yes, I was crazy to fall in love with them, but it was too late. I'd already lost my heart. I'd willingly given them free reign over every part of me. I had no clue how I was going to put myself back together once the week was done.

As if reading my mind, Nick held me tighter. "Shhh, don't cry, little one. We'll figure it out. I'm sorry, love, but it's going to hurt like hell... for all of us."

A scoff melded with my sobs. "How do you do always know what I'm thinking?"

"I don't know. It's crazy, but I sense what you're thinking. I've never been able to do that with anyone else before."

"I can, too," Dylan whispered. "It's never happened to me before either."

"Like I said, we'll figure it out," Nick assured.

Dylan's body shuddered as he lifted from my back, climbed off the bed, and silently strode to the bathroom. I knew he was as scared and confused as I—and maybe even Nick—was.

A part of me wanted to run after him, but what could I say? I didn't have any answers...didn't have words to ease his mind. Nick rolled to his side, taking me with him, then cupped the back of my head as I sobbed against his chest.

Long minutes later, Dylan climbed in behind me, draped an arm around my waist, and pressed his rugged body against my back. Neither of them said a word, they simply held me between their naked bodies while I struggled to stem the flow of my tears.

I felt raw. Exposed. There were no walls left to hide behind. They'd unfurled me sexually, but more frightening, they'd sliced me open emotionally as well. Though their bodies enveloped me, covered me in warmth and reassurance, I'd never felt so brutally naked and vulnerable.

Panic took root in my belly. I fought the urge to pry myself from their loving cocoon and lock myself away in the bathroom, to hide like a child. But I was no longer a child. I was a woman who had made the conscious decision to participate in this endeavor. I had to face the consequences of my actions like an adult.

I could spend the rest of our time together counting down the days until emotional Armageddon, or I could bask in the glorious gifts they longed to give. The choice was easy.

Forcing myself to stop crying, I sniffed and exhaled a deep breath. "I'm sorry, Sirs. I didn't mean to fall apart like that. It's just...that was the most incredible experience of my life."

"It was fucking earth-shattering for us too," Dylan whispered in my ear. "I've never felt anything like that before, and doubt I ever will again."

Nick nodded as his warm breath fluttered over my cheek. "Fan-fucking-tastic is what it was, pet."

"Is it going to be like that the rest..." *Dammit!* Why did I have to keep shoving reality in their faces, in *my* face? "If we do it again?"

"You mean *when*?" Dylan chortled. "I sure hope so. There's only one way to find out."

"Not yet," I moaned. "I need to recover first."

"Rest, little one. We've got lots of time to practice until we get it—"

The sound of a loud engine outside cut him off. Dylan rolled out of bed and strode to the window.

"What is that?" I asked.

"It's a snowblower," he replied, easing the curtain shut. "Kit's trying to clear off the porch of the main house. There's got to be five feet of snow out there, and the drifts are massive. It's gonna take hours for her to get a path cleared."

Nick groaned then dropped a quick kiss to my lips. "Guess we should go up there and help her."

"You can hang here if you want; I'll do it," Dylan offered.

"No, man. If we both go, we can get it done in half the time," Nick replied as he rolled away from me and stood.

The condom still clung to his semi erect cock, and I couldn't take my eyes off it.

"Kitten?" Dylan cocked his head and looked at me with a strange expression.

"Yes, Sir?"

"Do you have a fascination with soft cocks?"

"Umm." I felt my face warm. "I don't know if I'd call it a fascination. Okay, maybe it is. I've never..."

"You've never felt a cock that wasn't hard, is that what you're trying to say?"

I lowered my eyes and nodded.

"That's nothing to be ashamed or embarrassed about, little one. When we get back, we'll be more than happy to sate your curiosity. But your inspection will need to be quick. They won't stay soft for long with you touching them." Nick grinned.

"I'll do my best, Sir," I chuckled.

"You have our permission to say in bed, soak in the tub, or curl up on the couch by the fire," Dylan instructed. "I'll throw some more logs on before we head up to the house."

"Thank you, Sir."

Emotions and endorphins still pinged through my system so wildly, I opted to stay in bed and wallow in the sex-stained sheets. Hugging their pillows to my chest, I breathed in Nick and Dylan's distinct, intoxicating scents. And when I closed my eyes, it was as if they'd never left. As I stretched out in the center of the bed, muscles I never knew existed decadently throbbed. And as a satisfied smile curled my lips, I closed my eyes, and drifted off to sleep.

"Savannah. Savannah, honey?" Kit called, pulling me from the darkness.

Blinking the fog of sleep from my brain, I sat up with a gasp.

Kit stood at the side of my bed, and I was naked.

Gripping the covers tightly to my chin, my heart thundered in my chest as I glanced at the empty spaces beside me. It took a hot minute to remember they'd gone out to help her shovel snow. Grateful I didn't have to explain why I was naked in bed with them, I forced a smile.

"Is everything all right?" I asked.

"That's what I came to ask you," she chuckled. "The guys are still digging out the sidewalk. Bless their hearts, they've already cleaned off the porch. I came to see how you were feeling after the accident."

"Oh, I'm fine. I was a little sore the next day, but I'm good now."

"Oh good. Are the boys behaving themselves?" she asked with a tilt of her head.

"Yes, they've been perfect gentlemen." I nodded, struggling not to laugh.

"I'm glad. When they carried you in the day of the accident, I told them not to behave like a couple of rabid wolves around you." She winked. "So, you're really doing okay? You're not sore or anything?"

"No. Not at all."

Liar.

"Thank goodness. Is there anything you need?"

"Not that I can think of." I smiled.

Nothing but Dylan and Nick naked in bed with me again.

"All right. I'll let you rest. If you think of something you need, send one of those Neanderthals up to the house to fetch it for you."

I laughed. "I will, Kit. Thanks so much for checking in on me."

"It's the least I can do. I'm so sorry Mellie didn't make it. I know this vacation didn't turn out like you planned."

Oh, if you only knew.

"It's okay. Just knowing Mellie is safe and sound is all that matters."

"That's right. Get some rest, honey. I'll come check on you again from time to time."

"No," I blurted, then quickly flashed a big smile. "I mean, you don't need to take time away from your other guests at the house to brave the cold and come see me. I'm not doing anything but lazing around all day, relaxing. But if I do need anything, you'll be the first to know."

"Uh-huh." Kit issued a look of skepticism then smiled. "You mean you'll send Dylan or Nick to get it for you, right?"

"Yes. That's what I meant. Thank you."

With a tight grin still plastered across my mouth, Kit turned and left. It wasn't until I heard the front door of the barn close that I let out a massive sigh.

"Please don't come back down, Kit. God only knows what you'll likely walk in on."

The thought of Kit finding out what I'd been doing with Dylan and Nick shouldn't have bothered me. But it did. Not because I thought her a prude, but because ménages weren't readily accepted in conventional society.

The question of how people managed a threesome in their daily lives stuck in my head. From what I'd seen, it was hard enough for two people to make a stable relationship work. I imagined three would be next to impossible, especially for someone like me who was used to spending ninety-nine percent of my time alone. I'd probably go batshit crazy with Dylan and Nick hovering over me day in and day out. I'd never have a moment to myself. And why was I thinking about such ridiculous scenarios in the first place? In a few short days, my time with them would be nothing but a memory.

My stomach grumbled, a welcome distraction from my train of thoughts. As I climbed out of bed, a sweet burn throbbed between my legs. Humming in delight, I savored the glorious ache.

As I reached for my robe, my hand froze as a bewildering tug-of-war ignited in my brain.

If I covered myself, knowing they forbade it, I ran the risk of punishment. But if Kit decided to pop back in, how would I explain my nakedness? Indecision pinged through me, and I nibbled my bottom lip. Deciding I could toss on the robe, raid the fridge, then toss it back off before hopping back into bed without them knowing…I pulled it on and tied the sash.

But just as I stepped from my room, Dylan and Nick rounded the corner.

Shit!

Nick's brows shot up in surprise before an unhappy frown settled over his face. Beside him, Dylan cocked his head and scowled.

"We didn't take the rules with us when we left the barn," Nick chided as he and Dylan shed their coats and kicked off their boots.

"I know, but Kit was here a few minutes ago. I was afraid she might come back."

"She's inside the house," Dylan informed. "Besides, I'm sure she's seen a naked woman before."

"Yes, but it would have been totally out of character for me to be running around the barn naked. Especially when you two could have wandered back in at any minute. She would definitely find that suspect."

"Still worried about others' perceptions, I see," Nick grumbled.

"Come on, Nick. Normal people don't do what we're doing here."

"It's Sir to you, little one," he barked. "And *we* do it all the damn time."

"But I don't, Sir," I mumbled, worrying my fingers over the knot of my robe.

"And you're not comfortable at the idea of Kit finding out what you enjoy," Dylan stated flatly.

"No. It's nobody's business but mine, Sir."

"Take the robe off, little one. Now," Nick demanded.

As he stepped toward me and extended his hand, disappointment rolled off him in waves.

With a furtive glance toward the hallway, I untied the sash and slid off the robe before placing it in his palm. The cold air and his arctic stare sent goosebumps peppering my flesh.

"Thank you. Are you hungry?" Nick asked.

Wait. What? No edging? No spanking? No lecture?

"Yes, Sir."

"Then go sit by the fire and warm yourself while we fix some lunch."

"You may use the blanket, if you want." Dylan winked.

"Thank you, Sirs."

I hurried to the couch and sat down. The leather was warm, but I still wrapped the soft cotton blanket around me and tucked it under my feet. As Dylan and Nick worked in the kitchen, they talked so quietly I couldn't make out a single word. I had no doubt they were plotting some heinous type of punishment for finding me in my robe. Whatever they decided, I would willingly accept. I knew the risk I was taking when I dragged the damn thing on.

During lunch, neither said a word about me paying a penance. Instead, they talked about the *weather*. Kit had informed them that the freak snowstorm had passed and an abnormal warm front was coming in. The newscasters claimed all the snow would be gone in a day or two. From what I'd seen outside, a tropical blast from South America wouldn't be enough to melt the mountains of snow outside.

I t wasn't a heat wave from below the Equator, but a steady rise of temperatures that set its sights on the expansive farmland, leaving only a few patches of snow on the ground. The snow wasn't the only thing that had melted away. So had the days—far faster than I'd wanted.

"Are you ready yet?" Dylan called through my locked bedroom door.

I giggled, wondering if that poor man had an ounce of patience in him. "Almost, Sir. Just putting on my shoes."

"Nick's about to start gnawing the leather from the couch. Let's go, kitten. We're hungry."

I opened the door and smiled. "I'm ready. Thank you Sirs, for allowing me to primp in private. It's not every day I have two gorgeous men taking me out to dinner."

"You look.... fantastic. Damn, Savannah, you take my breath

away," Dylan approved with a wolfish grin. "Too bad we can't call for room service."

"Little one, you look stunning," Nick lauded as his gaze slid up and down my body.

"It's just a pair of jeans and a sweater, Sirs. But thank you." I couldn't help but grin. Their indulgent words warmed my heart.

"Well, Ma Kettle's doesn't sound like a five-star dining experience, but I'm afraid it's the only place to eat in the thriving metropolis of Duncan…population of seven hundred." Nick winked.

Both of them slid an arm around my waist, then escorted me out of the barn. The setting sun cast blue, purple, and red hues over the wispy clouds. Dylan opened the passenger door of my rental—a beefy, black Hummer—before helping me into the seat. Then climbed into the back, while Nick slid in behind the wheel. As we made our way into Duncan, I couldn't wipe the excited smile off my lips.

When I'd awoken that morning, wrapped in a tangle of heavy arms and legs, I'd made a silent vow not to dwell on the panic and fear that in two days my dream would be over. Instead, I focused on branding every remaining second with Dylan and Nick to memory.

Ma Kettle's, though quaint and clean, was exactly as I'd pictured. But what it lacked in ambiance was made up for by the delicious aromas filling the air. The sign on the front door boasted of home-cooked goodness. Since it had been years since I'd tasted a meal like my mom used to make, my taste buds tingled with anticipation.

After sliding onto the wooden bench of a big booth near the front door, our waitress Meg—a young girl, probably still in high school—greeted us with a warm smile. As she placed glasses of water and menus on the table, she rattled off the daily special, then scribbled down our drink orders before darting away.

Nick slung his arm around my shoulder and gently massaged my neck, skimming kisses over my cheek while he studied his menu. As Dylan looked over his menu, he trailed his fingertips up and down my arm, pressing kisses to my lips, as well. While their affection wasn't overt, my pussy clenched beneath their possessive touch.

When Meg returned, a look of shock widened her eyes before she eyed me with contempt. I was confused by her abrupt change of demeanor until Dylan lifted his hand from my arm and cleared his throat. Our PDA had earned Meg's disapproval, or jealousy. Though it shouldn't have mattered, I wanted the floor to open and swallow me whole.

"Are you all ready to order or what? The cook wants to go home," she curtly snapped.

"Meg," Nick began in a low, silky voice. "The sign on the door says you're open until ten o'clock. It's barely eight. While you might not approve of our unorthodox relationship, it's truly none of your business, and certainly no excuse for a pretty, young girl like you to be rude."

The way he complemented and scolded her at once was intriguing. Even more fascinating was watching Meg's expression soften and a bashful smile tug her lips. I was certain she'd start drooling over him any second.

"My deepest apologies. Why, I have no idea what came over me," she gushed, sizing up him and Dylan as if I didn't even exist.

"It's all right, dear. Everyone has a bad day."

Meg giggled and nodded before jotting down our order and floating away. As she passed the table of narrow-minded women, they turned and shot us repugnant glares.

I tensed and swallowed tightly. I didn't want to give in to embarrassment, but that didn't keep my heart from racing or my stomach from knotting.

"It's okay, kitten," Dylan whispered, cupping my hand. "It's a small town. They don't have anything better to do than gossip and judge."

"With your permission, Sirs, may I go to the ladies room?" I whispered.

"If you need to pee, yes. But if you're going there to hide, we will drag you out by your hair. Understood?" Nick warned as he stood and helped me from the booth.

"Yes, Sir."

I didn't bother telling him I planned to do both. I simply smiled, then gathered my nerve and walked the length of the diner to the ladies' room in back.

Leaning over the chipped porcelain sink, I splashed cool water on my face, then blotted it dry. Staring at my reflection in the mirror, I dragged in a deep calming breath.

"Ignore them. They're jealous and narrow-minded. They don't understand the bond I share with Dylan and Nick, and they never will. Don't give them the power to ruin the first real date you've had in months."

Bolstered by my pep talk, I exhaled a resolute sigh as the bathroom door opened.

An older woman, who'd been sitting at the table with the others, charged toward me with a disgusted scowl. As her lips curled in an angry snarl, her bottle-red hair shimmered in the harsh florescent lights.

"You're an abomination. You and those two men are nothing but sick, disgusting perverts. We're a respectable, God-fearing town that doesn't cater to whores. You all need to eat your food and leave."

A surge of white-hot anger quickly replaced the shock at her vile words.

"Who do you think you are...the morality police? I don't see a badge. Mind your own business, you narrow-minded, hateful old heifer."

"On second thought, leave now before I call the cops," she hissed.

"And report what?" I scoffed in a humorless laugh. "Friends having dinner? Sorry, lady, that's not a crime." My fists clenched into tight balls. I wanted to knock her on her self-righteous butt. "On second thought, why don't you leave? Go on home and get laid or dust off your vibrator and give yourself a much-needed attitude adjustment."

"Why, I never. Mind my words, missy, you're going to burn in hell, you filthy little whore." Her face turned beet red as she spun on her heel and stormed out in a huff.

My body shook in fury. I had never lost my temper or spoken so rudely to anyone in my entire life. It felt...wrong, yet strangely empowering.

Suddenly, every glorious moment I'd spent with Dylan and Nick solidified into a thick, black slab of shame.

No!

I was not going to allow her to taint the beauty the three of us shared. The hateful cow was not going to take away one iota of joy I'd experienced with Dylan and Nick.

"God-fearing, my ass," I hissed as I fisted a paper towel and dried my hands. "You can kiss my butt, you jealous hag. I'm going to plop my happy ass back in that booth and bask in the attention those two men want to give me and enjoy my dinner."

The words had no more left my lips than reality slammed through me. If, for some magical reason, I was to spend my life with Dylan and Nick, we would be assaulted with judgmental attitudes, vile comments, and condemning stares on a regular basis. Suddenly, what I'd been doing was all too real. And sadly, I wasn't equipped to handle the consequences of bringing my fantasy to life.

Why was I wasting time and brain cells on what ifs? In less than forty-eight hours, it would all be nothing but a memory.

Steeling my spine, I stepped from the bathroom, and with my head held high, I marched back to the booth. The rude cow sat at the table with her friends again, huddled in close and whispering like children. As I passed them, their caustic comments buzzed through the air like angry bees. Pasting on a *fuck you* smile, I swayed my hips and kept right on walking.

Nick stood, eyeing me with a knowing smirk. "Everything go all right in there?"

"Peachy, Sir," I quipped as he helped me into the booth beside Dylan. "If we're not too full after dinner, can I have dessert tonight?"

"Of course." Nick nodded. "What would you like?"

"A double-hard-on sundae with whipped cream," I said, flashing a cheeky grin.

"Only if you beg, kitten; only if you beg," Dylan chuckled.

As the women continued to shoot daggers our way, I kept a firm hold on my confidence. Yes, it was hard to ignore their judgmental and condescending expressions, but I refused to let them spoil my night.

Meg appeared numerous times—looking past me as if I were a ghost—to ask if Nick or Dylan needed anything else.

"Nick and I are going to take off in the morning to do some hunting," Dylan announced. "Will you be all right alone in the barn?"

"Of course. I'll be fine, Sir. Just...if you kill Bambi or anything, I don't want to know."

Nick laughed. "We'll be sure to cover it with a tarp. Happy?"

"I'd be happier if you hunted rocks instead of deer, Sir."

"We can't make venison chili out of rocks," Dylan chuckled.

I wrinkled my nose. "Ewww, yuck. Thanks, but I'll pass."

"Don't knock it till you've tried it." Nick grinned.

"We won't be gone long," Dylan assured. "We'll have the afternoon and part of the next day before we have to pack up and head home."

I took a sip of water to wash down the grief clogging my throat.

"No problem, Sir. Since my days of sleeping in are numbered, I plan on staying in bed as long as I can." I forced a carefree tone, while inwardly starting to slap bricks and mortar around my heart. I was going to need those walls all too soon.

Nick held me with a probing stare. All the while, I prayed he couldn't see the pain already seeping into my veins. If I could make it through the meal without my misery spilling over the table, it would be an Oscar winning performance.

The food on my plate made my stomach turn. The aromas in the diner now turned my stomach, and I'd barely touched my food. I hoped they wouldn't notice.

Meg reappeared at the table, striking a seductive pose and batting her lashes. "Are you two handsome men ready for dessert? We've got some gooey pies with rich, creamy topping."

I'd had enough. I couldn't take another second of her shameless flirting and sexual innuendos. Especially when my time with Nick and Dylan was quickly coming to a heartbreaking end.

"No thanks, Meg," I bit out. "Just between us, *I'm* their dessert, and I'm going to spoon feed them every inch of my body...all night long. Be a dear, and bring us the check. I don't think I can wait another minute to feel their hot hands, slick tongues, and naked bodies all over me."

"Rawwwwrrr." Dylan smirked as Nick closed his eyes, lowered his chin, and shook his head.

Meg blanched. Her jaw dropped open in shock before she pressed her lips in a tight, angry line and raced away.

"That wasn't nice, pet," Nick whispered in that decadent, whiskey smooth voice.

"She wasn't being nice either, Master. She was all but climbing into your lap."

"Yes, but you're the adult here, little one. She's just a child."

"She certainly isn't acting like one."

Between the judgmental bitch in the bathroom and Meg the *Playboy* bunny wannabe, my patience was shot. My hopes for a memorable night out had turned into a ghastly episode of *The Twilight Zone*.

Meg stood behind the cash register; her face bright red as she pounded on the keys.

"I'm going to go settle the tab. I'll be right back," Nick announced as he stood.

"I bet ten dollars she gives you her phone number," I hissed.

Nick spun on his heel and turned. Bracing one hand on the table and the other on the back of the booth, he leaned in. "Put your little green-eyed monster away, pet. It's unbecoming, and I don't like it. She's a child, and I'm *not* a monster."

"I didn't mean..."

"Hush. Not another word," Nick bit out. Crushing his lips to mine with an angry kiss, he turned and walked away.

"I didn't mean to suggest—"

"He knows. Relax." As Dylan nuzzled my cheek, his warm breath spilled over the shell of my ear.

"I'm fine," I murmured as shivers rippled through me.

"Not yet, but you will be as soon as we get you back to the barn," he purred in my ear.

Panties flooding, I turned my head, then, without asking for permission, I kissed his lip, and welcomed his tongue.

"Ah-hem," Nick cleared his throat. "You two ready to go or would you rather we get busy here on the table?"

Dylan swallowed my laugh as he reached up and pinched my nipple.

"Home," Dylan mumbled against my lips.

Nick gripped my hair and pried me from Dylan's mouth.

"Enough, little one, before I join in…in front of everyone," he growled.

Furtively dragging his hand over my beaded nips, my bones turned to putty.

"Yes. Home, please. Now, Masters," I anxiously seconded.

Chapter Nine

W hen we reached the barn, they guided me straight to my room where our clothes began flying through the air and pooling on the floor in our rush to get naked. As our hands, fingers, lips, and tongues urgently tangled, hungry growls and whimpers filled the air as we tumbled onto the bed.

Alternating between their swollen weeping shafts, they kept me busy worshiping every glorious inch. After prying my mouth off him, Nick pinned me to the bed where he and Dylan took turns feasting on my flowing pussy.

While Dylan laid siege to my clit with his teeth and tongue, burnishing my G-spot with his masterful fingers, Nick filled my mouth and whispered all the dirty things they planned to do as he rocked his thick cock over my tongue.

In a thrilling rollercoaster ride, they soared me to the peak, only to pull away and force me to tumble back to earth. Over and over, they methodically tortured me until I was sweat-soaked and mindless.

Grinding my pussy over Dylan's wicked mouth, Nick hissed and withdrew completely before fisting his shaft with a fierce grimace. "Get ready, little one. I'm going to stretch and fill your tight little ass.

Claim and fill you so full and deep you'll come harder and longer than you've ever come before."

"Yes, Master. Please…let me come. I'm on fire," I whimpered.

His growl of approval was like a soft caress. Dylan lifted from my pussy. Hunger etching his face, his mouth glistened. After snagging a handful of condoms and the bottle of lube from the nightstand, he climbed over me and positioned his cock in front of my lips.

Lifting my head, I wrapped my lips around him, sucking him in deeply. With a growling curse, he rocked his hips, thrusting impatiently to the back of my throat.

"Fuck. We've got to take her together…now!" Dylan barked.

As he repositioned me over his chest, I couldn't help but smile. Nick was usually the demanding one, but Dylan, who seemed to have run out of patience, had no compunction about showing it.

I reached up and plucked the condom from his fingers.

"Allow me, Master," I said with a sassy smirk.

"You're trying to kill me, aren't you, kitten?"

"No. I just want to put you in a coma." I grinned before opening the packet and rolling the condom down his hard shaft.

"Fuck me," Dylan hissed.

"As you wish, Sir." With a devilish laugh, I swung a leg over his waist, then eased down onto his steely girth.

Riding him with a slow, sultry roll of my hips, I heard Nick open another condom behind me. Splaying his broad hand between my shoulders, he pressed me down over Dylan's chest before glazing my puckered rim with lube. As he pressed one finger, then another, through my taut rim, explosions of bliss burst outward.

"Please, Master, hurry. I need to feel you inside me," I moaned, sliding up and down Dylan's shaft.

A sturdy slap landed across my ass, and I jerked, gasping in surprise.

"Patience, my sweet slut," Nick instructed, landing another firm slap across my ass. I gasped and jerked, then moaned when he added another finger. "You're not ready to take my cock up your ass yet."

"But I'm on fire," I whimpered, impatiently rocking against his embedded fingers.

"Yes, you are," Dylan growled. "Your pussy is hotter than lava. Tell me you're almost there, man."

"Getting closer," Nick replied between clenched teeth.

"She feels so good, I don't know how much longer I can hold back."

"Patience, fucker. You can hang."

"Easy for you to say, you're not the one whose balls are boiling."

"They will be soon," Nick chuckled, gliding his fingers from inside me.

I closed my eyes and inhaled a deep breath to prepare for his burning invasion. But when he sank his teeth into the cheek of my ass, I threw my head back and screamed.

"Now she's ready," Nick announced, pressing the tip of his cock against my ass. "Relax and let me in, little one. We're ready to take you to paradise."

He steadily pressed his bulbous crest through my rigid rim. After having them claim my ass numerous times over the past few days, my body knew how to respond. And as the exquisite burn coalesced into spine-bending pressure, a low moan rolled off my tongue.

Peering up at me, Dylan plucked, pinched, and rolled my nipples between his fingers and thumbs. "You are so fucking perfect, it's like you were made for us, kitten."

Brimming with joy, my heart swelled.

As Nick retreated and Dylan surged—over and again—I tossed my head back and basked in their savage indulgence. Like a summer storm, demand churned with each deliberate scrape Dylan dragged over my G-spot, and lighting splintered as Nick scraped the sensitized nerve endings of my narrow rim.

Lost and sailing in the pristine depths of ecstasy, I held nothing back. Grinding and moaning against their driving shafts, I welcomed the savage hunger they commanded.

Raw.

Open.

Exposed.

They claimed pieces of me that had never been touched before.

Though they bound my body to theirs, they'd set me free.

I could never go back to what I'd been before.

There was nothing of my former self left.

They'd redefined me beneath their masterful hands.

Like a Phoenix rising from the ashes, a new woman had been born.

Bold.

Proud.

Secure.

Willing, ready, and able to surrender it all to their fierce demands.

The power was indeed *mine*, but it was hollow... inconsequential without their dominant devotion.

Their passion.

Their strength.

Their love.

And I was safe.

Protected.

Treasured.

The savage heat pooling in my womb expanded through my limbs. Dylan's chest was glazed in our combined sweat. His dusky indigo eyes sparkled with desire, incongruent to the fierce grimace of restraint curling his lips. The magnitude of his struggle to stave off release was etched on his face.

As the mounting force of demand squeezed in all around me, my keening cries, mixed with panic and need, tore from my throat. In a mantra of pleas, I implored their permission to let the monstrous orgasm they'd created obliterate me.

"Nick?" Dylan barked in a gravelly voice.

"Fuck yes," Nick hissed, digging his fingers into my hips, maniacally thrusting his entire length into my ass.

"Now, kitten. Shatter for us. Shatter hard!"

As if his roared command possessed my soul, I let the orgasm's fury consume me.

My muscles seized, compressing around their driving shafts in rippling spasms, as screams of rapture tore my throat. Exploding from the annihilating crescendo splintering through me, their feral cries scorched my flesh as they followed me over. But instead of riding the crest and coming down, their driving cocks sent me soaring even higher.

"Again!" Nick growled. "Come again, our sweet, insatiable slut."

As a second, equally brutal orgasm crashed through me, an inhuman cry sailed off my lips. Spasms wracked my tunnels, milking the last ropes of come from their shafts.

Slowly sliding back to earth, I collapsed over Dylan's slick chest as aftershocks twitched and fluttered. Long minutes passed before our breathing evened out, and Nick gently eased from my ass. After climbing off the bed, he headed toward the bathroom while Dylan wrapped his arm around my waist and rolled me onto my side. Still coupled to his rigid shaft, he smoothed away the strands of hair stuck to my sweat-soaked face before pressing a kiss to my lips so reverent and tender, tears stung my eyes.

When Nick returned, Dylan eased from inside me with a groan, then strode to the bathroom while Nick gently cleaned me up. As he climbed into bed, I curled in close against his side and rested my head on his chest. Neither of us said a word. We didn't have to. For the first time, I could read his emotions as clearly as he could mine.

Content. Happy. Satisfied.

As I released a soft sigh, Nick chuckled. "My sentiments exactly."

Seconds later, Dylan joined us before meshing me between their warm bodies. I nuzzled Nick's neck like a sated kitten before their tandem snores vibrated my body. After the intensity of our carnal workout, I should have been sleeping as well, but I couldn't shut my brain off. The events at the diner wouldn't stop spooling through my brain.

Easing out from beneath their heavy limbs, I carefully crawled out of bed and padded from the room. Snagging the blanket off the couch, I wrapped it around me before starting a fire, then strolled to the kitchen and fixed a cup of tea.

Seated on the couch in front of the roaring fire, I sipped from my mug while my mind continued to whirl. This fantasy world we'd created was beyond anything I'd ever imagined. But reality, like sand in an hourglass, was slipping closer and closer by the second. In a few hours, Nick and Dylan would head out in the quest to kill Bambi, then return. After sharing another few hours of our incredible power exchange, we'd say our goodbyes and go our separate ways.

Tears stung my eyes.

Walking away from both amazing men was going to be the hardest thing I'd ever had to do. They'd stolen my heart; it belonged to them now, and I didn't want to contemplate how dark the coming days would be.

It was my own fault for falling in love with them. Though they'd never promised me anything more than they'd delivered, my hopelessly romantic heart was going to be shattered. Even though I knew there was zero chance of a happy ending with Dylan and Nick, I'd let the fairy tale take over all logic. I'd let naiveté get the best of me, and now I had to pay the price.

The experience at the diner rolled through my head again. And the bleak realization that our ménage relationship would be scorned by nearly everyone. Even, if by some miracle, Nick and Dylan wanted to forge a long-distance relationship, my skin wasn't thick enough to keep the insults and disapproving looks from slicing me to pieces.

But it was more than that. I wasn't capable of slaying their demons. Nick was still dealing with Paige and the wounds she'd left on his heart. And Dylan was still struggling with the horrors of war. While I knew all about artifacts and ancient cultures, I didn't know squat about healing the human psyche. Besides, I was clearly fucked up way worse than either of them. Why else would I be sitting alone in the middle of the night letting pointless scenarios spin through my brain? If I'd stuck to my plan and guarded my heart from the beginning, I wouldn't be worrying about leaving them.

While I didn't completely understand what Dylan and Nick gained by sharing me, I knew the way they fed off one another when we made love felt like the most natural thing in the world. But after being a part of that connection, I didn't know if I could ever be happy with just one man again. What I really wanted were the two Doms snoring in the other room.

"If I had a magic wand, none of us would ever have to say goodbye," I whispered, wiping a tear from my cheek.

Though it was a cold, hard depressing fact, I wasn't a magician.

Instead of mourning what I couldn't have, I started counting my blessings.

I was lucky Nick and Dylan had rescued me after the accident. And even luckier they brought life to the submissive within me. And though it was going to end in goodbye, my life would be richer and fuller because of them. I simply hoped gratitude would sustain me in the empty days ahead.

As another tear slid down my cheek, I closed my eyes and inhaled a ragged breath, then tried to welcome the familiarity of being alone. This quiet space where I could process my thoughts without confessing every emotion to be scrutinized like an all-you-can-eat-buffet for my insecurities was what I was accustomed to. It was familiar, but oh, how I was going to miss them. Swiping away another tear, I took a sip of tea. Though the ache within was inescapable, I had to come up with a plan to ensure I came out the other side of this with my sanity.

After long hours of joyriding my mental merry-go-round—which was not fun—I still hadn't come up with a painless exit strategy. With a heavy sigh, I closed the glass fireplace doors, then crept back to bed. Neither of them stirred as I snuggled between their rugged bodies.

Moonlight spilled through the window, illuminating Nick's face. Staring at him, I drank in every inch of his gorgeous tawny features. Memorized the fine lines at the corner of his eyes, the dark thick lashes caressing his cheeks, and the masculine arch of his full, broad lips. I could still taste his kiss. It took all my willpower not to trace his exotic cheekbone or thread my fingers through his silky hair.

Dylan snorted then turned on his side, wrapping a thick arm around my waist. Turning my head, I studied his features, too. He was every bit as blindingly beautiful as Nick. I knew Dylan's heart-stopping dimple and his blue, intoxicating eyes would haunt my dreams forever.

I had one more night to spend with them…just one.

It wasn't enough.

It would never be enough.

Tears slipped down my cheeks as a lump of anguish lodged in my throat. I softly sniffed, trying to hold back my sorrow, but I couldn't stem the flow. The ache in my heart felt insurmountable.

Suddenly, Nick's sat phone beeped. Bolting upright, he silenced the alarm while I quickly dried my tears. But when I sniffed, he snapped his head my way.

"What's wrong, little one?" he whispered, cupping my face in concern.

I couldn't do it…couldn't tell him I'd fallen in love with them and that I was falling apart at the seams.

"I had a bad dream…about my parents," I lied.

"Aww, pet. Do you want to talk about it?"

"No, Sir. I'm fine. I have the same nightmare from time to time. It always leaves me a little rattled." Guilt, for lying to him, pumped through my veins.

"We'll stay with you and not go hunting if you need us to."

"No. That's not necessary. It was just a dream," I assured, forcing a smile I didn't feel.

"Okay. We won't be gone long. In fact, we'll be back before you know it."

I forced a wider smile. "Then I'll roll over and go back to sleep."

"Okay, little one. We'll be back in time for lunch." Reaching over me, he shook Dylan's shoulder. "Get up, man. It's time to go hunting."

"What? Huh?" Dylan sat up but wasn't fully awake.

"Hunting. Time to go," Nick repeated.

"Oh, yeah." Dylan scrubbed a hand over his face, then smiled down at me. "Good morning, gorgeous. What are you doing awake?"

"I had a nightmare, but I'm fine now." Though my heart was dissolving into a million pieces, I smiled.

Dylan rolled over, caging me with his body before kissing my lips with a ferocious growl. "Keep the bed warm, kitten. We're gonna set it…and you on fire when we get back."

I clung to his blue eyes, twinkling with promise, longer than I should have. Thankfully, he didn't notice before leaping out of the bed.

But Nick did. He pinned me with an intense stare. "You sure you're all right?"

"Yes, Sir. I'm fine," I assured, cupping his neck and drawing him to my lips. "Go on and do your man stuff. I'm going to stay here and keep the bed warm."

"Not too warm, little one. You don't have permission to come without us." He smirked as his gaze delved deeper.

Keep the mask in place. No cracks. No fissures. And NO falling apart.

After a long moment, he winked and stood. I sprawled out my arms and legs, pretending I was enjoying all the space. But in reality, I was soaking up the traces of warmth and inhaling their masculine scents while dying a little inside.

Holding tight to every ounce of willpower I possessed, I watched as they got dressed. As soon as the front door of the barn snicked shut, I buried my face in their pillows and sobbed.

Outside, the pickup roared to life. And as the gravel crunched beneath their tires—matching my breaking heart—they drove away, taking all the peace and happiness they'd brought me with them.

There was no way I would be able to keep myself together when they returned. I'd barely been able to hold back my tears while they got dressed. I knew in my heart; these torturous minutes were only a precursor to the heartache to come.

My pitiful wails filled the air.

"It wasn't supposed to end this way," I wailed.

Clutching their pillows to my face again, I sobbed and breathed in their rugged scent.

Bold and sensuous.

Masculine and virile.

Powerful and perfect.

Commanding yet so tender.

"Why does it have to hurt so bad?"

Tossing the pillows aside, I leapt off the bed. Wrapping my arms around me to hold myself together, I paced the room as tears streamed down my face. Together, panic and pain consumed me.

"How am I supposed to stop loving them?" I sobbed. "I can't...I can't do this."

As I flopped onto the bed, their scents surrounded me. Memories, like strobes, flashed through my brain. And while sobs burned my throat, a heavy, black cloak of despair sucked the light from my soul.

I laid in the bed crying until my tears ran dry…until I was cold, empty, and numb inside.

Forcing myself off the mattress, I made my way to the bathroom and splashed cold water on my face. I raised my head and stared at my haunted reflection. Swollen eyes, rimmed red, matching my nose. An errant tear slid down my cheek.

"You've got to get a grip. This isn't the end of the world," I scolded myself.

No, but it sure as hell felt like it. Still, I had to get myself under control. I couldn't fall apart like this in front of them.

"I can't pull it off. I know I can't," I whined as I dried my face with a towel. Nick's scent clung to the fabric and another wave of tears slammed me. Sinking to the floor, my back against the tub, I cried some more.

There were only two options I could think of.

One, stay and confess that I'd foolishly fallen in love with them, which wouldn't do a damn thing but make me look pathetic and weak.

Or two, pack up and leave before they returned. Save my pride and run away like a gutless coward for not following the rules.

If I left, they'd never know how badly I'd fucked up.

Palming my tears, I stood and looked around the room. My toiletries sat on the shelf where Nick and Dylan had unpacked them.

These men had taken care of me with such devotion, not just the first night, but every hour of every minute we'd been together.

Stop it. You're never going to do the right thing if you keep torturing yourself. You fucked up. It's time to go before you make an even bigger fool of yourself, the voice in my head chided.

I had no other options. I had to leave now…go home and lick my wounds, or go down in an embarrassing ball of fire in front of them.

"No. I'm not about to let that happen."

After gathering my toiletries, I marched back to the bedroom. Tossing my suitcases onto the bed, I tried to keep my eyes from wandering over their pillows…over the empty spaces on the mattress where they'd made me feel like the center of their universe.

A mournful cry escaped my lips as I tugged on my clothes—the clothes they'd forbidden me to wear each day. Wiping away my tears, I cleaned out the closet and drawers, then stuffed everything in my suitcase. Hastily digging the rental key from my purse, I carried my belongings to the other room. My gaze stilled on the couch as memories of all the nights we'd spent curled up by the fire, talking, touching, kissing…and making love filled my mind.

"Enough!" I screamed, shoving the onslaught of memories down deep.

I rounded the island and rummaged through the utility drawer until I found a pen and notepad. Then I sat at the table and gripped the pen so tightly my fingers turned white.

Tears filled my eyes and blurred my vision. Clenching my teeth, I blinked them away. The time to fall apart was over. It was time to grow the fuck up. I wasn't some teenager in the throes of a stupid crush. I was a grown woman acting like a child.

"Stop it. Just fucking stop it!" I hissed.

Scrawling out the first thing that came to mind, I tore off the page, then carried it back to the bedroom before propping it on my pillow. Forcing myself not to look back, I gathered my luggage, then made my way down the long narrow hallway.

The rented Hummer sat alone in the gravel lot. It was a stark and haunting reflection of what I felt inside.

"You're taking away exactly what you wanted, Savannah," I tersely whispered. "Memories. That's all you get."

I pressed the fob to unlock the vehicle and heaved my luggage in the back. Then I sucked in a deep breath, hurried to Kit's front door, and pasted on a smile before ringing the bell.

When she pulled it open, a bright smile lit up her face. "Come on in. I'll make us some coffee. I guess it's kind of quiet in the barn with the guys out hunting."

"Actually, it's nice. I miss my alone time," I lied. "I just wanted to pop by and say…see you next year. I decided to head on home. There's some painting I want to get done in the spare bedroom, and I need to check my messages in case something's come up for work. It was great to relax and unwind, but it's time to get back to the grind."

Though the lies rolled off my tongue with ease, it became increasingly harder to keep the smile on my face. When Kit's brows furrowed, my heart thundered in my chest. I feared she'd seen through my mask.

"You drive safe. No more deer, you hear?" she warned.

I laughed, but it sounded hollow and fake, then wrapped her in a hug while promising I'd be careful.

Once on the road, I didn't stop shaking until I'd hit the four-lane highway. The sun warmed my skin, but I was frozen to the bone. I turned on the radio and found a rap station, then cranked up the volume. I hated rap music, but I didn't want to listen to sappy love songs that would make me cry and wreck. While the music blared with a heavy, chest-thumping beat, my head began to throb. It was a welcome distraction from the pain shredding my heart.

I tried not to wonder what Dylan and Nick's reactions would be once they returned and found the note. Would they be mad or grateful I'd saved us from an awkward goodbye? Maybe it was my own guilt, but I hoped they'd welcome a day to relax and do what they wanted instead of what they felt obligated to teach me.

When I hit the Missouri/Iowa line, I stopped for gas and a cold drink. As I rummaged through my purse for my wallet, my cell phone rang. I clutched the phone, staring at Kit's name on the caller ID. Indecision filled me. Surely, they hadn't come back from hunting so soon. I'd only been on the road a couple of hours. My finger hovered over the phone, but I chickened out and let the call go to voicemail.

As I climbed back into the Hummer, it rang again. Guilt and dread filled me as I checked the number. It was one I didn't recognize. Clenching my jaw, I turned the device off, then started the Hummer and pulled back onto the highway.

My hands trembled and anxiety bloomed. Was the unknown number Nick's phone? Were they mad? Were they hurt? Were they relieved? Maybe it hadn't even been them. Maybe it was a wrong number. Maybe they didn't even know I was gone.

"Stop it," I barked to my brain.

I knew if I continued rolling every fucking question over and over in my brain, I'd go insane before I reached Kansas City.

If I was more like Mellie, I could have stuck around and told them goodbye. But I didn't have the life experiences she had. I didn't have tools or solid ground to get a foothold in. I was the one who'd climbed inside myself after our parents died. I was the one afraid to love someone for fear they'd disappear or die and leave me with a heart so broken I couldn't mend it back together.

It was enough of a risk to love Mellie as much as I did. She traveled endlessly, and though every trip reminded me of a game of Russian roulette, I always mentally prepared myself the day she didn't make it home. We'd even made a pact. Each time she had to leave, she would call and tell me how much she loved me. We made sure we carried each other in our hearts, no matter where we went.

I loved my boss Myron and his wife Hellen. They, too, would die someday, leaving me to grieve and mourn because they were old. But I'd prepared myself as much as I could for that day as well.

But giving my heart to two men who might want it, but couldn't accept it was a whole level of grief I didn't know how to handle. I'd never learned how to pick up pieces of my broken heart and move on.

By the time I pulled into my apartment complex, I was emotionally and physically exhausted. My feet felt like bricks as I unloaded the Hummer. Dropping the luggage on my bedroom floor, I crawled into my bed and cried.

Cried for the Dominance they'd never give me again.

Cried for the peace and serenity they'd given me.

Cried for the safety and care they'd given me.

Cried for the punishment and pleasure they'd drowned me in.

I ached to hear their voices again. But I knew it would only prolong my heartache.

Instead of trying to quash the pain inside, I welcomed it…let it consume me so I could purge Dylan and Nick from my system.

I'd lived my ultimate dream for a few glorious days. But, oh, how I longed to go back and relive it all over again. To breathe in their scent, feel the comfort of their strong bodies next to mine, hear the praise of their decadent voices, and revel in their dominant command.

"Why does it fucking hurt this much?" I wailed. Tears soaked my pillow. And as I tried to purge them from my heart, the fear I would never be whole again wended through me.

When my tears dried up, I wiped my eyes and climbed out of bed.

In a listless haze, I wandered to the kitchen and made a cup of tea. My movements were mechanical, robotic. I ran on autopilot…dead inside.

As I looked around my apartment, I realized there was nothing there but a way of life I no longer wanted to go back to. My quiet oasis felt like a giant cavern. The silence I reveled in before was now a choking weight making it hard to breathe.

I sat at the kitchen table while the walls around me pressed in.

Gone were the rugged warm bodies that had held me tight.

Gone was the thrill of yielding to their command and granting them pleasure.

Gone were the reassuring touches and two words that sent my heart sailing…*Good girl.*

The ring of the cordless phone on the counter nearly jolted me out of my chair. I glanced at the answering machine beside it and the red light pulsing with messages. It rang and rang until the machine picked up.

I held my breath.

"Sanna? Honey, are you there? Please, baby, pick up if you're home. You're not answering your cell, and I'm going fucking bat shit with worry. Where are you? Come on baby, please pick up!" Mellie's anxious pleas echoed through the room.

Bolting out of the chair, I snatched up the receiver. "I'm here. I'm here. I'm sorry. I didn't mean to worry you," I frantically choked out as my voice cracked.

"Thank fuck. Dammit, Sanna. You scared the living shit out of me."

"I know, I know. I'm sorry. I wasn't thinking."

"What the fuck is going on? I got a call from Mr. Dreamy Voice, Nick. Sanna, he's pissed to the gills. What the fuck happened between you two?"

"Oh, Mellie. I fucked up. I fucked up big time." Tears spilled as I plopped onto my chair.

Through sobs, I explained the whole mess…the Dom/sub stuff… everything. I expected her to be shocked, but she wasn't. She understood which made me cry even harder. Her unconditional love was a balm to my jagged, raw nerves.

"Baby, part of submission is being honest. If you don't think they'd understand what you're feeling then they weren't the kind of Doms you need."

"How do you know?"

"Let's just say we're cut from the same cloth." She chuckled. "You don't think I'm this bossy and hardheaded *all* of the time, do you? Sanna...I'm a sub, too."

"Holy shit, Mel. Why didn't you tell me...like, years ago?"

"Get real. I didn't tell you because I was afraid you'd freak the fuck out and run for the hills, thinking I was some kind of kinky pervert."

"Yeah, well if I was in better shape, I wouldn't have told you, either." I sniffed.

"Well, we're both out of the closet now. What are you going to do about Dylan and Nick? They are *not* happy campers at the moment."

"There's nothing I *can* do! I'm not going to call and say, Oh, I'm sorry I didn't ask your permission before I ran away, but I couldn't handle telling you goodbye." I blew out a heavy sigh. "There's nothing left to say. It was a few days of Dom/sub fun, some amazing, mind-blowing sex, but...that's it. We're not going steady. I'm never even going to see them again, so what's the point? I'd rather run away than let them see what I've done to myself."

"Okay, so maybe it's more than you're comfortable confessing to them. They still have the right to know. And you shouldn't have packed up and walked out on them like that, without a word."

"I had to, Mel. I couldn't stay and fall apart in front of them. It would have been too fucking embarrassing."

"So, you didn't do anything embarrassing with them, say...sexually?"

I could feel the smile in her words. Logic. She was going to try to trip me up with logic. My own sister was pulling the same shit Dylan and Nick did.

"Don't go there. This is totally different," I warned.

"Well, *I* have to call him back. So, what do you want me to tell him?"

"*Why* do you have to call him back?" I gasped.

"Because I told him I would, once I finally talked to you. Honey, they're honestly worried about you."

"Shit!" I hissed. "Tell them I'm home safe and sound and…hell, I don't know. Tell them I said thanks."

"Thanks?" she barked.

"Yes," I said with a note of finality.

Mellie issued a heavy sigh, then mumbled she'd pass the message along.

"Do you want me to fly to KC and stay with you? You sound like you could use some company and a shoulder to cry on."

"No. I'm fine. Really. This shit will pass. I'll just go back to…"

To what? The idea of going back to the life I left behind a week ago chafed.

"Back to what?" Mellie pressed.

"Back to research."

"Myron closed the office," she reminded with a hint of doubt.

"I'm working on an article that I'm trying to get published. I've got tons of research that will keep me busy. Please, Mellie. I'm fine."

"All right," she sighed in exasperation. "But you'd better call me if you need me, understand?"

"You know I will. I love you, sis. Love you so much."

"I love you too, baby. Pour yourself a glass of wine and go relax in a long, hot bubble bath. You need it."

"I will. Talk to you soon."

As I hung up the phone, I cringed. Dylan and Nick were mad. That wasn't the reaction I expected. What did it mean?

"It means nothing other than you usurped their authority and took back your control," I groused.

Pinching the bridge of my nose, I tried to will away my pounding headache before dragging my cell phone from my purse. When I turned it on, there were over fifty calls from the same unknown number when I'd stopped to get gas.

"Nick," I whispered wistfully, then cursed and tossed it back in my purse.

Aimlessly wandering through my apartment, I stopped in the bathroom to take some aspirin but realized I hadn't eaten all day. My guts were already churning and burning with anxiety. The meds would only add fuel to the fire on an empty stomach. The refrigerator was empty. All I had in the freezer was a frozen dinner and a bag of peas. With a sigh, I slung my purse over my shoulder and headed to the store.

As I strolled through the aisles of the grocery store, I realized I should have stayed home and fixed the TV dinner. Though nothing looked appetizing, I grabbed a package of chicken breasts and vegetables for a salad, then swung by the bakery.

My favorite motto was…When in the throes of depression—eat cake!

But even that looked too sickeningly sweet. I knew when I turned my nose up at cake, I was in serious trouble. As I headed toward the ice cream section, my cell phone rang. Fear gripped my heart until I saw Mellie's name on the caller ID.

"Hello?"

"Hey. Don't be mad, but I had to check on you again. Are you feeling any better?"

"Aww, Mel. You know I could never hate you. I love you for being worried, but honestly, I'm fine. I'm at the store…getting cake," I lied.

"Julia Child would be so proud," she teased. "I wish I knew how to boil water. Thank god for delivery."

"So, what did Nick say when you called back?"

"He didn't answer, so I left a message telling him you were home and fine, and you said *thanks*. Cake, huh? The magical powers of flour, eggs, sugar and whatever else is in it will do you good."

"It will."

"You sure you're okay?"

"Seriously, Mel, I'm fine. I'm not where I want to be, but like Mom always used to say, *this shit, too, shall pass*."

But deep down, I knew it was going to take forever.

"It will, baby. And you'll be a whole lot happier once you join the club in KC and get out amongst other kinky people."

"How do you know there are clubs here?" I asked suspiciously.

"How do you think I learned about the lifestyle?"

"I see. Okay, then you'll have to tell me which one to join when I'm ready."

"I will when your heart heals."

We said our goodbyes before I checked out my groceries and drove back home.

As I slid my key into the lock of my apartment door, I noticed it didn't stick like usual. When I pushed the door open, an ominous chill slid up my spine. Reaching inside my purse, I fisted my can of Mace and thumbed the lock off as I set my groceries and purse on the welcome mat.

The interior was so dark, I couldn't see anything past my feet. Why had I pulled the curtains shut? *Because of your headache, dumbass.*

Hoping more light would fill the room, I pushed the door open wide, but it didn't reach the dark, murky corners. Peering into the still darkened room, the hairs on the back of my neck stood on end.

Chapter Ten

With a tentative step forward, I breached the portal. The canister of Mace lay hidden in my fist. Even as I tried to convince myself the sinister, prickly feeling was from lack of sleep and my emotional state of mind, I knew something was wrong.

I'd only feared for my safety once, but never in my own home.

I'd been working in an old courthouse in a sketchy part of town. It was late at night. Had it not been for the squeaky wooden floors, I never would have been alerted to the drunk coming up behind me. He'd somehow wandered in off the street and decided he was going to have sex with me…in a misguided, alcohol-induced way. Forcing me to the floor by my hair, he reeked in a vile combination of booze, feces, and vomit. I knew he was going to try to rape me on the spot. I fought like hell, but not only did the vagrant outweigh me, he was strong as an ox, even for being toasted out of his gourd. My screams alerted the ancient night watchman, who came to my rescue and began beating the delusional drunk with his trusty flashlight. It was the encounter that convinced me to take up karate.

You know what to do. Focus and listen.

Every cell in my body was on high alert. Trusting my intuition—screaming at the top of its lungs—I knew someone was in my apartment. But it was too dark for me to tell where the burglar was hiding.

If the prick wanted to abscond with my jewelry box, he wasn't going to make it past me. The only memento I had left of my mother was her wedding necklace. He'd have to kill me to steal it.

Behind me, a car horn honked. Without thinking, I glanced over my shoulder. Inwardly cursing myself for being distracted, I whipped my head around as a blurry figure rushed from the shadows. Strong hands gripped my arms and before I knew what was happening, my back was up against the closet door.

Swallowed into the dark abyss, I couldn't see the face of my attacker.

Crying out in panic, I bent my wrist and aimed the Mace toward his face, then pressed the button. The robber began to scream before releasing my arms and covering his face.

As his feral curses morphed with cries of agony, I bolted away from the door as he bent over, still clutched his eyes.

"Get on the ground, motherfucker, or I'll blow your balls off." I prayed he was too incapacitated to realize I wasn't holding a gun, but merely bluffing. "Do you hear me, asswipe? I said get your ass on—"

A second pair of beefy arms wrapped me from behind and squeezed tightly. I was pinned and helpless against a wide chest. Son of a bitch! They were working as a pair. It pissed me off. I didn't hazard to think there might be two burglars.

"Stop!" the prick who had me immobilized growled on the back of my neck.

Thinking fast, I let my body grow lax in his arms—as I'd been trained. Waiting for him to loosen his hold, I prayed he'd think I was out of fight. When the dumb shit kept me locked to his chest, I clenched my teeth and sucked in a breath.

"Not today, fuck face," I growled as I wrenched from his arms, then spun and clipped the side of his head with a roundhouse kick.

With a howling yell, he fell to the ground like a mighty oak.

Unwilling to stay and see if any more goons were waiting in the wings, I turned and raced toward the front door.

"Savannah! Wait!" roared the man still palming his burning eyes.

As my heart clutched, I froze mid-stride.

I knew that voice.

Dylan.

"Oh, no. Oh, shit. No. No."

I whipped around and yanked open the curtains, then raced to his side. His eyes were red and pouring tears, and his face was crumpled in pain.

"What the fuck are you doing here? Is that…Oh, no. No. No. Nick!" I screamed, racing to the other man still sprawled out on my living room floor.

"I'm going to get a fucking bar of soap and make you eat the whole damn bar, girl," he growled as he slowly sat up, rubbing the side of his face.

"Ohmigod! Ohmigod! I'm so sorry," I moaned. "Why did you grab me? How did you get in here? Why are you two here?" I screeched.

"Help!" Dylan cried out. "I can't see a fucking thing. Fuck! This shit burns!"

Rushing back to Dylan's side, I gripped his elbow and led him into the kitchen. Flipping on the light, I shoved his head over the sink and started flushing his eyes with cool water.

"Just keep rinsing, I'll be right back," I instructed before racing out of the kitchen to check on Nick.

He sat on my couch, holding his cheek and glaring at me as if I was the spawn of Satan.

"Where did you learn to fight like that, little one?"

A weak smile wobbled over my lips. "Karate class," I confessed as I hauled my purse and groceries inside the apartment and shut the door.

Nick looked like hell. Knowing that he'd soon be sporting a nasty bruise, I nervously nibbled my bottom lip. "Why didn't you two say something when I opened the door. I thought you were burglars or rapists. What are you two doing here?"

"Go check on Dylan. Do you have some ice?"

"Yes, come on," I replied as I helped him off the couch.

"I can walk. Not sure I'll be able to eat for a while, but I can fucking walk."

"Oh, Nick, I'm so sorry. If I'd known it was you…"

"It's Master or Sir, dammit. Clearly, you've forgotten how to address us as well as how to say good-fucking-bye," Nick thundered.

"But...I...thought," I stammered as a glorious, disapproving Dominant scowl lined his face. "Yes, Sir."

Butterflies set sail in my stomach. I wrapped my slender arm around his waist and led him into the kitchen before helping him sit at the table.

"How are you doing, Sir?" I asked rushing back to the sink, smoothing a palm over Dylan's broad back.

"Better. Fuck, this shit is wicked."

"I'm so sorry, Sir. I didn't know it was—"

"Us, yeah, we know. It's all right. I'm proud you can take out any *real* attackers."

"Easy for you to say," Nick grumbled. "She didn't break your jaw."

"It's broken?" I shrieked.

"No, but it sure as fucking feels like it is," he groused.

Tossing the chicken and ice cream into the freezer, I pulled out a squishy gel ice pack. After wrapping it in a towel, I pried Nick's fingers away, then gently pressed the cold pack against his face.

"I can't apologize enough, Sirs. If I'd known it was you two in my apartment, I wouldn't have done what I did."

"So, you didn't just kick our asses for fun?" Nick scoffed.

"Never, Sir. Why are you two here?" I asked as my head swiveled between the two like a metronome.

"Why are *you* here and not back at the barn with us?" Nick countered as his brows slashed in anger.

Averting his gaze, I placed a clean kitchen towel in Dylan's hands.

"Let me tell you how surprised—no, that's too tame. Let me tell you how *blindsided* we were when we came back from hunting early to spend more time with you, only to discover you'd not only packed up and gone, but also left us a fucking note behind," Nick roared as the veins in his neck bulged, and his face turned deep crimson.

I'd never heard Nick sound so infuriated, not even the day when I woke and heard him talking to George about his skanky ex, Paige. "The fucking Christmas card from my accountant has more heartfelt sentiments than the kiss-off note you left us."

Guilt and fear thundered through me as I watched Nick pluck the note from the pocket of his jeans. With a scowl, he began to read.

"Dear Sirs, thank you so much for a memorable week. I will fondly treasure our time together. Sincerely yours, Savannah." Nick tossed the paper onto the table as if it were on fire. "If you were *sincerely* ours, girl, your ass would have been in bed when we got back, like you'd promised. But *sincerely* you weren't. Is this tripe you wrote how you really feel about us? Or is it another smoke screen to hide how you truly feel?"

I had no idea how to answer his question, except to tell the truth, and I wasn't ready to do that. Luckily, Nick didn't give me a chance to respond before resuming his tirade.

"That's what you were doing this morning before we left, isn't it, pet? Blowing smoke up our asses and feeding us some bullshit story about a fucking dream? I gotta tell you, Savannah, you had me fooled. I honestly believed you. You looked right into my eyes and lied straight to my face."

Nick stood. Fury rolled off him in a potent wave. I inched back until my butt bumped up against the countertop.

"I'm sorry," I whispered, shrinking inside.

"I want an answer. Not a fucking apology!" Nick slammed his fist onto the table. "Is this--this glacial shit you wrote how you really feel about us?" His lips curled in an angry sneer as his eyes drilled into mine.

Tears welled and spilled down my cheeks as I shook my head. I couldn't speak because I couldn't swallow the lump of guilt lodged in my throat.

"Finally, we're getting somewhere." Nick crossed his arms over his wide chest. His dangerous gaze palpably peeled the flesh from my bones.

Dylan turned off the water and dried his face with the towel before clasping my elbow and leading me to the kitchen table.

"Sit down, kitten."

Steeling myself to get my ass handed to me, I complied.

"Do you know why we cut our hunting trip short?" Dylan asked.

His beautiful blue eyes were bloodshot and rimmed red. I glanced back at Nick with the ice pack to his swollen cheek and held back a sob. I'd done that to them. I'd inflicted pain on the two men who meant the world to me.

"No, Sir."

"You have *no* idea why we rushed back to the barn?" Nick asked in disbelief.

"No, Sir," I choked out.

"Come on, Dylan, let's go," Nick announced in a defeated tone.

As they turned and started toward the door, I launched from the chair in disbelief.

"Wait!" I yelled. They stopped and turned in tandem, blistering me with hot, angry glares. "You're leaving because I don't know the answer to your question? What do you want from me?"

"Obviously, something you're no longer willing to give." Nick's tone was arctic.

"What...you mean my submission?" I rounded the table.

"Stop," Dylan barked. "Not another step."

I froze. My heart pounded in panic and confusion. Nick narrowed his eyes and crossed his arms over his chest as his lips thinned to a tight angry line.

"Strip," he commanded.

"What?" I gasped.

"Oh, little one. Do. Not. Make. Me. Repeat. Myself. If you think the rules have changed just because we're on your turf, you're sadly mistaken."

"Strip," Dylan instructed.

Together, they squared their shoulders and clasped their hands behind their backs. Power, anger, and Dominance surged off their bodies. They wore their command like custom-tailored suits.

Every cell in my body melted like spun sugar.

I'd been a fool to think I could survive without this...without *them*.

I didn't know why they'd gone way out of their way to find me. All I knew was if they walked out the door now, I'd lose my mind.

The sun beamed through the wide window, casting a halo around their rugged bodies. They looked like angels but their expressions were born of the devil. Their jaws ticked in tandem as their stares flayed me open.

My fingers trembled as I began to unbutton my blouse. Movement at the window drew my attention. My heart slammed against my ribs as my neighbor passed by. Thankfully, he didn't glance at the big, plate glass window, but another neighbor might.

"Can I please close the drapes, Sirs?" I asked in a timid voice.

"No. It's now or never, kitten. Decide what you want."

Dylan's harsh and unfamiliar tone scared me. It also confirmed I'd been way off-base thinking they might be relieved I'd removed the burden of training me off their shoulders. There wasn't a happy bone in their bodies.

As I resumed working on the buttons, anxiety from being seen stripping in my living room warred with the unyielding need to make Dylan and Nick proud. As my clothing fell away, the barriers I'd build after leaving the barn crumbled at my feet. The same calm serenity I'd felt surrendering to their Dominance filled me once more.

They were bringing me back to life.

When I stepped out of my jeans, I inhaled a deep breath. Casting my eyes toward the floor, I lowered to my knees beside the kitchen table. An audible sigh poured from Dylan's lips. I yearned to raise my eyes and read their expressions to know if I had pleased them. Instead, I remained in the submissive pose as unnerving silence dragged on and on.

Sweat broke out over my upper lip, and a tremor skittered through my body.

Please don't leave. Please don't leave. Please don't leave.

I sensed retreating movement.

Fear and panic gripped my heart in a tight fist.

Tears filled my eyes as silent sobs shook my body.

Clearly, I'd failed their test.

As hope began dying inside me, I heard air escaping the cushions of my leather couch.

They hadn't left. They'd merely sat down.

My fading embers of hope reignited. Still, I knew the *real* test was yet to come.

Fighting the urge to peer up at their faces, submission won over want. Though fear and uncertainty whirred, the beacon of hope continued growing. Self-preservation and pride flew out the window. Pissed or not, they completed me in ways I couldn't fathom. I'd endure all the heartache on the planet to spend one more day beneath their command...their control.

Tears streamed down my face.

"Raise your head, little one," Nick demanded in a low, controlled tone.

I inhaled a deep breath then slowly lifted my chin. With matching hunger glistening in their eyes, they sat on the couch, legs spread, and elbows resting on their knees. I swallowed tightly. After several long, interminable seconds, Nick sat up and pointed a finger toward his shoes.

"Crawl to us, girl."

Do what?

The knee-jerk reaction to tell him to go to hell seared the tip of my tongue. I wasn't going to crawl like a dog to him, or anyone. Yes, I wanted to spend one more day with them, but not at the cost of my self-respect. As I opened my mouth to tell Nick where he could shove his request, I had a shocking epiphany.

This was the final test. The one that determined my fate, their fate, and the fate of any future we might have together.

Shoving down the caustic humiliation bubbling inside me, I leaned forward and positioned myself on all fours. Forcing my limbs to move, I choked back a sob and began crawling toward them. Inching closer and closer, I tamped down my pride and let the tattered threads of my submission knit through me.

"Head up. Eyes on us," Dylan commanded in a stern, uncompromising tone.

When I raised my head, the wide-open window flashed a neon sign of dread. I faltered for a moment then clenched my teeth, determined to see the lesson through.

"Move your ass, pet. You're trying what little patience we have left," Nick growled.

If this isn't a test, you can throw them out. My inner voice railed in defense of my crumbling ego. I issued a small nod, not at Nick's caustic command, but at the submissive longing burning within.

As I gazed up at their critical stares, a myriad of emotions tore through me. Anger. Debasement. Servitude. Embarrassment. Arousal. Fear. Contentment. The combination didn't make a lick of sense, but I continued crawling toward them, determined to see what happened next.

As I neared their feet, Nick leaned forward and threaded his strong hand into my hair. When he cinched a tight fist, sending prickles of pain and pleasure skipping over my scalp, a fluttering cry tore from my throat.

"Good girl. Kneel." Though Nick's voice was flat...void of the whiskey smooth timbre I'd grown accustomed to, his first two words made my heart sing.

"Dylan, would you mind closing the curtains? We need her full attention for this discussion," Nick asked, flipping on the lamp on the end table beside him.

"You're damn right we do," Dylan muttered before rising and jerking the drapes shut.

Relief that no one could gawk at my naked body did little to soothe my prickled nerves. As Dylan sat back down, he cupped my chin. With the broad pad of his thumbs, he wiped the tears from my cheeks and issued a heavy sigh. His jaw ticked as he released my face.

"Trust is very fragile. Once broken, it's hard to mend. Don't you agree?" Nick asked in a deep authoritative tone.

"Yes, Sir. I'm sorry."

"Don't give me another fucking apology, girl. Give me the truth. For once, just give me the truth." His eyes narrowed.

"I'll give you all the truth I have, Sir."

"Let's hope you *finally* do." He speared me with a look of disapproval so intense; I felt it to my bones. "Why did you run away from us this morning?"

My heart raced, and I began sweating more. "I didn't want you knowing I'd made a mistake."

"A mistake?" Dylan asked in a seething tone. "You think the time we shared was a fucking mistake?"

"No, Sir," I amended quickly. "I said *I'd* made a mistake."

"Go on," Nick prompted.

"I did a stupid and foolish thing." I swallowed tightly. I hated being forced to spill my guts. "With my heart, Sirs."

My gaze darted between them. I grew more confused as their expressions softened and slow smiles spread over their lips.

"What happened to your heart, little one?" Nick asked softly.

"I lost it, Sir. To both of you," I confessed.

"So, you fell in love with us, is that what you're saying?" Dylan arched his brows.

"Yes," I whispered, waiting for them to laugh at me for being so stupid and foolish.

Instead, Nick cupped my chin and forced my gaze. After searching my eyes for long, unnerving seconds, he exhaled a heavy sigh. "Did you ever happen to think that maybe we fell in love with you, too?"

My eyes widened as an explosion of hope blasted my system. "N-no, Sir."

"You've changed us. Changed us in ways we never imagined," Dylan confessed. "We came back early from hunting to talk to you about us."

"But when we got back, you were gone." Nick scowled. "We need to know what's in your heart, Savannah. If the note you left is truly how you feel, then we've wasted our time coming here."

The tortured sound of his voice coupled with the pain and fear flickering in his eyes ripped my heart to shreds.

"No, the note is…a lie," I sobbed. "I fell so hard…so fast… I broke the rules. I-I was afraid…afraid to tell you."

"Shhh, it's going to be all right, kitten. I promise."

Dylan's whispered vow only made me cry harder.

He plucked me from the floor, then settled me on his lap before wrapping his strong arms around me. I buried my face against his hard chest, and breathed him in. As his masculine scent—the one I feared was lost forever—blanketed every cell in my body, I clutched his shirt and cried like a child.

"We were so afraid we'd lost you, Savannah," Nick murmured, combing his thick fingers through my hair. "We haven't figured all the details yet. All we know is we want you in our lives. Do you want that, too…want to be with us?"

"Yes," I cried as all my pain, fear, and anxiety evaporated.

Nick tugged my hair and pried my face from Dylan's chest before crushing his lips to mine in a desperate and feral kiss. Drowning me in passion, he swallowed my sobs while Dylan gripped my nape, holding me in place.

"We love you, kitten," Dylan whispered in my ear. "We were afraid to say the words at Kit's. But not now. You need to know; you've done the impossible. You brought us back to life, Savannah. We want you to come back to Chicago with us…so we can figure out a way to make this work."

As Dylan's confession and invitation crowded my brain, he placed his hand over Nick's—still buried in my hair—in a double decree of ownership. As Nick reluctantly released my lips, Dylan swooped in and claimed my mouth with a kiss so teeming with love, my head swam.

They loved me, and they wanted me. Not just for a week, but hopefully, forever.

As another wave of tears, happy ones, crested through me, they pressed me between their powerful bodies and whispered reassurances and promises. When I finally gained control of myself, I realized their twin erections pressed against my flesh.

Hunger, wending with happiness, throbbed through my system.

"Please, Masters, I need to feel you inside me," I begged, wiping my eyes and casting them a hungry gaze.

"We'd love to squeeze inside your sinful pussy and ass," Dylan growled. "But there's a little matter of punishment we have to address first."

"Punishment?"

"Yes." Nick nodded. "You didn't think you could run away from us without suffering any repercussions, did you?"

"I-I…"

"Threatening to blow my balls off and calling us names earlier is going to cost you," Dylan said with an evil grin.

"Indeed. There's no way we can allow you to get away with calling us such vulgar names as motherfucker, asswipe, and fuck face." Nick smirked.

"But I didn't know it was you two. I thought you were burglars."

"We know that," Dylan assured. "But there's other things we need to address before punishment and...pleasure."

"What things?"

"Things like, whether or not you want to go back to Chicago with us."

"We know your boss won't open the office again until February," Nick stated.

"How did you know that? Did Mellie tell you?"

"No. The morning after your accident, you talked to her on the sat phone. We heard every word." Dylan winked.

"Ahh, yes. I'd forgotten about that."

"We'd like you to come home with us," Nick began. "We'd like to continue your training, and also see where this road might lead. If you can't or don't want to, we'll figure a way to schedule visits with you, every other weekend if possible."

"No. I want more...I want it all."

"So do we. Is there anything keeping you here...any responsibilities you need to take care of before February?" Nick asked.

"No," I whispered, tingling with anticipation.

Is this what spontaneity feels like?

"What do you need to do before we leave then, kitten?" Dylan's blue eyes sparkled with glee. And as his smile widened, his sexy dimple sank even deeper.

"I have to turn in the rental, go to the post office and forward my mail or stop it...or something. Then, I don't know...pack?"

Everything was moving at the speed of light. While it was exciting and thrilling and more than I'd ever dreamt possible, I was scared. Having aligned my life in rigid routine, such abrupt change was more than a bit daunting.

Still, something niggled in the back of my brain.

Nick said we would see where this new road would lead us. But he'd also made it clear their desire was to continue my training. They'd both professed to love me, but that was far different from being *in* love with me. Was Nick willing to expose his heart, to try to fall *in* love again? Or would he forever hold back to ensure it didn't get broken? And what about Dylan? Was this new arrangement his attempt to heal the scars he carried from war? Was he trying to regain the pieces of himself that were lost? They'd said I'd changed them, but I wasn't sure what I'd done to influence a shift *this* dramatic.

Was it possible to forge a new path in a little over two months? Then what? What would happen when I had to return to work? The separation would be ten times worse than the few hours I'd experienced since leaving Kit's.

"Tell us what you're thinking," Nick commanded.

I swallowed tightly and peered up at him. "I'm a little overwhelmed, Master. What happens when I have to come back home in February?"

His expression grew solemn. "Nothing's set in stone, Savannah. We'll deal with everything, one day at a time."

I pursed my lips as his words rolled through my brain.

For a man who'd vowed to protect his heart, he'd quickly tossed it into the ring. How had he changed his mind so quickly? Worse, I wasn't even supposed to know he'd made that vow.

Eavesdropping on their conversation that night in the barn had come back to bite me in the ass...my entire ass.

"We refuse to drag every crumb out of you, kitten," Dylan admonished.

Inwardly cursing myself for childishly playing possum in the first place, I blew out a heavy sigh.

"There's something I need to tell the two of you," I began, darting a guilty glance between them both. "I wasn't asleep that night in the barn. I heard your whole conversation."

Their bodies tensed in unison as palpable waves of shock and irritation rolled over me.

"Well, well," Dylan said, breaking the heavy silence. "You're just full of surprises, aren't you?"

"And then some," Nick drawled in curt agreement.

"I'm sorry, Sirs. I knew it was wrong when I did it. But I wanted to learn more about you both. I-I just didn't know how to ask."

Dylan scoffed. "It's easy, kitten. You open your mouth."

Though I'd earned their disapproval, I didn't like it.

"Yes, Master."

"What questions do you have after listening to our conversation?" Nick frowned.

Willingly planting my ass in the hot seat, I dragged in a deep breath as the flames grew higher and hotter.

"You said that I had changed you both. But Nick, Sir, you were never going to love again. And Dylan, Sir, you said you avoided commitment at all costs. Do you both still feel that way? I don't know...I'm not sure...I need to know where *I* stand in regard to your walls, Sirs."

"Evidently, your little ploy only caused you more insecurities, kitten." Dylan tsked.

I nodded as remorse seeped through me.

"When we told you we loved you, we meant with all our hearts." Nick's voice so soft and filled with adoration, I could barely look into his eyes. "Yes, you have changed us...changed everything we thought we wanted until *you* touched our lives. Without knowing, or trying, you opened our eyes and our hearts and changed us for the better."

Tears stung my eyes. Nick pressed a kiss so tender and reverent to my lips, my heart swelled as his love fused to my soul. A tiny whimper escaped my throat as he pulled away.

When I glanced up at Dylan. His expression was filled with pain. Fearing he wasn't ready to slice himself open like Nick, I cupped his hand and sent him a soft, understanding smile.

"I don't how to explain it, Savannah. All I know is the time we spent with you chased away the dark clouds that have been hanging over my head since I left Iraq. You've given me hope, kitten. That's something I never thought I'd feel again."

Tears slid down my cheeks as Dylan cupped my nape and pulled me in close to his lips. A gentle smile tugged his lips before he kissed me with the same love and passion Nick had.

A kiss so potent and claiming, all my fears and insecurities melted away.

Though blissfully ecstatic we had found each other and changed one another's lives, that unknown something still squirmed in the back of my mind.

As Dylan lifted from my lips, I kept my eyes closed to try to pinpoint the crux of the uncomfortable sensation.

The diner.

My heart thundered as the ugly experience roared to life inside me. If I hadn't been locked in Dylan and Nick's strong arms, I would have bolted off the couch to escape the inky embarrassment pumping through my veins.

"What's wrong?" Nick cupped my cheeks and held me in a stern, confused gaze.

"Nothing," I lied, watching as Nick arched his brows in warning. "I mean…" *Crap.* I couldn't keep pushing them away. The few hours I'd spent alone had been debilitating. "I'm sorry, Master. Something happened last night at dinner, in the ladies' room."

"What?"

"A woman came into the restroom shortly behind me. She was one of the women sitting—"

"We remember them. Go on," Dylan insisted.

"She called us perverts and said we needed to leave or she was going to call the cops. She said I was a whore and that I was going to burn in hell."

"What did you say to her?" Nick asked.

I nibbled my lip. I'd already earned a long session of edging for running away, but I feared telling them how I put the hateful cow in her place would only add more torture. Ignoring Nick's question wasn't an option. All I could do was hold out hope they'd *eventually* give me permission to come.

When I finished repeating the nasty things I'd said to the woman, both men tossed their heads back and laughed.

"Our first date didn't go very well, did it, kitten?" Dylan asked, still chuckling.

"We'll make it up to you, Savannah," Nick assured. "There's a wonderful Italian place that welcomes not only our kink, but also the kinks of others. We'd like to take you there when we get to Chicago."

"I'd love to." I grinned.

"Good." Nick smiled. "Then let's get started."

"Started with what?"

Dylan chuckled as he slid me onto Nick's lap. "I'll be right back."

As he walked out the door, I peered up at Nick. "Where's he going?"

"No more questions, little one," Nick instructed.

"But I'm trying to communicate. If I'm not allowed to speak, how can I do that, Sir?"

When he pinned me with a look of warning, I pressed my lips together and huffed.

Long seconds later, Dylan returned. The big, black duffel bag clenched in his fist answered all my questions.

"Show us where your bedroom is, kitten," Dylan demanded with hungry grin. "It's time to pay the piper."

When Nick lifted me off his lap and set me on my feet, my pussy was inches from his face. His gaze stilled on my closely cropped tuft of curls. My folds grew wetter by the second. His nostrils flared, and he licked his lips before turning toward Dylan. "I can smell her cunt. She's already wet for us."

"Please, Masters. No punishment. Just make love to me," I begged.

Nick stood and placed his hands on my hips, then turned me to face Dylan—now wearing a wry grin. As I opened my mouth to beg him, too, a harsh and painful slap exploded over my ass. As the burn rushed down my legs, I nearly purred.

"Save your breath." Nick chuckled. "You'll need to when you start begging us for...mercy."

"What are you going to do to me?"

"Painful pleasures," Dylan smirked.

"We'll never give you more than you can handle," Nick assured. "However, we need to make a few things perfectly clear. First and foremost, you belong to us. Running away is forbidden. You will not trick us by faking sleep or any other guise again. We will purge the negative body image you cling to, as well as your preoccupation with other people's opinions about our lifestyle. Negative thinking has no place in *our* relationship, nor does it promote your submission. And last but not least, you own the responsibility of communicating with us about *everything*. There will be no more yanking it from you like a fucking dentist."

"That will keep us busy for a long time." Dylan chuckled.

"But...I wasn't in the right frame of mind to explain how I felt at the barn."

"Because you chose pride over honesty," Dylan scolded, eating up the distance between us in two long strides.

"I know," I mumbled as both men wedged me between them.

My nipples drew up tight and hard. My clit throbbed as more slick juice coated my folds.

Their stern command turned me on like a light bulb. I was getting hotter and wetter by the second.

"If you keep choosing pride over honesty, your submissive journey is going to be one hell of a rocky road," Nick chided. "Regardless of what people think, what they say, or how they stare, Dylan and I will always protect you. Until you trust us with your emotions...the good, the bad, and the ugly, you'll never find the true peace and serenity we're trying to give you."

"We know you've been alone for a long time, but we won't tolerate bits and pieces, pet." Dylan scowled. "It's all or nothing. Do you understand?"

"Yes, Masters."

On one hand, I was relieved they didn't expect me to slough off my insecurities with the wave of a magic wand. But sharing every damn emotion with them seemed as daunting as the elephant of punishment still in the room.

"You're going to edge me, right?" I cringed.

"Not today, kitten," Dylan grinned, holding up the bag. "You've earned something more substantial. Now show us your room."

Chapter Eleven

B efore I could comply, Nick scooped me up in his arms and
followed Dylan as he swaggered down the hall.

"First door on your right, Sir," I directed while my hideous and
painful punishments crowded my brain. "It's going to be horrific and
painful, isn't it?"

"Only as much as it needs to," Nick replied in an unnervingly icy
tone.

"I've learned my lessons though, Master. I won't run away again.
I'll talk to you both about my feelings. I'll do better with my
insecurities. You don't have to punish me, I swear."

"Maybe we *want* to," Dylan goaded before stepping into my room.

"But making love would feel so much better," I urged.

"Oh, it will…eventually." Nick's lips curled in a feral smile.

Little Red's wolf had nothing on him.

"Stop trying to worm your way out it. You did the crime. It's time
to pay the fine." Dylan smirked, dropping the duffle bag beside
my bed.

"I think we start with her on her back." Dylan grinned.

"For now," Nick replied in a cryptic tone as he set me on the edge of the bed, then guided me back onto the mattress. "Your safeword is red. Close your eyes, little one."

A tremor rippled through my body as the sound of the heavy zipper sliced the air. While I knew the bag contained ropes, paddles, floggers, condoms and lube, I assumed it contained painful and unpleasant toys as well.

I closed my eyes and tensed.

The sound of soft zippers and rustling clothes told me they were stripping. I wanted to peek, but didn't dare. I was in enough trouble all ready.

Sending up a futile pray that my punishment be geared more toward pleasure than pain, I anxiously waited.

Suddenly, broad hands gripped my thighs and spread me open. Warm breath danced over my sodden pussy, and I moaned.

Gripping the bedspread in my fists, I trembled as I waited to feel a warm, wet tongue glide up my slit. Instead, fingers toyed with my folds, plucking and pulling in a maddening rhythm. I writhed and whimpered, inwardly begging for more.

Suddenly, white-hot pain bit into my folds.

My eyes flew open wide as a shrill scream exploded from my throat.

Writhing and bucking my hips, I tried to escape the fire, but strong hands held me to the bed. Tears burned my eyes as I gasped and tried to rise above the caustic fire consuming my sex.

"What the fuck are you doing to me?" I screamed as I slashed an angry glare at Dylan kneeling between my legs.

Nick's grip tightened around my thighs, growling at my expletive.

"Breathe, kitten. Ride it out," Dylan coaxed, strumming my clit.

"Use your safeword if you need it," Nick reminded in a voice laden with concern.

"I'm okay," I panted, peering back down at Dylan. "What did you to do me? It hurts…burns."

A wry smile curled his lips as he held up a clothespin.

I blinked and gaped. "You put a clothespin on my pussy lips?"

"Yes. Well…the first one anyway." He smirked.

"Y-you mean you're going to clamp on more?"

"Oh, yes. I'm just getting started."

"Clasp your hands behind your head and breathe," Nick instructed.

"I-I can't. It's too much. I've learned my lesson, Masters. Honest," I pleaded.

"Either use your safeword or clasp your hands behind your head. If you choose to do neither, you'll take the whole bag of pins," Nick barked.

I had no clue how many clothespins were in the bag. I only knew I didn't want to find out.

Locking my hands behind my head, I stared up at Nick as he climbed onto the bed and began tracing his fingertips around my pebbled areolas.

As Dylan attached another clothespin, Nick crashed his mouth over mine, swallowing my scream. Plunging his tongue past my lips, he swept deep, and as he carried me away from the pain, I moaned and tangled my tongue around his.

This was the submission of my dreams, this sweet, tender, possessive tranquility. But I knew more searing slashes of pain… Dylan's pain…his *punishment* was soon coming. Though I wondered if I could survive this riotous combination of heaven and hell, the need to please him surrounded me in a blanket of peace.

Handing over my pleasure and pain completed me.

When Dylan latched his mouth over my pussy, Nick devoured my muffled squeal of shock. While Dylan's grunts and wet sucking sounds filled the room, Nick cupped my breasts and thumbed my aching nipples. Soaring fast and hard, I whimpered and writhed as Dylan stabbed my pussy and lapped my clit.

Together, they plucked, pinched, and laved my flesh, driving me higher and higher, then obliterated my bliss with more insidious clothespins. With each biting pinch, Dylan assuaged the pain with his magical mouth while Nick's tongue and teeth laid siege to my nipples.

The demand to be set free from their sexual purgatory hummed through me like millions of bees.

Slowly easing from my pulsating pussy, Dylan gazed at my pussy with pride. "All done."

Nick lifted from my breast and admired the other man's handiwork with a smile. "Beautiful. Are you ready, brave girl?"

For what...I didn't know. But it didn't matter. The second they'd brought me into the room, I'd surrendered my heart, mind, body, and soul to them.

"Yes, Master."

"Good girl," he praised.

As those two magnificent, magical words zipped up my spine, I gazed into his smoldering eyes. "On your hands and knees, little one. We've claimed you. It's time for you to claim us."

I didn't know what he meant, but I was ready and beyond willing to find out.

As I started to sit up, agony engulfed my pussy. A cry of pain spilled off my lips as I looked down. A fan of clothespins encircled my sex. When I leaned up to get a better view, the wooden fingers dangled and clicked together, gnawing against my screaming flesh.

Even the slightest jostle sent the burn flowing down my thighs and up my stomach.

I begged and pleaded for Dylan to take away the pain with his mouth, but he simply shook his head, then nipped his teeth into my thigh.

"Suffer for us, kitten," he whispered in a raspy voice.

It was a slow and agonizing process, but I repositioned myself on all fours. My mouth was perfectly aligned with Dylan's weeping, purple crest.

"You haven't earned a treat yet, kitten," he growled, sliding his thumb into my mouth.

Floating in the same clouds that carried me away after orgasm, I licked and sucked his digit as if it were his shaft. The sound of a condom wrapper seeped into my brain before Nick began massaging cold lube against my puckered rim.

"You wear Dylan's pins nicely, little one," he murmured, then reached between my legs and fanned the wooden pins. Pain, like lightning, streaked through me. Biting down on Dylan's thumb, I rose to my knees and howled at the top of my lungs.

Tears spilled from my eyes, and sobs rocked my body as Nick pressed a wide hand on my back, guiding me down on to all fours again.

"Don't move again, little one," he instructed, emphasizing his command with an open-handed spank across my butt cheeks.

Jolting, I pathetically whimpered. "Take them off, please. Please. They hurt. They burn."

"You don't want me to do that yet, Savannah. Trust me," Dylan warned.

As Nick prepared my ass, the pain from the pins was replaced with pulses of pleasure. Focusing on relaxing, I moaned when his finger breached my rigid rim. The pleasure centers in my brain sputtered, and my muscles contracted around his invasion while he thinned and expanded my ultra-sensitized ring.

Dylan reached into his bag of magic tricks and extracted a long vibrating wand. He wasted no time plugging the device into a socket by my bed. The bulbous, round-tipped toy began to buzz. A wicked gleam danced in his eyes as he eased onto the bed beside me. And as he pressed the vibe between my legs, the dangling pins danced and came to life.

The wood absorbed the vibration and bit into my flesh like razors.

As pain careened through my system, my screams echoed off the walls, and my whole body shook.

"Are you going to run away, kitten?" he taunted.

"No," I wailed.

"No, you're not," Dylan repeated, dragging the vibe to my clit.

"Such a pretty little slut," Dylan praised.

When he plunged his fingers into my dripping core and began burnishing my G-spot, bliss vanquished all my pain.

I flew through the heavens as Nick squeezed in another finger. His murmured praise slid over me as sinister shockwaves of demand splintered through me. When he pressed his broad crest to my ass and squeezed inside me, a sweet burn spread through me on gossamer wings.

My tiny ring expanded and contracted, sucking at his crest in a blistering contest of consent and denial. While gasps and moans scraped my throat, Nick gripped my hips in a commanding hold as he fed inch after thick, hard inch fully inside me.

Alternating the vibe between the pins and my clit, and toying with my G-spot, Dylan held me prisoner...trapping me in a maddening realm of ecstasy and painful denial.

"Who do you belong to?" he asked, thrusting his fingers in and out of my wet core.

"Ahhh," I cried, wildly rocking on his hand and sliding over Nick's driving cock. "You, my magical Masters,"

"Yes, you do. We want all of you, Savannah. Not just the pieces you are willing to share, but *all* of you. No more secrets, sweet slut. We'd much rather drown you in pleasure, than punish you."

"Yessss," I hissed.

"Do you vow to give us your body to use and treasure as we see fit?" Nick growled, quickening his pace.

"Yesss, Master, yessssss," I moaned, desperately trying to hold back the surge rising inside me.

"Do you hand over your trust to *our* command?" Dylan growled, fanning the clothespins.

A scream rippled in the back of my throat. "Yes, oh god, yessss," I panted through the pain.

"Do you give us permission to climb inside your mind to soothe your fears, slay your demons, and protect you from the past, the present, and the future?"

Dylan's impassioned words ripped through my heart. Fresh tears filled my eyes and trailed down my cheeks. "Yes, Master," I sobbed.

"Who do you belong to, girl?" Nick barked.

"You...I belong to you both," I sobbed.

"Yes," he growled. "You're ours...all ours."

"Give us your heart, mind, body and soul, sweet sub," Dylan coaxed. "So we can give you our hearts, bodies, souls, and drown you in unconditional love."

"They're yours...all of me belongs to you both," I wailed.

"Then come for your Masters, sweet slave. Come, now!" Dylan roared.

Like a shooting star, ecstasy consumed me in a blazing ball of fire.

Colorful lights exploded behind my eyes. As I tossed back my head and cried out their names, Dylan quickly plucked the pins from my enflamed folds. Lightning streaked from my pussy and shot up my spine and as the intense pain left in the wake of the pins melded with the electrified pleasure of Nick's shuttling cock, Dylan's driving fingers, and the numbing vibe on my clit.

"Ours!" Nick's booming roar thundered through my entire body.

And as he slammed through my clutching rim and filled the latex with his hot seed, my whole universe shifted and meshed with Nick and Dylan's.

They were the air I breathed.

The blood that pumped through my veins.

The light in my eyes, to help me find my way.

The strength to shield and protect me.

The hope in my heart for a new and better life.

And though I never fathomed how lost and alone I'd been...they were my salvation.

"I love you, Masters," I sobbed, crumpling to the mattress.

Within seconds, I was nestled between their warm, steely bodies. Infused with their unconditional love. And being inundated with their praise.

After a long night of conversation, a little bondage, and a lot more sex, we woke early and returned the Hummer to the rental agency before stopping at the grocery store. Back at the apartment, my five-star chefs began preparing a gourmet breakfast of bacon, eggs and toast. As they cooked, I phoned Mellie, argued with my insurance company, did a quick load of laundry, and re-packed my suitcases.

On the way out of town, we made a brief stop at the post office to forward my mail, then climbed into their truck and headed to Chicago.

The ride was long, but not a second of it was boring. My Masters made great use of my mouth and pussy as they took shifts driving. And only once did Nick have to threaten me with the butt plug when I got a little sassy.

It was close to midnight before we reached the outskirts of Chicago.

JENNA JACOB

"Our house is about another thirty minutes north of the city, but I'll take us up Lake Shore Drive so you can see the lights on the water," Nick announced as I sat a little straighter, unwilling to miss the sights.

Nick soon pulled off the interstate and drove along a highway parallel to Lake Michigan. The full moon reflecting off the water was beautiful, but the sprawling mansions lining the coast shocked and intimidated me. I'd grown up in a modest blue-collar home. While I didn't want for much, we were far from rich. Clearly, the people living in the homes facing the lake were mega-loaded.

Nick made a series of left and right turns, then slowed on a street lined with large, mature trees. Streetlights cast eerie shadows through the thick foliage, allowing only brief glimpses of the impressive houses set back from the street. Some were totally obscured behind manicured hedge rows, but others were daunting and massive and clearly visible.

When he pulled into a cobblestone drive, the headlights flashed over a monstrous brick colonial mansion. My eyes grew wide as I glanced at the avant-garde metal sculpture poised in the center of the circular drive before all my attention fluttered back to the mammoth house with multiple windows all framed with black shutters.

"You live here?" I asked, unable to mask my astonishment.

"We live here, kitten," Dylan chuckled.

"Wow," I whispered in awe. "Do you have maids and a butler?"

"Yes, Rachel and Pablo live in the guest house out back," Nick replied with such a casual tone, I knew he didn't have a clue how utterly dumbfounded I was. "Rachel oversees the cleaning service and prepares our meals. Pablo maintains the landscaping, pool, and makes household repairs when needed."

"You have a pool?"

"And a stunning view of Lake Michigan." Nick grinned, then sobered at my shocked expression. "Don't let it overwhelm you, Savannah. It's just a house."

"Yeah, a huge mother..." I coughed. "I mean, a really big one, Master."

"Come on, let's go in and crash. We'll unload in the morning."

"Can I grab my toiletries, Sir?"

"No. It's late. We need sleep…well, eventually." He grinned.

The naughty gleam in his eyes told me sleep would be hours away.

Stepping into the wide foyer, I felt like Cinderella at the Prince's palace. Gleaming hardwood floors shimmered beneath a stunning crystal chandelier dangling from the elegant, coffered ceiling. Dark cherry woodwork lent a masculine yet inviting contrast against the beige walls.

As they took me on what Dylan referred to as the *ten-cent tour*, I marveled how each room was more stunning than the one before. Being a professional designer, I knew Mellie would appreciate the attention to detail throughout each elegant room. While I was overwhelmed by the sheer grandeur of it all, the dichotomy of the men and their home was beyond fascinating. Their surroundings were ostentatious, yet there wasn't a pretentious bone in their bodies.

"Come on, kitten, let's get ready for bed."

"How many bedrooms are in this…castle?"

Nick laughed. "There's six, but don't get too impressed. We bought it for a song when the market crashed. It's a nifty tax deduction, nothing more."

"It's a little late not to be impressed, Master. I was already there when you pulled into the driveway. The view of Lake Michigan…is whoa, beyond breathtaking."

"It soothes our savage beasts, that's for sure," Dylan agreed as we climbed the wide staircase. "Nick and I laid claim to a couple of the guest rooms. We've been saving the master suite for…well, for you."

"Me?"

"Yeah," he nodded. "We've always hoped someday we'd find a submissive to share our lives with. The master suite is reserved for the sub of our dreams…you."

The adoration in his tone gripped my heart. Never had I imagined being someone's dream, let alone the dream to two of the most amazing Masters on the planet.

Nick pushed open the double doors to the suite. I felt the weight of his gaze as he watched my reaction. I caught the smile curling his lips as my jaw dropped at the splendor laid out before me. Stepping into the room, my feet sank into plush white carpet. A massive four poster, mahogany bed was the room's focal point. It was larger than any bed I'd ever seen. It had to have been custom built. I couldn't stop myself from gliding my fingers over the ornate, carved accents, imagining what it would feel like to be bound to the sturdy spires.

Making my way across the room, I stopped to admire the white marble fireplace located next to a set of beveled lead crystal doors. Curious, I twisted the shimmering brass handles to discover a large balcony that overlooked a sparkling swimming pool, and beyond…a picturesque view of Lake Michigan.

After returning to the bedroom, I stood in silence, drinking it all in. There wasn't an inkling of masculinity to be found. It was bright and airy and ethereal, as if I'd stepped through a door to heaven. Pale peach and sage green accents highlighted the bedspread and curtains. Among the cozy looking loveseat and chairs, I noted the glossy marble-topped tables, adorned with fresh cut flowers, matching the nightstands flanking the big bed.

Tears stung my eyes as I gazed at the overstuffed ecru couch positioned in front of the fireplace, exactly like the couch in the barn.

"What do you think?" Nick asked, pulling me from my gobsmacked trance.

"It's…magical," I whispered with a soft sniff.

"You've not seen the best part yet." Dylan grinned as he breezed past me and stopped at a massive, mirrored armoire.

"What's in there?" I asked, having presumed it was a closet.

"It's where we hide the fun toys." He smirked, opening the door.

"Oh my," I gasped, gazing at the plethora of floggers, paddles, cuffs, gags, whips and vibes. Spying several sizes of butt plugs, I quivered and gulped. "You've got a lot of toys."

"Not as many as we have at Genesis." Nick smiled as he pulled me in close to his side. "Think of all this as educational equipment."

I giggled and brushed my fingers over the soft, thick falls of a heavy flogger. My clit throbbed as a shaky breath fluttered over my lips.

Nick plucked my turgid nipple through my shirt then leaned in close to my ear. "I think our toy closet turns you on. Is your pussy wet?"

"And then some, Master," I boldly confessed.

"Good. That's how we want you…wet, ready, needy, and willing to please us."

"Oh, I'm there, Sir. All the way." I peeled my attention off the toys and stared into his sexy, dark eyes.

A low growl rumbled in his chest as he spun me against his chest and claimed my lips in a hungry kiss.

"If you start this now, bro, we're never going to get any sleep," Dylan warned with a chuckle.

Nick's lips curled against mine, before he ended the kiss. "Who needs sleep?"

"We all do if we plan to go to Genesis tomorrow…err, tonight."

"You're taking me to Genesis?"

"Of course. We want you to fully learn and experience the lifestyle." Dylan nodded. "You need to feel the sexual energy in the air, hear the erotic sounds, smell the leather and sex, and most of all, meet our friends who share a love for kink."

"But I don't have anything to wear. I mean, I don't own fetish wear."

"We'll take you shopping after we get some sleep," Nick assured. "We'll get you some club wear, and anything else you want."

"I don't want anything except you two, Masters. You're all I need and want."

For the first time, I'd confessed what was in my heart without fear of rejection. It was freeing to feel so safe.

Dylan swirled me from Nick's arms and ushered me into a stunning bathroom. I grinned when I spied the oversized whirlpool tub, much larger than at Kit's. Elevated against one wall was a tier of marble stairs skirting its edge. Sprawled along another wall was a rainforest shower with crystal doors. Against the third wall was a long wide marble vanity. Three ebony marble washbasins with glimmering silver faucets sat poised beneath the biggest mirror I'd ever seen.

"The toilet is in here," Nick stated, opening the door to another large room with not only a toilet, but also a bidet.

The bathroom was bigger than my entire apartment. I couldn't wrap my head around the fact Nick and Dylan lived in these lavish surroundings.

No wonder Nick had Paige sign a prenup. Probably a damn good thing, too.

"Oh, and there's one important rule for the master suite, little one."

I could already figure out what rule Nick was talking about by the mischievous twinkle in eyes. "No clothes. Right, Master?"

Both men chuckled. "You're catching on quickly."

"I just want to make you the happiest Masters on the face of the earth." I sighed.

"You already make us happy, little one, but pushing your limits will no doubt make us even happier. And finding a way to keep you here forever…that would make us ecstatic."

Forever. I wasn't foolish enough to think it would truly last forever. All good things came to an end, eventually. And though I didn't want to start thinking about it, the day would come when I'd be forced to walk away from the two men who brought more joy in my life than I'd ever imagined possible.

Yes, I'd have to leave their magical castle and go back to my boring existence…my job, and my empty apartment. But, not today. I had months, not weeks, to live this fairy tale. Hopefully, it would be easier to say goodbye to Dylan and Nick once I got my fill of submission. Sadly, I knew in my heart, it would be a million times harder. The fear of how I would ever survive rolled through me.

"Savannah," Nick murmured. "What's wrong? You have that look again."

"What look, Master?" I asked, forcing a smile.

Nick scowled and Dylan heaved a heavy, disgruntled sigh.

"That…I'm going to pretend everything's all right and hope they don't notice, look," Nick growled as he ate up the distance between us before gripping my chin and tilting my head up. "We're not playing this game anymore, Savannah."

"It's not a game, Master," I whispered as Dylan swooped in behind me.

"Then what the hell do you call it?" Dylan snarled in my ear before sinking his teeth in the flesh of my neck.

As a million pinpricks skipped through me, I dragged in a deep breath.

"I don't know how to… how to tell you every thought that flutters through my brain. I'm not used to confessing the mass amount of crap that consumes me every minute of every day."

"Then you'd better get used to it, because that's exactly what we expect."

Nick's eyes blazed with doubt and irritation. When I glanced over my shoulder, Dylan's reflected the same emotion. Their displeasure drove a spike through my heart.

"I'm worried about how I'm going to survive leaving in a few months."

"Hopefully, you won't want to," Nick replied with furrowed brows.

"I already know I don't *want* to, but I'll have to, Sir."

"Do you want some popcorn?" Dylan snarled in my ear.

"Popcorn?" I repeated in confusion.

"Yes. Since you're already sitting in the theatre, projecting the movie's unhappy ending, before it's barely started, I figured you might want some popcorn."

Dylan's snarky condescending tone pushed all my hot buttons. Spinning to face him, I slapped my hands on my hips and lifted my chin. "I'm not projecting the worst. I'm simply stating the facts. I have a job, an apartment, and responsibilities to—"

"To whom?" Nick interrupted.

"To my boss, Myron."

"Isn't Myron a grown man?" Dylan asked.

"Yes, but he's old and—"

"And you're not his mother," Nick stated in a patronizing tone.

"Stop belittling me. Both of you," I bit out.

"There she is." Nick chuckled.

"What are you talking about?" I asked, still fuming but totally lost.

"You," he glowered. "The spunky, sassy spitfire who cusses like a sailor. Ever since you realized it was us after beating the shit out of us yesterday, you've been walking on eggshells. It's about time the real you emerged again. Trust me, the real you is a whole lot more erotic and challenging than the little Miss Perfect we rode up here with."

"Little Miss Perfect?" I sneered. "I can't win with you two. I wasn't trying to be perfect. I was trying to *please* you."

"You honestly don't think you please us?" Dylan scoffed.

"In bed? Yes. Outside the sack? I honestly have no fucking clue."

"Strip," Nick growled as he eased in beside Dylan.

Peeling my clothes off with a disgruntled sigh, I sent them a brittle smile. "I suppose you want me to kneel at your feet now, right?"

"No. We want you to march your sexy naked ass to the kitchen," Dylan growled.

"I don't remember how to get there. Sir," I snapped.

Though I knew I was simply digging myself in deeper, I couldn't mask my snarky tone. Once ticked off, it took me more than a couple minutes to cool off. But it was more than that. I was tired and wanted to go to bed, but mostly, I was out of my element—in a new city, a new home—and suffocating with angst.

"Follow me." An evil smile tugged Nick's lips as he turned and headed out the door.

Apology searing the tip of my tongue, I trailed behind him along the hall and down the stairs, all too aware of Dylan right behind me.

When we reached the spacious kitchen with its shimmering stainless steel appliances, Nick open a cupboard and pull out a box of instant rice. I watched in confusion as he sprinkled a pile of white pellets on the ceramic tile.

"What—"

"Not another word, little one. In fact, not another sound. Lock your hands behind your head and kneel," Nick barked, pointing to the thick pile of dry rice.

Clenching my jaw, I followed his instructions. I'd barely gotten into position before the hard granules bit into my knees like hundreds of sharp teeth. The longer my body weight pressed against the innocuous specks, the more painful it became. I tried not to wiggle, but it was physically impossible.

The more I wiggled, the more potent the agony became. Both men leaned against the counter, their ropey arms crossed over sculpted chests, watching me as I fought the urge to cry out.

"You please us more than any woman we've ever known," Nick began, ignoring my whimpers of discomfort. "Yet, you don't believe it, at least not in your heart. Do you think we're lying to you when we praise you, little one?"

"No, Sir," I whispered.

"You not giving us a chance to succeed is unfair to our entire relationship. You have to communicate your feelings with us. If you harbor the tiniest doubt about how much we love you, we need to know. Closing yourself off, anticipating goodbye, is the kind of negativity that will destroy our relationship. If you want us in your life, then you've got to give us a chance. None of us know what the future brings, but I know one thing, neither of us want to lose you. I told you we'd figure everything out, and we will, because we love you. We can't be any clearer about our feelings than that. But it's up to you to decide if you'll believe us in your heart, or not."

I closed my eyes and sighed as my shoulders slumped. "I do believe you, Master, and I love you both so much it scares me. I don't want to leave, but can't keep from worrying. Being with you both is so perfect, I find myself waiting for the other shoe to drop," I confessed, hissing as the pain radiated up my thighs and began climbing my spine. "Is my punishment over?"

"No, kitten. The rice is a tool meant to drill us, our words, and our expectations into your soul. We've coddled, edged, denied, and talked. Maybe a little torture will force you to understand we can't take your trust, honesty, and communication…you have to willingly give them to us." Dylan squatted down and held me with a pleading stare. "Don't let your worries steal your chance for happiness, kitten."

Tears stung my eyes. They'd talked to me about releasing my control until they were blue in the face, but I still clung to it in so many ways. I was slamming the door in their faces before I'd given myself the chance to actually live the fairy tale.

"They're all I know, Masters. They protect me from getting hurt," I softly confessed.

"Did it hurt when you ran away from us?" Nick asked, squatting beside Dylan and leveling his tormented eyes on me.

I nodded as fat tears slid down my cheeks. "More than I'd dreamed possible, Sir."

"We don't want to hurt you, little one. We want to love and protect you."

"Then get me off this fu...wicked rice, please, Master?" I begged with a loud sniff.

"First, we need a promise, kitten," Dylan taunted. "No more locking up destructive worries and fears inside yourself."

"I'm trying, Master, I really am. It's not easy for me."

"We know, but you're not alone anymore. You don't have to handle everything by yourself. You have two strong Masters who can't wait to shoulder your fears. We've been over this time and again."

"I know. I know." I nodded, wishing I could find the magic key to unlock my fucking insecurities. "I'll try harder for you, I promise."

"Try harder for *all* of us. Trust and honesty aren't only for our benefit. It's for yours, too," Nick murmured wiping a tear sliding down my cheek with the pad of his thumb.

As he stood, pieces of rice crunched beneath his shoes. The sound was eerily reminiscent of the echo of gravel beneath their tires and the beastly grief that consumed me when they left the barn to go hunting.

Terrified of living through that unholy despair again, a surge of panic slammed through me. Nick's words screamed through my brain...*I told you we'd figure everything out, and we will, because we love you.*

As peace forced the dread from my system, Nick banded an arm around my waist and lifted me off the rice. Still crouched beside me, Dylan brushed the embedded bits from my knees.

"I'm sorry I disappointed you, Masters."

"We're not disappointed, kitten," Dylan assured as he stood and slung his arm around my waist as well. "We're construction workers. Not being able to build a solid foundation as quickly as we want is...frustrating."

With a whispered apology, I clutched them both and rested my head on Dylan's shoulder and Nick's chest.

"Rice is evil. I'd rather endure edging," I murmured, darting a glance between them.

They both chuckled. Nick kissed the top of my head. "Come on, little one. Let's get some sleep. I think we're beyond exhausted."

When I climbed into the enormous bed and their naked bodies surrounded me, I savored their familiar warmth. Before drifting to sleep, I smiled at the soft snores coming from the two men who owned my heart.

Chapter Twelve

Dawn was breaking when I opened my eyes to find Nick's mouth teasing my hardened nipple. A soft purr rolled from the back of my throat, and I stretched, arching into his mouth with a silent plea. Dylan lay snoring with a leg wrapped around mine in possessive claim. Nick tugged the turgid tip between his teeth. My needful moan stirred Dylan awake. A wicked smile played over his lips when he rolled to his side to watch.

"Does his mouth feel good, kitten?"

"Mmm, yes, Master."

"Is your pussy wet for us, sweet slut?" Dylan taunted.

"Ahhh," I gasped. "Yes, Master. Wet and so hot."

"That's how we like it, kitten. Spread your legs, I need your sweet honey on my tongue."

Without hesitation, I complied. Dylan climbed between my thighs and quickly latched his mouth over my pussy. As he plunged his tongue deep inside my core, he burnished my clit with the tip of his nose, chasing desire through my veins. My needy whimpers floated through the air while Nick lifted from my nipple and studied my responses with a dark, scrutinizing stare

"I love watching you soar, little one. Your expressions are so pure…so innocent…so fucking erotic," he moaned, plucking and pinching my pebbled nipples.

"Please, Masters…make love to me," I begged, writhing beneath the growing inferno.

"As much as I love watching you soar, I love hearing you beg, even more," Nick growled as he straddled my chest and brushed the slick tip of his hard cock over my lips.

I stared at his tawny smooth flesh, seductive dark eyes, and his sleep-tousled hair glistening midnight-blue as the morning sun streamed through the curtains.

He was beyond stunning.

A dreamy sigh spilled off my lips. I gazed at his glorious cock— swollen and dripping for attention—and breathed in his masculine scent. As I opened my mouth and started to stick out my tongue, Dylan lifted from my pussy.

Whimpering at the loss of his decadent tongue, I watched him ease off the bed.

"More, Master Dylan. Please."

"Easy, pet. He'll be back. He's just getting us some condoms," Nick assured, cinching a hand in my hair. "Open those pretty plump lips for me, sweet slut. I need to feel your wicked mouth around me."

Tingling with excitement, I engulfed his glistening crown. As his slick spice ignited my tastebuds, Dylan gripped my hips and drove his thick cock inside my weeping core.

With a muffled scream, my body bowed sending Nick's fat shaft deeper down my throat.

Filled.

Loved.

Treasured.

Sensations swamped me. Inundated with their potent and intoxicating power, I mentally screamed to the heavens in bliss. Claiming me in a rhythm anchoring me to them each sinful second, I urgently sucked and swirled my tongue around Nick's cock while my pussy gripped at Dylan's surging shaft.

As I writhed and groaned, basking in the searing sensations they awakened inside me, Nick held me in a savage stare as he stroked my cheek. The command and love shimmering in his dark eyes melted my heart.

Soaring higher and higher, Dylan's strummed my clit as his bulbous head scraped the magical bundle of nerves deep inside me. Their grunts, moans, and hisses of pleasure melded with Nick's raspy praise.

Release burned like hot coals as I struggled to hold my orgasm back.

"Nick," Dylan barked.

"Yes. Fuck yes," he hissed as fire flared in his eyes. "Come, little one. Now!"

Gripping my hair tighter, Nick's thick crest slammed against the back of my throat. Pinching my lips around the base, I felt him expand over my tongue before he erupted, showering my throat, and bathing my tongue in his hot, slick seed.

Ecstasy exploding inside me, Dylan tore from my pussy and savagely gripped my hips before manically, shuttling his thick cock in and out of my clutching core. Frantically panting through my nose, I gulped Nick's seed as Dylan roared…flying headlong with me into oblivion.

Milked dry, Nick eased from my lips. His reddened shaft glistened with my saliva. With a gratified curse, he flopped down on the bed beside me. Dylan stayed coupled deep inside me as rippling aftershocks quaked our bodies.

With sweat trickling down his face and his wide chest heaving with each gasping breath, Dylan was as beautiful as a Viking god. But what stole my breath was the raw, unequivocal love shimmering in his blue eyes.

For the first time, I could see his beautiful soul. Dylan had ripped off the mask of humor, decimated his walls, and sliced himself wide open for…*me.*

"I love you, Master."

The words rolled off my tongue as if I'd spoken them a thousand times. As his expression softened and tears glistened in his eyes, he eased from my pussy and launched onto the bed. Pinning me beneath him, I felt the desperation rolling off his chiseled body as he dragged in a ragged breath and held me with a piercing stare.

"Say it again, kitten," he demanded. "I need to hear to say it again."

My heart swelled, and tears stung my eyes. "I love you, Master. I love you…I love you…I love you."

"I love you, too, kitten. I love you so fucking much," he growled as his mouth crashed over mine, leveling my soul with a blistering kiss.

Nick caressed my face before brushing a kiss over my cheek. "We'll never get tired of hearing that, little one, just as we'll never get tired of showering you with all the love we hold in our hearts for you."

Through asking what I'd done to deserve their intense love; I wrapped my arms around Dylan's burly chest and returned his fiery kiss.

"You two keep swapping tongues," Nick chuckled. "I'm going to go fill the tub."

As Nick swaggered to the bathroom, Dylan grudgingly eased from my lips and smiled down at me. "You complete us, Savannah."

"You two complete me, as well."

"Good, because we're never gonna let you go," he quipped with a crooked grin as he rolled away and lifted me off the bed with him. "Come. Our bath awaits, my sweet, sultry siren."

When we entered the bathroom, I couldn't help but grin. Nick lounged with his eyes closed in a tub of billowing bubbles. His dark skin was a stunning contrast to the fluffy white suds.

"Not one word, my sweet slut. This foo-foo scented shit is *all* for you," Nick scoffed, slitting one eye open.

As I bit my lips to keep from laughing, he extended his hand. Accepting his chivalrous offer, a giggle escaped as I stepped into the tub. Without warning, he drew back a wet hand and landed a sizzling slap across my ass.

"Owww! That hurt," I huffed with a playful pout.

"*Owww* is not your safe word, girl. Besides, I look forward to spanking your ass a lot more." Nick smiled. Sitting up, he snaked an arm around my waist and pulled me to his chest beneath the water. Bubbles exploded into the air as I yelped and giggled.

"Promise?" I taunted, grinding my ass on his erection.

"Indeed," he hissed, thrusting his hips and driving his cock between my tender folds.

Lord, the man had stamina. He was hard as cement. I could have sworn the water heated another twenty degrees as his cock pulsed against my clit.

As Dylan climbed into the tub and eased in behind me, I rested my head on Nick's chest. When Dylan wrapped his arms around me, tangling us as one—a striking testament of our commitment—I sighed and closed my eyes.

"How do you feel, little one?" Nick asked, squeezing sweet, floral scented shower gel on a washcloth.

"Small," I whispered. It was the only word that adequately expressed the myriad of emotions flowing through me.

Dylan brushed the hair from my neck before pressing his warm lips to my neck. "Good, that's how you're supposed to feel."

With a languid moan, I closed my eyes as they washed my boneless body. Passing me back and forth while praising and kissing me, their hands never left my skin. After positioning my arms on a fluffy towel, they bent me over the side of the tub and gently washed my tender folds and backside. I rested my head on my arms and closed my eyes.

Nick leaned in close to my ear as he traced a fingertip over my butt cheek. "You're still wearing the imprint of my hand. It makes me want to mark you even more."

As I softly purred, jets of water pounded in fury against my sensitive and still swollen clit. A cry of surprise tore from my throat as I lurched onto my knees. As Nick cinched a hand in my hair, Dylan pressed a firm hand against the small of my back. Together, they held me in place while the water hammered my tender nub.

"You're going to come for us again," Nick taunted.

"I can't," I whimpered as pain and pleasure pounded my system.

"You can. And you will," Dylan growled. "You'll do anything we ask, because you live to please us, don't you, sweet slut?"

Like a relentless tongue, the jets lashed my clit. "Yes," I pitifully mewled.

Soaring faster and harder than ever before, the strumming water warred with my determination to please them. With their twin erections melded against my hips, their deep voices urged me to soar higher. And when they buried their fingers inside my pussy and ass, panic meshed with the demand thundering through me.

"So hot. So precious," Nick whispered as keening cries raked my throat.

"Let it swallow you whole, kitten. Shatter for us."

As permission tumbled off Dylan's lips, my universe exploded in a blinding orgasm. I shrieked as the thundering release seized me. Clamped around their driving fingers, my entire body stiffened as I dissolved beneath the brutal crushing onslaught of ecstasy.

"Fucking stunning," Dylan murmured, gently pulling me away from the jets.

When their fingers eased from inside me, I collapsed onto the towel and slowly floated back to earth. Spent and exhausted, I didn't have the strength to open my eyes when they lifted me from the tub. I simply purred as a thick towel was wrapped around me. I knew by his familiar, protective embrace, and familiar scent, Dylan was the one cradling me in his arms.

"Sleep," I whimpered.

Nick chuckled as Dylan carried me from the bathroom and placed me on the bed. Together, they gently dried my skin, then eased a pillow under my head before darkness pulled me under.

The sound of deep laughter dragged me from sleep. Squinting against the bright sunlight filling the room, I watched Dylan kick the door shut behind him as both men strode toward me carrying silver trays brimming with food.

Tantalizing aromas hit me as they placed the trays on the marble-topped coffee table.

My mouth watered as I sat up and scampered out of bed. Hurrying toward them, I reached for a strip of crispy bacon when Dylan swatted the back of my hand.

"Not yet, kitten. There's a few more rules in this room than simply being naked."

"You're not going to feed me like a child again, are you, Masters?" I moaned.

"Should I get the dog bowl from the armoire?" Dylan asked Nick with a scowl.

"You have a *dog bowl* in there?" I gaped.

"Indeed, we do," Nick replied with a staunch nod.

I didn't bother masking my reaction. "I know some subs find great joy in puppy, pony, and piggy play. And far be it from me to judge anyone, but crawling on my hands and knees is too much."

"We've already discovered how much you hate humiliation." Dylan winked.

"Then why did you suggest the dog bowl, Sir?"

"To remind you there are worse things than being hand-fed." Nick smirked.

"So, it was a trick?"

"No," Nick frowned. "It was a push. That's our job."

With a nod, I knelt on the thick carpet beside the low table.

"Good girl," Dylan praised, running his fingers through my hair. A knowing smirk tugged one side of his mouth as a rush of heat streaked between my legs.

They each took a seat in the matching Parsons chairs, then smiled at me with such raw adoration, my heart skipped a beat.

While I didn't understand their desire to feed me, when I took the first bite of crispy bacon from between Dylan's fingers, the heat in his blue eyes was all the reason I needed.

As Nick prepared the coffee, a soft chuckle rolled from his tongue. "I still can't get Rachel's shocked expression out of my head."

"What was she shocked about, Master?" I asked before taking a sip of coffee from the mug he lowered to my lips.

"She couldn't figure out why there was a pile of rice on the kitchen floor when she came in this morning," Nick replied.

I felt my face warm. "What did you tell her, Master?"

"I told her what we did to you last night."

"You did what?" I gasped. Mortification filled me. I'd have to face the woman at some point. God, how embarrassing and awkward the introduction would be now.

"Relax, kitten. She knows of our…proclivities. She's just never been exposed to them until now."

"So, you've never brought a sub home from the club before, Sirs?"

"Never," Dylan emphasized with a note of finality.

"But what about all the toys in there?" I asked, nodding toward the armoire.

"We've been saving them for you." Nick cupped my cheek. "You're the first…and our last if we have anything to say about it."

My heart swelled. "I'm honored, Master."

"So are we," Nick said with a dazzling smile that always sent my blood pumping.

After breakfast, they carried up the suitcases from the truck. As I unpacked my bags, Nick and Dylan hauled in clothes and toiletries from their respective rooms, claiming ownership of the suite as a triad. More than once, tears filled my eyes at the fairy tale unfolding before me.

Nick eased in behind me and kissed my neck. "It is magical, isn't it?"

"How can you *always* read me like a book, Master?" I laughed. Turning in his arms, I pressed a soft kiss to his lips. "Thank you. Thank you for all this and everything you've both given me."

"I'm just lucky that way. And you're welcome, precious."

"No. *Thank you* for being brave enough to give us your power." Dylan stepped in front of me and brushed a kiss over my lips. "We've been searching for you for a long time."

"A very long time," Nick emphasized. "Now, let's go buy you something sexy to wear tonight."

"Where are we going?" I asked, giddy with excitement.

"Club Genesis," Dylan reminded, nipping the lobe of my ear.

"I know *that*, Master. I meant, where are we going shopping?"

"We'll stop at Gurnee Mills, then hit a few shops along the Magnificent Mile. But first, we're going to take you to a couple special boutiques. Ones that cater specifically in club wear." Dylan winked.

"Permission to get ready?" I asked with a gleeful grin.

"Go, little one. Make it quick," Nick laughed at my over-enthusiastic mien. "Just tell me you're not one of those women who take a day and a half to get ready to go somewhere."

I laughed. "No, Master. I'll be ready in thirty minutes, tops."

Dylan issued an exaggerated groan. "She only takes a half a day, bro."

"Very funny, Sir." I rolled my eyes as I rushed to the bathroom.

After my anticipated prickly introduction to both Rachel and Pablo, we set out on our shopping quest. Our first stop was a corset shop. I was fitted and cinched, squeezed and bunched, and left wondering how they expected me to breathe or even sit in the rigid garment.

After several adjustments, I was able to at least draw in a deep breath. Nick explained how I would grow accustomed to the garment over time. He promised that neither he nor Dylan would cinch it too tight in the beginning. Reason being, Dylan explained, was they didn't want me passing out during my first visit to the club.

I modeled an emerald brocade corset with a hand-beaded neckline. The approval straining beneath their jeans made me feel sexy, provocative, and empowered.

I'd never known there were shops that only sold fetish wear and kinky toys. I'd ordered my vibe off the internet because I'd been too chicken to shop the adult chain stores in Kansas City. With wide-eyed wonder, I strolled the store, checking out all the toys and sexy clothing. By the time we left, I had more outfits than I could wear in a lifetime, and Dylan and Nick had more toys to add to their collection.

Hours later, after they insisted on buying me a whole new wardrobe of vanilla clothing, we drove to the Italian restaurant they had talked about at the barn.

Maurizio's was situated between two large brick buildings in an older part of Chicago. As we walked through the front door, I prepared myself for judgmental stares and insults. Instead, we were met with smiles and waves from several of the diners sitting at tables and booths. Suddenly, I remembered what else Nick had said about it being a *wonderful, Italian place that welcomes not only our kink, but also the kinks of others*. The anxiety that had been pinging through me vanished.

"Hey, Nick, Dylan. Where the hell have you two been?" asked the sandy haired man behind the bar.

"Hey, Scotty." Dylan waved with a broad smile. "We just got back from our annual hunting trip."

"Glad to know you missed us," Nick laughed as he wrapped his arm around my waist and led me to the bar.

"And who do we have here?" Scotty asked, a playful smile spread over his lips.

"Savannah, this is Scotty. Scotty this is *our* Savannah," Dylan introduced, his chest expanding.

"So, you finally found her, huh?" Scotty winked.

"Indeed, we did." Nick preened.

"Took you two jokers long enough," the bartender laughed before turning his full attention to me. "Savannah, it's a pleasure to meet you. And may I be the first to say that these two fuck-nuts don't deserve a woman as gorgeous as you."

"Bite me," Dylan growled as I bit back a giggle.

"Don't listen to him, little one. He's just jealous that we found you first," Nick added with an arrogant smirk.

"Busted." Scotty laughed. "Take a seat wherever you'd like. Carla will be out in a sec to take your order and hey...congratulations."

"Thanks, man." Nick beamed.

"Thanks, bro." Dylan nodded.

I simply smiled as I cast a wistful glance at my two gorgeous Masters.

After we'd squeezed together in one side of a booth, a short, dark-haired waitress with a bright smile took our orders. And after Dylan teased her about her new boyfriend, she laughed and scurried away.

"So, you two come here a lot, don't you?"

"Who are you talking to, girl?" Dylan asked arching his brows.

"Oh, I mean, Sirs." I glanced nervously to the couple seated near our booth and lowered my head. "Sirs."

"What was that, kitten? We didn't hear you."

"I said, Sirs," I whispered. My gaze was glued on the older, sophisticated-looking woman and her handsome son. Silently praying she wouldn't choke on her manicotti. I was confused when the woman simply arched a brow before a soft smile spread upon her lips.

"If you'd like, we can arrange it for you to stand on the table and shout out the proper way to address us," Nick threatened.

I flashed him a look of fear. "No, Sir. I'd rather not do that."

"Then speak up and address us the proper way you were trained."

"I'm sorry, Masters, I'm not used to…exposing my submission like this."

"The only people here are those in the lifestyle, Savannah. It's the reason we brought you here, so you wouldn't be judged or insulted."

"You mean, all these people are in the lifestyle?"

Before either of them could answer my question, an older man with a shiny bald spot came through the door. A bubbly, petite blonde clutched his elbow, laughing as if her father had told some hilarious joke.

"George!" Nick called with a wave of his hand.

George and Leagh? I blinked. Neither of them looked anything like I'd imagined. I stared at the couple and tried to envision them together…as in *together*. Though I knew George was light-years older than Leagh, it was still hard to wrap my head around them as a Dom/sub couple.

"Nick," George answered. As a wide smile spread over his wrinkled face, they approached our table. "Glad to see you made it back in one piece."

The old man appraised me for a brief second, then turned his attention back on Dylan and Nick. Leagh's focus remained fixed on me. Her eyes flickered as a knowing smile spread across her petite mouth.

"May I, Master?" the young blonde asked in a low whisper.

"After Dylan and Nick have made introductions, you may ask their permission, precious."

The feisty girl rolled her eyes and bobbed her head from side to side as if silently screaming, *get on with it already.*

A laugh accidentally slid off my lips.

"She doesn't need any help getting into trouble, kitten," Dylan warned.

"Aww, I'm not that bad," Leagh protested with a disingenuous pout.

"No, you're worse," George growled, tugging a red ball gag from his pocket and dangling it in Leagh's face.

Though I knew we were among like-minded people, I skipped a

nervous look around the room. The prim woman seated next to us eyed the swaying ball gag, then placed her fork on her plate and dryly announced, "A red ass is what she needs."

"Oh, come on, Mistress Ivory. I'm behaving," Leagh protested with an impish grin.

Mistress? Wow, Dylan wasn't lying; the whole place was crawling with Doms and subs.

"For now, girl, and I say that without much faith in the minutes to come," the Mistress smirked.

I studied the young man sitting beside her. Even as Ivory spoke, his focus remained fixed on the plate of food in front of him.

Definitely her sub.

But the longer I watched the young man, the more I worried I wasn't showing the proper respect to my Masters or to George and Ivory as well. Even if I was a newbie, I didn't want to look like one. And I certainly didn't want my actions reflecting badly on Dylan or Nick.

Terrified I might be embarrassing my Masters, uncertainty crawled through me like a colony of ants. Tensing, I cast my eyes to the table.

Dylan brushed the hair from my shoulder and leaned in close to my ear. "Relax. You're doing fine, love. We only require strict protocol inside the club. Lift your chin and stop hiding from our friends, kitten."

His warm breath and reassuring words sent waves of relief sailing through me. And as he clasped my hand in his beneath the table—a much needed anchor as well as a boost of confidence—my worries vanished.

I raised my head and smiled as Nick introduced me to George, Leagh, and Mistress Ivory, then cast an inquisitive glance at the young man still staring at his plate. I didn't understand why Nick hadn't introduced him as well.

"Ignore him," Mistress Ivory said with a wave of her hand. "My boy, Dark Desire, won't be joining in on any conversations until he learns to watch his sassy mouth."

The gaze she cast on him was so cold and disapproving, I felt sorry for the young man. But as Ivory turned her attention our way again, her boy peeked at me beneath his dark lashes and smiled.

Making sure no one was looking, I smiled back. Though I'd just met or semi-met Dark Desire and Leagh, I felt a bizarre bond with the two. As if we were all a part of the same team or something. I desperately wanted to pull them aside and ask if what I felt was normal, but I knew this wasn't the time or the place.

"Hey, we never did get that snowstorm you were talking about."

"Consider yourself lucky." Nick shook his head. "It was a bitch."

"Masterrrr," Leagh whined, hopping like an impatient bunny.

"Dammit, girl, you're going to be the death of me," George grumbled. "You may ask."

Leagh squealed, then lifted onto her toes and planted a wet kiss on his cheek.

"Thank you, Master." She cleared her throat, loudly, then clasped her hands behind her back with an impish grin before casting a hopeful glance at Dylan and Nick.

I wanted to giggle at her well-practiced and transparent manipulation.

"Sirs? May I please have permission to speak to your beautiful sub?"

"Now that didn't hurt, did it?" Dylan teased.

Leagh clutched her hand around her neck. "Like broken glass lodged in my throat, Sir."

"It's a wonder you didn't choke." Nick smirked. "And yes, girl, you have our permission to speak to Savannah."

"Oh goodie! Thank you, Sirs." Without warning, she leaned across the table and tossed her arms around me in an awkward hug. As soon as she touched me, I felt a warm, sincere friendliness bubbling inside her.

"It's so nice to meet you, and I'm thrilled Sir Dylan and Sir Nick have finally found a girl to share." Her excitement made me grin. "But I gotta tell ya, there are gonna be submissive hearts breaking all over Genesis now. These two hunks have been making our sub sisters drool for years. They're going to be green. *Green*, I tell ya."

"Leagh," George interrupted. "That's enough, my little hellcat."

"Well, thank you, Leagh...I think," I snickered.

"Oh, yeah, it's a good thing they found you. I can already tell you'll be able to handle them. Trust me!" She winked.

"We'll leave you in peace to enjoy your lunch now," George announced with a weary sigh. "Glad you're home safe and sound. Savannah, it's been a pleasure meeting you, girl."

"Likewise, Sir." I smiled.

Before turning away, George leaned down and, under his breath, said to my Masters, "Keep her."

"We plan to." Nick beamed as George and Leagh made their way to a table in the center of the restaurant.

"Just for the record, I totally agree with George." Mistress Ivory nodded with a cheeky grin. "Just sayin'."

Nick chuckled, then announced with a proud smile, "She'll be accompanying us to the club tonight."

"Oh, good. I look forward to watching you two work her." Ivory grinned.

Suddenly, the bottom fell out of my stomach. *Work her? What the hell did that mean?* I snapped my head and looked at Dylan in confusion.

"She means she's going to enjoy watching us scene with you, kitten."

"You mean, people are going to watch us, Sir?"

"Of course, little one," Nick replied as he turned in the booth, shielding me from the other patrons. "Is there a problem with that?"

"I-I...I thought we would be doing things in your private room, Sir."

"Oh, we will, after." Dylan grinned.

As I began worrying about what they intended to do to me in the crowded dungeon, the waitress placed our drinks and three heaping bowls of salad on the table. My stomach rolled when the scent of Italian dressing wafted up my nose.

Trust them, Sanna. You've got to let go and trust them. They love you.

I hesitated, then picked up my fork. "You okay, little one?" Nick asked.

"Yes, I'm just scared," I bravely confessed.

"Do you trust us?" he asked, dark eyes drilling into me.

"Yes," I answered without an ounce of reservation.

"Then you don't need to be scared. We'll protect you, Savannah. Even as we test your limits, we will always protect you."

As he cupped my chin and softly kissed my lips, a blanket of peace washed over me.

"I fucking love you," he murmured against my mouth.

I nside the lobby of Club Genesis, voices and laughter filled the air as we stood in line to be checked in. Dylan and Nick beamed with pride as they introduced me to everyone around us. Though I felt naked in only my corset and short, ruffled skirt, I smiled and greeted each person, inwardly praying I didn't have to remember all their names.

Muffled sounds of paddles and whips filled the air, growing louder as members passed through a thick curtain near the front of the line. I was anxious to see what lay beyond in the next room.

Antsy and self-conscious about the amount of cleavage and skin I was exposing, I couldn't stop tugging at my trench coat around me.

"You look stunning, little one. Stop fidgeting," Nick growled in my ear.

"I'm trying, Master," I whispered, nibbling my bottom lip.

"Stop stressing. Think of everyone around us as a big extended family." Dylan smiled.

"Seriously, Master. I doubt my Aunt Emily, the crazy cat lady of Tulsa, is into this stuff."

"I thought you only had Mellie?" Dylan asked in confusion.

"We don't talk to Aunt Emily for a reason," I chuckled. "She's crazy. I mean, full-on bonkers. Like, little white coat with funny sleeves crazy. My own dad wouldn't even talk to her, and she was his *only* sister."

"So, does mental illness run in your family, kitten?" Dylan sobered.

"No!" I hissed in a hushed whisper.

When he and Nick started to laugh, I rolled my eyes and grinned.

"I got you to relax just a bit, didn't I?" Dylan winked with an ornery grin.

I sent him a grateful smile, then kissed his cheek. "Yes, Master. Thank you."

Looking around at the growing group of lifestylers, I found solace in knowing there were so many others like me in the world. The submissives were welcoming and eased my angst—at least, until I spied the big, burly biker-looking dude dressed in leather standing at the podium near the big curtain. Tattoos covered his beefy arms, and his expression was tight and stern. Beside him was a beautiful woman with thick red hair and enchanting green eyes. She smiled and talked to the members as they reached the podium. On the other side of the imposing man stood a young man with long, blond hair. His infectious giggles and overt gestures made me smile.

"Who are they?" I whispered to Nick.

"That's Daddy Drake, his submissive and life partner, Trevor. The woman is who we've been anxious for you to meet. That's Emerald."

"Are they a threesome, too?"

"No," Nick shook his head. "Emerald isn't Drake's sub, she's simply under his protection. She doesn't have a Master yet, so she goes to Drake if she has a problem or needs help with her submission."

"I bet nobody messes with her. That guy is massive and scary looking," I whispered under my breath.

"Drake's a good guy, and a good friend. His single tail skills are impeccable," Nick praised.

"When he and Trevor scene, it's a sight to behold," Dylan added.

I frowned. Was Dylan talking about us watching them have sex? Did *everyone* in the club have public sex? Surely, they didn't expect *me* to have sex with them while everyone watched, did they? I had no idea what to expect. My mind raced like a lab rat in a maze.

As I continued to stare at the threesome behind the podium, Emerald looked my way. She glanced at Dylan and Nick before a broad smile spread over her full, red lips. I watched as she leaned over and whispered into Drake's ear. He raised his eyes and leveled me with a stare. I felt myself shrink like a violet in the desert. Swallowing tightly, I cast my eyes toward my black stilettos.

"What's wrong, pet?" Nick mumbled in my ear.

"I don't know if I can do this," I confessed.

"We're not throwing you to the wolves, little one. We will be right by your side every step of the way," Nick whispered before peppering kisses along my jaw and down my neck.

Centering me with his affection, I held tight to my courage as they led me to the podium.

Drake's intimidating scowl morphed into a happy grin as he welcomed Nick and Dylan. Though the man didn't frighten me as much as he had, that didn't stop me from trembling when he shook my hand.

Trevor and Emerald each welcomed me with excited grins and warm hugs.

"Emerald, with Drake's permission, of course, we'd be grateful if you could help Savannah with the submissive side of life."

As she pinned Drake with a pleading stare, I held my breath.

"You may." The big man nodded.

"I'd be honored, Sir Nick," she respectfully replied, then turned and flashed me a smile that could have lit up all of Las Vegas.

In the ten seconds since we'd met, I knew, without a shadow of a doubt, I wanted to learn everything Emerald could teach me.

"We have sub meetings every Saturday morning from nine until noon, here at the club," she began. "Don't be shy. Come and join us. We talk about a lot of different topics. Some of the information will help you now, and some will help you further down the road. Plus, Trevor and I always compete to see who makes the most sinful munchies."

"She doesn't kick my ass often, but she *does* make the best brownies on earth," Trevor laughed then blew a kiss to Emerald.

"Thank you. I'd really like that...if I have permission," I said, glancing between my Masters.

"We wouldn't have asked for Emerald's help otherwise." Dylan smiled.

After signing a long waiver of legal mumbo-jumbo, Dylan slid my coat off and tossed it over his arm. And Nick pulled back the heavy, red curtain.

I held my breath.

Chapter Thirteen

My heart lodged in my throat as the curtain fluttered closed behind us. I tried to take in every sight, sound, and sensation, but I couldn't. I was in BDSM overload. Having read about dungeons, it was plain to see that their friend—Michael, Mika, Mitchell; hell, I couldn't remember his name—had spared no expense. The club was gorgeous, and massive. Numerous stations lined the walls, each occupied with subs enjoying a plethora of sensations by their Masters and Mistresses.

Dozens of tables filled the center of the room, each adorned in ambient candlelight, where members sat, watching and talking in low voices while sipping drinks. The sweet scent of leather, combined with the musky tinges of sex, hung heavy in the air.

Dylan stowed my coat, then he and Nick ushered me toward a gleaming mahogany bar, waving and smiling to members along the way. A tiny blonde woman with twinkling blue eyes and enormous boobs moved efficiently behind the long counter, filling plastic cups with ice, sodas, and juices.

Nick leaned in and whispered against my ear. "That's Sammie. She's our resident Domme and bar Mistress extraordinaire. Come on, let's get a drink."

I nodded, still trying to absorb the fact that I was actually inside a BDSM club. As we sat down on the tall barstools, I continued trying to take everything in.

"There you two are," Sammie greeted with a saucy and sassy smile. "I thought you'd gone off and forgotten us. Oh, and who do we have here?"

Her blue eyes danced over my face before admiring my corset with an approving smile.

"Sammie, this is our girl, Savannah," Nick gloated, his smile growing wider.

"It's a pleasure to meet you, Savannah." She extended a petite hand. Her long nails were painted a blood red color.

"A pleasure to meet you as well, Ma'am." I smiled with a soft shake of her tiny hand.

"Oh, such good manners, too," Sammie winked. "You two better hang on to this one."

"We fully intend to," Dylan assured with a beaming smile.

"Good to hear. What can I get you all to drink?" she asked with a wink.

Nick ordered sodas for us, then spun me around on my stool until I faced the stations.

"Watch, little one," he instructed as he rested his wide hand on my bare knee.

Dylan draped his arm around my shoulder. Sheltered in their protective, possessive touch, I felt brave, safe, and totally at peace.

As I sipped my drink, I focused on the different sizes and ages of the subs. Most were naked, but didn't seem bothered by it at all. I couldn't understand how they weren't at least a little embarrassed. If they were, they certainly didn't show it.

A big, beautiful woman and her Master walked to one of the stations with a tall, wooden frame. As her Master began assembling his toys, she undressed, then stood waiting for his instruction. Her ankles were nearly the size of my thighs, and her cellulite-pitted flesh and rolls sagged and swayed. While some might find her naked form repugnant, I was awed by her grace, stunned by her self-assurance, and envious of her bravery. It shamed me to realize I lacked the confidence she readily displayed.

The crack of a whip drew my attention to the other side of the dungeon. I blinked in surprise when I recognized Mistress Ivory and her sub, Dark Desire. Tethered to a cross, Dark held his head high. Pride radiated in his posture. Mesmerized, I watched Ivory coil the long leather whip into the air before landing it with a deafening *whack* against his narrow ass cheeks. As a bright red stripe bloomed and his loud cry of anguish pierced the air, goosebumps skipped over my arms.

"It's okay, kitten. Dark enjoys pain," Dylan assured.

"I don't think I'd ever enjoy something that brutal, Master." I cringed.

"There she goes," Nick murmured. A hint of admiration resonated in his tone.

I turned to see what he was talking about. The Master—of the large woman cuffed to the frame—whispered in her ear as he skimmed his hand over her bare flesh. Gripping a long, leather flogger in his other fist, the man stepped back and began brushing the leather falls over her back and butt cheeks. A wistful smile curled on her lips. In a matter of seconds, her eyes turned glassy as her face glowed in ethereal serenity. Beauty transcended her physical form; lost in her submission, she was the most breathtaking woman I'd ever seen.

"Oh, wow," I marveled.

"Remember when I told you submission comes in all ages, little one?" Nick paused as I nodded. "Well, it also comes in all shapes and sizes. I wanted you to watch so you would understand. It's not the body that makes the submissive, but what's inside the heart. That's where the true beauty lies."

Nick's words contained an almost magical tone. The woman had not only gifted her submission to her Master, but to everyone in the club watching them. As Nick stroked my cheek, we watched the woman as she sailed away to subspace. Her expressions kept me enthralled. Every clip of the flogger seemed to send her deeper into that silent white space I'd experienced at the barn. The same sublime and surreal clouds I longed to be floating on again.

"I'd love to be as…free as she is, Master."

JENNA JACOB

"Do you feel brave, kitten?" Dylan asked with a sly smile.

"How brave, Master?" I gulped, realizing I'd just opened a dangerous door.

"Would you like to soar again?"

"If I can keep my clothes on, yes, Master," I bargained.

"What makes you think you get to make the rules, little one?" Nick's brow arched; his eyes flashed in warning. "You'll have to take off your skirt."

"Technically, you'll still be covered...you're wearing that sexy, black thong," Dylan growled and snapped his teeth like a hungry wolf.

"I don't know if I can get up in front of all these people," I confessed in a thin voice.

"We'll be right there with you. You don't have to look at any of them. You can close your eyes and pretend we're alone. Can you do that for us?"

Dylan's expectant look rocked me to the core. The need to please and reflect their Dominance in a positive light gnawed my system. I knew their job was to push my limits. If I only yielded to the things I wanted or liked, I was only submitting to myself...not them.

Swallowing my fear, I nodded. "I would love to, Master."

As their eyes ignited in pride and smiles of delight stretched their lips, my courage spiked, and I started to ease off the barstool.

"Hold on a minute, little one," Nick chuckled. "Your eagerness pleases us immensely, but we need to discuss the scene. But first..."

Cupping my nape, he held me in place before his lips crashed over mine. I swallowed his growl and basked in his raw, commanding kiss. Long seconds later, he lifted from my mouth and held me with a stern, Dominant expression that sent heat rolling up my body.

"You'll remove your skirt before we cuff you to a St. Andrews cross, like the one Ivory has Dark tethered to. The members of the club will only be able to see the back of you while we flog and caress you. Your safeword is red, and we expect you to use it if you need to. Are you comfortable and accept the things I've described?" Nick asked quietly, but firmly.

"Yes, Sir."

The pride in his dark eyes set my heart soaring.

"I'll be right back," Nick announced as he stood and strode toward a wide archway near the bar.

"Where is he going?"

"Our private room to get the flogger." Dylan winked.

"Can we play in there, instead?"

"Later. When our cocks get so hard we can't stand the pain, we'll take you to our room and sink balls deep inside your tight, hot body."

As Dylan pressed a slow, sensual kiss to my lips, sizzling images of him and Nick thrusting their hard shafts in my pussy and ass had me humming with desire.

"It'd be nice to start there, first." I smirked when he eased back.

"We want you to fly first, our greedy little slut."

Dylan plucked the drink from my hand, then helped me off the barstool before nodding across the dungeon. "Come. Nick's waiting for us at the station over there."

My heart thundered in my chest, and my knees trembled. I had no clue where my courage had run off to. As Dylan wrapped a steadying arm around my waist, Nick—standing at the cross, hands behind his back in a familiar and powerful, Dominant stance with his long, black hair spilling over his wide shoulder—sent me a reassuring smile, and my courage returned.

His stunning command sent a shiver skipping through me. As Dylan guided me toward the cross, I peered up at him. Head held high, possessive pride etched his face. The powerful Dominance radiating off them was beautifully blinding.

My Masters.

My guides.

I squared my shoulders and raised my head. They'd chosen me to be their submissive. It was time for me to prove they'd made the right choice.

As we reached the station, Nick pulled me against his chest. As his warm breath spilled over the shell of my ear, he softly whispered, "Sweet, brave and beautiful slut, you please us. Words can't express how much we love and treasure you, little one."

A lump of emotion gathered in the back of my throat.

"Take off your skirt," he murmured, nipping the lobe of my ear.

Still soaring from his praise, my fingers trembled as I peeled the black ruffled skirt off my hips. Dylan stood behind me, protectively shielding my bare ass from members' eyes.

"This will help you soar faster for us." Nick smirked, dangling a black satin blindfold from his fingers.

"Thank you, Master," I said on a grateful exhale.

"Remember, the whole time, we'll be right here with you." I shivered as Dylan's breath wafted over my nick. What's your safeword, kitten?"

"Red, Master."

"Good girl," he murmured as Nick placed the blindfold over my eyes.

"Relax, little one. Let us set you free."

Together, they secured downy-lined cuffs to my wrists and ankles. I could feel the members watching us...hear them whisper Dylan and Nick's names. Anxiety bloomed, but as a broad, heated hand pressed against my lower back—guiding my breasts and stomach to the cool wood—it melted away.

"We're going to warm you up, now," Nick announced. "Fly, little one. We'll be right here to catch you and ease you back to earth."

As soon as he stepped back, I mourned the loss of his body heat, and the safety and reassurance of his words.

As they caressed, squeezed, and spanked my ass cheeks, their whispered praise floated over me like snowflakes. But when the soft, heavy flogger brushed over my backside, I yelped in surprise. It didn't hurt. In fact, it strangely soothed me.

"You're doing beautifully," Dylan praised. "Focus on the rhythm... let it carry you away."

Following his instructions, I focused on the leather falls raking and warming my flesh. Short minutes later, I drifted away, surrounded by peace. Time ceased, and all thoughts evaporated.

Between the lulling rhythm of the flogger, their strong hands caressing and soothing the growing burn from my flesh, and their deep, rich voices bathing me in continual praise, I soared among the clouds in warmth and serenity.

From time to time, they meshed their hot, rugged bodies against my back in a silent reminder that I was anchored to the chains of their Dominance.

A tug at my torso pulled me from the clouds, and confusion sullied my brain. When the constricting corset fell from my body, it took several seconds before I realized that, aside from the scrap of lace covering my pussy, I was naked. A wave of panic crested through me. My mind was so saturated in bliss, I forgot all about being bound to the cross, or that no one could see my breasts—still pressed to the wood.

Instinctively, I tried to cover myself with my hands, but couldn't.

Obliterated beneath an onslaught of panic, I thrashed, trying to break free.

"RED!" I screamed, jerking impotently against my shackles.

"Savannah!" Nick's thunderous voice boomed in my ears. "Stop, pet. We're here. It's okay. You're okay."

But I wasn't okay. The icy hands of panic gripped my throat and stole my breath.

"Back away, Nick. You too, Dylan. You guys know the rules."

A new wave of panic slammed through me as a deep-voiced man ordered my Masters to abandon me.

"No!" I cried, struggling with such force the cuffs bit into my skin. "Don't leave me! Please don't leave me, Masters!"

"We're right here, little one," Nick reassured before whispering several curses.

The blindfold was peeled from my eyes. A man I'd never seen before, stepped behind the cross to face me. As he raised his hands and cupped my cheeks, I jerked away.

"Don't touch me," I cried. "I don't know you."

The man immediately dropped his hands. "Okay. Okay, calm down, girl." Understanding was written all over his face, but did nothing to calm the riot inside me.

"Please, don't look at me. I'm...naked," I whimpered as tears spilled down my cheeks.

"I'm not looking anywhere but your beautiful eyes," he replied calmly, holding me with a steady stare. "My name is Tony. I'm a dungeon monitor. I just need to ask you some questions, okay?"

I nodded and mewled, "Where are my Masters?"

"We're right behind you, kitten," Dylan assured. "Try to calm down and talk to Tony. We're not going anywhere."

"Can you hug me? I need to feel you," I whimpered.

"We not allowed to yet, little one," Nick bit out. "Answer his questions, and we'll hug you until hell freezes over."

Your name is Savannah, right?" Tony asked, never breaking eye contact.

"Yes."

"I need you to focus on me. Can you do that?" His voice was so serene, yet I couldn't grasp onto any semblance of tranquility.

"Tony, can you hurry? Please?" Nick's appeal was fraught with anxiety.

"Patience, man. You know I have to assess."

"Fuck," Dylan spat.

"Chill out, you two, or we'll have to go to Mika's office and sort this out," Tony warned, pinning both men with a stern stare.

I didn't like him threatening my Masters.

"What do you want to know?" I sniffed as anger now warred with the embarrassment flooding my system.

"Are you physically or mentally hurt?"

"No," I curtly replied. "Dylan and Nick would never hurt me."

"Then why did you call your safeword?"

"Because I was embarrassed, but now, I'm just...humiliated." I lowered my chin, acutely aware everyone in the club had heard my childish meltdown, and was now watching the ensuing aftermath. "Can you get me out of these cuffs now?"

Tony gave me a sympathetic shake of his head. "In a minute. I realize you hit a hard limit, but I have to make sure you're physically and mentally all right."

"I'm fine. I just freaked out."

"Don't beat yourself up, pet. That's why your Masters gave you a safeword. Some subs won't use theirs. They're afraid of failing their Masters. I know Dylan and Nick, and I know they're proud of you for using it."

"We are," Dylan assured.

"And now that they know you hit a hard limit, they'll help you through it."

As Tony smiled and subtly nodded to my Masters, a soft cotton blanket was draped over my bare shoulders.

"Thank you, Emerald," Nick said before pressing his warm body against my back...surrounding me in his blissful heat while protectively shielding me.

"We'll get you back to our room as soon as we can, okay?"

Peering up into his sad eyes, I started to cry. "I'm so sorry I failed you."

"Oh, Savannah. You didn't fail us." He pressed his lips against my neck. "We're the ones who are sorry, little one."

Dylan moved in beside me, and stroked my cheek while Tony released my wrists from the cuffs.

"We didn't mean to scare you. We would never have turned you around and shared your naked body with anyone here," Dylan assured.

The guilt and anguish written all over their faces tore my heart to shreds. They were blaming themselves for my insecurities.

"It's not your fault, Masters. It's not. I snatched my trust back, and—"

"We need to have a chat, you two," Tony interrupted grimly.

"We know," Nick drawled. Stepping back, he reached into his pocket.

"But they didn't do anything," I protested.

"It's club rules...part of the protocol," Dylan said with a tight smile.

"Emerald, will you please take Savannah to our room? We'll be along in a couple of minutes."

"Of course, Nick, Sir." She nodded and accepted the key, then tucked the blanket around me, covering up my breasts with an understanding smile.

"But I want to stay with you two."

It didn't take a genius to figure out I'd gotten them in trouble.

"This will only take a couple of minutes. Emerald is going to stay with you in our room. We trust her implicitly; you can too. We'll be back to talk to you as soon as we get things straightened out here," Nick calmly and quietly explained.

"It should only take a few minutes," Dylan assured.

"Less than that," Emerald scoffed as she tucked an arm around my waist and guided me toward the archway.

I cast a worried glance over my shoulder. Their grim expressions sliced like a knife.

Cheeks blazing in embarrassment, I dropped my chin and kept my head down as Emerald led me down a long hall lined with doors.

"How much trouble did I get them in?" I murmured.

Emerald stopped and gaped at me. "Oh, Savannah. They're *not* in trouble. And you didn't do anything except what you were *supposed* to. Every person in this club knows and highly respects Sirs Dylan and Nick. They also know you're a newbie. You not only showed everyone in the dungeon you're smart, brave, and have the heart of a good submissive, but also that Dylan and Nick are doing a kick-ass job of teaching you about the power exchange."

"They are? How?"

"Because you called your safeword when you got scared. Sir Tony was telling you the truth. A lot of subs, especially new ones, are afraid to use their safeword. Because they're still holding on to their control…their power. They're not being honest, and that's not good. Eventually, it will mess a sub up in here," she said, tapping her temple.

As guilt began bleeding from my system, I knew why Nick had been so adamant about introducing me to Emerald.

"Thank you. Thank you," I murmured, hugging her tightly. "I really needed to hear that from another sub."

"You're welcome." She grinned before sliding the key into the lock of the door in front of us.

Shoving the door open, she flipped on the light.

Having another sub ushering me inside wasn't at all how I'd envisioned seeing my Masters' private chamber for the first time. But that was all on me. I knew they'd wanted my first experience in the dungeon to be a beautiful and rewarding experience. But I'd fucked that up, royally, and ruined their whole scene. In hindsight, I knew no one had seen anything but my back and butt cheeks.

I felt horrible. I'd screamed my safeword as if they'd stripped me bare so they could put me on display. But they hadn't.

They did what they were supposed to do…push my limits.

I should have trusted them more. The fact I hadn't worried me deeply.

"Here, sister. Put this on." Emerald held out a white silk robe with the word *Genesis* embroidered on the breast pocket.

"I feel like such a fool."

"Don't. You didn't do anything wrong." Emerald frowned, tying the sash of the robe before plopping down on the big bed and patting the mattress. "Come on and sit down. Let's talk."

"I don't know what happened…my corset came off and I freaked out," I sighed, flopping down beside her.

"You hit a limit is what happened. They're not just physical. Everyone has mental triggers too…ugly little buttons that when pushed freak us the hell out."

"But if I'd trusted them more, that dungeon manager guy… Tony—"

"Dungeon *monitor*," she corrected with a smile. "Tony was only doing his job."

"If I didn't get them in trouble, why is he still talking to them?"

"Your Masters are *not* in trouble. They're simply explaining what led up to you calling your safeword."

I might not have gotten them in trouble, but that didn't erase the fear of them rejecting me, or deciding I wasn't capable of submitting to them the way they wanted and needed. I knew Emerald was trying to help talk me off the ledge, but until Dylan and Nick walked through the door and forgave me for messing up our first scene, nothing on the planet was going to ease my angst.

"Trust me, Savannah. Sir Tony and your Masters are simply going through the safety precautions Genesis has in place. Without them, none of us would be able to play in a safe, sane and consensual environment."

"Do you honestly think they're not going to be so disappointed…so mad at me for what happened, they're not going to walk through the door and dump me?"

"Not in a million." Emerald wrapped me in a tight hug and pulled me close. "I've seen the way they look at you. They're head over heels in love with you. In all the years I've known them, I've never seen them so happy. You bring them to life. They're not going to release you. Ever. Especially not over this."

She was so certain how my Masters were going to react, and though I desperately wanted to believe her, my worries remained.

"Okay, listen, if they let you go, I'll have Daddy Drake kick their asses before every other Dom in the place lines up to do it, too. How's that sound?" She grinned.

Emerald blew my mind. I'd just met her, and she was showering me with so much understanding, acceptance, and love, I wasn't sure how I could repay her.

"I already did that," I groaned.

"Did what?"

"Kicked their butts."

"You what?" she gasped. "Oh, honey…spill the tea. I've got to hear this."

"It's a long story. Let's just say it was an all-star example of fight or flight. I keep choosing fight, like I did out there." An exasperated huff rushed from my lips.

"You'll have to tell me about it one of these days, but first, you need to stop beating yourself up. Or I'll be forced to bring Daddy Drake in here to convince you that you did the right thing."

"No thanks, he scares the crap out of me."

"Oh, pfft," she said waving her hand. "He's nothing but a giant teddy bear. He likes to look all bad-ass to intimidate people."

I couldn't help but chuckle at the way she described the leather-clad Dom. It was going to take a long time before I saw any teddy bear-like qualities in that man.

"You're worrying over nothing," she said as Nick and Dylan burst through the door.

My heart leapt to my throat as they both froze and stared at me. Still fearing they'd reject me, I jumped from the bed. As they opened their arms and hugged me tight against their steely chests, sobs of relief and joy seeped from my throat.

"With your permission, Sirs, I'll go now," Emerald murmured.

"Of course, pet, and thank you," Nick said, voice cracking with emotion.

"Anytime, Sir. Savannah is a love. I can't wait to see her again on Saturday," Emerald stated before closing the door behind her.

"Yes, you are a love. *Our* love," Dylan growled as he laid siege to my lips.

"Don't start that yet," Nick chided. "We need to discuss what happened out there.".

I moaned in regret as Dylan released my lips. I didn't want to talk. I wanted to stay right where I was—wrapped in their safe, loving arms.

I dried my eyes as they led me to the bed. After the three of us sat, Nick kissed my temple and cleared his throat.

But before he could speak, I began a speech of my own. "I know you're disappointed and upset with me. I'm sorry I embarrassed you, and myself, by calling my safeword."

"We are not disappointed, upset, or embarrassed, Savannah," Nick thundered, cupping my chin. "We are relieved to know you won't hesitate to use your safeword. That's what it's there for. But…"

There it was…a big fat ugly *but.*

I knew what was coming next.

"But you don't want me as your submissive anymore, right?" I asked in a fearful whisper.

"What?" they asked in unison, slashing me with identical looks of confusion and shock.

"No. But I'm going to put a ball gag in your mouth if you interrupt again," Nick growled.

"Grab a hammer so we can knock the insecurities out of her system, too." Dylan scowled.

I closed my eyes, wishing we'd stayed home instead of coming to the club. Instead of them dissecting my fears, we could have been naked, making love until the sun came up.

"Think long and hard before you answer, Savannah," Dylan continued. "Do you trust us?"

Yes, I did trust them, I just hadn't shown it. I'd been too self-conscience to climb down off the ledge once I'd scaled it.

"Yes, Master. I trust you with my life."

"If you trusted us, you wouldn't have freaked out. You would have known that we'd protect you with our last dying breath." Nick frowned. "We were going to block your body...keep you flush against the cross until the session was done before wrapping you in a blanket, and bringing you here...to this room."

"We know your buttons, kitten. The fact you think we'd purposely push them during your first public scene confirms you truly don't trust us."

As an anvil of regret flattened my heart, I shook my head.

"Tell us what went through your head when you realized we'd removed your corset," Nick instructed.

"I was floating, then suddenly, I was yanked back, but everything was foggy. It took a few seconds before I realized I was naked. I could hear people talking, but I wasn't sure where I was. It was like...have you ever had one of those dreams where you're standing in front of a bunch of people giving a lecture or something and you realize you're totally naked?"

Nick smirked and nodded.

"It was like that, but I knew I wasn't dreaming. What I didn't know, because I couldn't see anything, was if I was facing them, like in that messed up dream, or still facing the cross. Before I could figure that out, I screamed my safeword. It was a knee-jerk reaction, because I was scared. I'm sorry."

"We're sorry, too, kitten. We thought we had the scene under control...had you where we wanted...floating peacefully out in space, but we were wrong. We're sorry."

The remorse etching his face and slathering his words stabbed my soul.

"No. No, it was my faul—"

"Enough," Nick barked. "We all fucked up, we're all sorry, and we're all responsible. Instead of sitting here apologizing, we need to implement safeguards so it doesn't happen again."

"How?" I whispered. "I don't know how to stop a panic attack once it starts."

Nick's expression softened. "To make sure we don't do anything to trigger that panic attack before it starts, little one."

"Exactly." Dylan nodded. "We'll start by explaining everything, and I mean, *everything* we're planning to do to you during the scene."

"At least, in the beginning," Nick interjected. "As time goes on, and your trust in us grows, we'll toss in a few…surprises."

"Let's not get ahead of ourselves, man," Dylan drawled. "If that doesn't work, we'll scene at home, alone, and try again some other time."

"You mean, we won't be coming to club?"

"No. We'll still come; let you observe other subs…while working on your self-confidence outside the club."

I exhaled in relief. "Thank you, Master Dylan. Can I come to the sub meetings on Saturday mornings? I'd like to talk to Emerald more. She really helped me while we were waiting."

"Absolutely." Nick nodded. "We want you attending those meetings regularly. But right now, we need to hold you, Savannah."

They both wrapped their arms around me and lowered me onto the bed, then took turns kissing me senseless. The heat of their bodies and the passion of their mouths and tongues annihilated the tendrils of uncertainty still lingering inside me.

Long minutes later, we came up for air and laid in a tangle of limbs…taking.

"I need to apologize to Sir Tony," I muttered. "I yelled at him."

Dylan chuckled. "You're not the first sub to do that."

"But you didn't curse him, like a few of the others have." Nick grinned.

"Why do they yell and curse him? He seems like a kind and compassionate person."

"He is, and a very respected sadist."

"Sadist. You mean like Mistress Ivory?"

"She goes by Lady Ivory here, but you're addressing her correctly as Mistress, kitten." Dylan reaffirmed. "But no, Ivory isn't even in the same ballpark as Tony when it comes to doling out pain."

"Hence why some subs yell and curse him." Nick chuckled.

"You're making Sir Tony sound scarier than Daddy Drake."

JENNA JACOB

"You don't need to be afraid of either of them, little one," Nick assured. "Tony has a stable of pain sluts who thoroughly enjoy the pain he provides."

"Speaking of being thoroughly enjoyed," Dylan grinned. "You up for some private play time, kitten?"

A broad smile spread across my lips. "With my two amazing Masters? Always."

Nick rolled off the bed and extended his hand. "Will you fly for us again?"

"Oh, yes, Master," I purred, sliding my fingers into his palm.

As Nick helped me off the mattress, Dylan bolted up and eased in behind me before peeling the robe off me. Pressing soft kisses over my shoulders and down my spine, he sent ripples and goosebumps of anticipation skating through my system.

With a devilish grin, Nick pulled a wooden suspension frame out from against the wall before leveling me with a serious stare. "We're alone, but you will use your safeword again, if needed. Understood?"

"Of course, Master. But I won't need it now."

"Don't be too sure about that," Dylan growled as he tweaked my nipple.

I hissed, then whimpered, as shards of fire rippled through my breast and shot to my core.

"Arms up, kitten. I've wanted to do this since I wrapped the first strand of rope around you at the barn." Fire blazed in his blue eyes as he gathered several bundles.

"Shibari?" I wistfully asked.

"Yes. Shibari, and a little torment." He smirked as Nick positioned me under the frame.

Chills skittered through me. As Dylan wrapped the first strand of rope around my wrists, I closed my eyes.

Nick cupped my cheeks in his warm hands and skimmed his lips over mine before claiming me in a raw, passionate kiss.

Sailing higher with each scrape of his tongue while he tugged and pinched my nipple, I floated away as rope and knots bound my arms and torso. When Dylan cinched the soft cotton between my legs,

214

purposely dragging it back and forth over my clit, I cried out and rocked my hips, while he tied a teasing knot at my throbbing bud.

"You can grind your hot little pussy against that all you want," Nick taunted. "Just remember, you don't have permission."

"Yes, Master," I breathlessly moaned without stopping.

A squeal of surprise tore from my throat as I was hoisted into the air. Suspended beneath the frame, and poised like a cupid, I spun in a slow circle. As Dylan and Nick stood back, admiring their work, lust shimmered in their eyes, and wolfish smiles curled their lips.

"How does it feel to be floating off the ground?" Dylan asked as he and Nick started peeling off their clothes.

"Incredible, Master," I sighed. "I feel like I'm flying."

Though the ropes were tight, they were placed in such a way that my weight was evenly distributed. There was no pain, no pinching, just sublime compression holding me off the ground. Though I wanted to close my eyes and float away in the peace and serenity sluicing through me, it wasn't incentive enough for me to miss the opportunity of watching my Masters strip.

As they stood before me, naked, hard, and ready, a contented sigh slid from my lips.

Cupping my bound limbs, they spun me back and forth, taking turns guiding their weeping cocks in and out of my mouth. Greedily sucking their thick cocks, I breathed in their potent musk, savoring their individual flavors bursting over my tongue while they toyed and teased the knot on my clit.

Giving into the demand rising inside me, I sailed toward the stars. As I sucked and swirled my tongue over Nick's driving shaft, Dylan clutched my thighs and spread my legs before wedging his head between them. Tugging the knot with his teeth, he slid his tongue under the rope and stabbed my melting core.

As my cry of delight vibrated over Nick's length, he cinched a fist in my hair and bit out a curse before quickly shuttling his cock in and out of my stretched lips. A low growl rumbled from deep in his chest as he thrust to the back of my throat and stilled. Letting out a beastly roar, his slick, hot seed showered my throat and spilled over my tongue. I gulped and swallowed while Dylan's tongue, teeth, and fingers destroyed my quivering pussy.

While the familiar numbness climbed through my tethered limbs, I milked Nick dry with keening cries of need. He abruptly pulled from my mouth before cradling my face in his hands.

"Open your eyes, little one, so I can watch you shatter." His voice was hoarse and ragged.

As I forced my impossibly heavy lids open, he was kneeling in front of me, wearing an expression so overflowing with love, I wanted to cry.

"Now, our beautiful girl. Come for us... Now."

Dylan suckled my clit and strummed my G-spot, masterfully sending me over the edge. And as lightning splintered my veins and thunder rolled through me, Nick claimed my mouth and swallowed my screams.

As Dylan's wicked mouth lifted from my spasming core, Nick tore from my mouth, and turned my quaking body my other Master's way. Dylan gripped my hair, then speared his swollen crest past my lips. Pummeling the back of my throat in a manic rhythm, his feral cry splintered the air as I guzzled the thick ropes exploding from his cock.

Dylan gripped the frame, panting, as I sucked him dry while aftershocks sizzled through me. Nick released the ropes with great care, then eased me down, back on my feet. Flying and sated, I sagged against my bindings. Dylan's hot body supported mine as Nick extricated me from the ropes. They carried me back to the bed and snuggled close.

Surrounded in their potent aftercare, I closed my eyes, marveling at the absolute joy and completeness they brought to my life.

After several long hours nestled in their arms, we finally rolled out of bed and got dressed. With Nick on one side and Dylan on the other, we strolled back into the dungeon. I was so happy and relaxed, I didn't even care what the members might think about my earlier freak out. As we headed toward the big, red curtain, we passed Emerald, sitting at a table with a group of people. She smiled and flashed me a knowing wink. I was thrilled, honored even, that she'd been the one to help me through my first submissive crisis. She definitely had her submissive shit together. And though it was completely absurd, I felt a bond with her, one I hoped would grow stronger. What I didn't understand was why such a beautiful, smart, and impressive sub didn't have Master.

When we arrived back at the house, I sat at the kitchen table while my gifted Master Chef Masters prepared a breakfast of pure nirvana. I scarfed down everything on my plate as we laughed and swapped stories of our lives before destiny intervened on that cold, deserted Iowa road.

~

A s sunlight peeked through the side of the curtain, I woke and snuggled deeper against my Masters. I wanted to pinch myself to make sure I wasn't dreaming as I gazed at their gorgeous, sleeping expressions. Nick's hair lay tangled in a blue-black web across his pillow. Unable to resist, I softly threaded my fingers through his soft, silky mane and sighed in contentment.

"Morning, little one," he whispered with a crooked smile.

"I thought you were asleep," I whispered.

"Nope. We've both been awake for about an hour," Dylan grinned before growling like a lion and pouncing on top of me, pinning me beneath him.

"Wait. Wait. I need to go pee, Master," I giggled as he nibbled my neck.

"So go," Nick laughed.

"Not that again, Sir," I groaned.

"Relax. We're not into water works," Dylan assured as he rolled off me. "Go."

"Thank gawd," I said, tossing off the covers before racing to the bathroom.

Taking time to brush my teeth, I was rinsing my mouth when they swaggered through the door.

"When you're done, grab a shower and get dressed. We're meeting a friend for breakfast," Nick announced, starting the water for me.

"Who, Sir?"

"It's a surprise," he replied cryptically.

A short time later, we grabbed our coats and began walking along the shoreline of Lake Michigan. We hadn't gone far before Dylan steered me toward a big, beautiful mansion. As we climbed the stairs to a massive wooden deck, a handsome, dark-skinned bald man opened a set of etched French doors and flashed a blinding smile. After embracing Dylan and Nick in a bro-hug, he stared at me with the most gorgeous amber eyes I'd ever seen in my life.

"You're just as beautiful up close as you were from far away last night."

My cheeks warmed as I softly smiled.

I didn't remember seeing him at the club, but then again, I was so nervous I didn't make eye contact with a lot of the members.

"Savannah, this is Mika. He's a good friend of ours, who also happens to own Genesis," Nick announced with a broad smile.

"Oh." I blinked. "It's an honor to meet you, Sir. Genesis is…it's amazing."

"Thank you. It's a pleasure to meet you, as well. But for the record, you've never met me, and you don't know who I am." Still flashing a dazzling smile, Mika arched a brow in warning.

"I beg your pardon?"

"Remember our discussions about anonymity?" Dylan asked.

I nodded, wondering what that had to do with the owner of Genesis.

"Mika is a phantom," Nick interjected with a chuckle. "He guards his anonymity at all costs, both in and out of the club. Only a chosen few of us know his true identity. He wishes to keep it that way. So, we're trusting you to honor his wishes. Understood?"

"Of course, I understand now, Sirs. I won't say a word to anyone. I promise."

"Thank you." Mika winked. "This needs to remain our little secret."

"It will," I assured anxious to get home and start peppering my Masters with the zillion questions now fluttering through my brain.

As Mika led us inside, I was once again surprised how seemingly ordinary people lived in such opulent surroundings. The mansion was gorgeous and screamed Dominance with its rich masculine décor. I kept expecting a harem of submissives to descend the wide staircase and fall at his feet. But none appeared, and I started wondering if he lived in the massive house alone.

When we reached the dining room, a buffet table laden with steaming foods waited for us. The huge, mahogany table—complete with candelabra, and four place setting of fine bone China, crystal stemware, and polished silverware—looked like something out of a museum. Wondering if I'd ever grow accustomed to such grandiose surroundings, I filled a plate and sat between Dylan and Nick.

It didn't take long before I found myself laughing at the three Doms playful banter. In truth, Mika was as down to earth as my Masters, which did wonders to ease my angst. Well, until they started discussing my freak-out in the dungeon last night.

"Have you ever tried to analyze why nudity is a hard limit for you, Savannah?" Mika asked without an ounce of judgement.

"No, Sir. As far as I know, there's no logical reason for it. I mean, I was never de-pants or forced to streak through the halls at school."

The three of them chuckled as Mika nodded. "Sometimes, there aren't any *reasons* for triggers. They just are. Don't let it bother you, Savannah. Everyone has them."

It was as if Mika had climbed inside me last night and knew how horrible I'd felt.

"We'll soon find out if it's a trigger worth disarming." Nick pursed his lips.

"*Worth* disarming? What does that mean?" I asked.

"It means working through the limit or leaving it alone if it doesn't enhance your submission."

"At least, for now," Dylan added. "As you grow and learn, your limits will change. What's a hard limit now might be a soft limit in the future."

"How do you determine if it's worth disarming or not? Is there some kind of test?"

"Funny you should ask." Nick smirked.

The knowing and unnerving glance the three men shared made me suddenly lose my appetite.

"What's going on?" I asked, pushing my plate away.

"I've offered to help your Masters test your limit and observe them while they work you in my dungeon down the hall," Mika announced in a matter-of-fact tone.

Heat rolled up my chest and singed my cheeks. The thought of Mika watching me felt a hundred times more intimate than a whole club of strangers. Surely, Dylan and Nick weren't going to accept his offer...were they? Darting a panicked glance between them, their expectant expressions answered my question. They were a hundred and ten percent on board.

Someone shoot me, please, I inwardly prayed.

Our friendly, innocent breakfast had taken an embarrassingly wicked turn.

As a punch of panic set my fight or flight reflex on fire, the knee-jerk reaction to tell Mika where he could shove his offer seared the tip of my tongue.

Suddenly, Nick's words screamed through my head. *If you trusted us, you wouldn't have freaked out. You would have known that we'd protect you with our last dying breath.*

This wasn't a lesson in nudity or embarrassment. It was a lesson of trust.

If they accepted Mika's offer and stripped me bare in his dungeon, they'd guard and protect my insecurities...cover and conceal my flesh, and wrap me in their Dominant care, like they'd planned to last night.

"Savannah?" Nick's voice sliced through my churning thoughts.

"Yes, Sir?"

"Come, sit on my lap, little one," he instructed, scooting his chair back and patting his thighs.

As soon as I'd situated myself, he wrapped me in a fierce hug.

"You did it. You stopped your fears before they could consume you, didn't you?"

The level of pride permeating his voice and glistening in his eyes split me wide open.

As I nodded, Nick cupped my nape and drown me in a spine-bending kiss.

"Amazing job, kitten," Dylan whispered beside me.

Cupping Nick's hand, Dylan slowly eased me from Nick's mouth before devouring me with an equally dizzying kiss.

"Stunning breakthrough, Savannah," Mika said, arching a brow at my Masters. "I rescind my offer. She passed the test, with flying colors I might add, before she even took it."

Dylan eased into my chair, then dragged my plate between him and Nick, hand-feeding me as the three men continued heaping me with praise. When brunch was through, we adjourned to Mika's study. After hours of talking, laughing, and Doms ribbing Doms, we said our goodbyes and stepped out onto the massive deck again.

"I forgot to ask," Nick said to Mika. "You, Drake, and Trevor are coming for Thanksgiving again this year, right?"

"We wouldn't miss it for the world." Mika grinned.

"Is Emerald coming?" I asked excitedly.

Chapter Fourteen

"No!" Mika barked.

I jolted and blanched at his fierce tone and intimidating scowl.

Mika exhaled with a powerful huff. "I'm sorry, girl. Emerald doesn't know who I am, and she never will."

Why not? The question gonged through my brain, but I knew better than to ask. Instead, I simply nodded as Dylan and Nick each slung an arm around my waist.

"Come along, little one. I need to go home and spend the afternoon working off breakfast—"

"In bed," Dylan added with a dirty grin.

A shiver rippled through me, not from the cold, but from anticipation. Lurid images of us naked, thrusting and writhing, danced in my head as we slowly plodded over the sand. Growing more impatient by the second, I flashed them a playful smile.

"Race you," I challenged before sprinting toward the house.

"Minx!" Dylan roared with a laugh.

As they gave chase, I glanced over my shoulder. Dylan's sexy dimple and Nick's dark hair flowing in the wind made it hard to breathe. Their soul-stealing beauty had me turning around and running back toward them. As they sprinted toward me, I threw out my arms in surrender. But instead of slowing and wrapping me in their glorious embrace, they ran right past me and started laughing like a couple of loons.

Scoffing in disappointment, I watched them and quickly realized they weren't racing me…they were competing against each other.

"Hey! A hug would have been nice," I yelled, then rolled my eyes and raced after them.

Nick was the first to slap a palm on the banister of the deck. Coming up behind them, I slowed and watched Dylan shove him away, declaring himself the winner.

A mischievous glint skipped across Nick's eyes as he crouched down and charged, driving his shoulder into Dylan's ribs. They both tumbled to the grass with a grunt.

Nick sprang to his feet and gripped the railing again with a triumphant grin. "Who's the winner now?"

"Kiss my ass, fucker," Dylan laughed, brushing the grass off his jacket.

My big bad Doms acted like a couple of six year olds, and all I could do was laugh.

Two weeks later, I helped Rachel prepare a Thanksgiving feast of biblical proportions. Standing at the counter, mashing the potatoes, I thought about the previous Thanksgiving. Mellie and I had fixed a traditional holiday meal in the tiny kitchen of my apartment. My heart ached. I missed her. This was the first Thanksgiving we'd spent apart. She promised to try to visit over Christmas, but Enrique—who, surprisingly, was still her *flavor of the month*—wanted to spend it with his family in South America.

When the doorbell rang, Rachel shooed me out of the kitchen to go play *hostess*.

Unable to shake my melancholy from missing Mellie, I was quiet through most of the dinner. Thankfully, Trevor's gregarious nature and never-ending energy and stories took the focus off me. Dylan and Nick didn't seem to notice my reserved demeanor.

It was easy to see why Trevor and Emerald were such close friends. They shared the same glass-half-full attitude. I was glad we were becoming good friends. I'd never really had a best friend growing up.

While everyone continued talking and eating, my thoughts skipped like a flat rock across a pond. Frustrated for not being able to engage with my new friends gathered at the table, I searched for the crux of my reticent mood.

It didn't take long to find it as my conversation with Tony, yesterday after the submissive group meeting, plowed through my head.

After confessing my fear of being naked in public, and my Masters' goal to erase those fears, Emerald had excused herself. After a brief conversation with Dylan and Nick, she headed toward the bathroom. When the meeting was over, Sir Tony, the dungeon monitor I'd yelled at during my epic freak-out, strolled up and sat at the table with me, Emerald, and Trevor.

"Hello again, Savannah." he smiled. "Emerald has asked me to join her after the meeting was over. I'm not sure if I'm here in Dominant capacity or a professional one."

"Oh, sorry, Sir. Professional, if you don't mind," Emerald replied. With a nervous smile, she clasped my hand beneath the table. "Sir Tony is a psychologist. I thought maybe he could help shed some light on your fear of being naked in public."

My mouth suddenly went dry, and my heart raced. I darted an anxious glance to my Masters, still seated at the bar. Dylan winked and Nick smiled before they both nodded, giving me permission to spill my guts

Great.

"Do you mind me asking some questions?" Tony arched his brows.

"No, Sir," I lied.

"After your parents died, did you start actively looking for men to date?"

How did he know my parents were dead?

Clearly, Emerald wasn't the only one who'd been talking to Tony. Nick and Dylan had undoubtedly been twisting his ear, too.

Traitors!

"No, Sir. I…"

"If you'd rather to talk to Sir alone, we can leave," Trevor volunteered, no doubt sensing the angst rolling off me.

"No, please stay. I don't have anything to hide," I reassured, gripping his hand beneath the table. Anchored to them both, I drew in their strength and support.

"I've dated a couple of times, but Dylan and Nick are my first real boyfriends…man friends…lovers…Masters," I said, struggling to find the appropriate label.

Tony blinked in surprise, then silent studied me as if pondering the mystery of life itself. Anxiety spiked. I wondered if I was so fucked up a professional couldn't even fix me.

The corners of his mouth twitched as he leaned in and steepled his fingers. "Would you have any problem taking your clothes off in front of Emerald?"

His question caught me off-guard. I blinked, then looked at her. "No, Sir."

"How about Trevor? Can you take off your clothes in front of him?" Tony continued.

"Yes."

"Are you sure? He's a man," Tony challenged.

"He's a submissive," I corrected.

"And I'm gay," Trevor said with a dramatic wave of his hand.

"And he's gay." I grinned.

"What about Drake?"

I instantly sobered and shook my head. "No, Sir. He scares the cra…crackers out of me."

"What about me?"

"I-I can't do that, Sir."

"No. I'm sure your Masters would rip my balls off."

"And…shove them down your throat," Trevor added with a laugh.

"I don't understand. Why am I okay stripping for Emerald and Trevor, but not you?"

"I was hoping you'd ask that." Tony winked. "Though it's only been a few weeks, you've created a bond with Emerald and Trevor. You trust them. You don't trust me, and you shouldn't because you don't know me."

"I didn't trust my Masters the night I freaked out, but I should have."

"Why?"

"Because I knew...I *know* they'd never purposely hurt me."

"You're right. They wouldn't. But I'm going to back up a bit. By your own admission you don't like letting people in." When I opened my mouth to argue, Tony held up his hand. "It's not a bad thing. In fact, it's perfectly understandable. I think you're afraid to let people in your heart because you're afraid they'll die and leave you, like your parents did. It's safer to lock up your heart than to open up and be vulnerable. Subconsciously, being vulnerable has the potential to rip you apart as much as loving someone who gets ripped from your life."

"Little one?" Nick murmured, placing his hand over mine and dragging me back from my musing over Tony's words.

"Yes, Sir?" I swallowed tightly worried he'd asked me something I'd have to beg him to repeat...and pay the price for.

"Would you go in the kitchen and tell Rachel we're ready for coffee in the study, please?"

"Of course, Sir." I nodded, then stood and excused myself from the table.

As we sat by a roaring fire in the study commiserating about our full bellies, I sipped my coffee and listened to the flow of conversation. My fear of Daddy Drake had been for nothing. Like Emerald had said, the man was a big teddy bear. In fact, the way he and Trevor bantered was funny as hell. Snuggled between Dylan and Nick, I listened, and laughed, and finally relaxed.

Mika had a wicked sense of humor. He was far less reserved than the first time I'd met him. Dylan and Nick had answered *most* of my questions about the club owner, but not all. When I discovered Drake, Trevor, and Mika had been friends long before the idea of Genesis had even been hatched, their palpable bond made perfect sense.

But when the trio began discussing the slave Mika lost several years ago to brain cancer, my heart ached for the man. Having loved and lost, he'd vowed to never claim another sub. If anyone in the room understood the need to protect your heart from complete annihilation again, it was me.

Still, question about Mika's vehement reaction the day I'd mentioned Emerald's name continued spooling through my brain. His hatred toward my new friend seemed way over the top. Though it was none of my business, there was something bizarre about the whole thing.

～

The days passed in a blur, and the weather turned bitter. I spent every Saturday morning learning volumes about submission. My Masters were pleased with my growth and seemed eager to answer my questions evoked by the classes. Before I'd even realized it, my trust in them had grown deeper and stronger, just like my need to please them.

Christmas morning, I woke to an empty bed and the doorbell ringing incessantly. After tossing off the covers, I rushed to the bathroom, then tugged on my clothes before bounding down the stairs.

As I reached the foyer, Drake stood in the doorway wearing a red, velvet Santa suit, and a scowl, while Trevor danced around him, dressed like an elf and singing *Merry Christmas*. Clutching my stomach, I plopped down on the stairs, consumed by laughter.

Drake turned and pinned me with a big, bad, Santa-Dom glare.

"And just what do you think you're laughing at, pet?" Drake growled. "You know Santa has a list for insolent subs. If your name is on it, girl, then Santa knows how naughty you've been and you're likely to get something you don't like."

"Oh, I'm sure I'm on that list, Santa, because I've been a wicked, naughty girl…numerous times. Just ask my Masters. They get naughty with me all the time." I laughed so hard, tears leaked from my eyes.

"That's it!" Drake barked as he slung the big red bag off his shoulder and set it on the floor. "No bunny flogger for you."

"I can't help it, Sir," I choked through my howls of laughter. "I've never seen a Dominant Santa before. It's…it's…hilarious." Laughing even harder, Drake narrowed his eyes and began to dig through the large red bag. Trevor stood behind him with a hand pressed to his mouth, smothering his grin. Dylan and Nick watched with expressions of disbelief while merriment danced in their eyes.

"Hilarious, am I? You may not think so when you're cuffed and helpless beneath the crack of this whip." Drake pulled a plaited red and black single tail from his Santa bag.

"Uh-oh, sister, you're in trouble now," Trevor warned with a child-like giggle.

"Oh, Santa," I begged over-dramatically as I bounded off the steps. "Please don't give my Masters a whip. My lily-white ass will never survive."

"We already have three," Dylan announced with a devilish grin.

"But not for me, right, Masters?" I asked, innocently batting my lashes.

"Not today, little one, but we'll work up to it."

The conviction in Nick's voice sent tendrils of dread wending through me.

The doorbell rang again, keeping me from fixating on my Masters whipping my ass. As Trevor pulled it open, Mika stood on the porch, brushing snow off his coat before stepping inside. His eyes grew wide, and he started laughing when he saw Drake and Trevor.

"What kind of fucking holiday spirit got into you two?" Mika laughed.

"Don't laugh, Sir, or Santa will give you horrible gifts. Like a nasty whip," I said in a stage whisper, nodding toward the whip in Dylan's hand.

"I've already got dozens of those, but I'd be interested in seeing if Santa brought me a bottle of Glenfiddich," Mika replied, peering into the red bag.

"Though you're the baddest boy on the list, I think there's something in there for you," Drake grinned as the pair shared a bro-hug.

"You say that like it's a bad thing." Mika grinned, shucking off his coat and placing it in my waiting hand. "Thank you, Savannah. Regardless what Santa thinks, you're a good girl."

"Thank you, Sir." I grinned.

As I hung up his coat, the doorbell rang again.

"I've got it," Trevor announced, dancing toward the portal.

A second later, Sammie crossed the threshold, arms filled with gifts.

"Let me help you, Mistress," Trevor offered as I dashed to help him relieve her of the packages. "Under the tree, Sirs?" he asked Dylan and Nick.

"Please, dear boy." Nick nodded.

"What tree?" I asked in confusion, trailing after Trevor.

"The one we put up in the study this morning, kitten," Dylan called out behind me. "Next year, we'll drag your sexy ass out of bed to help us."

"A Christmas tree?" I squealed, excitedly racing past Trevor.

After my parents died, Mellie and I spent cozy but subdued Christmases together, not bothering to put up a tree. A pang of sadness pierced my heart that she wasn't here—but in South America with Enrique—to celebrate the holiday with me, but Dylan and Nick were doing everything in their power to make it a special day for me.

I skidded to a halt in the study and stared at colorful lights and beautiful decorations on the massive tree. Then, I dropped my gaze to the mound of presents beneath it.

"Here, please take these, Trevor. I'll be right back."

Shoving more presents in his arms, I turned and raced to the media room and gathered the gifts I'd hidden for my Masters. I hurried back to the study and helped him place Mistress Sammie's presents beneath the tree as the Dominants strolled into the room.

Quickly finishing my task, I ran to Dylan and Nick and hugged them fiercely. "The tree is gorgeous. Thank you. Thank you both so much."

"We're glad you like it." Dylan smiled and kissed the top of my head.

"Is Emerald spending Christmas alone?" Mika asked Drake. A hint of anguish flashed over his amber eyes.

"No. She's spending it with George and Leagh," Drake replied.

As Drake tugged off the Santa suit and beard and eased onto the long, leather couch, Trevor dropped his chin and clenched his jaw.

My gut told me there was history between Mika and Emerald, and out of all the people in the room, I was the only one in the dark as to what had happened.

"Savannah, Trevor, would you please go to the kitchen and bring in the coffee and sweet rolls for us?" Nick asked, breaking the awkward silence that had settled over the room.

"Right away, Sir." I smiled, dragging Trevor out of the room in a tight hug.

Once safe inside the kitchen, I pulled him next to me. Giving a cursory glance around the room, I leaned in. "Okay, what the hell is up with Mika and Emerald?"

"Nothing, and don't ask me anymore about it, please," Trevor begged in a tiny whine.

An immediate rush of guilt slammed me. "I'm sorry. It's none of my business. I shouldn't be prying."

"Don't be sorry. It's just... I can't say anything." He sighed.

While I filled two silver carafes with coffee, Trevor arranged the cream, sugar, and mugs on a large silver tray.

"So, there *is* something going on, right?"

"No. The only people who know or have ever seen Mika are all in the study. Emerald doesn't even know he exists."

Though that tidbit of insight confused me even more, I bit back the urge to ask more questions as I placed the carafes on the tray, then handed Trevor the platter of sweet rolls.

"Last one in the study gets to serve." I grinned, lifting the tray of coffee.

"Hell no, I'm not racing you. I'll drop something." Trevor shook his head in mock fear. "Are you trying to get my ass whipped?"

"Like you wouldn't enjoy it?" I scoffed.

"No. I'd love it." He giggled.

After returning to the study and serving the Doms, Trevor knelt at Drake's feet while I settled on the floor between my Master's legs. Together, they caressed and stroked my hair, cheeks, and shoulders with their warm fingers. Hands down, it was already the best Christmas of my adult life.

While everyone sipped coffee and devoured the pastries, the Dominants discussed everything from toys and techniques to protocol. But when they started talking about politics and religion, things quickly heated up, especially when Trevor raised his hand.

"What is it, boy?" Drake thundered after a long tirade about homophobes and organized religion.

"Can we open presents now, Master? Pretty please?"

"Are you purposely trying to change the subject, boy?" Drake scowled.

Worried for Trevor's backside, I held my breath.

"As a matter of fact, I am." He thrust out his chin defiantly. "I don't want you stroking out on Jesus's birthday."

"I'm going to fire up your insolent ass when we get home, boy," Drake snarled.

"Oh, goodie. Santa got my letter!"

As Trevor grinned and clapped, Drake sank a mighty paw in Trevor's long, blond hair, then tugged his head back before dropping a sizzling kiss over his lips.

"And therein lies the problem with pain sluts." Sammie grinned. "The only way to punish them is to ignore them."

Releasing his boy with a hungry growl, Drake nodded. "You may ask Masters Dylan and Nick if it's time to distribute the gifts, my sassy slut."

After leaping to his feet, Trevor wiggled his ass in Drake's face. When the big Dom landed a firm slap, Trevor whimpered in delight.

"I fucking love you two." Mika chuckled, shaking his head.

"We love you, too, Master," Trevor replied, blowing the club owner a kiss before sobering quickly.

Placing his hands behind his back, he lowered his gaze and approached my Masters in a stunning display of respect and submission.

"Master Dylan and Master Nick, if it pleases you, may Savannah and I have your permission to pass out the presents...pretty, pretty, pretty please?"

"He *does* know how to be a good slut, after all," Drake tsked.

Though his tone dripped with sarcasm, a blind man couldn't miss the pride and love in the big man's eyes.

"Yes, Trevor, you sweet boy, you may." Dylan smiled with a nod.

The words had no more left my Master's lips, than Trevor tossed all protocol out the window and jumped up and down, squealing in excitement.

Grabbing my hand, he pulled me off the floor, and grinned. "Let's do this."

"Boy!" Drake bellowed in a scary, feral cry.

Trevor froze. The happy smile fell from his face as he slowly turned toward Drake and lowered his gaze to the floor. The room turned so quiet, you could have heard a pin drop.

"I don't remember them giving you permission to touch their sub, do you?" Drake chided.

"No, Master. I'm sorry. I got carried away in the moment." Slowly turning his head, Trevor sent Dylan and Nick an apologetic grimace. "I'm sorry, Sirs."

Nick nodded in appreciation. "You're fine. You have our permission to touch Savannah...respectfully, any time."

"Thank you, Nick." Drake nodded before turning a stern glare on his sub. "Trevor?"

He raised his head and swallowed tightly. "Yes, Master."

"Enjoy yourself, boy." Drake beamed.

Trevor's face lit up brighter than the tree. Jumping up and down like a kangaroo on crack, he thanked Drake and Nick, then dragged me to the tree.

The next hour was a blur of paper ripping and bows flying as we unwrapped the mountain of presents. For the first time in years, I felt like a child again.

Nick and Dylan were speechless when they opened the custom-made floggers—each with their initials scrolled into the handles—that Emerald had secretly helped me order from a Dom at the club. And their eyes lit up at the matching boxes of pervertibles I'd scoured long and hard to find. Dylan held up the innocuous wooden pasta paddle I'd found at a gourmet foods store, then flashed a smile filled with the promise of a red ass.

"They're not really lifestyle toys," I said softly. "But they reminded me of our time at the barn."

"They mean the world to us, little one, just like you do." Nick smiled. "The days we spent at Kit's are the catalyst of where we're at now. Thank you, love."

He leaned down and captured my lips in a soul-stealing kiss before Mika stood and pulled a stack of envelopes from his back pocket.

"Please wait and open them together, if you don't mind," he instructed as he strode around the room, handing one to each of the Dominants. When all the envelopes had been distributed, he smiled and nodded.

"Oh, holy hell," Drake blinked, reading the message on the small square of parchment.

"What is it, Master?" Trevor asked, easing up and tilting his head toward Drake's hands.

"Oh, Mika," Sammie giggled. "This is going to be a blast!"

Craning my neck, I tried to read what was on the paper Dylan and Nick each held.

"A fucking kinky cruise?" Nick choked as he stared up at Mika. "Are you serious?"

"Yep. I've rented the whole damn boat. Mark your calendars now. The week of August fifteenth, we'll be spanking our way through the Caribbean. I plan to invite the club members as well, but you all are my guests of honor," Mika preened. "I've booked you all suites."

My heart skittered with excitement, then died as reality wrapped it in its icy hands.

As everyone chattered excitedly, I sat silently, forcing the smile to stay fixed on my lips, and my body relaxed.

By the time August rolled around, I'd be nothing but a distant memory to Dylan and Nick. I'd be back in Kansas City, combing through dusty courthouses while my Masters soaked up the sun and fun.

Blinking back the tears stinging my eyes, I felt someone watching me. Looking up, I watched Trevor's brows slash in confusion. Subtly shaking my head, I sent him a silent plea not to say anything to draw attention my way. He nodded faintly, then pasted on a bright smile.

"Oh, I almost forgot. You have one more present, little one," Nick announced as he palmed my nape. "Climb on up here, love."

I couldn't imagine another gift as I took inventory of the presents spread out before me. There were nipple clamps, butt plugs, sexy lingerie, and a vibe—that came with a strict warning to never be used when my Masters weren't present.

As I climbed onto Nick's lap, Dylan reached into his pocket, and pulled out a little red velvet box. My heart drummed against my ribs as he clasped my hand, opened my palm, and placed it in my hand.

"We love you, Savannah. No matter what the future holds." Dylan's smile wavered. "You are branded to our hearts and souls. We want to spend forever with you."

Stroking a knuckle down my cheek, he pressed his lips to mine with a kiss so overflowing with love, it stole my breath.

As Dylan lifted from my mouth, Nick fisted my hair and turned me to face him.

Déjà vu flooded my veins as flashbacks of the day they'd come to my apartment...and held me this very way.

"We might not know what the future holds, little one. But make no mistake, we'll do everything in our power to keep you right here, between us," Nick vowed before crashing his lips over mine with an equally spine-bending kiss teeming with love.

When he grudgingly ended the kiss, Nick smiled and nodded toward the box.

My hands trembled as I lifted the lid.

Inside lay a gold necklace with three delicate hearts entwined.

Tears filled my eyes and slipped down my cheeks, as a soft moan slid from my lips.

"It's beautiful," I choked.

"This is us, kitten. Joined together, no matter what," Dylan whispered.

"Wear this always, little one."

"Wear it and think of us," Dylan murmured. "No matter where you are or what you're doing."

I nodded as my tears continued to fall.

"Good girl," Nick whispered.

As the two magical words tossed my jumbled emotions to the four corners of the world, I bit back my sobs as they worked together and clasped the delicate chain around my neck.

"Oh, Masters...I love you. I love you both so much," I whispered, strumming my fingertips over the hearts.

"Who's ready for Christmas pizza?" Trevor blurted, wiping away his own tears.

"Christmas what?" I choked out a watery laugh.

"Pizza." Dylan smirked. "We kick Rachel out of the kitchen on Christmas, and though Nick and I could cook, we don't want to. Not on Christmas. So, every year, we eat pizza."

"They're heathens," Sammie drawled, rolling her eyes. "But I humor them. After all, they *are* men."

"You could cook for us," Mika countered her insult.

"Oh, for shit's sake. You know I can't boil water. I'd burn down the whole kitchen." She laughed.

Drying my cheeks, I stared at the triple hearts nestled between my breasts.

The doorbell rang again before the room turned eerily silent.

"I'll get it," Dylan volunteered, launching off the couch.

A look of panic careened over Mika's face. "Who else is coming?"

"Not who...what," Nick cryptically replied.

"What's going on?" I quietly asked him.

"You'll see. Patience." He smirked.

All eyes turned, expectantly watching the doorway. We didn't have to wait long before Dylan reappeared carrying an envelope and biting back a grin.

"It's for you, Savannah."

"Me?" I blinked, rising to my feet. I lifted the envelope from his hand. There was no return address on it, simply a label with my name. "What is this? Who's it from?"

"Open it and find out." Nick smiled as he and Dylan cinched an arm around my waist.

Ripping the paper open, I pulled out a note. As I flipped it open, I instantly recognized my boss, Myron's, handwriting. As I began to read, my heart lodged in my throat.

My dearest Savannah,

Words can't describe how thrilled Helen and I are that you have found two young men to fill your life with love. While it's outside the conventional ways, I applaud you for giving your heart to both these, caring, compassionate, and upstanding young men. All I have ever wanted for you, dear, is to find the kind of love that Helen and I have been lucky enough to share all these years.

After talking to your young men and Mellie, Helen and I nearly jumped for joy. Both Dylan and Nick sang your praises for hours, then explained their hearts and lives would be broken if you had to leave Chicago. Since you hadn't told me a thing about them, I placed a call to Mellie. After she confirmed you'd fallen fast and hard, Helen and I sat down and talked. We knew it was time to finalize the dreams we'd been putting on hold.

That leads me to the reason for this letter. We want you to stay in Chicago and build a life of love and happiness with Dylan and Nick. Believe it or not, I'm finally going to retire. I've been putting off the decision, because frankly, I couldn't find it in my heart to close the company and leave you unemployed. You're like a daughter to us, Savannah.

Dylan and Nick assured me they'd help you find a new job in Chicago, and support you a hundred and ten percent if you wanted to keep working. Their reassurance, and Helen pestering me for years to travel abroad while we still can, prompted me to make my decision.

I will miss you, sweetheart, but I know the new life you're about to start living is the stuff story books are made of. I do have one condition that's non-negotiable. We expect an invitation to your wedding.

If you ever need anything... anything at all, we're simply a phone call away.

Best wishes to you three. May your life be filled with as much magic and happiness as Helen and I have shared.

All our love,

Myron.

Dumbfounded and numb, I plopped down on the couch and read the letter over...then again.

"I know you're probably upset with us, little one," Nick began as he eased down beside me. "But it was the only solution Dylan and I could come up with to keep from losing you. I know we went behind your back...broke your trust, and kept secrets from you."

"We could say we're sorry, but that would be a lie," Dylan murmured, joining us on the couch. "We've tried, but neither of us can wrap our heads around the idea of letting you go. You left us once...we can't go through that again."

"What did you say to Myron?" I asked, trying to dissect and compartmentalize the flood of emotions flowing through me.

Nick chuckled. "The truth. I told him you swept us off our feet. That the week we spent with you at Kit's was the single most life-altering experience we've ever had."

"He put us through the wringer for the first thirty minutes. He knows more about our lives than we do." Dylan flashed that sexy dimple in a pleading, scared smile. "Don't be mad, Savannah. We want and need you. We'll do anything in our power to make this work."

"I don't have a job anymore," I mumbled.

As I continued reeling with the knowledge that Myron had put his life on hold to ensure I was taken care of, the realization of what my Masters had orchestrated...the desperation of their need to build a life with me, slammed my system.

Tingles of joy exploded through me, sending my heart soaring.

"I don't have to leave you and go back home," I breathlessly whispered. "I can stay," I screamed, launching off the couch with a childish giggle. I danced around the room.

"Yes. Yes you can, kitten." Dylan laughed.

Dragging them both off the couch, I wrapped them in a tight hug. As cheers went up around the room, I closed my eyes and exhaled a mammoth sigh of relief.

"This is the best present I ever had, Masters. Thank you. Thank you so much." I peppered their faces with kisses.

"We're just glad you're not pissed, little one." Nick grinned.

"How could I be pissed? You two have made all my dreams come true." Tears of joy filled my eyes as another revelation plowed through me. "I can go on the cruise now."

"We wouldn't have gone without you." Dylan frowned.

Nick drew back his hand and landed a hard spank to my ass. I jolted and yelped as he leveled me with an unhappy glare. "You've been keeping your feelings from us again, haven't you?"

"Not keeping, Master, saving. I was saving them to share with you later…when the three of us were alone."

I darted a glance around the room, drinking in the smiling faces… well, all except Mika. A bittersweet expression lined his face as he stared out the window. My heart grew heavy knowing that, once upon a time, he experienced the same unadulterated bliss still pinging inside me. The emptiness and pain of having it ripped from his life had to be staggering.

"Dude," Dylan barked, drawing my focus back to my amazing Masters. "She's staying. Our girl's fucking staying."

As he extended a fist, Nick laughed and nodded as they bumped fists. "I know." He grinned. "It's fan-fucking-tastic!"

"So, who's ready for Christmas pizza?" Dylan called out.

Weeks after my life-altering Christmas surprise, my feet still weren't touching the ground. Gone was the nagging worry of leaving my masters, replaced by happiness and an invigorating sense of freedom.

The last week of February, we took advantage of the break in the winter weather and drove to Kansas City to clean out my apartment. We spent two days loading up a U-Haul, then

enjoyed a delightful dinner with Myron and Helen. They were already making plans to fly to Paris as soon as Myron wrapped up a few loose ends and officially closed the office. They were both delighted to finally meet Dylan and Nick, and spent hours talking about excavation and artifacts.

Helen joined me when I took a trip to the ladies' room. I was shocked when she gleefully asked what being loved by two men at once was like. When I told her, I was pretty sure our girlish giggles could be heard throughout the fancy restaurant.

While it was harder than I expected to say goodbye to them, Dylan and Nick's invitation for them to come visit helped ease my sadness. After assuring us they would, I shared one final, poignant embrace with the couple and kissed their cheeks.

As soon as we returned to the hotel and entered our suite, Dylan and Nick began peeling off my clothes. A tingle of excitement zipped up my spine, and a smile spread over my lips. I was hopelessly lost when they undressed me with such tender care.

"I hope I'm as good of a boss as Myron," Nick stated, loosening his tie.

"You're a wonderful boss, I'm sure," I said, unbuttoning his shirt.

"Would you like to take some dictation to find out, little one?"

"It's a conference call, fucker," Dylan announced, strolling from the bathroom. "You'll have to take it from both of us, kitten."

"I'm assuming I won't need a note pad or pen, Sirs?" I asked with a saucy grin.

"No, you won't," Dylan growled. "You'll have to take it all down...by memory."

With a sassy wink, I eased to my knees and spread my legs in proper submission fashion.

"Your preparation is luscious, Miss Carson. Now let's see if you can handle the workload." Nick smirked.

"Whatever you slam me with, Mr. Masters, I'm sure I will fulfill my duties."

I bit back a giggle. I'd *so* wanted to call him Master Masters, but wasn't sure he'd find it half as funny as I did. Peeking up beneath dark lashes, I watched Dylan undress. The thick muscles on his arms rippled and bulged, and a contented sigh escaped my lips when his hard cock sprang from his trousers.

"I see you're getting comfortable for our *dictation* session, Mr. Thomas."

"Indeed, I am. I wouldn't want anything spoiling your *oral* abilities."

Six months ago, role play was nothing but a fantasy. Everything had happened so quickly. I sometimes felt as if I'd taken over someone else's life. But then I realized things hadn't changed, I had. I'd opened myself up for the new experiences they heaped on me because I knew I was safe and protected, and loved unconditionally.

My need to please them had grown exponentially as well. And even though nothing I'd read prepared me for all the things they'd taught me, I now understood the true meaning of the power exchange, and the true beauty of my submission.

"You know, Sirs, this would be a whole lot more realistic if you allowed me to get dressed again."

"No!" they barked in unison.

"Alrighty, then." I smirked.

"Wipe that devilish smile off your face, Miss Carson, and spread your legs for inspection," Nick growled, stepping closer as he stroked his fat erection. "We need to see if you're up to the *task* we have in mind for you."

Lifting my ass high in the air, I lifted my arms over my head, then bent and pressed my forehead to the carpet.

"Well, well… what do we have here?" Dylan tsked, dragging a finger up my slit. "You're wet…dripping wet, Miss Carson."

"Yes, Mr. Thomas," I replied, praying he'd put his fingers on me again.

"Why are you're wet?" Dylan asked, skimming a fingertip over my ass cheeks.

"Because you excite me, Sirs."

"We excite you, hrmm? When did this first start happening, Miss Carson?" Nick asked, gliding his cock down my spine.

"Since the first time I saw you both." It wasn't a lie.

"Do you have fantasies about us?" Dylan asked, tracing my folds with his finger.

"All the time, Sir," I replied as tiny tremors skipped through me.

"Tell us about them, Miss Carson…in detail," Nick whispered close to my ear.

I mewled, wishing they'd just shut up and fuck me.

"Tell us," Dylan demanded, plunging two fingers deep in my core.

"Ahhhh, that, Sir. I dreamed about your fingers, your tongues, and your cocks. Devouring me. Claiming me. Driving deep inside my pussy and ass."

"Is that what you want us to do, Miss Carson?" Nick's voice was thick.

"Yes, Sir. Please. All that and more."

"More? Do tell, Miss Carson," Dylan taunted. "Clearly, you've fantasized about more than us filling your silky cunt and tight ass."

Nick fisted my hair and lifted my head from the floor before painting my lips with pre-come. I opened my mouth to welcome him in, but he simply pinched my nipple and slapped his wet crest against my cheek.

"Oh gawd, please, Sir."

"Tell us," Dylan demanded as he pulled from my pussy and slapped my ass.

"That, Master… I mean, Mr. Thomas."

Landing another sharp spank, then another, I moaned and writhed.

"Yes, please. Spank me. Hard. Fuck me. Hard."

They'd driven me half out of my mind. The room was thick with sexual tension. My tunnel contracted against the emptiness. It was maddening.

"You want us to use you…slide our cocks inside your pussy and your ass, and make you come?" Dylan taunted, spreading my folds with his thumb and finger before his hot breath spilled over my quivering slit.

"Ahh, yes, Master. Please. Please," I begged.

As he stabbed his tongue through my dripping core, I cried out and shamelessly ground myself against his face.

"Stunning," Nick whispered as his silky hair fanned out over my back. "Open your mouth, Miss Carson, and suck me to the back of your throat."

Dylan spread the cheeks of my ass apart and swirled his wet tongue over my puckered rim as I gobbled Nick's cock like it was my last meal.

Growling like an animal, I sucked and slurped Nick's cock as the shocking sensations Dylan conjured crawled up my spine.

"You like Dylan's tongue on your tight puckered hole, girl?" Nick asked in a low, silky voice.

"Yes, Master. Yes. More, oh god, please."

Gliding his tongue in and out, over and around, Dylan sent me spinning on a carousel of carnal splendor. The ride so sublime, I never wanted it to end.

When I lightly dragged my teeth over Nick's pulsating veins before flicking my tongue on the sensitive spot beneath his thick crest, his curses of pleasure vibrated through me.

"My sweet slut, you keep doing that thing with your tongue and this is going to be over before it begins," he warned, thrusting himself to the back of my throat.

Dylan's fingers delved deep into my core and his thumb burnished my swollen clit. All the while, he danced his decadent tongue over my sensitive ribbed flesh. Nick wasn't the only one primed for detonation. Dylan had me crawling out of my skin.

Trying to focus my attention on the driving cock in my mouth was futile. Keening out muffled cries of distress, I wiggled my hips. I was going to topple over if Dylan didn't ease up. But he didn't. He simply chuckled, sending vibrations cascading over my gathered rim, and catapulting me even higher.

Struggling to contain the blistering orgasm bubbling too close to the surface, I released Nick's cock with an audible pop.

"I can't hold it, Masters. Please. It's too big."

"Not yet, kitten," Dylan growled as he stabbed his tongue through my electrified rim.

Nick gripped my mane and filled my mouth with his cock.

White flashes of light strobed behind my eyes.

Unable to stop myself, I surrendered, and shattered.

Consumed by the powerful explosion, I quaked and whimpered. And as ecstasy consumed me, I knew, in the back of my mind, coming without their permission was going to cost me…cost me big.

Chapter Fifteen

As wave after wave of blinding bliss crashed through me, Nick's cock swelled on my tongue before he released a thunderous roar and showered my throat with thick ropes of come. Dylan removed his tortuously delicious fingers and tongue before gripping my hips and driving his cock, balls deep, inside my clutching core. While I gulped the slick seed still spilling over my tongue, Dylan pummeled my pussy as if he had a point to make. He'd never taken me with such punishing power, and it turned me on like a freaking light bulb.

"You didn't have permission, kitten," he bit out, gliding his fingers over my sensitive, swollen clit. "So, now you get to keep coming and coming until we've decided you've had enough."

Nick stroked my cheek. "Keep sucking, sweet slut. I want to be nice and hard when I fuck your ass after Dylan's done coming in your cunt.

Oh, hell. They're going to fuck me to death.

"So. Fucking. Hot. And. Tight," Dylan bit out with each solid thrust.

Gliding his fingers over my screaming nub, he dragged me back up the craggy peak. My tunnel clenched around his driving shaft as I continued bobbing up and down Nick's cock. Seconds later, my keening cries reverberated up his length, while I struggled to hold back.

With a bitter curse, Nick pulled from my mouth before Dylan shuttled in and out of my pussy as if possessed. Without warning, my muscles seized and another, more powerful orgasm crashed through me. While Dylan shouted and spilled his seed, I tossed my head back and screamed as we shattered together.

As I lowered my head to the carpet, gasping for breath, Dylan eased from my core and dropped to the floor beside me.

But before I could even start floating back to earth, Nick splayed his broad hand to the small of my back and dropped a glob of cold lube to my backside.

Without a word, he started squeezing his thick crest through my delicate ring.

"Master!" I cried as pain and pressure, like shards of glass, exploded outward.

He didn't stop...didn't pull back, simply continued pressing his thick tip through my screaming rim.

"Open for me, little one. Take my cock inside your tight ass," he commanded, landing a succession of stinging slaps across my orbs.

Electrified and dazed, he bombarded me with so much pain and pleasure, I could only cling to one or the other. As my body and mind spiraled into another dimension, I gripped the carpet, praying it would anchor me.

When his bulbous tip finally penetrated past my agonizing ring, I arched my back, forcing his thick shaft deeper inside me.

"Yes, fuck yes!" I cried, rocking back and forth on my hands and knees. "Harder, Master. Fuck me harder. Give it all to me, pleaseeee."

"Fuck me," Dylan mumbled, kneeling beside me before teasing my burning clit. "Talk to him, Savannah. Tell him how you like it. Tell him how good it feels."

"Dylan," Nick roared.

"No worries, bro. I'm already hard as granite watching and listening to this."

"Talk to me, sweet slut," Nick taunted. "Tell me how you want it, baby."

"Please, Master. Please. I need you deep, and rough. Slam your fat cock inside me, please. Don't hold back. I need…faster. Harder."

As I begged Nick to defile me every way known to man, he cursed and granted my wishes. His balls slapped at my pussy as I sailed headlong, fucking him back like a wild animal.

"Rub her clit, man. I've got an idea," Dylan announced as he jumped up and hurried away.

"Hurry," Nick barked. "I'm not going to last. She's too hot, too tight…too fucking perfect."

As Nick pounded deep in my ass, he circled his fingers over my clit. I'd stopped wondering how they could draw so many orgasms as another one sliced through me. And as my muscles constricted around Nick's shaft, an inhuman cry tore from his throat. I could feel his spasms along the tender walls of my clutching tunnel as he filled the condom.

As he released the biting grip of my hips and eased from my ass, my legs gave out.

Melting against the carpet, I gasped and panted as my body continued to quake and hum.

"Not yet, kitten. We're just getting started," Dylan warned, flipping me over before tugging the black duffle bag to his side.

"I-I can't…I c-can't come any…more," I gasped.

"Sure, you can," he assured, sliding two high-backed chairs toward my feet.

Blinking through the sexual haze coating my brain, I groaned when he lifted my calves onto the seat of the chairs. After tying my ankles to the wooden rungs, he reached back inside the toy bag and pulled out the big, electric vibe.

I gasped and shook my head, muttering, "No. No."

"Oh, yes. Yes, kitten. Forced orgasms."

"But, Master…"

Before I could begin begging for mercy, Dylan flipped the switch and pressed the vibe to my clit. Nick gripped my wrists in one hand and dragged my arms above my head.

Bound and splayed, I was helpless and at their mercy—a mercy I knew they wouldn't grant until my punishment was through.

"You have a safeword if you need it, little one," Nick soothed, plucking and pinching my nipples with his free hand.

Using the fiendish vibe, Dylan dragged another blistering orgasm from me. Screaming, I arched my back as the thunderous release rolled me under. Though my clit was on fire, and my pleasure centers warred between bliss and pain, he kept the toy pressed to my clit, forcing me up and over, again, and again.

My eyes were open, but I couldn't see...couldn't focus.

My throat was raw.

My voice was gone, and my screams were nothing but strangled whispers.

Though my brain had shut down, my body continued to respond as orgasms—no longer defined—layered one on top of the next in an endless loop of tortured bliss.

Suddenly, the vibe lifted from my clit and fell silent.

Hands, warm and loving, brushed the wet strands of hair from my sweat-soaked face.

"You'll control your orgasm next time, won't you, little one?" Nick asked as his handsome face slowly came into focus.

Unable to speak, I merely nodded.

"Good girl," Dylan praised, releasing the rope from my ankles.

Nick lifted me off the floor and into his strong arms. My head lolled against his chest while my boneless arms flopped at my sides. Murmuring praises, he carried me across the spacious suite and into the bathroom, where the sound of running water filled my ears.

"Such a gorgeous, hot mess," Dylan cooed, brushing his lips against mine. "Keep floating, kitten, we're going to take good care of you."

Floating.

Yes, I was definitely floating, but not in fluffy clouds. I was drifting in an ethereal, pristine place inside myself...one that consumed my body as well as my mind.

Nick gently lowered me into the massive spa tub. The silky, jasmine-scented water felt good, but not as much as being sandwiched between their naked, hard bodies and drowned in their praises.

That was sheer heaven.

～

Spring turned into summer. When Dylan and Nick weren't working, we spent our days by the pool and our nights exploring Dominance and submission at Genesis. They kept their promise of pushing my limits...driving me to new and exciting levels with care and consideration for my *naked in public* trigger.

I thought about finding a job, but I was enjoying my unlimited vacation too much. As they'd promised Myron, Nick and Dylan were supportive of my choice, and even more supportive when I asked them to teach me how to cook—though, most lessons ended with us naked.

They plied me with pleasure, introducing me to so many new and exciting experiences—both in and out of bed—I sometimes forgot how boring and void my life had been before I met them. They wined and dined me at exclusive restaurants where little to no attention was given to their open affection. And I soon discovered my fears of condemnation and judgement had been a total waste of time.

Mellie—no longer with Enrique—visited often, instantly bonding with my Masters.

My life and everything and everyone in it were perfect, until one sunny summer morning.

The ring of Nick's cell phone jolted us from sleep. When he answered and didn't say anything, I could tell by the horrified expression on his face that something was dreadfully wrong.

Dylan, obviously reading his alarmed expression, rolled out of bed and began getting dressed.

"We'll be there in a couple of minutes," Nick replied somberly before ending the call and turning toward Dylan. "Mika asked us to come over right away."

"What's going on?" Dylan asked, tugging a tee over his head.

When Nick opened his mouth, unable to speak, I knew it was really bad.

"I'll get some clothes on," I said, tossing off the covers.

"No." Nick cringed. "Sorry, love. He only wants Dylan and me." Though his voice was calm, worry blazed in his eyes.

"W-what's happened?" I whispered.

Nick exhaled a heavy sigh and scrubbed a hand through his hair.

"What the fuck's going on, man?" Dylan demanded.

"Emerald was attacked in Drake's private room last night at Genesis."

"What?" I gasped as my stomach twisted in a knot of fear. "I-is she…all right?"

"I think so."

"Oh, fuck," Dylan groaned. "Who the hell attacked her?"

"That new guy that just joined, Jordon something. He's a fucking psychopath. He played Drake to get to Emerald, then used a razor blade flogger on her ass. Cut her up pretty bad. Mika, Tony, James, and Drake busted into the room and saved her, then Martin rushed over and stitched her up in Mika's office."

"Oh my god," I whispered as tears stung my eyes.

"*Mika* went in with them?" Dylan asked incredulously.

"Yeah. And spent the night at her place to take care of her."

"He stayed the night?" Dylan gaped.

"Will someone please tell me what the fuck is going on between Mika and Emerald?"

"Language, little one," Nick growled.

"I'm sorry, but my best friend was attacked, Dylan's beyond shocked that Mika *revealed* himself to Emerald…like it's some kind of cardinal sin. What's the big fucking deal?"

"I know you're upset; we all are. But if you don't watch your mouth, we'll spend all night forcing orgasms out of you. Do I make myself clear?"

"Crystal, Master," I bit out.

"If you'll calm down, I'll explain. Can you do that for me, girl?"

Like a blow torch, Nick's condescending tone set me on fire. It was hauntingly reminiscent of the cocky lawyers who all but patted my head as they talked down to me simply because I was a woman and thought my expert opinions didn't matter because the *big boys were handling it.*

Though I knew he hadn't meant to, Nick had just pounded my biggest hot button.

It was on.

"I think I can manage that Master, thanks."

His brows slashed in an angry scowl at my cynical reply.

"Time out, you two. Aside from this getting us nowhere, it's not helping Mika or Emerald," Dylan interjected with the voice of reason. "We're all worried, but jumping down each other's throats is only going to make matters worse."

Nick scrubbed a hand over his face, then eased onto the bed beside me and gathered me into his arms. "I'm sorry, little one. What I'm about to tell you cannot leave this room. Understood?"

I nodded and cupped his cheek. "I'm sorry, too, Master."

Placing his hand over mine, Nick kissed my palm. "Mika has been *infatuated* with Emerald since she joined Genesis years ago. For reasons of his own, he never wanted her to see or talk to him."

"That doesn't make sense. If he has feelings for her—"

"It's a long story. Some of it we can share, some of it we can't. We'll discuss it when we get back, but right now, Dylan and I need to get over to Mika's. He's in bad shape and needs to talk."

"Okay, but can I at least call Emerald and see how she's doing?"

"Not yet. Trevor and Drake are with her now. They'll take good care of her. I promise."

I opened my mouth to argue, then mulishly pressed my lips together.

"We're not asking you to ignore your friend," Dylan murmured, stroking a hand through my hair. "We're just asking you to wait until we have the details of what happened, and how Mika wants to proceed. We'll share what we know when we get back home."

His compassionate tone and gentle touch melted me to the bone.

Without a word, Nick stood and quickly started getting dressed. We'd never fought like that before, and his silence sliced me in two.

In need of space, I climbed out of bed and slid on my robe. I found solace with a cup of coffee in the kitchen until Dylan strolled into the room.

"He's not mad at you, kitten."

"Yes, he is," I said, staring into my mug.

Dylan plucked me from the chair, then sat and settled me onto his lap. Swaddled in warmth and security, I nuzzled my cheek against his chest and breathed in his familiar scent.

"Because you were scared and upset and got a little mouthy, you think what…that he doesn't want you anymore?"

"No. Yes. I don't know," I moaned.

Dylan cupped my cheek and forced my gaze. "I do. The answer is *no*. If you truly think otherwise, I'm going to turn you over my knee."

"I know," I whispered.

"Just because there are three of us in this relationship doesn't mean we're not going to disagree or fight like couples. The bottom line is, we're all human. We're all upset and worried about what happened to Emerald. And because Nick and I know the whole story, we're doubly worried about Mika."

"Is he going to be okay?"

"I think so…eventually. We'll do all we can to help him…cope. But while we're gone, I want you to erase, burn, and bury any fear that Nick doesn't want you. He does. He wants and loves you with every breath in his body, just like me."

"Oh, little one," Nick moaned as he entered the kitchen and quickly ate up the distance between us. "Is that what you think, love?"

He knelt beside us and cupped my face. The sorrow in his eyes felt like a sledgehammer to my heart.

"I'm sorry for arguing with you, Master," I whispered, blinking back my tears.

"Don't be. You're as worried as we are. I let my own fears get the best of me. I'm sorry. There's no way the three of us are going to go through life without making each other mad. But trust me. No fight or disagreement is going to change the way I feel about you. I love you, Savannah, with all my heart. That will never change. Ever."

His words were a balm of salvation. Relief flooded my veins.

"Oh, Master," I moaned, launching from Dylan's lap and into Nick's arms.

"It's okay, little one," he assured, hugging me tightly.

"As long as we're together, we can weather any storm, kitten," Dylan said, caressing my back.

After they left for Mika's, I tried to stay busy to keep my angst at bay. But as the hours ticked by, I ran out of ways to escape my worries. Stepping outside, I drank in the sun and watched for them along the shoreline. Long minutes later, I tossed off my robe and dove into the pool. I hoped swimming laps would burn off my nervous energy.

As I reached the shallow end, Dylan and Nick stood at the opposite end of the pool looking haggard and exhausted. Gliding through the water with powerful strokes, I neared the ladder.

"Wait," Dylan said, holding up a hand. "Don't get out. We're coming in."

They quickly stripped off their clothes, then dove into the pool. With a playful tug, Nick pulled me underwater, then wrapped me in his arms before pushing off the bottom and launching us up to the surface.

Dylan impatiently moved in behind me and meshed his chest against my back with a heavy sigh. My mind raced with questions. But before I could ask, they held me close and began revealing the details of Julianna, aka Emerald's attack.

Mika's reasons for wanting to stay invisible were complex but completely bewildering. Personally, I thought he was being a total douchebag, but I kept that opinion to myself. Yes, the death of his sub had caused him massive trauma, but hiding his feelings for Julianna wasn't doing him any favors.

But what bothered me most was finding out I couldn't call or talk to her until Mika granted permission. To me, keeping her sequestered from her friends seemed as harsh as the attack she'd endured. I wanted to see her...talk to her...help take care of her. But Dylan and Nick denied my pleas.

A part of me wanted to march down the beach and give Mika a piece of my mind. He wasn't her Master. He shouldn't get to call the shots. He'd hidden in the shadows, for years, watching and wanting her like a stalker.

When I found out he had sex with her last night, I nearly lost my shit. What kind of monster did that to a woman who was in such a vulnerable place? Add the fact that he'd torn out of her house after, like a scared pussy, made me want to kick his ass.

I could do it, too. I had a black-belt in Karate.

Needless to say, I lost all respect for Mika then.

Dylan and Nick knew I was livid, but made me promise not to say a word, or interfere in anyway. I grudgingly agreed, but wasn't happy about it.

The following week was nothing short of depressing. Genesis felt as hollow and void as my former life without Julianna. Drake looked vacant, as if the light had been sucked from his soul. The absence of his imposing demeanor made my heart hurt. Dylan and Nick confided that Drake had been reaching out to Julianna daily, only to hear one excuse after the next as to why she couldn't see him.

Trevor wasn't fairing much better. His best friend had figuratively been bound and gagged by the oh, so powerful Mika. Even Drake was keeping his sub completely out of the loop. And Trevor didn't bother to try to hide the dark circles under his eyes.

The whole situation was a cluster-fuck of biblical proportions.

After spending a few subdued hours at the club, Dylan, Nick, and I climbed into bed and snuggled together until we all drifted off to sleep.

A short time later, Nick's cell phone rang, jolting us awake.

Quickly glancing at the clock on the nightstand I wondered who in their right mind was calling at three in the morning. Dragging the device to his ear, Nick answered in a groggy voice, then seconds later, bolted out of bed, and flipped on the bedside lamp.

"No. Fuck. No. Is he alive?" The anguish in his voice made my blood run cold.

"Who are you talking about?" Dylan demanded, rolling out of bed and rushing to Nick's side.

"Mika's been shot," he announced, pressing the phone tighter against his ear. "Did she get shot, too?"

"She? She, who?" I demanded, but I feared I knew the answer.

"No. Julianna is okay. She's at the hospital with Drake and Trevor. Mika's father just arrived, as well," Nick relayed. "Sorry, George. Go on."

Nick dropped on the edge of the bed as if his legs could no longer support his weight, then engaged the speaker option on his phone. The three of us huddled around the device as George's grief-ridden voice filled the bedroom.

Silent sobs wracked my body and tears spilled down my cheeks as George relayed the horrific details.

In his attempt to right his wrong, Mika discovered that Julianna had convinced herself she was no longer a sub. After consulting Drake, they enlisted help from Sammie—who had been picking her up and bringing her to Mika's office for days. After finally making a breakthrough earlier that night, Mika had been escorting Julianna to her car when Jordon—the monster who'd attacked her—threatened her with a gun. Mika pulled his own weapon and killed Jordon, but not before taking a bullet to the chest.

Mika had died in the ambulance, en route to the hospital, but the EMTs had been able to revive him. By fate or some divine miracle, he'd made it through surgery but was in critical condition at St. Agnes Hospital.

George answered Nick and Dylan's questions as best he could while I struggled to pull myself together. While thrilled Julianna was alive, guilt for all the ugly, venomous assumptions I made against Mika pumped like a thick, oily sludge through my veins. He'd not only gone to great lengths to repair the emotional damage he'd done to Julianna, but he'd also sacrificed his own life to protect her.

"Mika is the most stubborn prick I know. He'll pull through. I know he will." The conviction in Dylan's voice bolstered fragments of hope inside me.

"Thank you for calling, George. We're on our way," Nick assured before ending the call.

When we rushed inside the ICU waiting room, several members from Genesis were there to lend support, along with Emile—Mika's father—Drake, Trevor, Sammie, and Julianna who was curled up in the Domme's arms sleeping. Sending Nick a pleading stare, my heart skipped a beat when he solemnly nodded.

I hurried across the room and sent Sammie a weak smile.

"Wake up, baby," she softly murmured, rousting Julianna awake. "There's someone here to see you."

When she raised her head and lifted her lids, I wanted to cry. She looked utterly defeated. Her chin quivered as she climbed off

Sammie's lap and tossed her arms around me with a fierce hug. She'd lost so much weight; I could feel her bones.

"How are you holding up, love?" I whispered in her ear.

Easing back, she wiped the tears from her cheeks and shook her head. "I've been better."

"I know…you poor thing."

"Not me. Mika." She sighed. "I was so terrified, I couldn't move. I didn't know what to do. But Mika did. He was so brave…so determined to save me. I-I would have died if not for him."

"That's fine, go ahead and hog Savannah's lovin' all for yourself. I see how you are," Trevor quipped with a smiled that didn't reach his eyes as he hugged us both.

"I'm gonna get some coffee. With all these subbie butts in my face, my hand's itching to grab a whip." Sammie winked and stood. "Sit and visit, pets. What do you want me to bring you from the cafeteria, Julianna?"

"Nothing yet, Ma'am. Thank you," she said, shaking her head.

"You need nourishment, girl. Don't make me sic Drake and Emile on your ass. Understand?" Sammie whispered, pinning her with a bad-ass-Domme glare.

"Yes, Ma'am," Julianna sighed in resignation.

Julianna refused to leave the hospital. So, Trevor and I stayed with her, day and night, enticing her to eat and sleep.

Dylan had been right. Mika was indeed stubborn. He recovered so quickly, the medical staff was shocked. In no time, he was back home recuperating with Julianna at his side. His near-death experience had changed him. Mika was no longer a ghost, but a dedicated Master to his devoted slave.

Epilogue

The champagne was flowing as we left the port of Miami.

Mika stood on deck, dressed as a dashing pirate, wearing a smile that rivaled the sun. Julianna—tucked in close to his side—wearing a sexy wench costume, glowed with pride. The sunlight reflecting off the golden collar adorning her throat sent shimmers of light all around.

With his extended kinky family gathered before him, Mika raised his glass. "To all you scurvy landlubbers, it warms me heart to share this adventure with ye."

"If you keep talking like that, Master, I'm going to start begging you to rape and pillage me," Julianna giggled.

"Aye, me sexy wench. Have no fear. I'll be driving me bone in your bountiful booty soon."

Julianna gasped and her cheeks flushed crimson as Mika swooped in for a powerful kiss.

Long seconds later, he released her and smiled.

"I'm glad you're all here to share a week of debauchery on the high seas." Mika suddenly sobered. "There aren't words to express the love and gratitude in my heart for everything you've done for Julianna and I these past few months. Being shot was one of the worst things I've ever been through. But at the same time, one of the best. I understand now how precious and short life really is. I hope you'll all follow my lead, and spend time doing what you love, with the people you love.

Mika dropped his gaze to Julianna, who quickly wiped a tear from her cheek.

"Thank you all. I truly love each and every one of you." Mika raised his glass, swallowed the bubbly liquid, then tossed it over the side of the ship. "Let the spankings begin!"

We all cheered and laughed. As I clinked my glass against Dylan's and Nick's my heart sputtered. The love reflecting in my Masters' eyes was more blinding and breathtaking than the sun sinking to the horizon over crystal blue water.

The dinner buffet was to die for, and I ate until I ached. As we dressed in our spacious suite before going below deck to join in the dungeon festivities, I begged Nick, who was cinching up my corset, not to make it too tight.

"Relax, little one. The only suffering you'll have to endure is beneath *our* hands."

His deviant chuckle made my blood heat. But when I turned and saw both of my Masters dressed in dark suits, flames of arousal flared and sizzled through me.

Thankfully, we didn't stay in the dungeon long.

After returning to our room, they kept their promise. I willingly suffered, over and over, until we lay in a tangle of limbs, sated and sweating, panting and boneless, and quivering in sublime aftershocks.

The sound of voices and a strange noise woke me. Easing from beneath my Masters' warm bodies, I padded to the balcony and stepped outside. A few suites down, Julianna was leaning over the side of the ship, heaving her guts while Trevor held her riot of curls in his fist.

Oh no, she's seasick.

Tossing on my robe, I grabbed the room key and a bottle of water from the mini fridge before hurrying out the door. I rushed down the hall to find the door of Mika and Julianna's suite wide open, and I darted inside. As I joined them on the balcony, I brushed my hand over Trevor's back. He turned his head and sent me a weak smile as worry danced in his eyes.

"Aww, honey," I moaned, patting her back. "Seasick?"

Wiping her mouth with the back of her hand, she shook her head with a worried expression.

If she wasn't seasick...

"Ohmigod! You're pregnant?"

"She won't take the test," Trevor chided, flipping his hand in the air.

"Why not?" I asked, keeping my voice low.

"Because Mika and I haven't ever talked about kids."

"Where *is* Mika?"

"He and a couple other Doms are decorating the dungeon for tonight," Trevor answered for her.

"I don't know if he *wants* babies. What am I going to do?" Julianna moaned, pressing a palm to her stomach as a fat tear slid down her cheek.

Hugging her tightly, I kissed her forehead. "We're gonna find out. Come on. Follow me."

"Where are we going?" Trevor asked, wrapping his arm around Julianna's waist.

"The medical bay. They're got to have a pregnancy test on board."

"Savannah, I can't." Julianna blanched.

"Yes, you can. Trev and I will hold your hand. And if the test comes back positive, we'll stay by your side when you tell Mika."

"I'm scared," Julianna whispered.

"I know you are, but we've got your back," I vowed.

Keeping our eyes peeled for Mika and Drake, we hurried down the hall, around the corner, and darted into the medical bay. To our surprise, the doctor was nowhere in sight. While Trevor stood in the portal, as lookout, Julianna and I quickly started searching through the cabinets and drawers.

"Found it," I announced.

Opening the box, the three of us squeezed inside the little bathroom before handing Julianna the plastic wand.

"Pee on this," I whispered, guiding her down onto the toilet. "No matter what the results are, it's going to be okay."

"I don't know if I can pee with an audience," she moaned.

"This might help," Trevor winked.

Turning sideways, he inched toward the sink and turned on the faucet. It worked like a charm. Julianna thrust the stick toward me, wiped herself, then squeezed her eyes shut. With Trevor peering over my shoulder, we stared at the little results window as a bold plus sign appeared.

"Oh, sister!" Trevor squealed.

"What does it say?" Julianna groaned as she stood, trembling.

"You're gonna have a baby." I grinned and hugged her tight.

"I'm gonna be an uncle," Trevor announced with glee.

The blood drained from her face, and her eyes rolled to the back of her head as her body slumped against mine.

"Oh fuck!" I cried. "Trevor. Quick. Go get Mika."

Though we were packed in the little room like sardines, Trevor managed to wiggle through the door. As I drug Julianna toward the exam table, and somehow lifted her on to the mattress, I could hear his bare feet thudding on the carpet as he raced down the hall.

"Come on, Julianna. Wake up," I frantically whispered, patting her face.

Short minutes later, Mika burst through the door with Trevor hot on his heels.

Fear flashed in Mika's eyes when he saw Julianna lying still on the bed.

"Julianna...no, baby no." he moaned, then glared at Trevor and I— clinging to each other, and shaking like leaves. "What the fuck happened to her?"

"S-she passed out on us, Sir," I replied.

"Where?"

"I-in the bathroom," I stammered, pointing toward the little room.

"Why was she in the bathroom...why were the *three of you* in the bathroom?" he asked, narrowing his angry eyes on us.

"I can't tell you that, Sir." I whispered.

"What do mean you can't tell me?" he thundered.

Annihilated by the rage rolling off him, I swallowed the whimper of fear lodged in my throat. But before I could reply, Julianna moaned.

Whipping his head toward her, Mika stroked his dark hand down her pale face as her eyes fluttered open.

"Easy, love. I'm here. I've got you, precious," Mike whispered softly.

"Master," she whimpered.

"Shh, my love. It's okay. You're going to be fine," he assured before glaring at us again. "Trevor, I want you to go wake up Drake, Nick, and Dylan. Tell them I need them here, now, boy."

Peeling his arms off me, Trevor swallowed tightly. "It was nice knowing you, sis," he whispered before sprinting out the door.

"Don't be mad at them, Master," Julianna begged. "They didn't do anything wrong. This is all my fault."

"What's your fault, love?" Mika asked, gently brushing the curls from her face.

Julianna sent me a pleading stare. "Show him, Savannah."

"You sure?" I whispered.

"For fuck's sake. Tell me what the hell is going on here," Mika barked.

As his thunderous tone vibrated through me, I jolted, then raced to the bathroom and retrieved the stick. Hurrying back into the exam room, I thrust it toward him and sent Julianna an apologetic grimace as Trevor, Drake, Dylan, and Nick rushed through the door.

"I'm sorry, Master," Julianna whispered as tears slid from the corners of her eyes.

"What's going on here, kitten?" Dylan demanded, confusion and worry written all over his face.

"I... I—"

"Fuck. Me. Holy. Shit," Mika screamed.

Julianna covered her face with her hands and began to wail.

"What is that?" Drake barked.

Mika's eyes filled with tears as Julianna curled into a little ball, and wailed.

"I-I'm going to be a father!" Mika yelled with elation, holding up the wand.

As cheers and congratulations filled the air, Julianna continued howling. With a frown, Mika lifted her into his arms and cradled her to his chest before easing onto the exam table. Though he peppered her wet face with kisses and murmured reassurances, Julianna couldn't stop crying.

Shaking his head in dismay, a smirk tugged his lips as he stood and placed her on the floor at his feet. Assuming the same, commanding stance I'd grown to love from my own Masters, Mika barked, "Present yourself, slave."

"I-I c-can't," Julianna sobbed.

"You will present to me now or I'll…" As the threat died on his lips, Mika skipped a bewildered glance at the three other Doms. "What the fuck can I do to a pregnant sub?"

"Love her, man. Love her hard." Nick laughed.

"I already do." Mika grinned before a mischievous glint flickered in his eyes. "Present yourself, or you'll go nine months without an orgasm, slave."

His threat lit a fire inside Julianna. She quickly tucked her legs beneath her and assumed a stunning submissive pose.

"Much better," Mika praised as he knelt in front of her and cupped her chin. "Open your eyes and look at me, girl."

As she opened her red, swollen eyes, I nearly gasped. The last time I'd seen so much fear reflected in them was at the hospital after Mika had been shot.

"I love you, pet. I love that our baby is growing inside your belly. You've showered me with your gift of submission, but this…" he said, placing his hand on her stomach. "Is the most magnificent present you could ever give me."

Julianna opened her mouth to speak, but only managed to cry even louder. Mika chuckled and wrapped her in his arms before pulling her to his chest and peppering her face with kisses.

Drake wrapped a beefy paw into Trevor's hair. "What do you want us to do with these two?"

As Mika pursed his lips, silently pondering, waves of guilt crashed through me.

Swallowing back my fear, I lifted my chin and dragged in a ragged breath. "This was all my idea, Sir. Julianna was afraid to take the test, but I forced her. Trevor didn't do anything but hold her hair while she puked. Please don't punish him. I'm the one to blame."

I darted a glance at my Masters and immediately wished I hadn't. Disapproval and anger lined their faces.

"I'm sorry for disappointing you, Masters," I mumbled, casting my guilty gaze toward the floor.

"If you were mine, I'd take you to my suite or the dungeon and use you hard," Mika chuckled.

My eyes grew wide as I jerked my head up with a gasp.

"I think that's a marvelous idea." Dylan's icy grin sent a shiver coiling up my spine. "Let's go, kitten. You've caused enough trouble for one day.

As he clasped my elbow, Nick stepped in front of me with a devilish smile. "I think we need to push a few buttons while we're at it."

As he started sliding the robe off my shoulders, I squeezed my eyes shut and quivered.

"If it will erase your anger of me, I'll do anything, Master."

Dylan eased in front of me and pressed my back against Nick's wide chest before nuzzling his lips to my ear.

"I vote we take you to our suite, sink balls deep inside your tight, hot holes, and start practicing, so one day you'll give us the same incredible gift Julianna just gave to Mika."

Heart soaring, I tossed my arms around his neck and giggled. "Really, Master? Really?"

"Practice makes perfect, little one." Nick smirked.

"And it's fun, too." Dylan grinned.

Looping an arm around Nick's neck, I hugged them both with all my might.

"Use me, please ,Masters. Use me hard for hours," I begged.

"Not so fast, kitten," Dylan warned. "You're still going to be punished."

"B-but, I—"

"Stuck your nose where it didn't belong," Nick growled, fisting my hair. "Instead of encouraging Julianna to talk to Mika, you took control that wasn't yours and forced her to take the pregnancy test. Yes, you've earned a punishment...tonight, in the dungeon."

My heart raced in fear as they ushered me from the room, down the hall, and back to our suite. The second the door closed behind us; they started lecturing me. Then, after hours of putting me through an emotional guilt-laden wringer, they left me alone to... *Think about my actions.*

For two interminable hours, I sat on the bed worrying. Though I knew it wouldn't do any good, I couldn't stop.

When we entered the dining room later for dinner, my stomach was in knots. Picking at the food on my plate, my mind whirled. They were going to punish me in the dungeon...in public, *and* push my buttons.

Was I going to taste the sting of a whip for the first time? I didn't know.

As the thought of them stripping me naked careened through my brain, the fear they'd dole out another session of forced orgasms sent panic soaring within. If given the choice between public nudity or forced orgasms, I'd willingly take my own clothes off. My poor pussy and clit hadn't stopped aching for days after they'd spent all night torturing me with that nasty vibe.

Unable to force a morsel of food past my lips, I set my fork down and raised my head.

"I'm sorry for letting you both down today, Masters. Can you please forgive me instead of punishing me?" I asked, swiping away the tear trickling down my cheek.

"You've already been forgiven, kitten," Dylan assured.

"Then why are you still going to punish me?"

"We'll explain in the dungeon," Nick replied as he stood and offered me his hand.

Heart in my throat, I placed my fingers in his palm and forced myself to stand.

Without a word, they led me to the dungeon. The room was packed, yet not a soul was at any of the stations. Everyone was seated in rows of chairs, facing an empty cross...to watch *me*.

I was nearly hyperventilating when Dylan and Nick led me to the front of the crowd. Unable to look at the faces of those who were eagerly waiting my punishment, I cast my gaze to the floor.

"Thank you all for coming this evening to witness Savannah's punishment," Nick solemnly stated.

As whispered murmurs buzzed in my ears, I raised my head to see Mika's father Emile rise from his seat.

"Go easy on her, Nick. Thanks to your girl, I now know I'm going to be a grandpa," he cried, tossing a fist pump in the air.

Collective laughter, cheers, and applause filled the room. Even my Masters laughed. I, on the other hand, was too scared to even smile.

"Congratulations, Emile," Dylan called. "But as all Masters, Doms, Dommes, and Tops know, we're sometimes forced to correct bad behavior."

Murmurs of agreement flowed over me.

"Such is the case tonight," Nick added before turning toward me. "We've had numerous discussions about honesty and trust, haven't we, little one?"

"Yes, Master," I whispered.

"Keeping secrets is the same as lying."

"And lying erodes trust," Dylan added. "Once trust is lost, it's very hard to regain."

"I know, Master, but I wasn't purposely keeping secrets from either of you. I know I should have come to you two, first, but there wasn't time."

I inwardly prayed the sincerity in my voice would finally penetrate their hearts and they'd forego this humiliating punishment.

"I don't know, Dylan," Nick said, rubbing his chin. "Do you really think she means it?"

"I do, Master I swear," I implored.

"Silence, little one. I wasn't asking you, I was asking Dylan," he chided.

"I don't know, bro. I'm not sure I trust her to tell the truth." His lack of faith in me pierced my heart like a knife. "Is there even a punishment worthy enough to make up for what she did to us?"

Fighting the urge to fall to my knees and beg their forgiveness, I darted a panicked glance between them. When I saw the mischief dancing in their eyes, I instantly knew they were setting me up.

For what? I had no clue.

I only knew Dylan's words were cutting me deeper by the second. Whatever punishment I had to endure paled in comparison to the pain consuming my heart.

Show them how much you love them...do it.

It had been a long time since that little voice in my head had guided me.

Deep down, I knew there was nothing I wouldn't do to prove my love, devotion, and submission to them. Determination and conviction pumped through my veins as I fixed my gaze on the back wall and stepped forward.

Plucking the knot at the sash of my robe, I brushed the silky fabric off my shoulders. As it puddled to my feet, the crowd gasped while Dylan whispered a reverent curse.

Anxiety and fear thundered through me as I skipped a gaze over the crowd.

The smiles, tears, and nods of encouragement from my friends... my family, teemed with pure, raw, and unequivocal *love*.

As Nick sank a fist in my hair, yanked my head back, and crashed his lips over mine, Dylan gripped my nape and dragged his tongue up my neck before pausing at my ear.

"We fucking love you, kitten. Love you with all our hearts."

When Nick released my lips, Dylan claimed them with a powerful, dizzying kiss.

"With more than our hearts, little one. We love you with our fucking souls," Nick murmured before nipping my ear lobe.

I was safe, loved...and whole.

When Dylan released my mouth, Julianna stood in the front row. Tears streamed down her face as she sent me a watery smile. "You're gorgeous, Savannah."

A few rows behind her, Tony stood. Wearing a smile so wide I thought it would split his face, he raised a thumbs up, then began to clap.

Suddenly ,the entire room started applauding as their yells of encouragement flowed over me like warm sunshine. A shy smile tugged the corners of my mouth as a tiny laugh spilled from my lips.

Turning, I faced my Masters.

I branded the pride and awe etched in their faces to my soul before I lowered my chin and eased to my knees. Spine straight, I spread my legs and placed my hands—palms up—on my thighs before dragging in a quivering breath and peering up at them.

The raw and pure unconditional love beaming in their eyes was blinding.

"I kneel at your feet, stripped of all barriers inside and out, to prove my love, desire, and need to please you are the only things that matter in here." I touched a finger to my head. "And in here," I said, placing my palm over my heart. "Nothing else on this earth means more to me than making you both happy and filling your lives with love."

As Nick and Dylan bent and surrounded me, their eyes were filled with tears.

"We love you, too, kitten...more than life itself," Dylan murmured.

"Love you and want you in our lives forever," Nick choked softly. "We're so fucking proud of you."

Burying his face against my neck, he repeated, *we love you*, over and over as Dylan nuzzled my ear.

"You're ours forever, kitten. You're our salvation, Savannah...you saved us from ourselves, sweet girl. We love you...love you until the end of time."

"I'll love you both right back...until the end of time," I whimpered.

As tears of joy spilled down my face, Nick scooped me into his arms and captured my lips in a sublime, heart-stopping kiss.

"Sorry, all, but...punishment's been canceled. Nick and I are taking our brave, beautiful slave back to our suite to do sinfully wicked things to her all night."

The room erupted in laughter and cheers as my Master's carried me away and down the hall. When we reached our room, Dylan closed and locked the door behind him while Nick lowered me onto the bed.

And as my beautiful, powerful, and commanding Masters gazed down at me, I saw every emotion vividly reflected in their eyes.

Pride.

Hunger.

But best of all…

Love.

With a sassy smile I opened my arms and invited them to consume me.

Thank you for reading **Consume Me**. I hope you enjoyed Dylan, Nick, and Savannah's journey. Yes, the ride was steamy and bumpy, but necessary for them to find their happy ever after. If you did, I'd love for you to leave a review and recommend this book to all your friends.

And if you'd like to be the first to hear about my upcoming releases and read exclusive excerpts, please sign up for my **newsletter**. Oh, and if you want to let your hair down, get a little rowdy, and grab some freebies, join my private Facebook group **Jenna Jacob's Jezebels**. I'd love to see you there!

Wait until you see what's happening next at Club Genesis…

SEIZE ME

Worlds collide and desires smolder when a powerful sadist tries to heal the broken heart of a reluctant submissive.

SEIZE ME
Club Genesis - Chicago, Book 3

He climbed inside my mind and controlled my every craving.

I'm **Leagh Bennett**—kept woman. The unexpected death of my lover shatters me, but when his family discovers our relationship, their cruel vengeance nearly destroys me. Homeless, penniless, and grieving, I seek refuge at Club Genesis to mourn and face an unknown future alone.

When **Tony Delvaggio**, panty-melting psychologist and the club's savage hotshot, forces me to confront my anguish, I tell myself his probing questions are purely professional. But his whiskey-smooth suggestions break through my defenses and ignite desires I never knew existed. Frightened, I push Tony away. But he's relentless, delving into my psyche until I'm letting him even deeper into my body and my heart—where I've let no man before. His raw passion shocks and devastates me. And soon, I'm falling too hard to resist…

But when my past returns and danger threatens, I'm forced to choose between running again or surrendering my all and letting Tony… *Seize Me*.

Previously published as *Master of My Mind*.

Here's a sneak peek of *SEIZE ME*…

I stood beneath the faded green awning, staring at the gleaming mahogany casket. The sparkling brass handles mocked the warmth that had been ripped from my soul. A cold rain splattered upon the canopy while somber-faced friends gathered beneath it to show their respect. Across the gravesite, seated in fabric covered folding chairs, I watched as the well-rehearsed tears spilled down the cheeks of his ex-wife. His hateful daughter tried to soothe the ice queen's theatrics. Neither woman was there to mourn the loss of the man I loved but to masquerade as grieving victims until the fat inheritance landed in their laps.

The monotone voice of the minister resonated in my ears. None of his words of comfort penetrated the numb void that had consumed me for days. I was all but dead inside; just as dead as my beloved Master, who would soon be lowered into the black earth hollowed out below him. And God help me, I wanted to go with him. Not because I wanted to die, but because I couldn't imagine life without him.

The honorable George Bartholomew Marston, State Supreme Court Justice for the past four decades, was being laid to rest. I felt as if I was outside my own body. Friends and family stood in a line before passing the casket one last time, placing blood-red roses atop the gleaming wooden box. I felt as if I'd been transported into a macabre movie, one I could barely watch but helplessly had to endure.

George's best friend and fellow judge, Reed Landes, stepped up to the coffin; his eyes were rimmed red, and the distinguished man's chin quivered. I swallowed back a sob. Pain wrapped its icy hands around my heart and squeezed. It was almost time to say goodbye; however, that was beyond my comprehension.

A firm, steady hand enveloped my shoulder. Glancing up, I gazed into the compassionate amber eyes of Mika LaBrache; friend, Dominant, and owner of the BDSM club, Genesis. I'd spent countless hours basking in my Master's adoration at Mika's club. His submissive, Julianna, dabbed at the tears on her cheek before smoothing a hand over her very pregnant belly. I couldn't ignore how life mirrored death. A new life grew inside her. A life that she and Mika would love, protect, and cherish—while the man who'd loved, protected, and cherished me was gone. It was so fucking unfair.

"It's time to lay your rose on the casket, Leagh." Julianna wrapped her fingers around my arm as I glanced down at the dark red rose gripped in my fist. Opening my hand, tiny red dots blossomed in the center of my palm. The thorns were smeared in crimson. It seemed like hours had passed since Trevor handed me the flower. Strange, I had no recollection of it piercing my flesh.

"I can't do it," I choked, swallowing back the tears I'd held inside for days. Even knowing a part of me would be interred with George forever did little to ease my devastation. Sucking in a ragged breath, I willed myself to remain strong. I refused to allow George's ex or daughter to revel in my pain or glean the depth of my love for him. They'd only use it as a weapon against me.

It had been humiliating enough, while standing on the church steps, when George's ex-wife demanded I be barred from the memorial service. Luckily, Drake, an imposing leather Dom from Genesis, leaned down and whispered something into the haughty bitch's ear. She'd sputtered and paled before she'd jerked her nose in the air and stormed inside the chapel. If it hadn't been for Drake's intervention, I never would have gathered the courage to attend the devotion. I'd shielded my grief from the hateful shrew then; I wasn't about to let her see a chink in my armor now.

With a nod of understanding, Mika lifted the rose from my palm and set it atop the copious pile of flowers adorning the casket. When he returned, Julianna wrapped her arm around my waist, attempting to lead me from the gravesite. My entire body froze. I couldn't move. I didn't want to. Stepping from beneath the awning meant I'd be forced to face a future without George. Even more unbearable was the fact that I would be leaving him alone, entombed in the cold black earth.

"Can you give us a little help here?" Mika murmured to Tony Delvaggio, the familiar Dom, Sadist, Dungeon Monitor, and resident shrink of Genesis.

He was a hulk of a man who always called me "brat" to my face—and meant it. The same one who set butterflies dipping and swooping in my stomach every time I caught him staring at me in the club. He was erotic beyond words, turning submissive heads—collared or not—every night at Genesis. Tony always sent my pulse racing, even now. It was ridiculous for him to affect me in such a way. Stupid even. I'd always been civil to the man, because he was a Dom and a friend of George's, but his intense nature made my skin itch in a very uncomfortable way.

Julianna stepped aside as Tony slid a thick arm around my shoulder. He was warm and solid. I tried to ignore the way he made my heart skitter.

"I've got her, Mika. You just keep Julianna and that little bun in the oven dry. We'll meet you back at the cars."

Tony raised his umbrella. It opened with a whoosh before he maneuvered me from beneath the canopy. Somehow, I put one foot in front of the other while I focused on Mika escorting Julianna up the hill. He held her close to his side—protective and adoring—enveloping her in comfort, reassurance, and love.

Anguish sliced deep. George was gone, yet Julianna still had all the things I longed for. Even though she was one of my closest friends, envy burned, spreading like a cancer through my veins. Tears stung my eyes as I cast my gaze toward the ground. The wet, brown grass blurred.

"Just a bit farther, Leagh," Tony encouraged. His voice was husky and deep.

Glancing up at the man, he smiled, but it didn't reach his eyes. Sorrow and pity replaced his usual piercing gaze. "Are you going back to the church for the luncheon?"

I shook my head. I couldn't stomach the thought of sharing a meal, let alone the same air, with George's pretentious ex-wife, Sloane, and his hateful, spoiled daughter, Hayden. "I just want to go home."

"No problem. I'll take you."

After settling me into his car, Tony jogged toward Mika. Through the rain splattered windshield, I watched the two men exchange a few words before Tony hurried back and climbed in behind the wheel. As he started the engine, I couldn't help but exhale a heavy sigh. The funeral was over. Yet the anxiety and fears that had eaten at me for the past four days weren't gone. They'd simply been replaced by new ones.

A long, unrelenting list spooled through my head. Most pressing, I had to find a job and a new place to live. Since Hayden was George's only heir, I wouldn't be welcome in his stately mansion after the will was read. Even though his elegant home on the shore of Lake Michigan had been my legal residence for the past two and a half years, his vile daughter would force me out as soon as she possibly could. I had a little reprieve, though. Reed Landes, the executor of George's estate, had assured me that I was welcome to stay until Master's affairs had been settled. But the clock was ticking, and time was running out. The fairy tale was at its end.

Staring out the foggy window, I watched the scenery rush past while I tempered the growing ache to crawl into bed, snuggle between the sheets, and absorb the waning vestiges of George's scent. Hold tight to his ghost for as long as possible before I had to find a way to say goodbye.

"If you need someone to talk to...someone to help you work through the stages. My door is always—"

"What stages, Tony?" I cut him off with a scathing glare. "There are no stages. There's nothing but a hole in my heart the size of the universe. There's not a damn thing you can do or say to wake me up from this nightmare."

He cast a sideways glance and pressed his lips in a narrow line while waves of tension rolled off his body, filling the scant distance between us. No doubt, he was pissed at my snippy reply. Good. Maybe he'd shut up and drive and stop making me feel like one of his patients.

"The stages of grief, Leagh," he replied, dashing my dreams of a silent trip home. "You're not ready to move past denial and anger yet. I get that. I'm simply extending the offer. When the time comes and you're ready to start healing again, I'm here if you need to talk."

"Healing?" A humorless laugh escaped my lips. "I'm trying to survive ten seconds at a time without falling apart at the seams. I haven't even started thinking about healing."

"There's nothing wrong with falling apart. It takes time, but it will get better."

"I'm not sure I want it to," I murmured as he turned onto the long driveway.

It was my first trip back to the house since George died. Julianna and Mika had whisked me away to stay with them after Master's body had been taken to the mortuary. I didn't want to stay there alone. At the time, the thought of roaming from room to room, assaulted by his memories, seemed painfully masochistic. But now, I yearned to wrap the precious times we'd shared around me, savor them, and mourn the loss of my best friend, alone.

When Tony parked in front of the red brick and mortar steps, I turned to face him. "Thanks for the ride and, um, for the offer to pick my brain. I'm going to pass for now, but I'll see you around."

Cold rain pelted my face as I hurried from the vehicle. Aware of Tony waiting for me to get inside safely, I dug out the keys from the bottom of my purse. Glancing up, I noticed an envelope taped to the front door with my name scrolled in feminine penmanship.

I slid my key into the lock, but it wouldn't turn. When I tried a second time, my heart sank. No doubt Hayden had done her worst. Tearing the note from the door, I pulled out the pages from within and began to read.

Ms. Bennett,

Please find enclosed a Restraining Order forbidding you from this property. There will be no other form of communication to you from either of us. My mother and I refuse to acknowledge your disgusting association with my father. Be advised that his upstanding reputation in the community, and courts, shall remain unblemished. Should you make any slanderous remarks hinting otherwise, we will file suit against you for defamation of character.

Your personal property is exactly where it belongs—on the side of the house—in the trash. Take what you can salvage and leave. You will be arrested for trespassing if you set foot on these premises ever again.

Good riddance. May you rot in hell!

Hayden Marston

As I stepped back from the door, the rain dripped from my hair and slithered like cold fingers down my spine. Stunned by the note's contents, I forced myself to re-read it once, then twice, while my guts turned to liquid. A tingling wave of panic spread through my limbs, and the tears I'd courageously fought for days filled my eyes and spilled down my cheeks.

"Leagh? Is everything okay? What's that letter say?"

Turning toward the sound of Tony's voice, I saw his torso poised between the partially opened car door and the frame. I knew he was watching me, even though his face had blurred from my tears.

Realizing that all my belongings were shoved into the trash, I dropped the papers, my keys, and my purse and sprinted toward the side of the house. A desolate cry, like a wounded animal, tore from my throat and echoed in my ears.

Panting and crying, I flipped the lid of the garbage receptacle open. The scent of feces and decay permeated my senses. Stumbling back, I gagged and sucked in a breath of fresh air before peering inside. Paper plates filled with dog excrement had been placed on top of open and leaking cans of pungent tuna fish and tomato paste, while raw and broken eggs jiggled as drops of rain landed upon the slippery membranes. A bottle of Italian salad dressing lay on its side, dripping oil and vinegar, mixing in with the sludge. Gazing at the putrid concoction, I spied some of the expensive clothing Master had given me as gifts saturated in the pungent muck.

Rage roared through me. Staring into the slurry, I remembered how George would pull packages with big red bows from behind his back. *"I like to spoil you with pretty things, my wild little tiger."*

Anguish stabbed, slicing deep. Turning, I spotted a long branch that had fallen from the bare oak tree. Plucking it from the ground, I carefully slid the forked bough beneath the plates of dog poop and tossed them onto the grass. Spearing the sleeve of my favorite Chanel blouse, I lifted it from beneath the slimy mixture. The dusty pink silk had been completely shredded. It was totally ruined.

Rooting around the amalgam, I shoved my wet hair from my face, desperate to find one piece of salvageable clothing. But every item had been obliterated by Sloane and Hayden's savagery. Why had they done such a vile thing? It wasn't as if I'd stolen the man away from either of them. It was my understanding that Sloane had wanted out of the marriage. At least that's how George had explained it. He'd been relieved to be rid of the shrew. The bitch's venomous cruelty made no sense whatsoever.

When I spied the handcrafted wooden box that stored my collar, hope soared. Using the branch, I lifted it from the barrel and carefully lowered it to the ground. Easing open the lid, I gasped. My treasured leather collar had been cut to bits, mingled among slivers of mutilated photographs. Every treasured snapshot of me and George had been reduced to confetti. My whole world tilted on its axis.

Dropping the lid down, I threw my head back. An inhuman cry of anguish erupted from deep in my belly, and fury exploded outward. Seeing red, I shoved the receptacle onto its side and fell to my knees. Tears streamed down my face as I poked through the slop, cursing and screaming, in search of one minuscule memento of my life with George that the malicious bitches hadn't destroyed.

"Hey. Stop, Leagh. Stop!" Tony commanded, wrapping me in a bear hug from behind and strangling my hot rage. Pinning my arms against my sides, he rendered me immobile. I shrieked and struggled, resenting the hell out of his interference.

"Calm down. There's nothing left for you here."

"I know that, dammit! Do you think I'm blind? Those whores destroyed it all. They took every piece of him away from me. I have nothing. Nothing!" I screamed.

"Come on. Let's get you out of here."

"No!" I snapped. "There's got to be something in there. Something they haven't ruined. Let me go. I need to find it. I need to find...*something*."

"Don't do this, sweetheart. Don't let them wreck your soul. Come on. We need to get out of the rain."

"Fuck you! Fuck them! Fuck the rain! Fuck everything!" Ranting, I tossed the stick aside and clawed from Tony's grasp. Scooting away, tears flowed as Sloane and Hayden's malice shredded what was left of my heart.

Tony crouched, staring at me, as rain dripped down his face. His wet, dark hair was plastered against his head. And his dark tailored suit had grown wrinkled and soggy. Gazing into his eyes, I watched his concerned expression transform into a sympathetic frown. My blood boiled.

"I don't need you or your damn pity. Go away. Just leave me alone."

"Pity?" Tony shook his head. "It's definitely not pity, and there's no way in hell I'm leaving you here. Not like this."

"You have to. Get out. It's for your own good. You can't be here if they come back."

Narrowing his eyes in suspicion, he tilted his head. "Why not?"

"Because I'm going to kill them. I'm going to take the knife or scissors or whatever they used to shred everything I owned and I'm going to slice their fucking throats. That's why!"

Tony's eyes widened for a fraction of a second before he eased toward me. "You can't do that, Leagh. You'd spend the rest of your life in jail. George wouldn't want that."

"I don't care. Don't you get it?" I sobbed. "I don't care about anything anymore."

My shoulders slumped, and every cell in my body succumbed to the piercing shards of grief. Wilted and sobbing, I gazed into Tony's chocolate eyes, feeling more alone than I ever had in my life.

"But I do, angel," Tony whispered in a soft plea as he pulled me to his chest. I clung to him as if he were a lifeline, one I wasn't sure I deserved but was grateful for, nonetheless. "I'm taking you home with me. We'll figure out the rest later."

I wanted to fight him…kick and scream until he left me to wallow in my misery. But most of all, I wanted to howl at George for leaving me alone, scared, and unprotected. Yet, I couldn't find the strength. I was exhausted and suffocating beneath the injustice of it all. Without challenge, Tony plucked me off the ground, cradled me in his arms, and carried me back to his car.

SEIZE ME
Club Genesis – Chicago, Book 3

CLUB GENESIS - CHICAGO
Awaken Me
Consume Me
Seize Me
Arouse Me
Ignite Me
Entice Me
Expose Me
Bare Me
Unravel Me
Command Me
Tame Me
Tempt Me

If you want another panty-melting BDSM adventure, I've got you covered…FREE

THE BETRAYAL
The Unbroken Series: Raine Falling, Book 1 - **FREE**

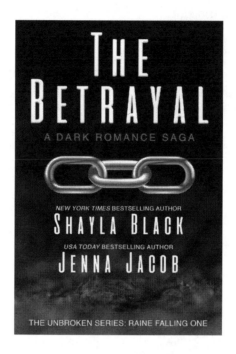

Two friends. One woman. Let the games begin…

Raine Kendall has been in love with her boss, Macen Hammerman, for years. Determined to make him notice her, she pours out her heart and offers him her body—only to be crushingly rejected. When his very sexy best friend, Liam O'Neill, sees Hammer refuse to act on his obvious feelings for her, he plots to rouse his pal's possessive instincts by making Raine a proposition too tempting to refuse. He never imagines he'll fall for her himself.

Hammer has buried his lust for Raine for years. After rescuing the runaway from an alley behind his exclusive club, he's come to crave her. But tragedy has proven he'll never be the man she needs, so he protects her while keeping his distance. Then Liam's scheme to make

Raine his own blindsides Hammer. He isn't ready to give the feisty beauty over to his friend. But can he heal from his past enough to fight for her? Or will he lose Raine if she gives herself—heart, body, and soul—to Liam?

ABOUT THE AUTHOR

USA Today Bestselling author **Jenna Jacob** paints a canvas of passion, romance, and humor as her alpha men and the feisty women who love them unravel their souls, heal their scars, and find a happy-ever-after kind of love. Heart-tugging, captivating, and steamy, her words will leave you breathless and craving more.

A mom of four grown children, Jenna, her husband Sean, and their furry babies reside in Kansas. Though she spent over thirty years in accounting, Jenna isn't your typical bean counter. She's brassy, sassy, and loves to laugh, but is humbly thrilled to be living her dream as a full-time author. When she's not slamming coffee while pounding out emotional stories, you can find her reading, listening to music, cooking, camping, or enjoying the open road on the back of a Harley.

CONNECT WITH JENNA
Website - E-Mail - Newsletter
Jezebels Facebook Party Page

ALSO BY JENNA JACOB

The Cowboy's Second Chance At Love

The Cowboy's Thirty-Day Fling

The Cowboy's Cougar

The Cowboy's Surprise Vegas Baby

BRIDES OF HAVEN

The Cowboy's Baby Bargain

The Cowboy's Virgin Baby Momma - Includes Baby Bargain

The Cowboy's Million Dollar Baby Bride

The Cowboy's Virgin Buckle Bunny

The Cowboy's Big Sexy Wedding

THE UNBROKEN SERIES - RAINE FALLING

The Broken

The Betrayal

The Break

The Brink

The Bond

THE UNBROKEN SERIES - HEAVENLY RISING

The Choice

The Chase

The Confession

The Commitment

STAND ALONES

Small Town Second Chance

Innocent Uncaged